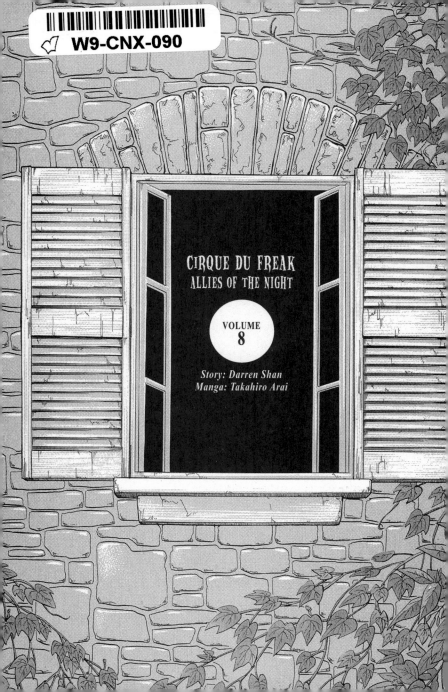

CIRQUE DU FREAK

ALLIES OF THE NIGHT

VOLUME
8

Story: Darren Shan
Manga: Takahiro Arai

A SUMMARY OF HUNTERS OF THE DUSK:

DARREN, MR. CREPSLEY, HARKAT, AND VANCHA HAVE GONE ON A JOURNEY TO FIND AND DEFEAT THE DREAD VAMPANEZE LORD THAT THREATENS THE LIVES OF ALL VAMPIRES. AFTER A VISIT WITH THE MYSTERIOUS LADY EVANNA, WHO HOLDS CLUES TO FINDING THE VAMPANEZE LORD, DARREN RETURNS TO THE CIRQUE DU FREAK FOR THE FIRST TIME IN SIX YEARS. MEANWHILE, THE VAMPIRES STUMBLE UPON A GROUP OF TRAVELING VAMPANEZE, BUT DESPITE A SNEAK ATTACK, THE VAMPIRES UNWITTINGLY ALLOW THE VAMPANEZE LORD HIMSELF TO ESCAPE. DARREN LEAVES THE CIRQUE, BUT WHERE WILL HIS TRAVELS TAKE HIM NEXT?

CIRQUE DU FREAK 8
CONTENTS

CHAPTER 65: THE SCHOOL INSPECTOR

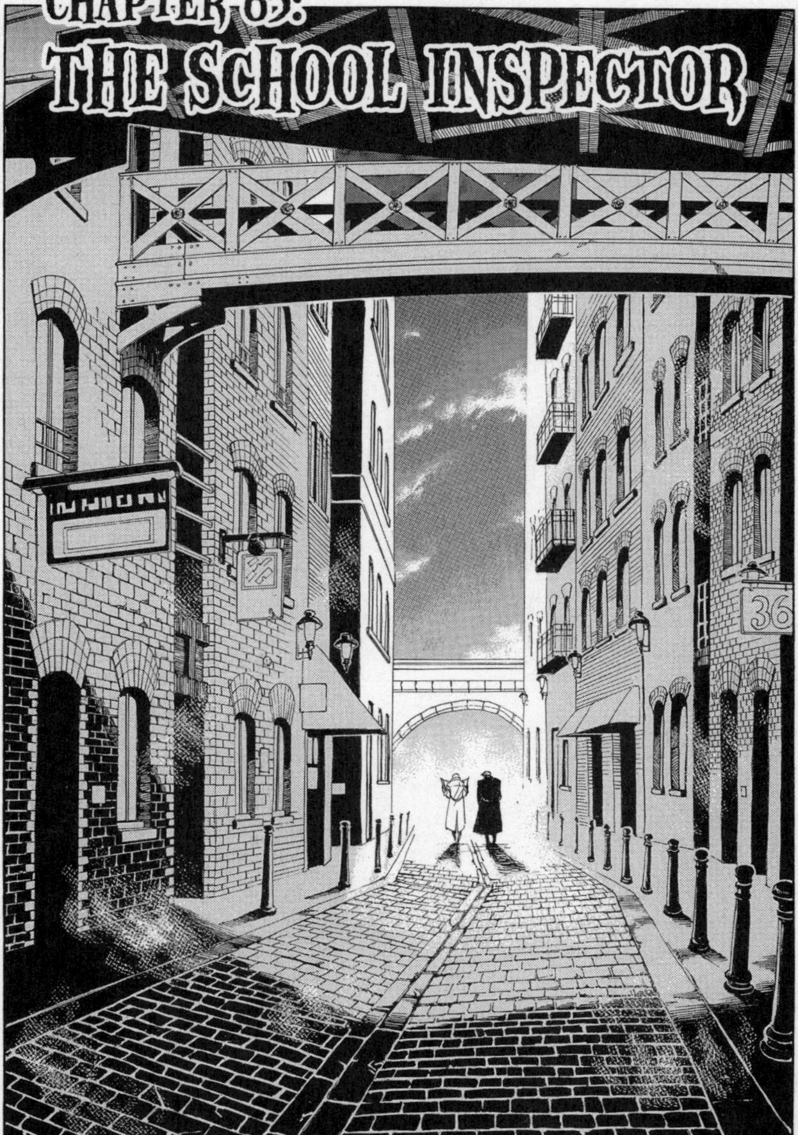
36

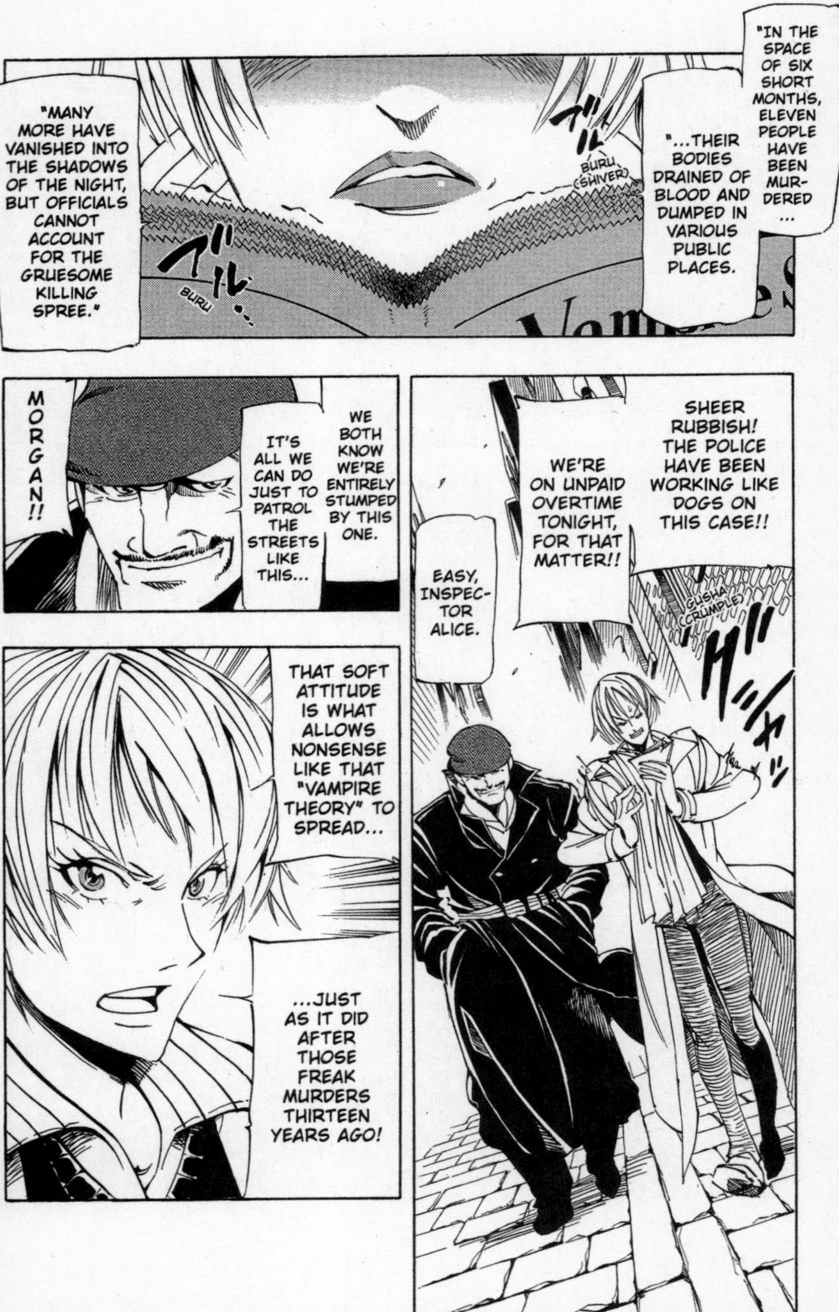
"IN THE SPACE OF SIX SHORT MONTHS, ELEVEN PEOPLE HAVE BEEN MURDERED...
"...THEIR BODIES DRAINED OF BLOOD AND DUMPED IN VARIOUS PUBLIC PLACES.
BURU (SHIVER)
"MANY MORE HAVE VANISHED INTO THE SHADOWS OF THE NIGHT, BUT OFFICIALS CANNOT ACCOUNT FOR THE GRUESOME KILLING SPREE."
BURU
SHEER RUBBISH! THE POLICE HAVE BEEN WORKING LIKE DOGS ON THIS CASE!!
WE'RE ON UNPAID OVERTIME TONIGHT, FOR THAT MATTER!!
GUSHA (CRUMPLE)
EASY, INSPECTOR ALICE.
MORGAN!!
WE BOTH KNOW WE'RE ENTIRELY STUMPED BY THIS ONE.
IT'S ALL WE CAN DO JUST TO PATROL THE STREETS LIKE THIS...
THAT SOFT ATTITUDE IS WHAT ALLOWS NONSENSE LIKE THAT "VAMPIRE THEORY" TO SPREAD...
...JUST AS IT DID AFTER THOSE FREAK MURDERS THIRTEEN YEARS AGO!

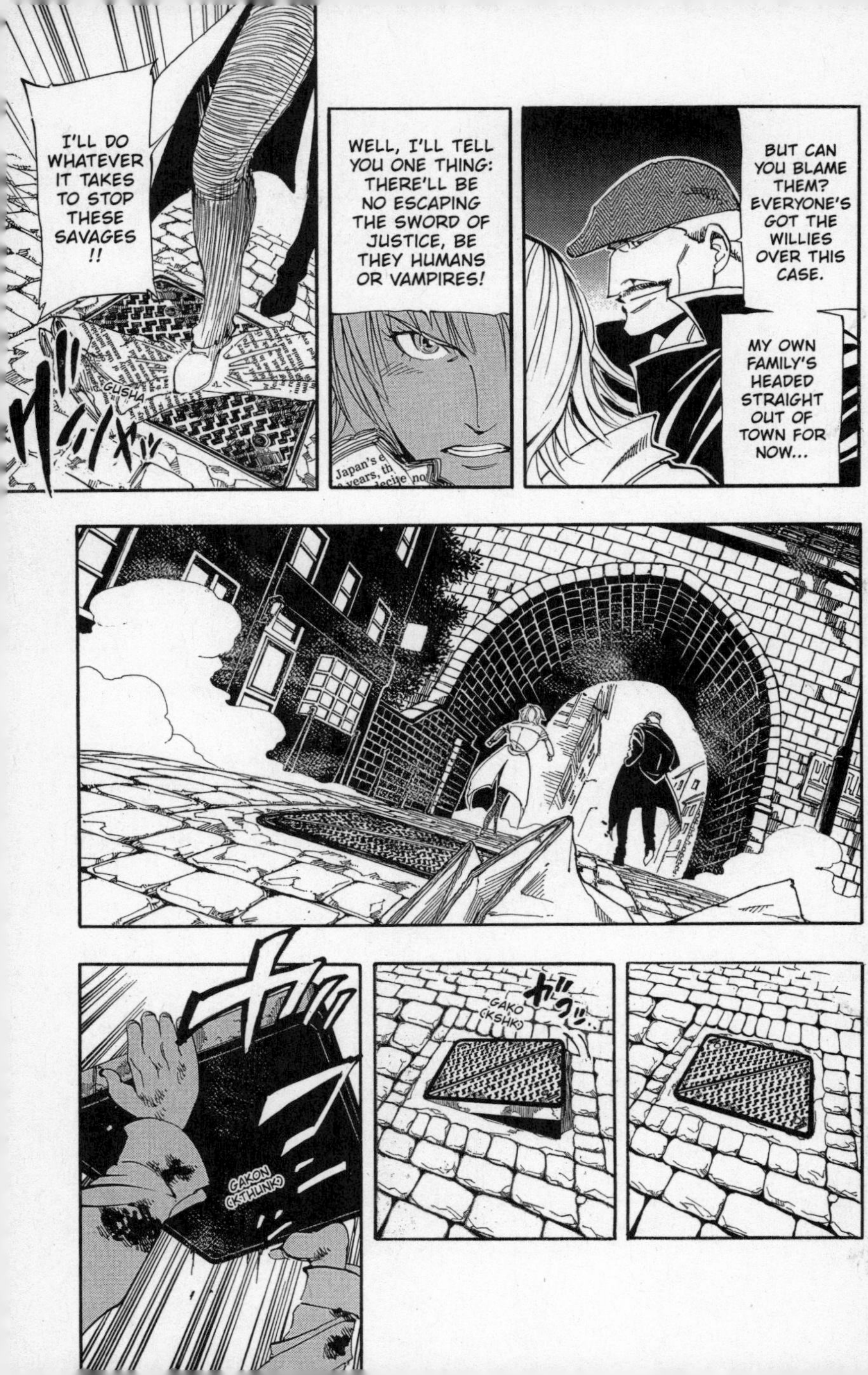
BUT CAN YOU BLAME THEM? EVERYONE'S GOT THE WILLIES OVER THIS CASE.
MY OWN FAMILY'S HEADED STRAIGHT OUT OF TOWN FOR NOW...
WELL, I'LL TELL YOU ONE THING: THERE'LL BE NO ESCAPING THE SWORD OF JUSTICE, BE THEY HUMANS OR VAMPIRES!
I'LL DO WHATEVER IT TAKES TO STOP THESE SAVAGES !!
GUSHA
GAKO (KSHK)
GAKON (KTHUNK)

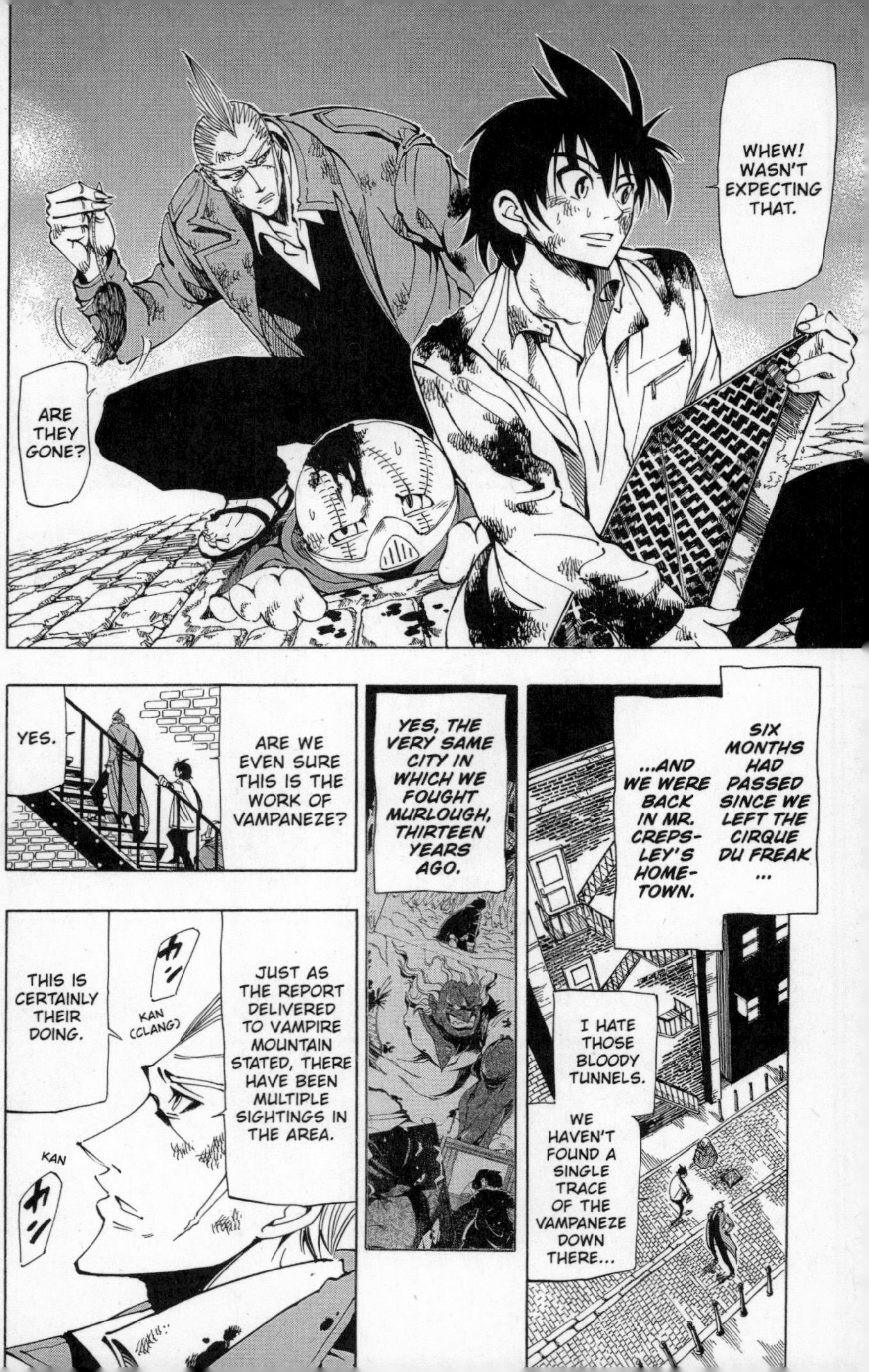
WHEW! WASN'T EXPECTING THAT.
ARE THEY GONE?
SIX MONTHS HAD PASSED SINCE WE LEFT THE CIRQUE DU FREAK ...
...AND WE WERE BACK IN MR. CREPS-LEY'S HOME-TOWN.
I HATE THOSE BLOODY TUNNELS.
WE HAVEN'T FOUND A SINGLE TRACE OF THE VAMPANEZE DOWN THERE...
YES, THE VERY SAME CITY IN WHICH WE FOUGHT MURLOUGH, THIRTEEN YEARS AGO.
ARE WE EVEN SURE THIS IS THE WORK OF VAMPANEZE?
YES.
JUST AS THE REPORT DELIVERED TO VAMPIRE MOUNTAIN STATED, THERE HAVE BEEN MULTIPLE SIGHTINGS IN THE AREA.
カン
KAN (CLANG)
THIS IS CERTAINLY THEIR DOING.
KAN
カン

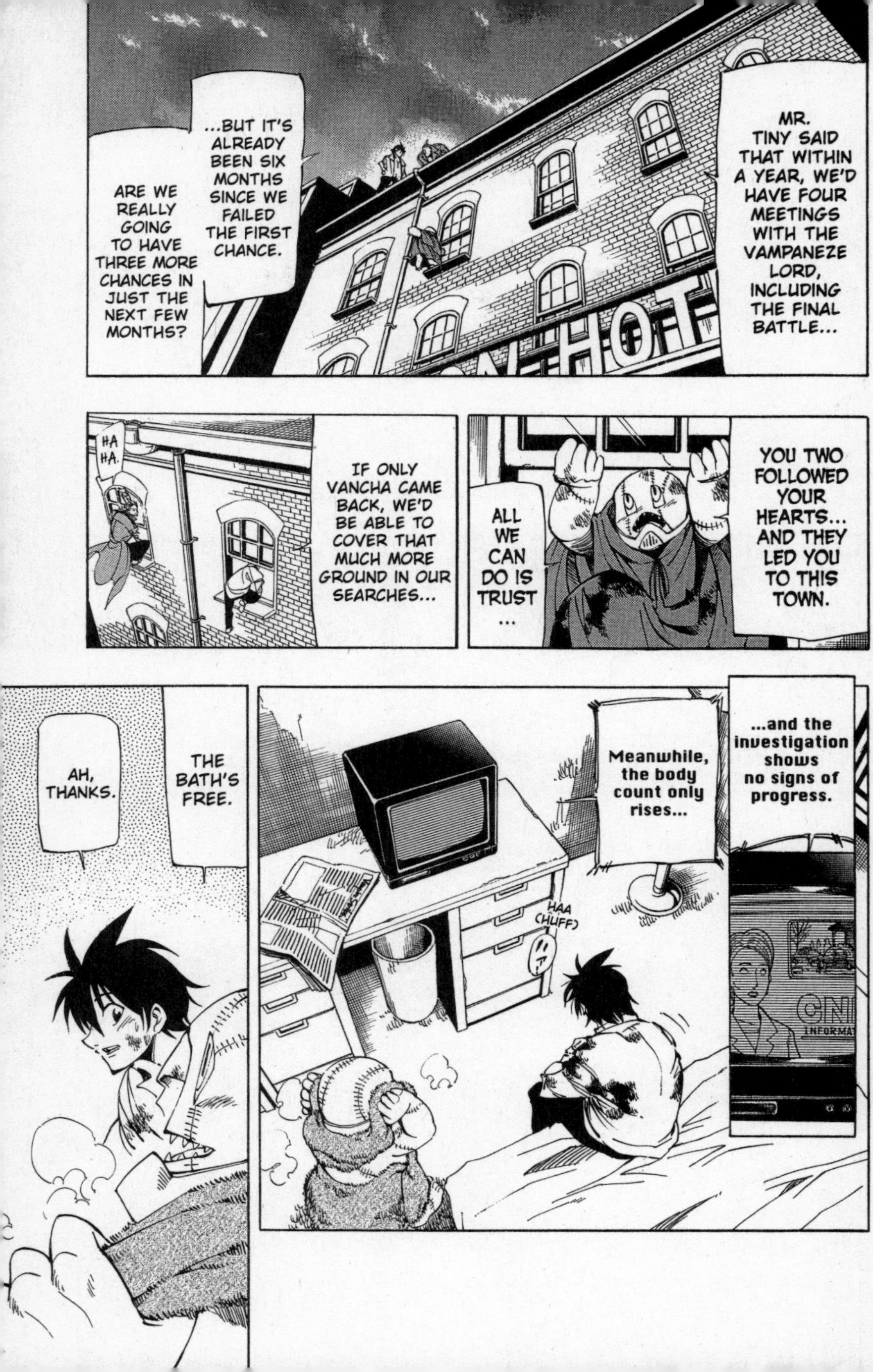
MR. TINY SAID THAT WITHIN A YEAR, WE'D HAVE FOUR MEETINGS WITH THE VAMPANEZE LORD, INCLUDING THE FINAL BATTLE...
...BUT IT'S ALREADY BEEN SIX MONTHS SINCE WE FAILED THE FIRST CHANCE.
ARE WE REALLY GOING TO HAVE THREE MORE CHANCES IN JUST THE NEXT FEW MONTHS?
YOU TWO FOLLOWED YOUR HEARTS... AND THEY LED YOU TO THIS TOWN.
ALL WE CAN DO IS TRUST ...
IF ONLY VANCHA CAME BACK, WE'D BE ABLE TO COVER THAT MUCH MORE GROUND IN OUR SEARCHES...
HA HA.
Meanwhile, the body count only rises...
...and the investigation shows no signs of progress.
HAA (HUFF)
THE BATH'S FREE.
AH, THANKS.

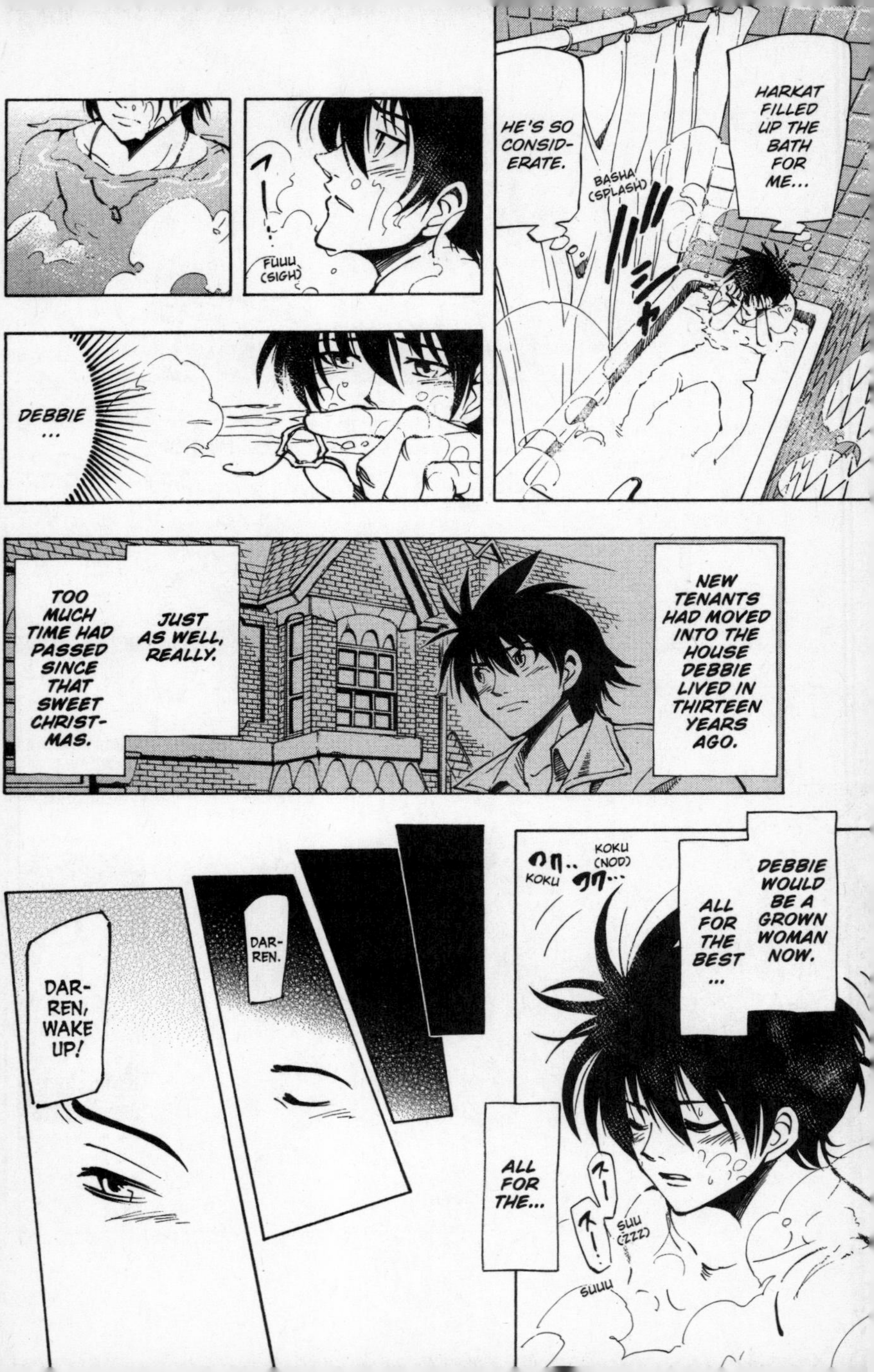
HARKAT FILLED UP THE BATH FOR ME...
HE'S SO CONSID-ERATE.
BASHA (SPLASH)
FUUU (SIGH)
DEBBIE ...
NEW TENANTS HAD MOVED INTO THE HOUSE DEBBIE LIVED IN THIRTEEN YEARS AGO.
JUST AS WELL, REALLY.
TOO MUCH TIME HAD PASSED SINCE THAT SWEET CHRIST-MAS.
DEBBIE WOULD BE A GROWN WOMAN NOW.
ALL FOR THE BEST ...
KOKU (NOD)
KOKU
ALL FOR THE...
SUU (ZZZ)
SUUU
DAR-REN.
DAR-REN, WAKE UP!

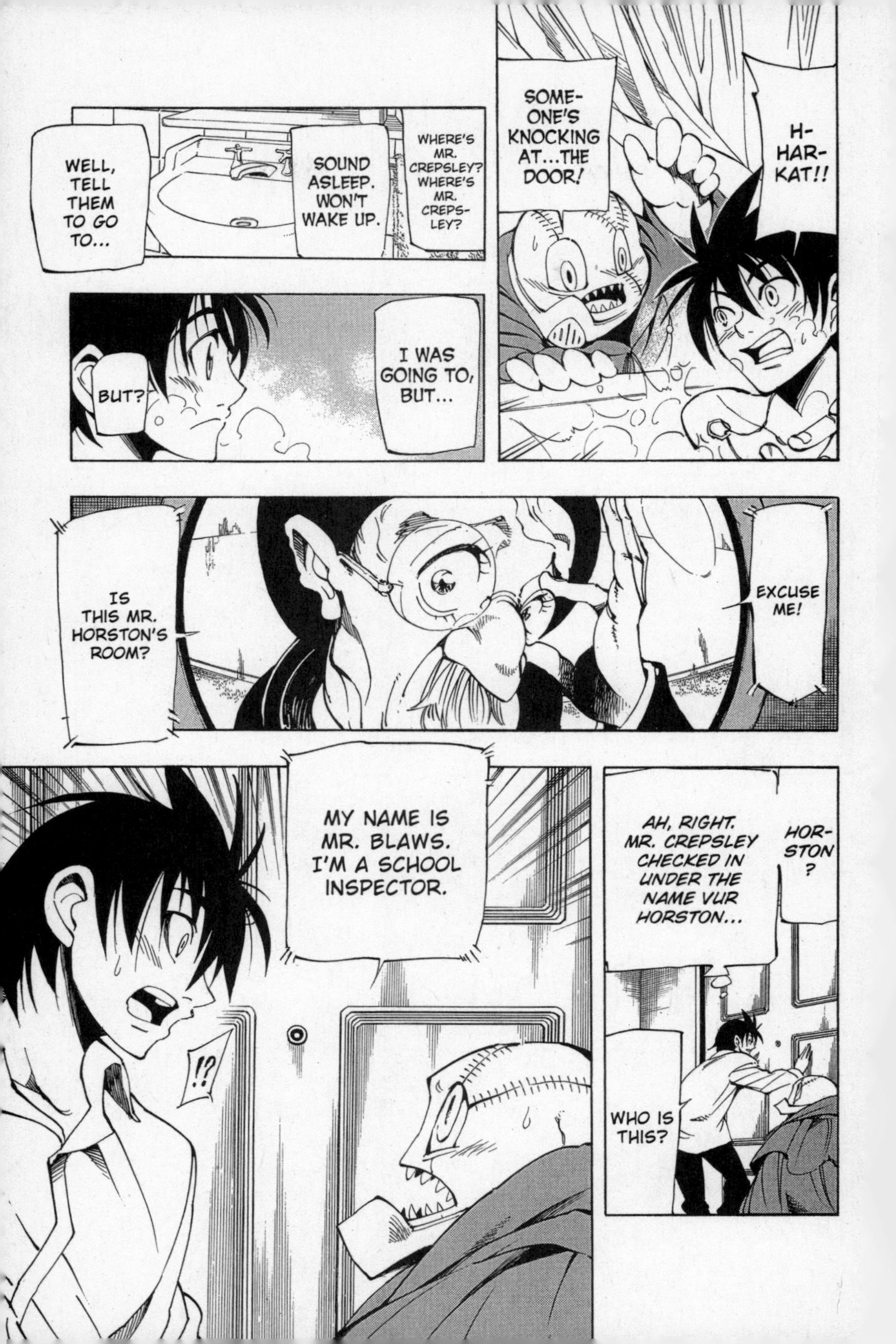
H-HAR-KAT!!
SOME-ONE'S KNOCKING AT...THE DOOR!
WHERE'S MR. CREPSLEY? WHERE'S MR. CREPS-LEY?
SOUND ASLEEP. WON'T WAKE UP.
WELL, TELL THEM TO GO TO...
I WAS GOING TO, BUT...
BUT?
EXCUSE ME!
IS THIS MR. HORSTON'S ROOM?
HOR-STON?
AH, RIGHT. MR. CREPSLEY CHECKED IN UNDER THE NAME VUR HORSTON...
WHO IS THIS?
MY NAME IS MR. BLAWS. I'M A SCHOOL INSPECTOR.
!?

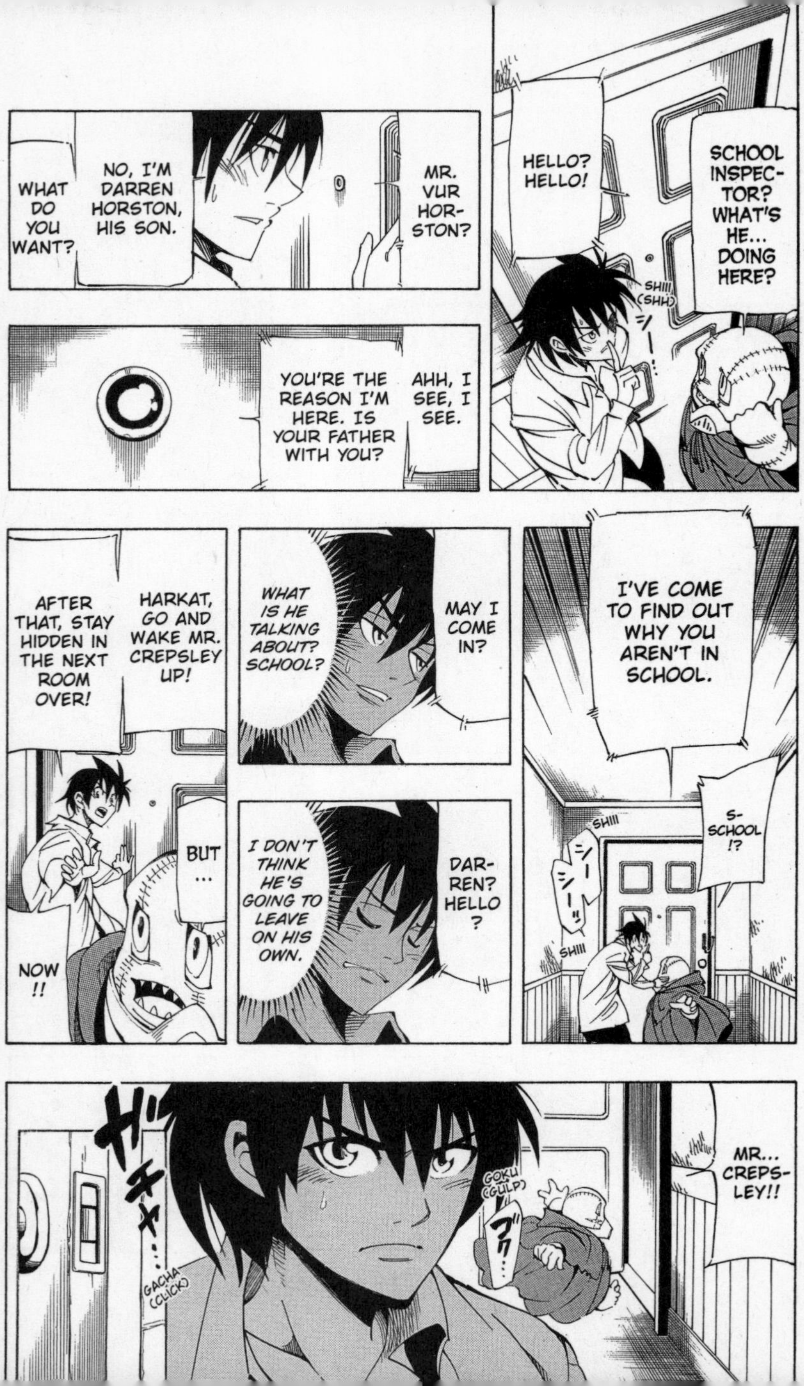

SCHOOL INSPECTOR? WHAT'S HE... DOING HERE?
HELLO? HELLO!
SHIII (SHH)
MR. VUR HORSTON?
NO, I'M DARREN HORSTON, HIS SON.
WHAT DO YOU WANT?
AHH, I SEE, I SEE.
YOU'RE THE REASON I'M HERE. IS YOUR FATHER WITH YOU?
I'VE COME TO FIND OUT WHY YOU AREN'T IN SCHOOL.
S-SCHOOL!?
SHIII
SHIII
MAY I COME IN?
WHAT IS HE TALKING ABOUT? SCHOOL?
DARREN? HELLO?
I DON'T THINK HE'S GOING TO LEAVE ON HIS OWN.
HARKAT, GO AND WAKE MR. CREPSLEY UP!
AFTER THAT, STAY HIDDEN IN THE NEXT ROOM OVER!
BUT...
NOW!!
MR... CREPSLEY!!
GOKU (GULP)
GACHA (CLICK)

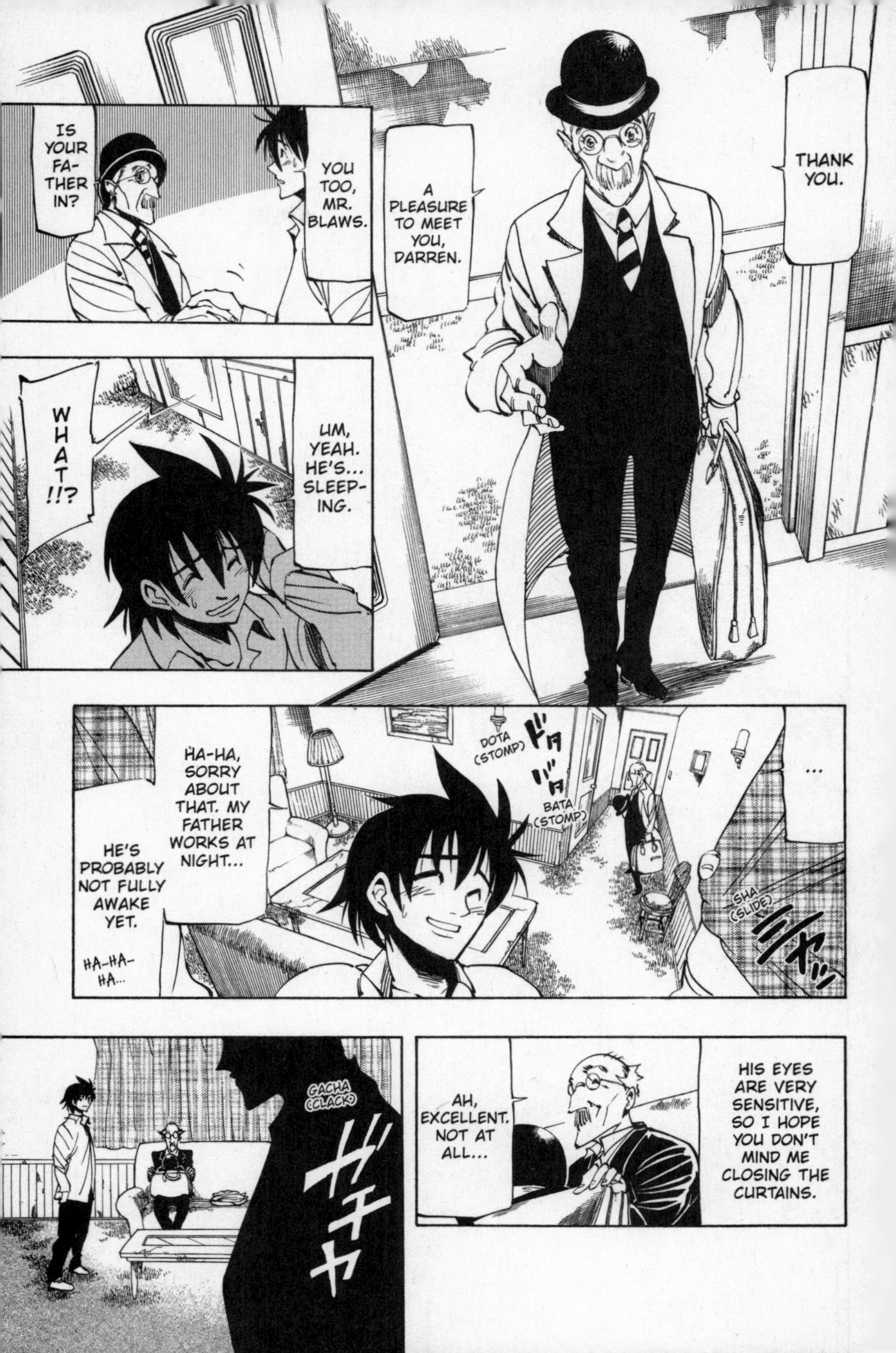
THANK YOU.
A PLEASURE TO MEET YOU, DARREN.
YOU TOO, MR. BLAWS.
IS YOUR FA-THER IN?
UM, YEAH. HE'S... SLEEP-ING.
WHAT!!?
...
SHA (SLIDE)
シャッ
DOTA (STOMP)
ドタ
BATA (STOMP)
バタ
HA-HA, SORRY ABOUT THAT. MY FATHER WORKS AT NIGHT...
HE'S PROBABLY NOT FULLY AWAKE YET.
HA-HA-HA...
HIS EYES ARE VERY SENSITIVE, SO I HOPE YOU DON'T MIND ME CLOSING THE CURTAINS.
AH, EXCELLENT. NOT AT ALL...
GACHA (CLACK)
ガチャ

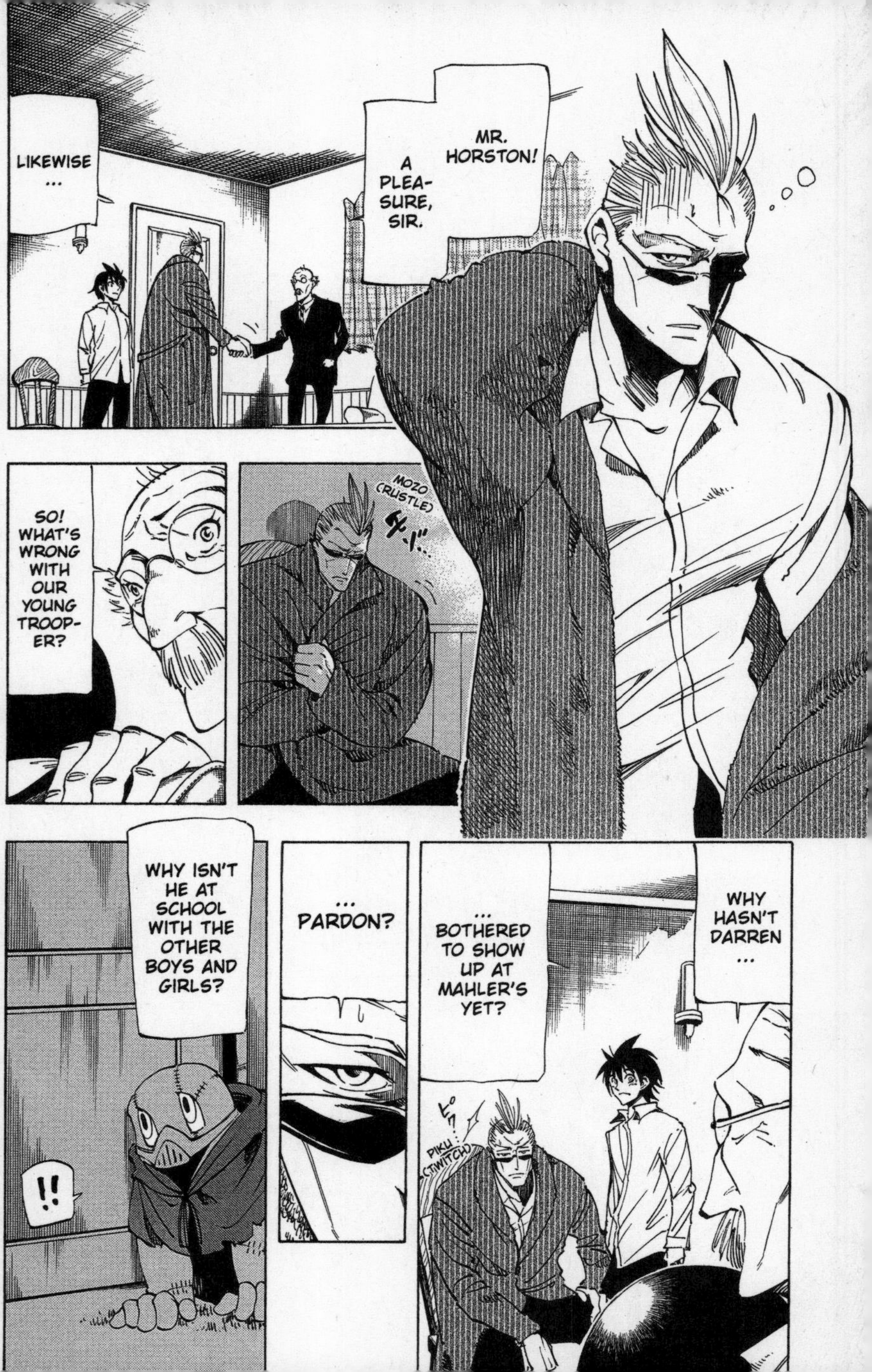
MR. HORSTON! A PLEASURE, SIR.
LIKEWISE ...
MOZO (RUSTLE)
SO! WHAT'S WRONG WITH OUR YOUNG TROOPER?
WHY HASN'T DARREN ...
... BOTHERED TO SHOW UP AT MAHLER'S YET?
PIKU (TWITCH)
... PARDON?
WHY ISN'T HE AT SCHOOL WITH THE OTHER BOYS AND GIRLS?
!!

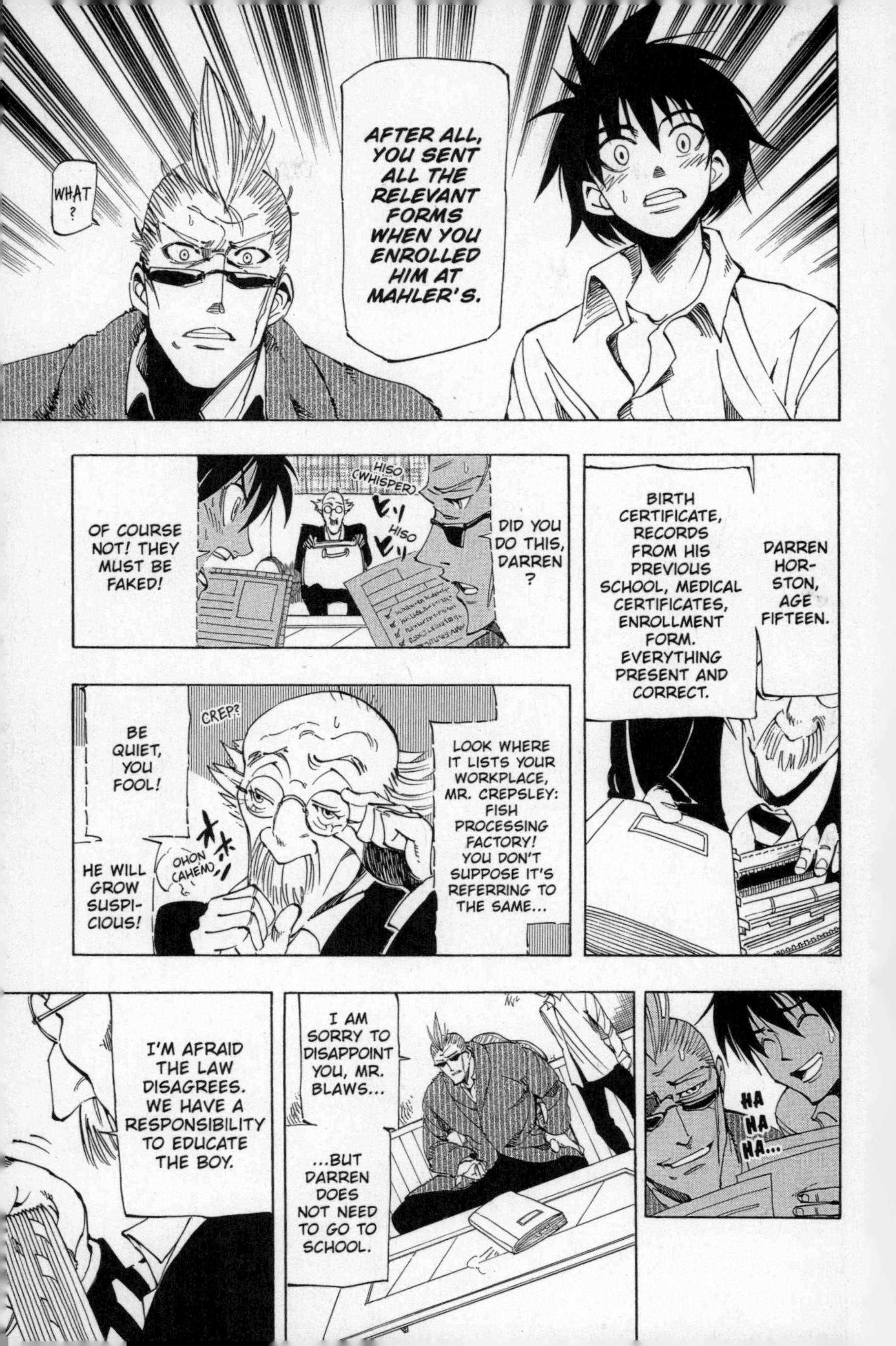
AFTER ALL, YOU SENT ALL THE RELEVANT FORMS WHEN YOU ENROLLED HIM AT MAHLER'S.
WHAT ?
DARREN HORSTON, AGE FIFTEEN.
BIRTH CERTIFICATE, RECORDS FROM HIS PREVIOUS SCHOOL, MEDICAL CERTIFICATES, ENROLLMENT FORM. EVERYTHING PRESENT AND CORRECT.
HISO (WHISPER)
DID YOU DO THIS, DARREN ?
HISO
OF COURSE NOT! THEY MUST BE FAKED!
LOOK WHERE IT LISTS YOUR WORKPLACE, MR. CREPSLEY: FISH PROCESSING FACTORY! YOU DON'T SUPPOSE IT'S REFERRING TO THE SAME...
CREP?
BE QUIET, YOU FOOL!
OHON (AHEM)
HE WILL GROW SUSPICIOUS!
HA HA HA...
I AM SORRY TO DISAPPOINT YOU, MR. BLAWS...
...BUT DARREN DOES NOT NEED TO GO TO SCHOOL.
I'M AFRAID THE LAW DISAGREES. WE HAVE A RESPONSIBILITY TO EDUCATE THE BOY.

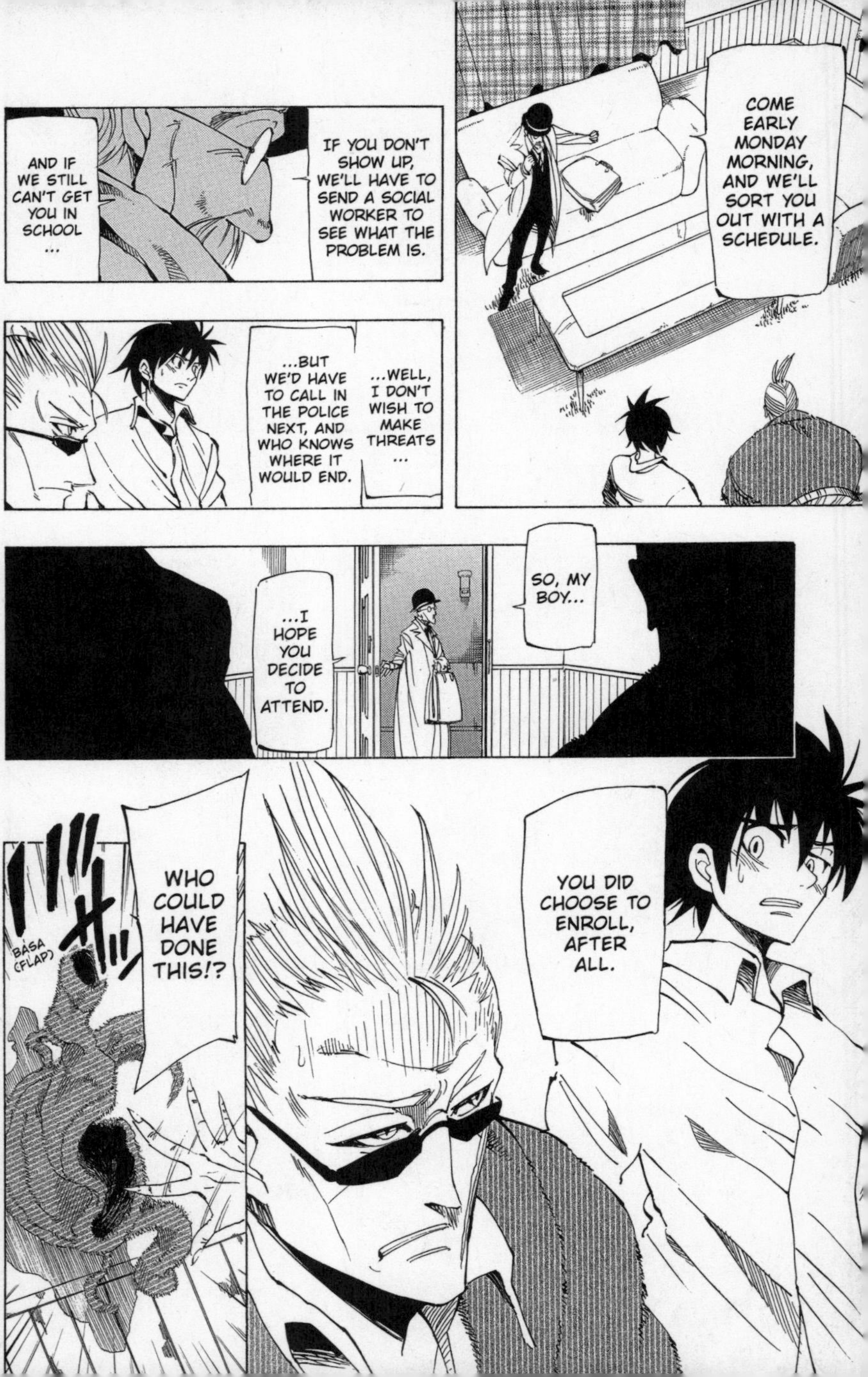
COME EARLY MONDAY MORNING, AND WE'LL SORT YOU OUT WITH A SCHEDULE.
IF YOU DON'T SHOW UP, WE'LL HAVE TO SEND A SOCIAL WORKER TO SEE WHAT THE PROBLEM IS.
AND IF WE STILL CAN'T GET YOU IN SCHOOL ...
...WELL, I DON'T WISH TO MAKE THREATS ...
...BUT WE'D HAVE TO CALL IN THE POLICE NEXT, AND WHO KNOWS WHERE IT WOULD END.
SO, MY BOY...
...I HOPE YOU DECIDE TO ATTEND.
YOU DID CHOOSE TO ENROLL, AFTER ALL.
WHO COULD HAVE DONE THIS!?
BASA (FLAP)

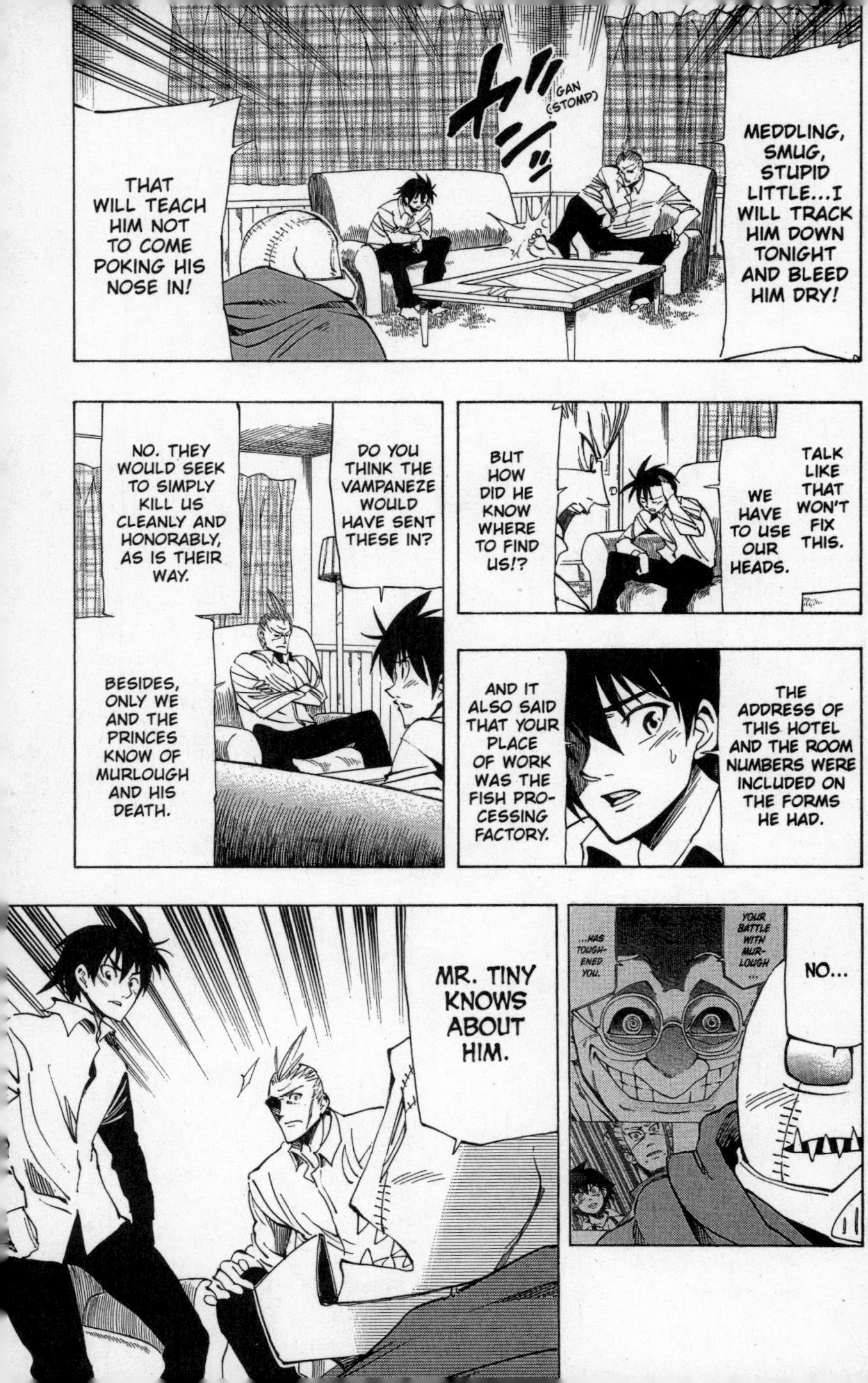
MEDDLING, SMUG, STUPID LITTLE...I WILL TRACK HIM DOWN TONIGHT AND BLEED HIM DRY!
GAN (STOMP)
THAT WILL TEACH HIM NOT TO COME POKING HIS NOSE IN!
TALK LIKE THAT WON'T FIX THIS.
WE HAVE TO USE OUR HEADS.
BUT HOW DID HE KNOW WHERE TO FIND US!?
THE ADDRESS OF THIS HOTEL AND THE ROOM NUMBERS WERE INCLUDED ON THE FORMS HE HAD.
AND IT ALSO SAID THAT YOUR PLACE OF WORK WAS THE FISH PRO-CESSING FACTORY.
DO YOU THINK THE VAMPANEZE WOULD HAVE SENT THESE IN?
NO. THEY WOULD SEEK TO SIMPLY KILL US CLEANLY AND HONORABLY, AS IS THEIR WAY.
BESIDES, ONLY WE AND THE PRINCES KNOW OF MURLOUGH AND HIS DEATH.
NO...
YOUR BATTLE WITH MUR-LOUGH...
...HAS TOUGH-ENED YOU.
MR. TINY KNOWS ABOUT HIM.

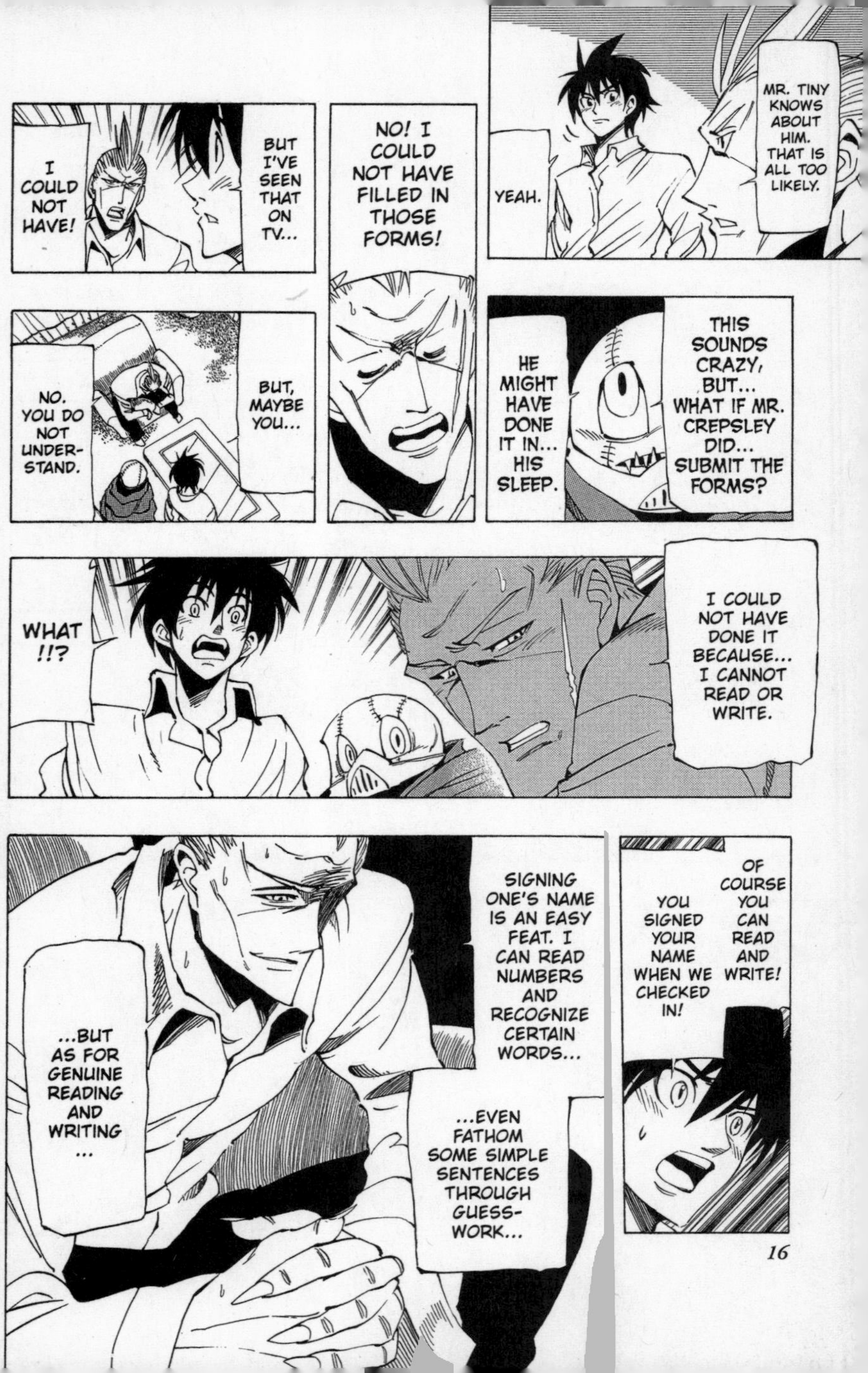
MR. TINY KNOWS ABOUT HIM. THAT IS ALL TOO LIKELY.
YEAH.
THIS SOUNDS CRAZY, BUT... WHAT IF MR. CREPSLEY DID... SUBMIT THE FORMS?
HE MIGHT HAVE DONE IT IN... HIS SLEEP.
NO! I COULD NOT HAVE FILLED IN THOSE FORMS!
BUT I'VE SEEN THAT ON TV...
I COULD NOT HAVE!
BUT, MAYBE YOU...
NO. YOU DO NOT UNDERSTAND.
I COULD NOT HAVE DONE IT BECAUSE... I CANNOT READ OR WRITE.
WHAT !!?
OF COURSE YOU CAN READ AND WRITE!
YOU SIGNED YOUR NAME WHEN WE CHECKED IN!
SIGNING ONE'S NAME IS AN EASY FEAT. I CAN READ NUMBERS AND RECOGNIZE CERTAIN WORDS...
...EVEN FATHOM SOME SIMPLE SENTENCES THROUGH GUESS-WORK...
...BUT AS FOR GENUINE READING AND WRITING ...

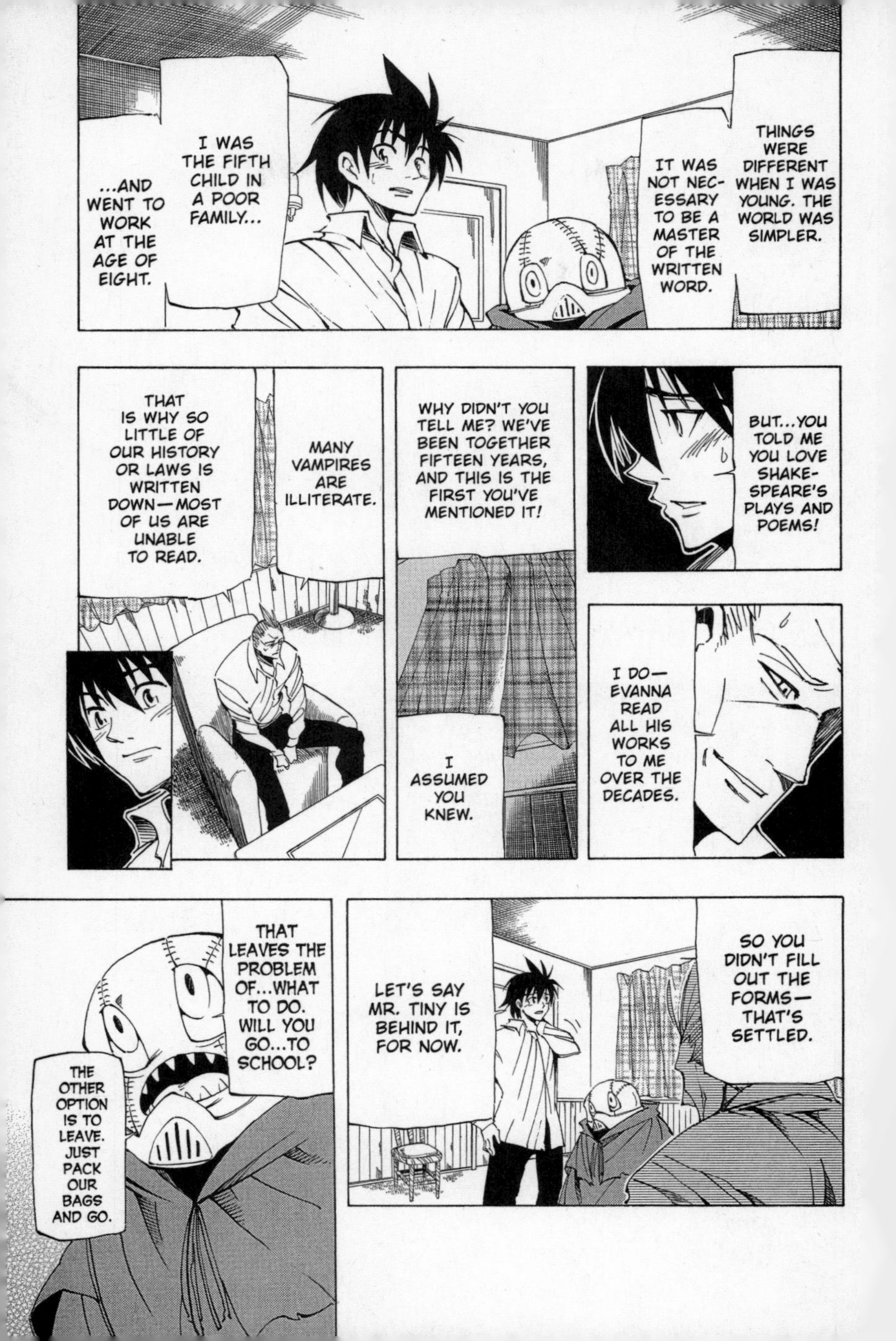
THINGS WERE DIFFERENT WHEN I WAS YOUNG. THE WORLD WAS SIMPLER.
IT WAS NOT NECESSARY TO BE A MASTER OF THE WRITTEN WORD.
I WAS THE FIFTH CHILD IN A POOR FAMILY...
...AND WENT TO WORK AT THE AGE OF EIGHT.
BUT...YOU TOLD ME YOU LOVE SHAKESPEARE'S PLAYS AND POEMS!
I DO—EVANNA READ ALL HIS WORKS TO ME OVER THE DECADES.
WHY DIDN'T YOU TELL ME? WE'VE BEEN TOGETHER FIFTEEN YEARS, AND THIS IS THE FIRST YOU'VE MENTIONED IT!
I ASSUMED YOU KNEW.
MANY VAMPIRES ARE ILLITERATE.
THAT IS WHY SO LITTLE OF OUR HISTORY OR LAWS IS WRITTEN DOWN—MOST OF US ARE UNABLE TO READ.
SO YOU DIDN'T FILL OUT THE FORMS—THAT'S SETTLED.
LET'S SAY MR. TINY IS BEHIND IT, FOR NOW.
THAT LEAVES THE PROBLEM OF...WHAT TO DO. WILL YOU GO...TO SCHOOL?
THE OTHER OPTION IS TO LEAVE. JUST PACK OUR BAGS AND GO.

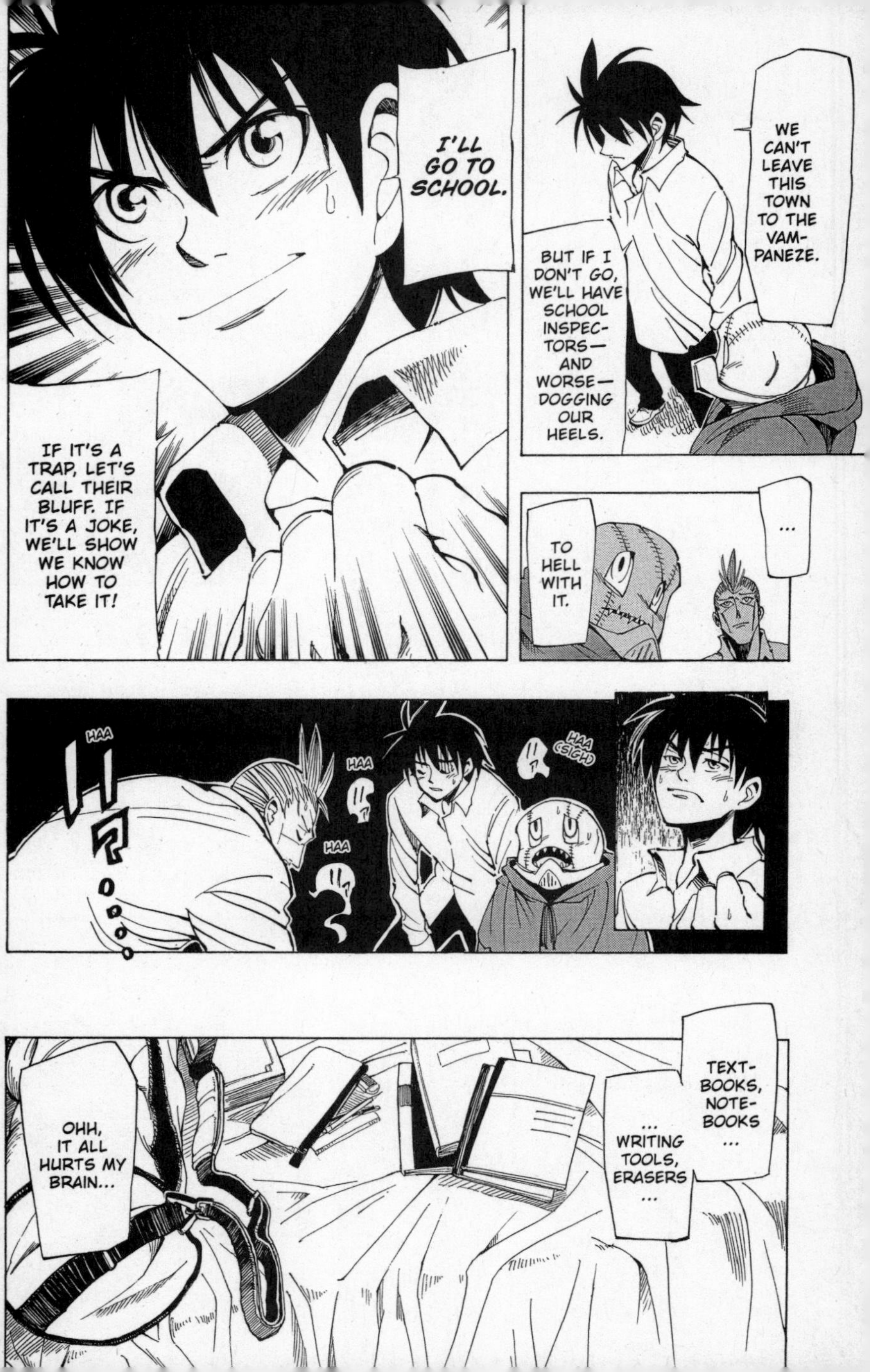
WE CAN'T LEAVE THIS TOWN TO THE VAM-PANEZE.
BUT IF I DON'T GO, WE'LL HAVE SCHOOL INSPEC-TORS— AND WORSE— DOGGING OUR HEELS.
...
TO HELL WITH IT.
I'LL GO TO SCHOOL.
IF IT'S A TRAP, LET'S CALL THEIR BLUFF. IF IT'S A JOKE, WE'LL SHOW WE KNOW HOW TO TAKE IT!
HAA (SIGH)
HAA
HAA
HAA
TEXT-BOOKS, NOTE-BOOKS ...
... WRITING TOOLS, ERASERS ...
OHH, IT ALL HURTS MY BRAIN...

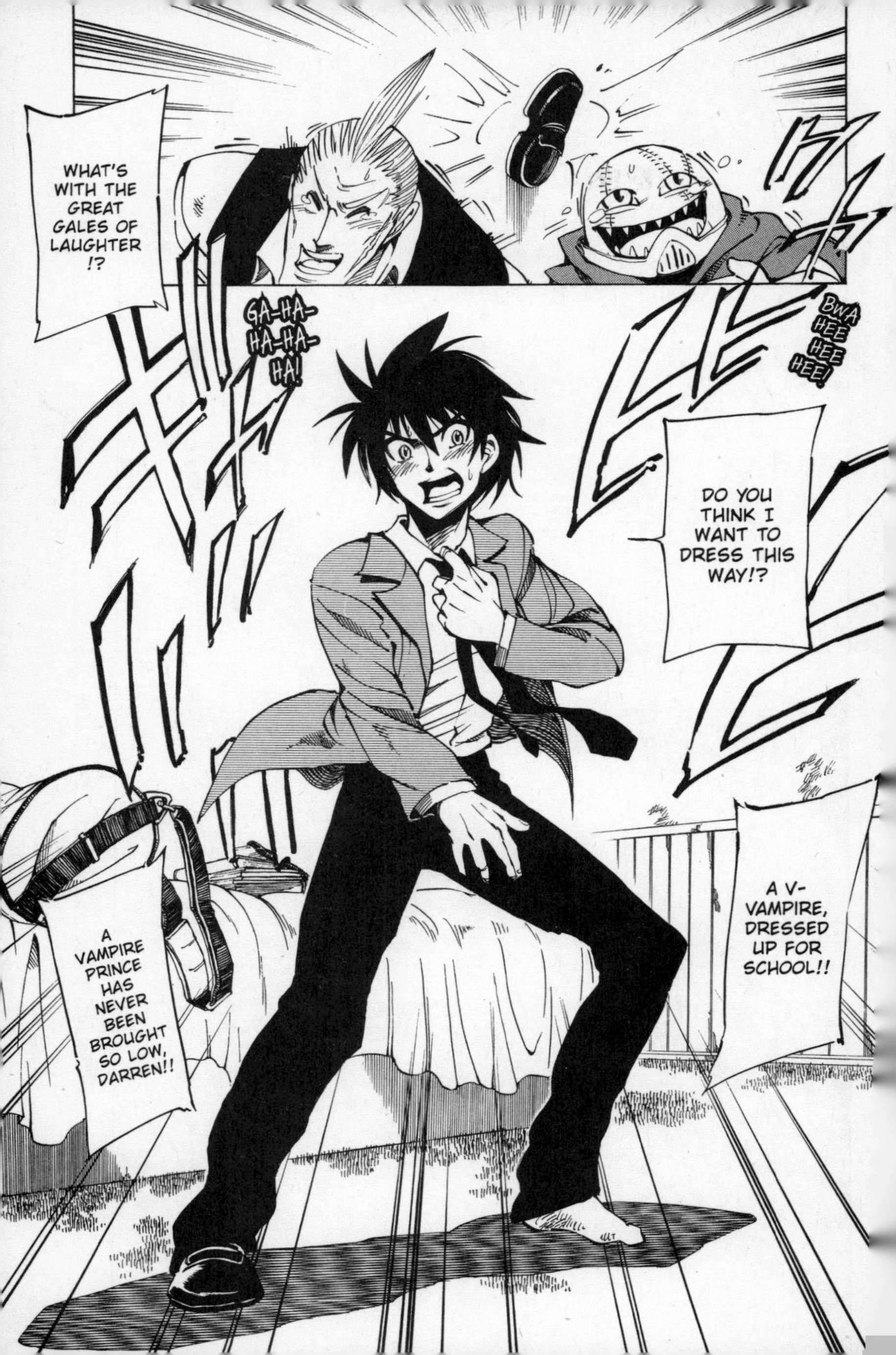
WHAT'S WITH THE GREAT GALES OF LAUGHTER!?
BWA HEE HEE HEE!
GA-HA-HA-HA-HA!
DO YOU THINK I WANT TO DRESS THIS WAY!?
A V-VAMPIRE, DRESSED UP FOR SCHOOL!!
A VAMPIRE PRINCE HAS NEVER BEEN BROUGHT SO LOW, DARREN!!

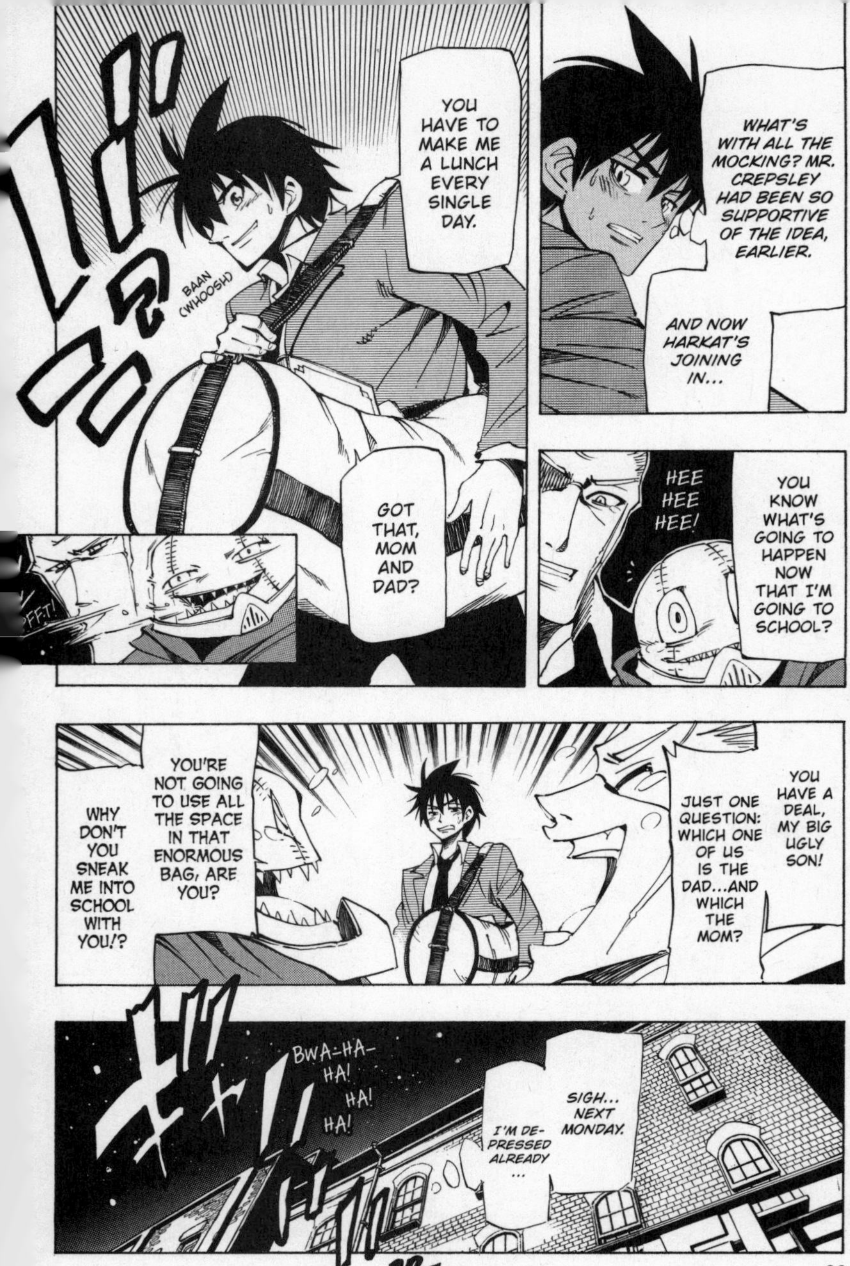
WHAT'S WITH ALL THE MOCKING? MR. CREPSLEY HAD BEEN SO SUPPORTIVE OF THE IDEA, EARLIER.
AND NOW HARKAT'S JOINING IN...
YOU KNOW WHAT'S GOING TO HAPPEN NOW THAT I'M GOING TO SCHOOL?
HEE HEE HEE!
YOU HAVE TO MAKE ME A LUNCH EVERY SINGLE DAY.
BAAN (WHOOSH)
GOT THAT, MOM AND DAD?
FFT!
YOU HAVE A DEAL, MY BIG UGLY SON!
JUST ONE QUESTION: WHICH ONE OF US IS THE DAD...AND WHICH THE MOM?
YOU'RE NOT GOING TO USE ALL THE SPACE IN THAT ENORMOUS BAG, ARE YOU?
WHY DON'T YOU SNEAK ME INTO SCHOOL WITH YOU!?
SIGH... NEXT MONDAY.
I'M DE-PRESSED ALREADY ...
BWA-HA-HA! HA! HA!

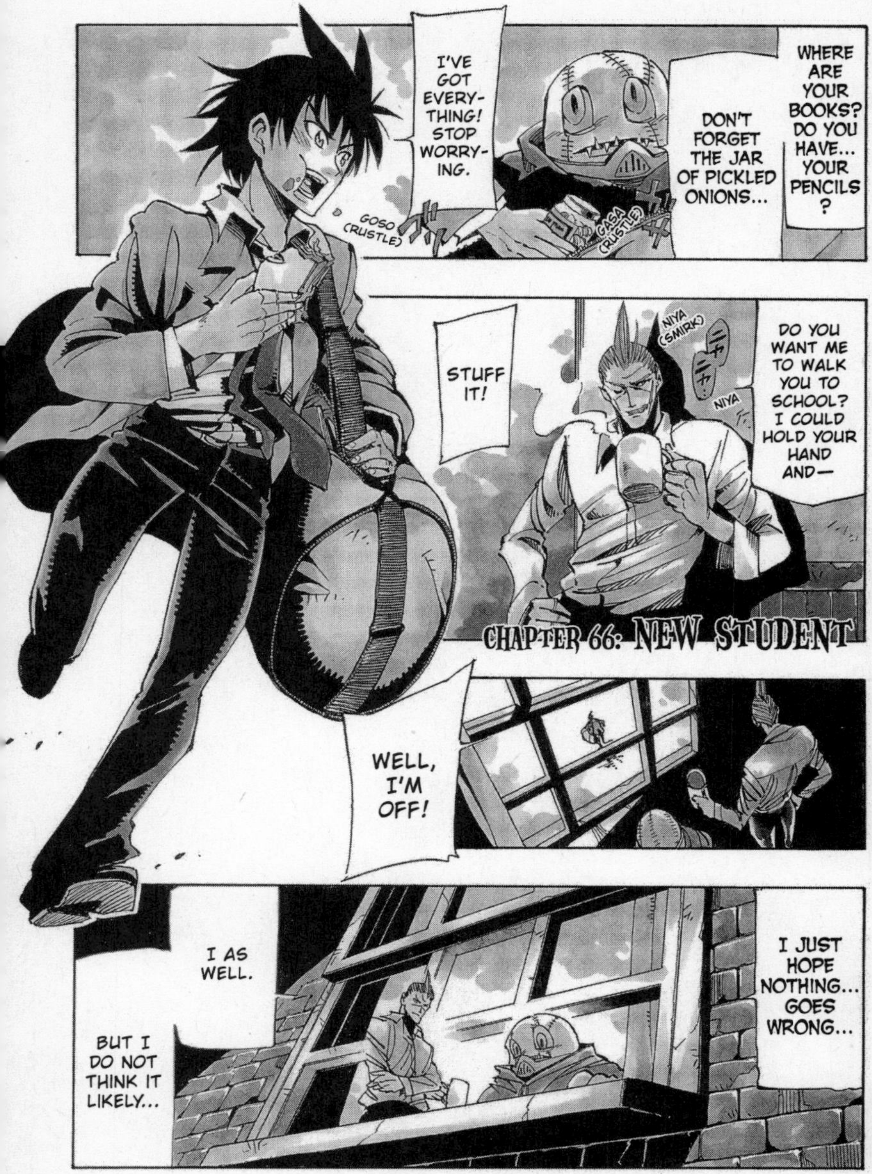
WHERE ARE YOUR BOOKS? DO YOU HAVE... YOUR PENCILS?
DON'T FORGET THE JAR OF PICKLED ONIONS...
GASA (RUSTLE)
I'VE GOT EVERYTHING! STOP WORRYING.
GOSO (RUSTLE)
DO YOU WANT ME TO WALK YOU TO SCHOOL? I COULD HOLD YOUR HAND AND—
NIYA (SMIRK)
NIYA
STUFF IT!
CHAPTER 66: NEW STUDENT
WELL, I'M OFF!
I JUST HOPE NOTHING... GOES WRONG...
I AS WELL.
BUT I DO NOT THINK IT LIKELY...

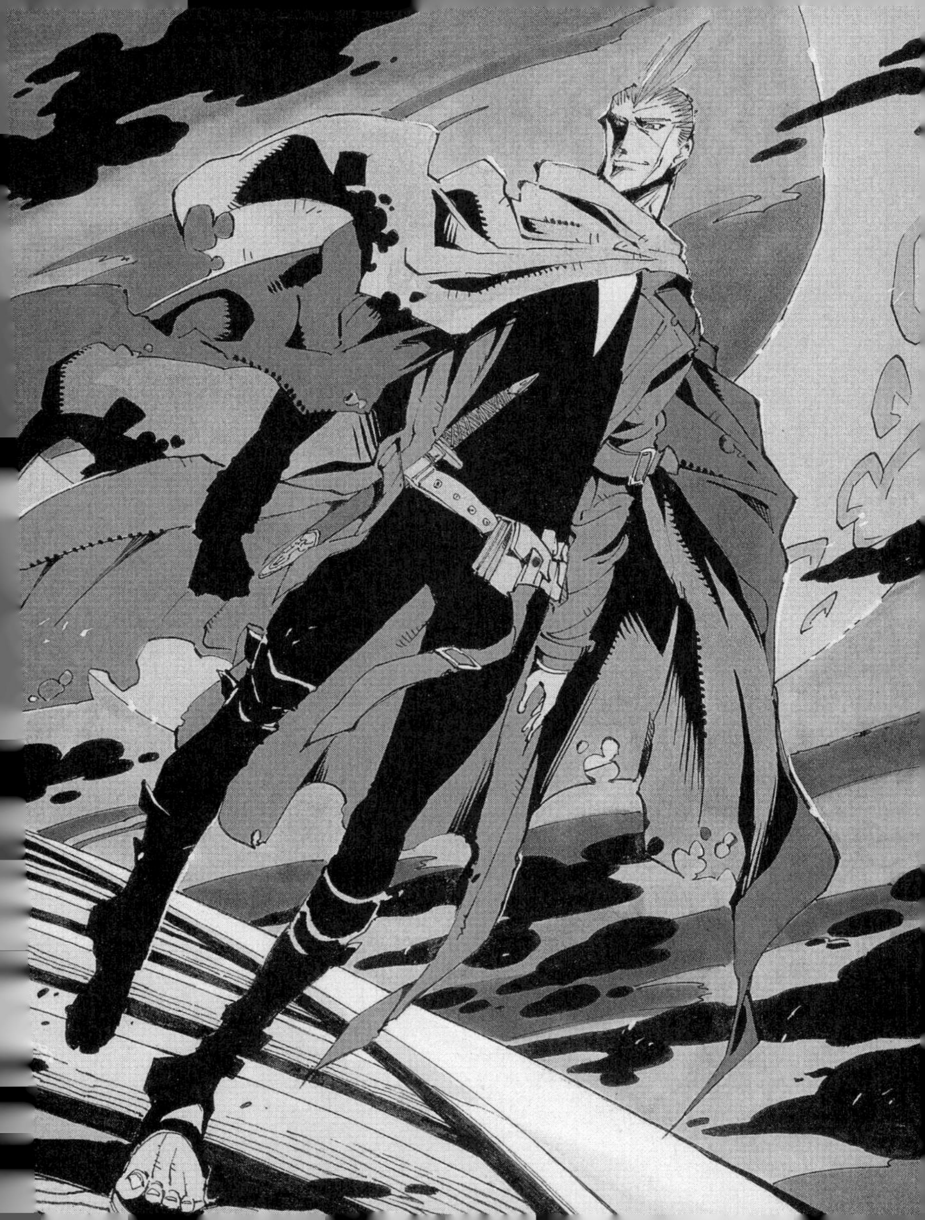

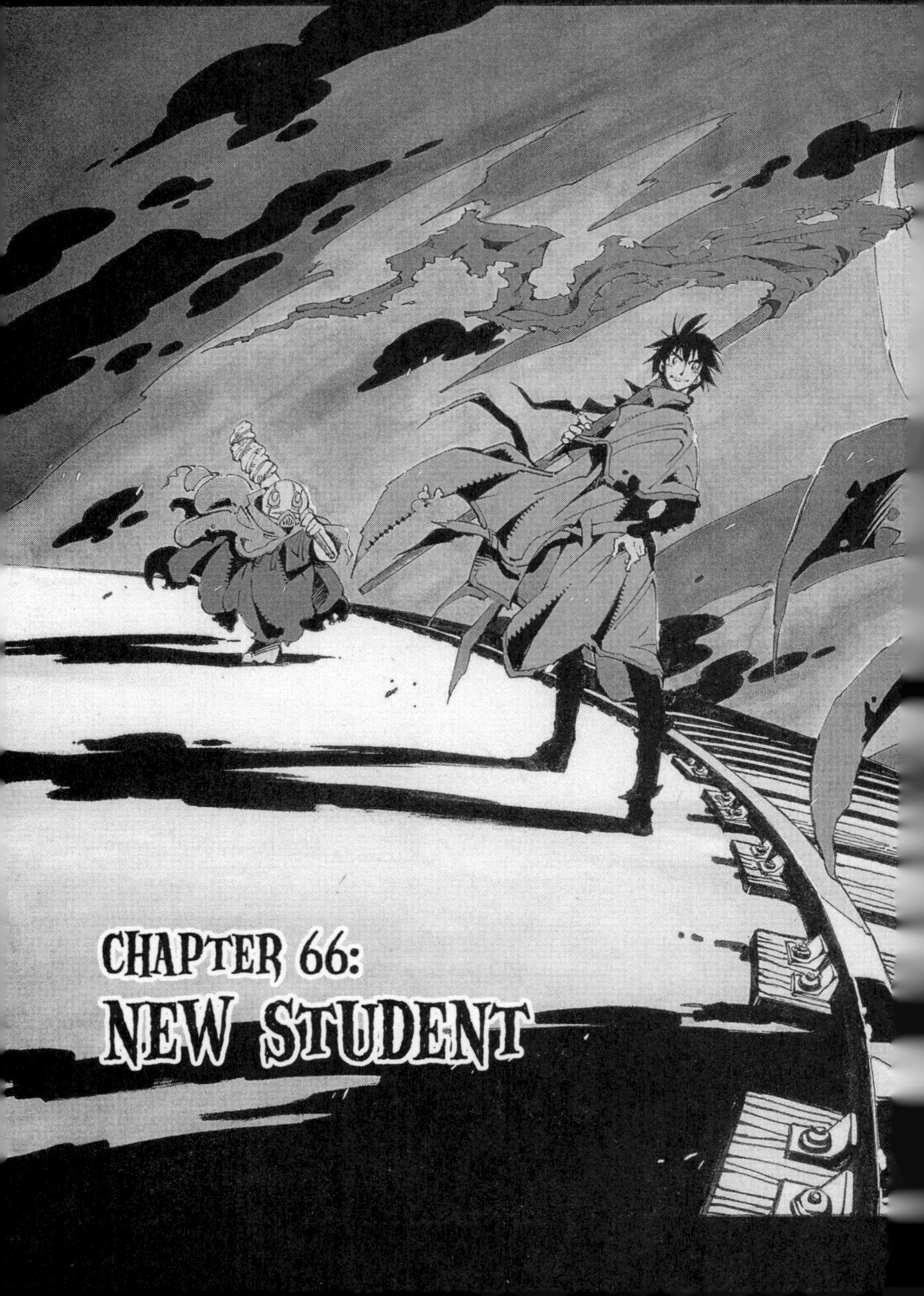
CHAPTER 66:
NEW STUDENT

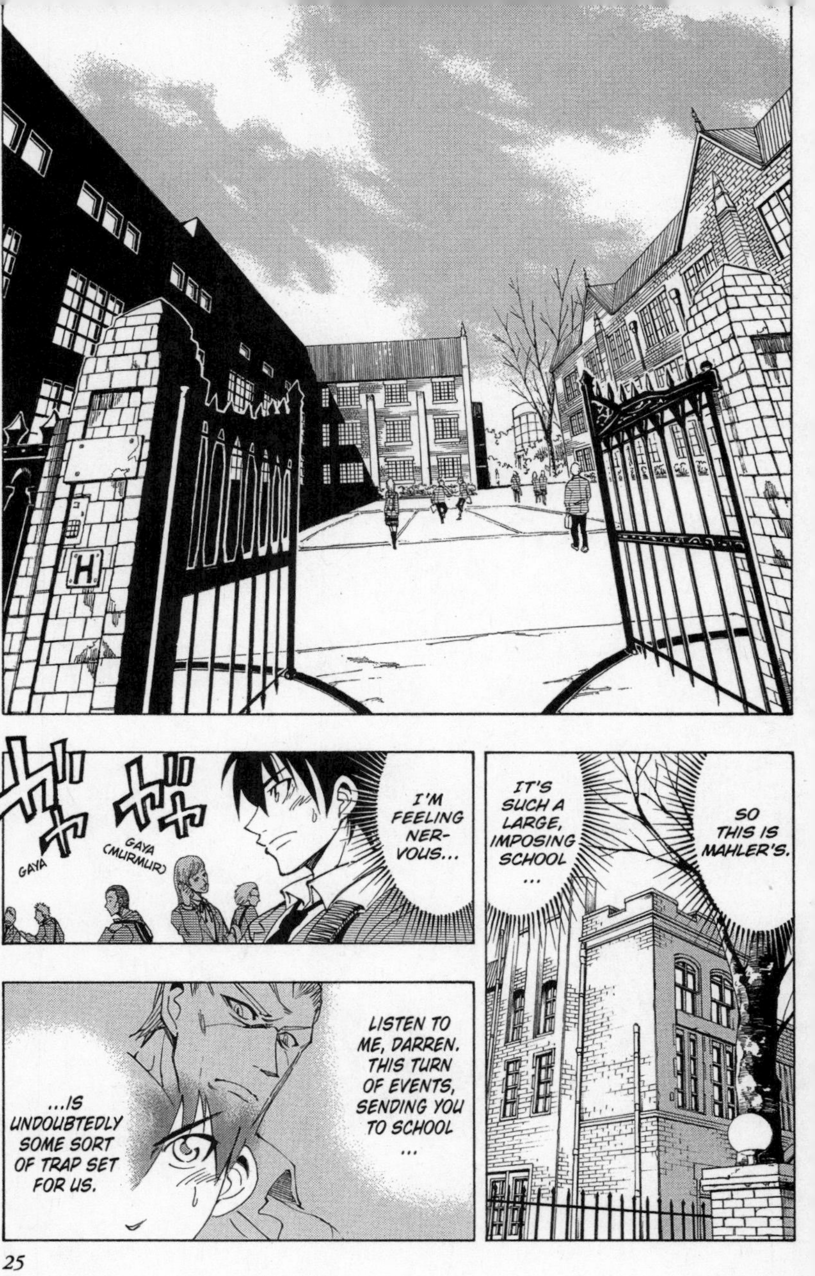
SO THIS IS MAHLER'S.
IT'S SUCH A LARGE, IMPOSING SCHOOL...
I'M FEELING NER-VOUS...
ガヤ
GAYA (MURMUR)
ガヤ
GAYA
LISTEN TO ME, DARREN. THIS TURN OF EVENTS, SENDING YOU TO SCHOOL...
...IS UNDOUBTEDLY SOME SORT OF TRAP SET FOR US.

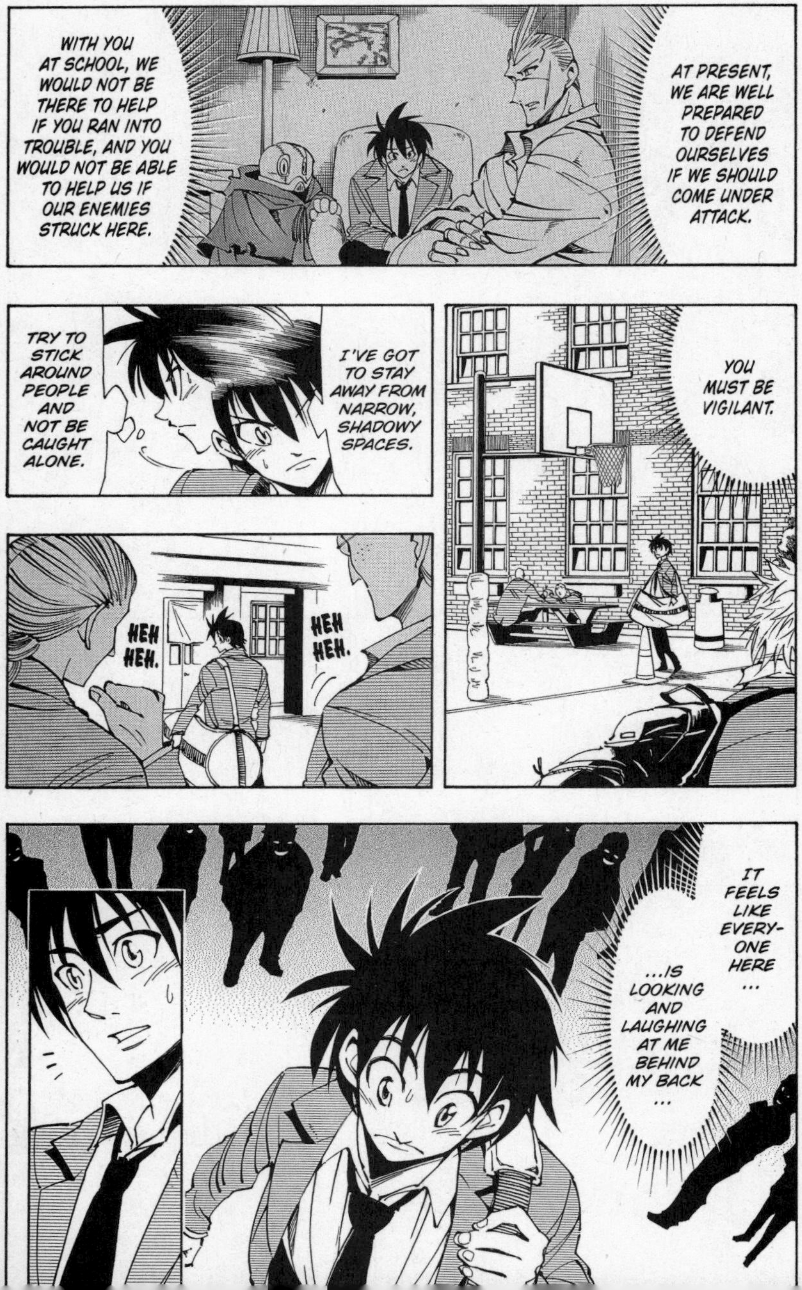
AT PRESENT, WE ARE WELL PREPARED TO DEFEND OURSELVES IF WE SHOULD COME UNDER ATTACK.
WITH YOU AT SCHOOL, WE WOULD NOT BE THERE TO HELP IF YOU RAN INTO TROUBLE, AND YOU WOULD NOT BE ABLE TO HELP US IF OUR ENEMIES STRUCK HERE.
YOU MUST BE VIGILANT.
I'VE GOT TO STAY AWAY FROM NARROW, SHADOWY SPACES.
TRY TO STICK AROUND PEOPLE AND NOT BE CAUGHT ALONE.
HEH HEH.
HEH HEH.
IT FEELS LIKE EVERY-ONE HERE ...
...IS LOOKING AND LAUGHING AT ME BEHIND MY BACK ...

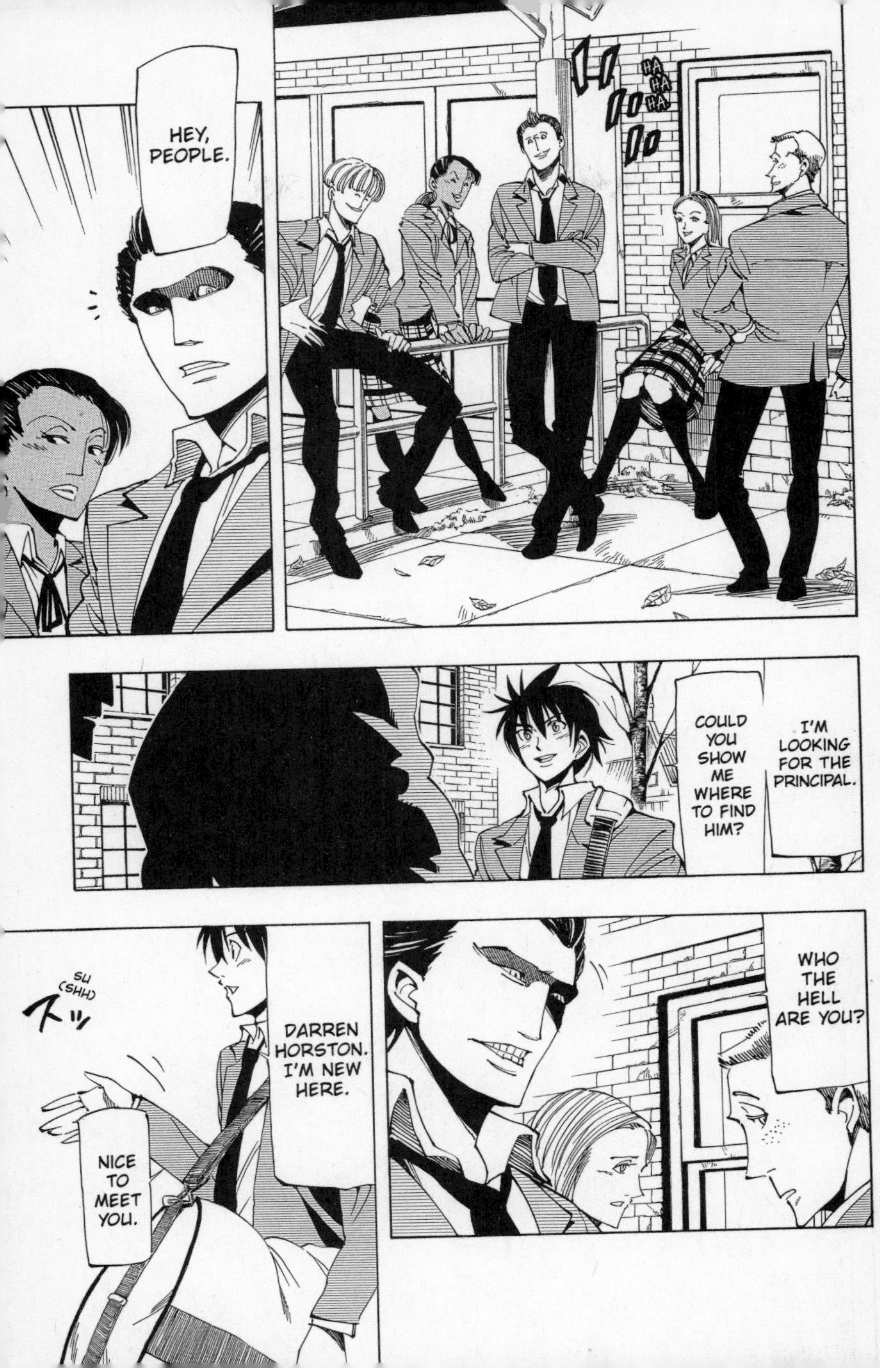
HA HA HA
HEY, PEOPLE.
I'M LOOKING FOR THE PRINCIPAL.
COULD YOU SHOW ME WHERE TO FIND HIM?
WHO THE HELL ARE YOU?
DARREN HORSTON. I'M NEW HERE.
SU (SHH)
NICE TO MEET YOU.

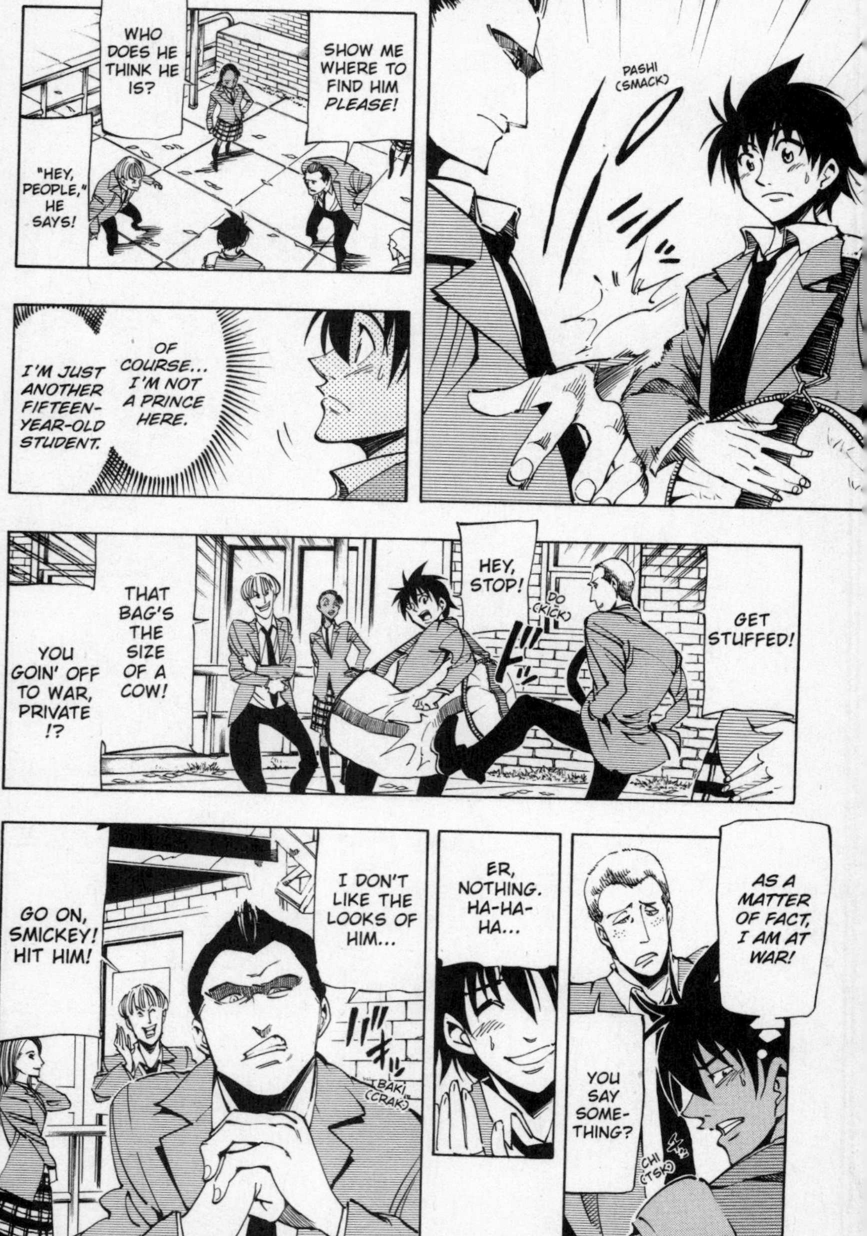

PASHI (SMACK)
SHOW ME WHERE TO FIND HIM *PLEASE!*
WHO DOES HE THINK HE IS?
"HEY, PEOPLE," HE SAYS!
OF COURSE... I'M NOT A PRINCE HERE.
I'M JUST ANOTHER FIFTEEN-YEAR-OLD STUDENT.
GET STUFFED!
DO (KICK)
HEY, STOP!
THAT BAG'S THE SIZE OF A COW!
YOU GOIN' OFF TO WAR, PRIVATE!?
AS A MATTER OF FACT, I AM AT WAR!
YOU SAY SOME-THING?
CHI (TSK)
ER, NOTHING. HA-HA-HA...
I DON'T LIKE THE LOOKS OF HIM...
BAKI (CRAK)
GO ON, SMICKEY! HIT HIM!

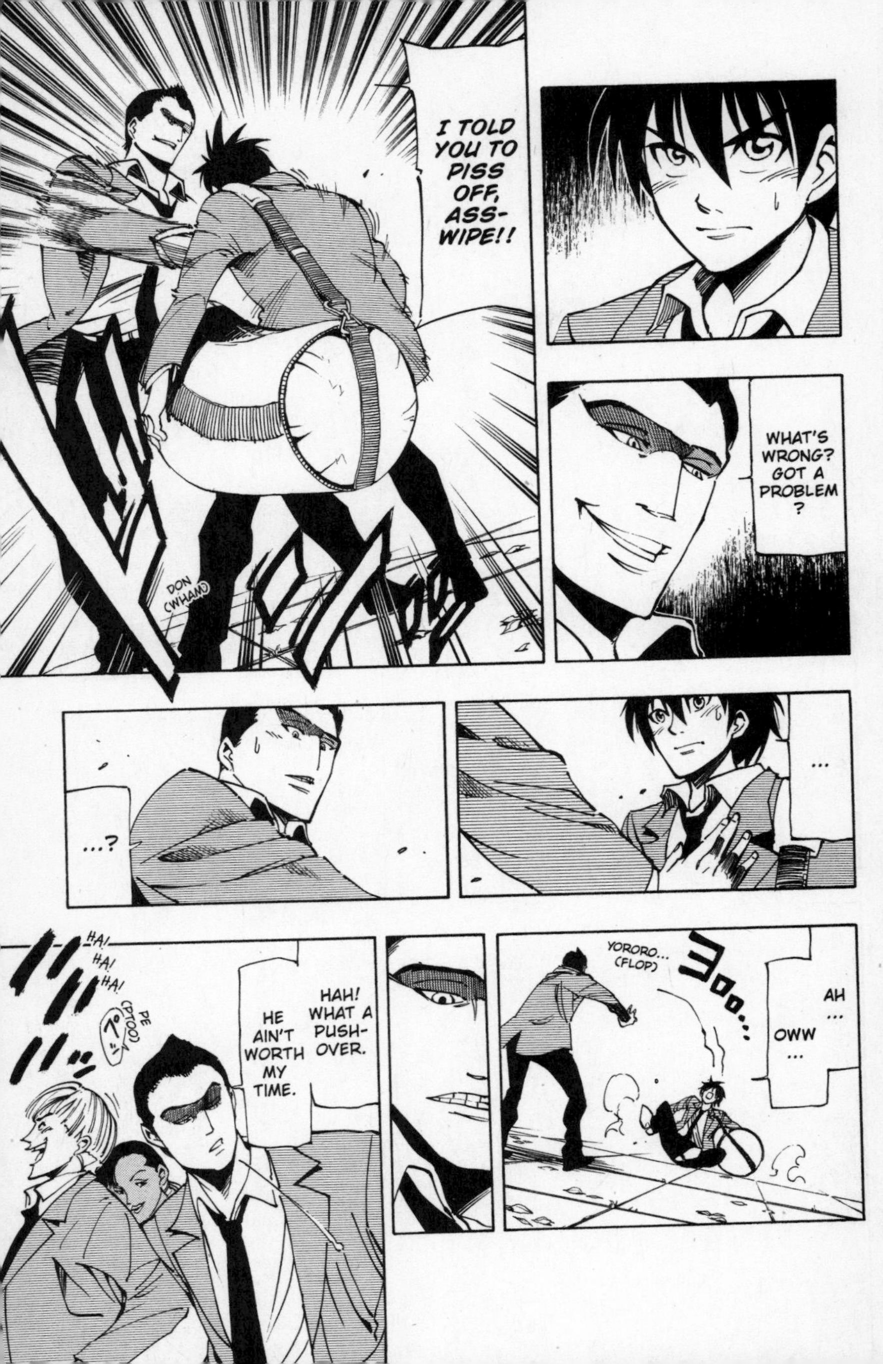
WHAT'S WRONG? GOT A PROBLEM?
I TOLD YOU TO PISS OFF, ASS-WIPE!!
DON (WHAM)
...
...?
AH ... OWW ...
YORORO... (FLOP)
HAH! WHAT A PUSH-OVER.
HE AIN'T WORTH MY TIME.
HA! HA! HA!
PE (PTOO)

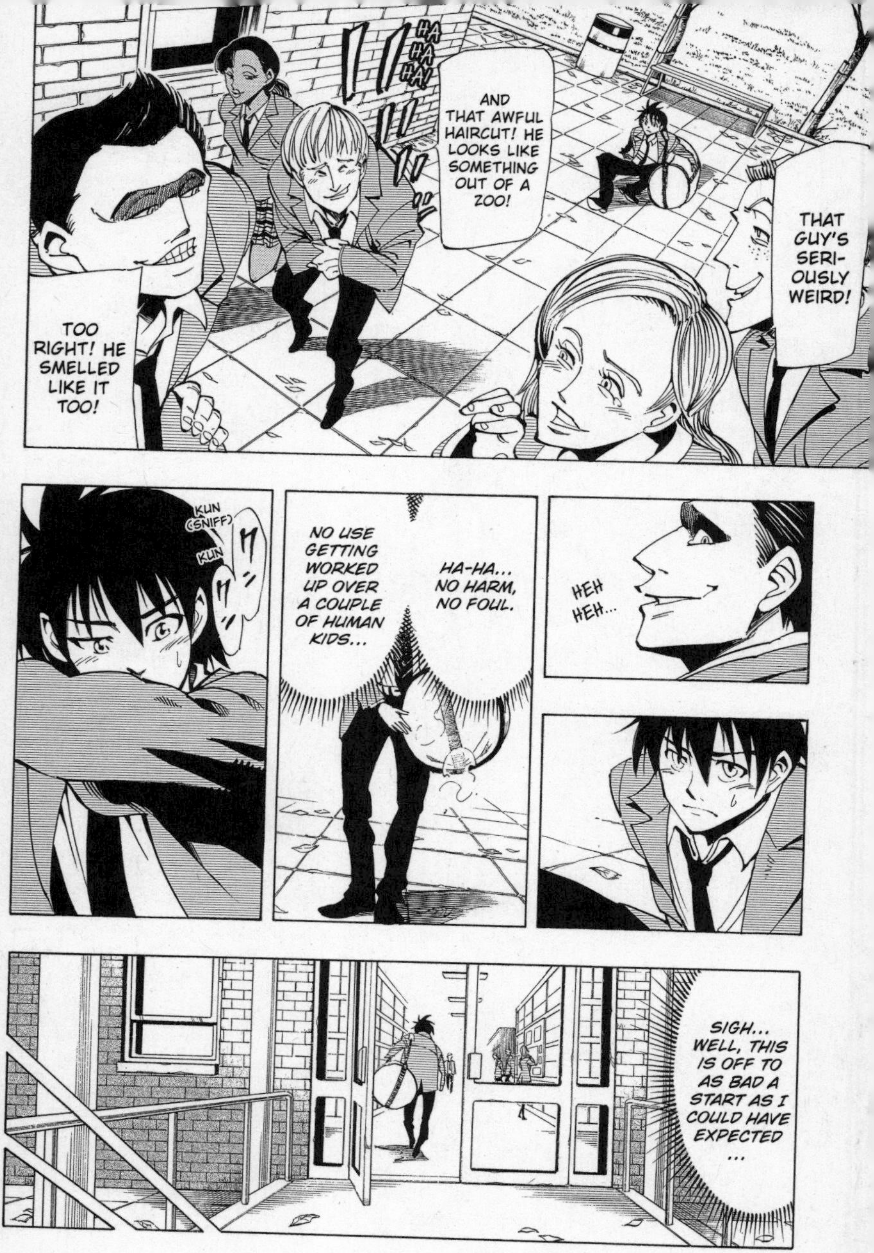
THAT GUY'S SERIOUSLY WEIRD!
HA HA HA!
AND THAT AWFUL HAIRCUT! HE LOOKS LIKE SOMETHING OUT OF A ZOO!
TOO RIGHT! HE SMELLED LIKE IT TOO!
HEH HEH...
HA-HA... NO HARM, NO FOUL.
NO USE GETTING WORKED UP OVER A COUPLE OF HUMAN KIDS...
KUN (SNIFF)
KUN
SIGH... WELL, THIS IS OFF TO AS BAD A START AS I COULD HAVE EXPECTED...

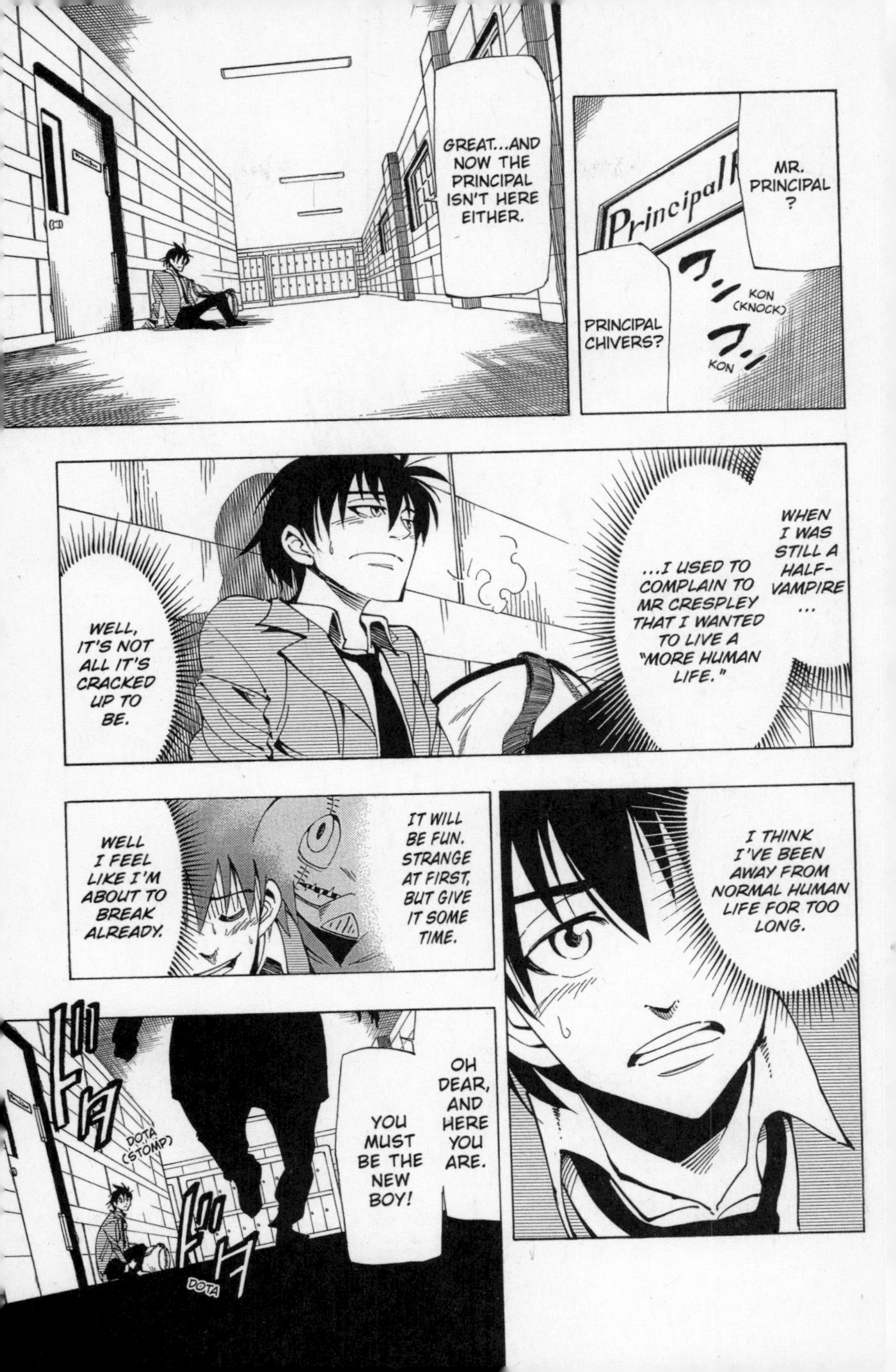
Principal
MR. PRINCIPAL?
KON (KNOCK)
KON
PRINCIPAL CHIVERS?
GREAT...AND NOW THE PRINCIPAL ISN'T HERE EITHER.
WHEN I WAS STILL A HALF-VAMPIRE ...
...I USED TO COMPLAIN TO MR CRESPLEY THAT I WANTED TO LIVE A "MORE HUMAN LIFE."
WELL, IT'S NOT ALL IT'S CRACKED UP TO BE.
I THINK I'VE BEEN AWAY FROM NORMAL HUMAN LIFE FOR TOO LONG.
IT WILL BE FUN. STRANGE AT FIRST, BUT GIVE IT SOME TIME.
WELL I FEEL LIKE I'M ABOUT TO BREAK ALREADY.
OH DEAR, AND HERE YOU ARE.
YOU MUST BE THE NEW BOY!
DOTA (STOMP)
DOTA

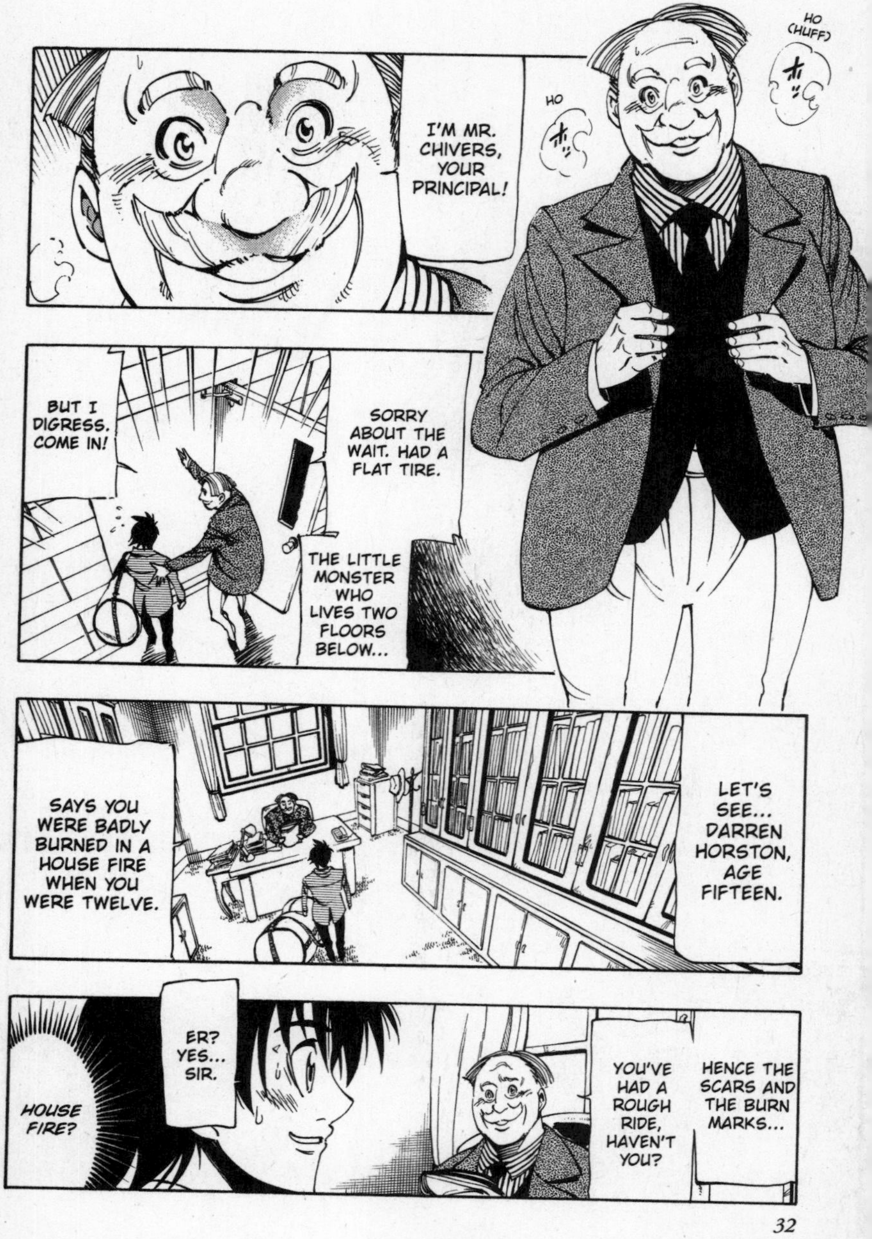
HO (HUFF)
HO
I'M MR. CHIVERS, YOUR PRINCIPAL!
SORRY ABOUT THE WAIT. HAD A FLAT TIRE.
THE LITTLE MONSTER WHO LIVES TWO FLOORS BELOW...
BUT I DIGRESS. COME IN!
LET'S SEE... DARREN HORSTON, AGE FIFTEEN.
SAYS YOU WERE BADLY BURNED IN A HOUSE FIRE WHEN YOU WERE TWELVE.
HENCE THE SCARS AND THE BURN MARKS...
YOU'VE HAD A ROUGH RIDE, HAVEN'T YOU?
ER? YES... SIR.
HOUSE FIRE?

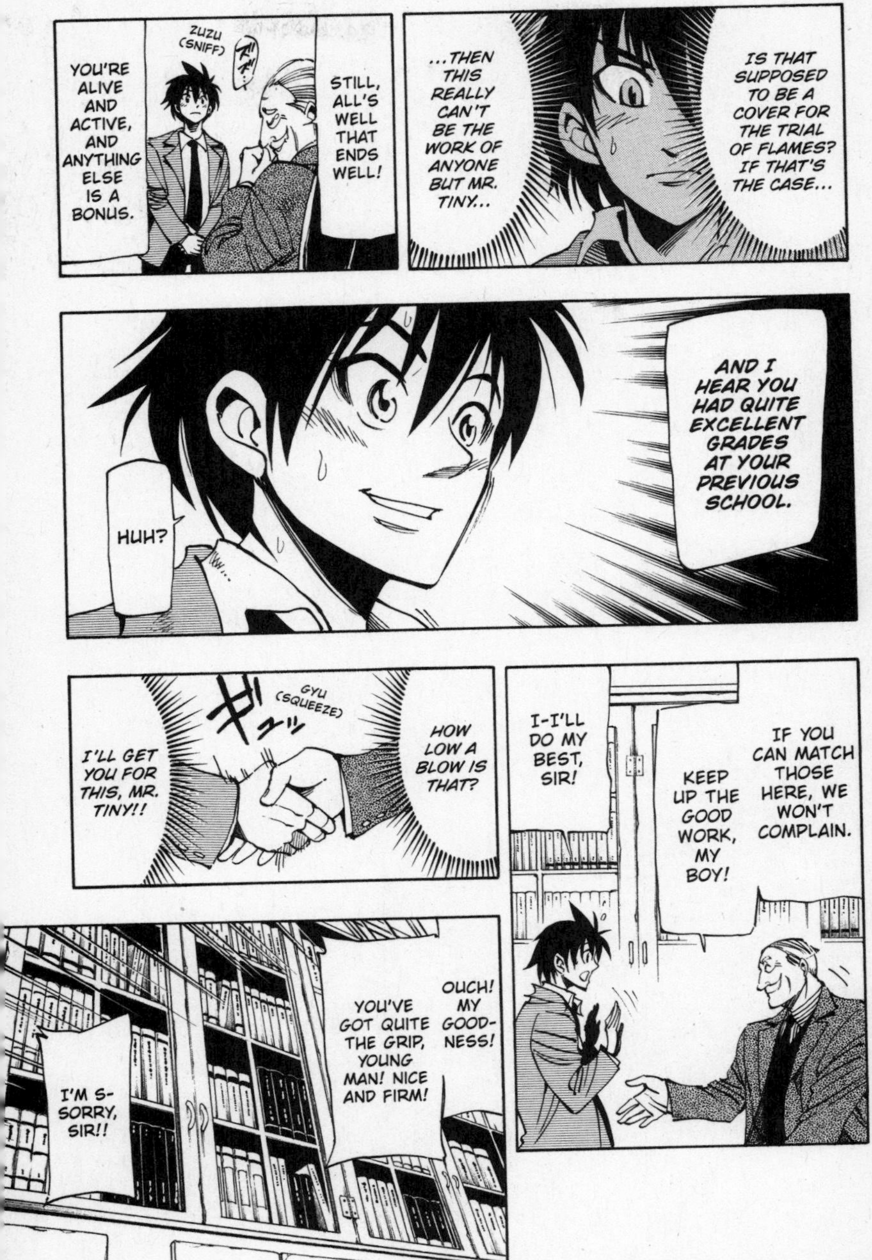
IS THAT SUPPOSED TO BE A COVER FOR THE TRIAL OF FLAMES? IF THAT'S THE CASE...
...THEN THIS REALLY CAN'T BE THE WORK OF ANYONE BUT MR. TINY...
STILL, ALL'S WELL THAT ENDS WELL!
ZUZU (SNIFF)
YOU'RE ALIVE AND ACTIVE, AND ANYTHING ELSE IS A BONUS.
AND I HEAR YOU HAD QUITE EXCELLENT GRADES AT YOUR PREVIOUS SCHOOL.
HUH?
IF YOU CAN MATCH THOSE HERE, WE WON'T COMPLAIN.
KEEP UP THE GOOD WORK, MY BOY!
I-I'LL DO MY BEST, SIR!
HOW LOW A BLOW IS THAT?
GYU (SQUEEZE)
I'LL GET YOU FOR THIS, MR. TINY!!
OUCH! MY GOODNESS!
YOU'VE GOT QUITE THE GRIP, YOUNG MAN! NICE AND FIRM!
I'M S-SORRY, SIR!!

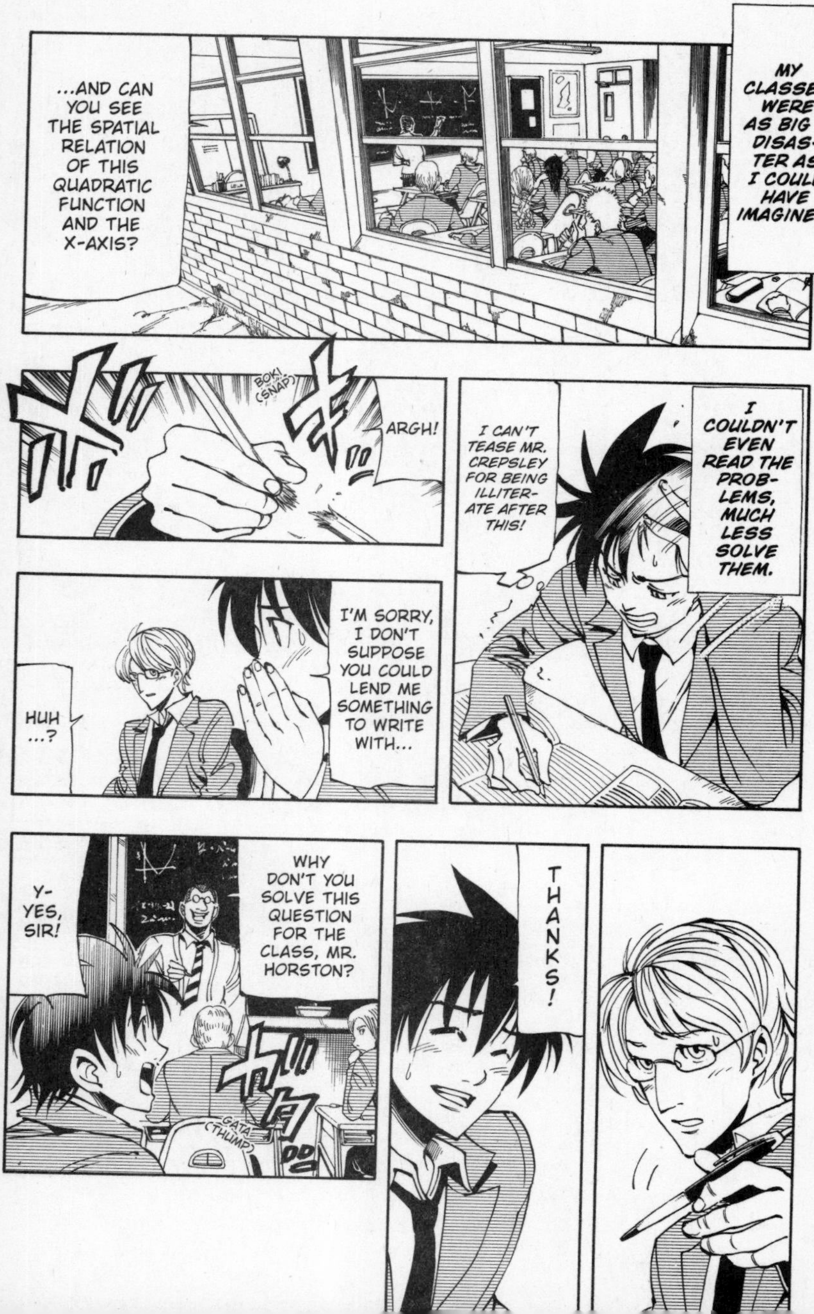
MY CLASSES WERE AS BIG A DISASTER AS I COULD HAVE IMAGINED.
...AND CAN YOU SEE THE SPATIAL RELATION OF THIS QUADRATIC FUNCTION AND THE X-AXIS?
I COULDN'T EVEN READ THE PROBLEMS, MUCH LESS SOLVE THEM.
I CAN'T TEASE MR. CREPSLEY FOR BEING ILLITERATE AFTER THIS!
BOKI (SNAP)
ARGH!
I'M SORRY, I DON'T SUPPOSE YOU COULD LEND ME SOMETHING TO WRITE WITH...
HUH ...?
THANKS!
WHY DON'T YOU SOLVE THIS QUESTION FOR THE CLASS, MR. HORSTON?
Y-YES, SIR!
GATA (THUMP)

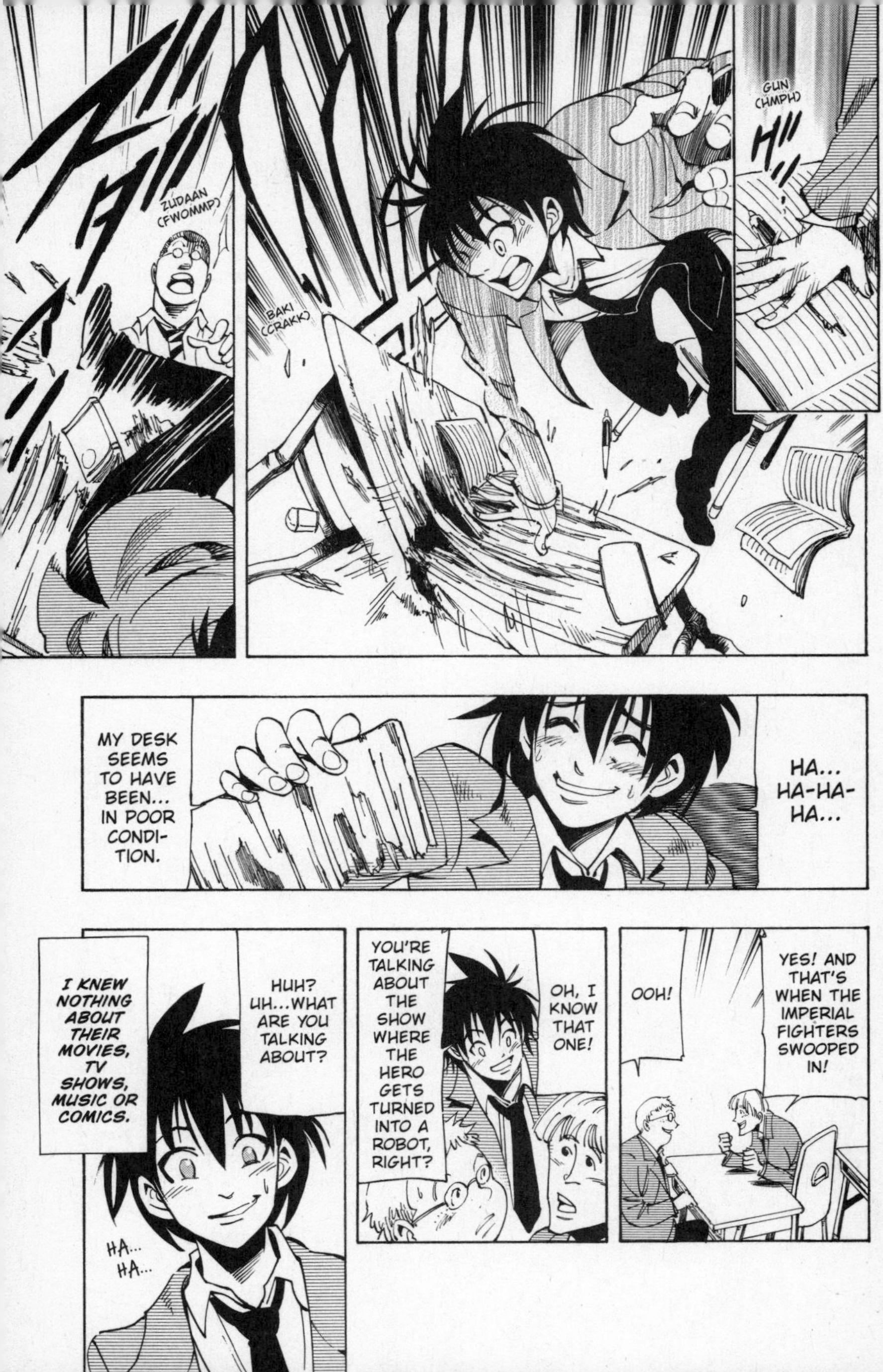
GUN (HMPH)
BAKI (CRAKK)
ZUDAAN (FWOMMP)
HA... HA-HA-HA...
MY DESK SEEMS TO HAVE BEEN... IN POOR CONDITION.
YES! AND THAT'S WHEN THE IMPERIAL FIGHTERS SWOOPED IN!
OOH!
OH, I KNOW THAT ONE!
YOU'RE TALKING ABOUT THE SHOW WHERE THE HERO GETS TURNED INTO A ROBOT, RIGHT?
HUH? UH...WHAT ARE YOU TALKING ABOUT?
I KNEW NOTHING ABOUT THEIR MOVIES, TV SHOWS, MUSIC OR COMICS.
HA... HA...

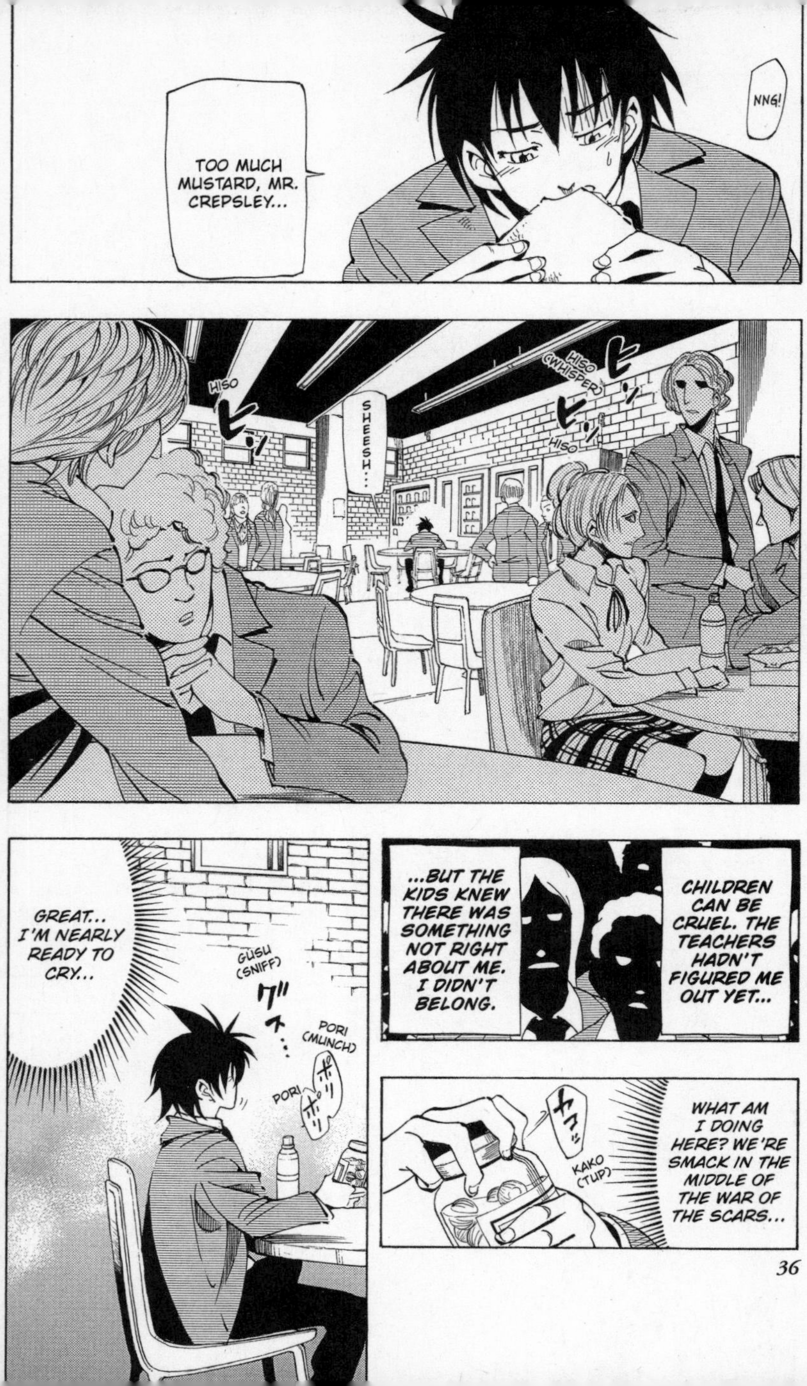
NNG!
TOO MUCH MUSTARD, MR. CREPSLEY...
HISO (WHISPER)
HISO
SHEESH...
HISO
CHILDREN CAN BE CRUEL. THE TEACHERS HADN'T FIGURED ME OUT YET...
...BUT THE KIDS KNEW THERE WAS SOMETHING NOT RIGHT ABOUT ME. I DIDN'T BELONG.
WHAT AM I DOING HERE? WE'RE SMACK IN THE MIDDLE OF THE WAR OF THE SCARS...
KAKO (TUP)
GREAT... I'M NEARLY READY TO CRY...
GUSU (SNIFF)
PORI (MUNCH)
PORI

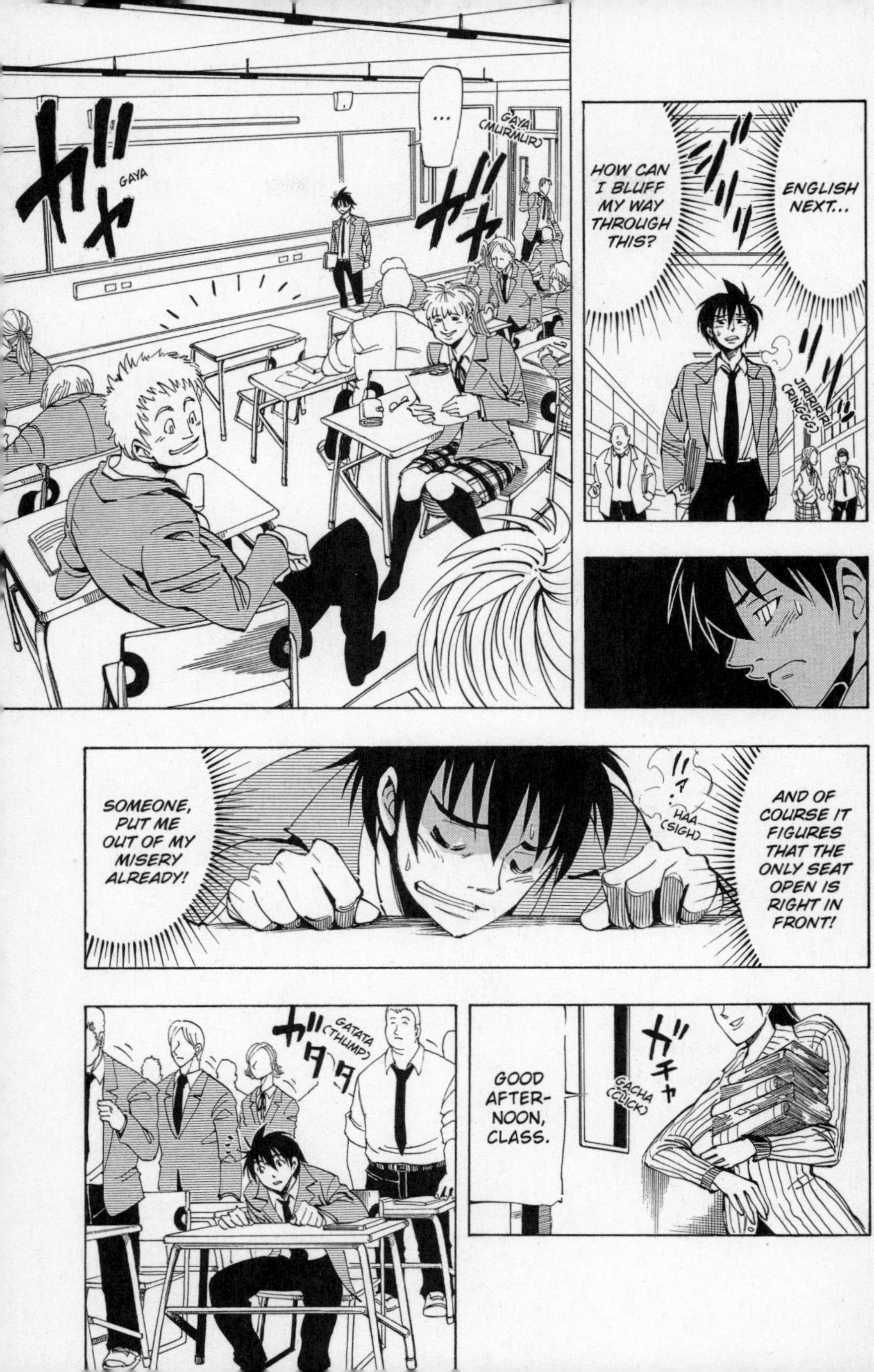
ENGLISH NEXT...
HOW CAN I BLUFF MY WAY THROUGH THIS?
JIRIRIRI (RINGGG)
...
GAYA (MURMUR)
GAYA
AND OF COURSE IT FIGURES THAT THE ONLY SEAT OPEN IS RIGHT IN FRONT!
HAA (SIGH)
SOMEONE, PUT ME OUT OF MY MISERY ALREADY!
GACHA (CLICK)
GOOD AFTERNOON, CLASS.
GATATA (THUMP)

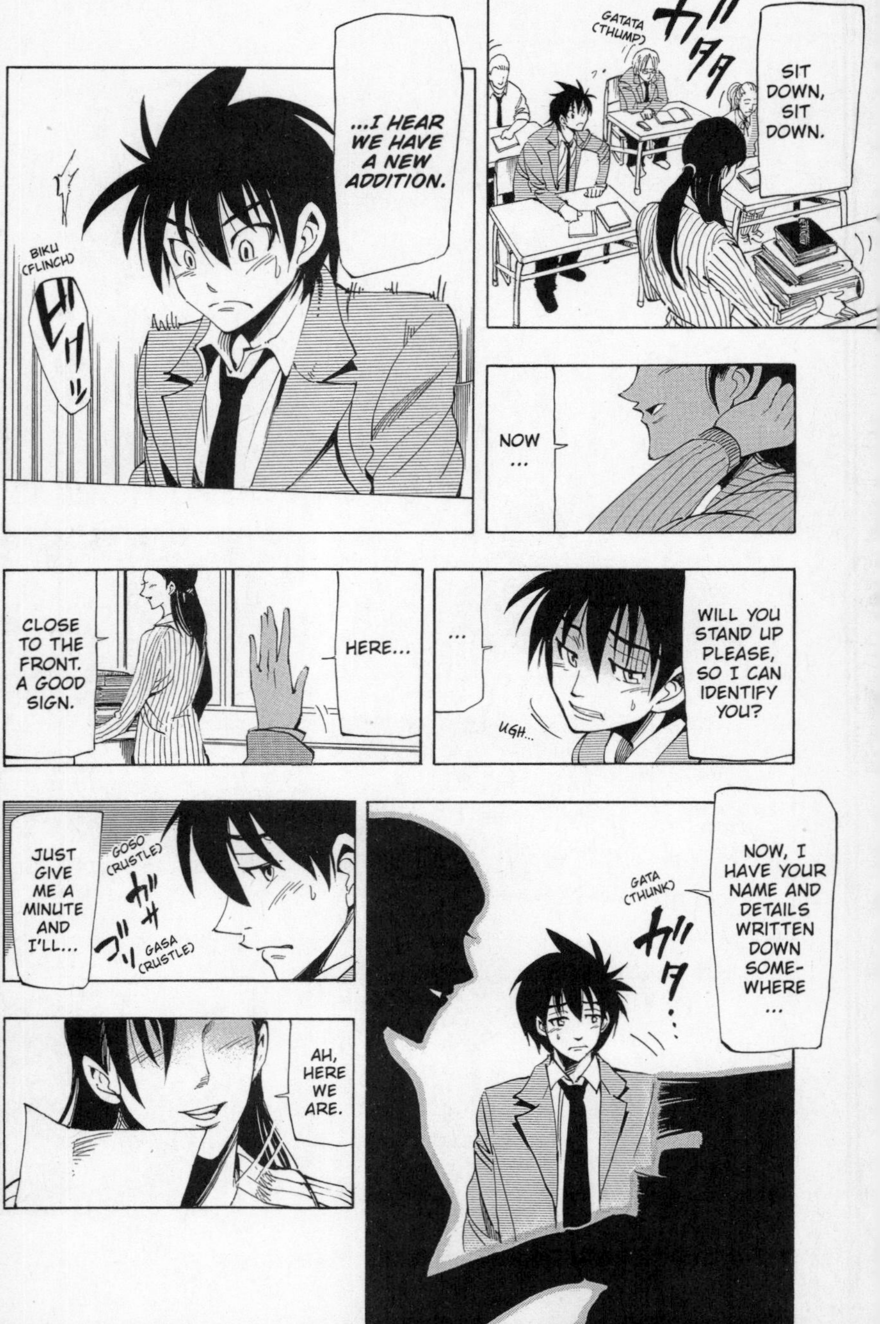
SIT DOWN, SIT DOWN.
GATATA (THUMP)
NOW ...
...I HEAR WE HAVE A NEW ADDITION.
BIKU (FLINCH)
WILL YOU STAND UP PLEASE, SO I CAN IDENTIFY YOU?
...
UGH...
HERE...
CLOSE TO THE FRONT. A GOOD SIGN.
NOW, I HAVE YOUR NAME AND DETAILS WRITTEN DOWN SOME-WHERE ...
GATA (THUNK)
JUST GIVE ME A MINUTE AND I'LL...
GOSO (RUSTLE)
GASA (RUSTLE)
AH, HERE WE ARE.

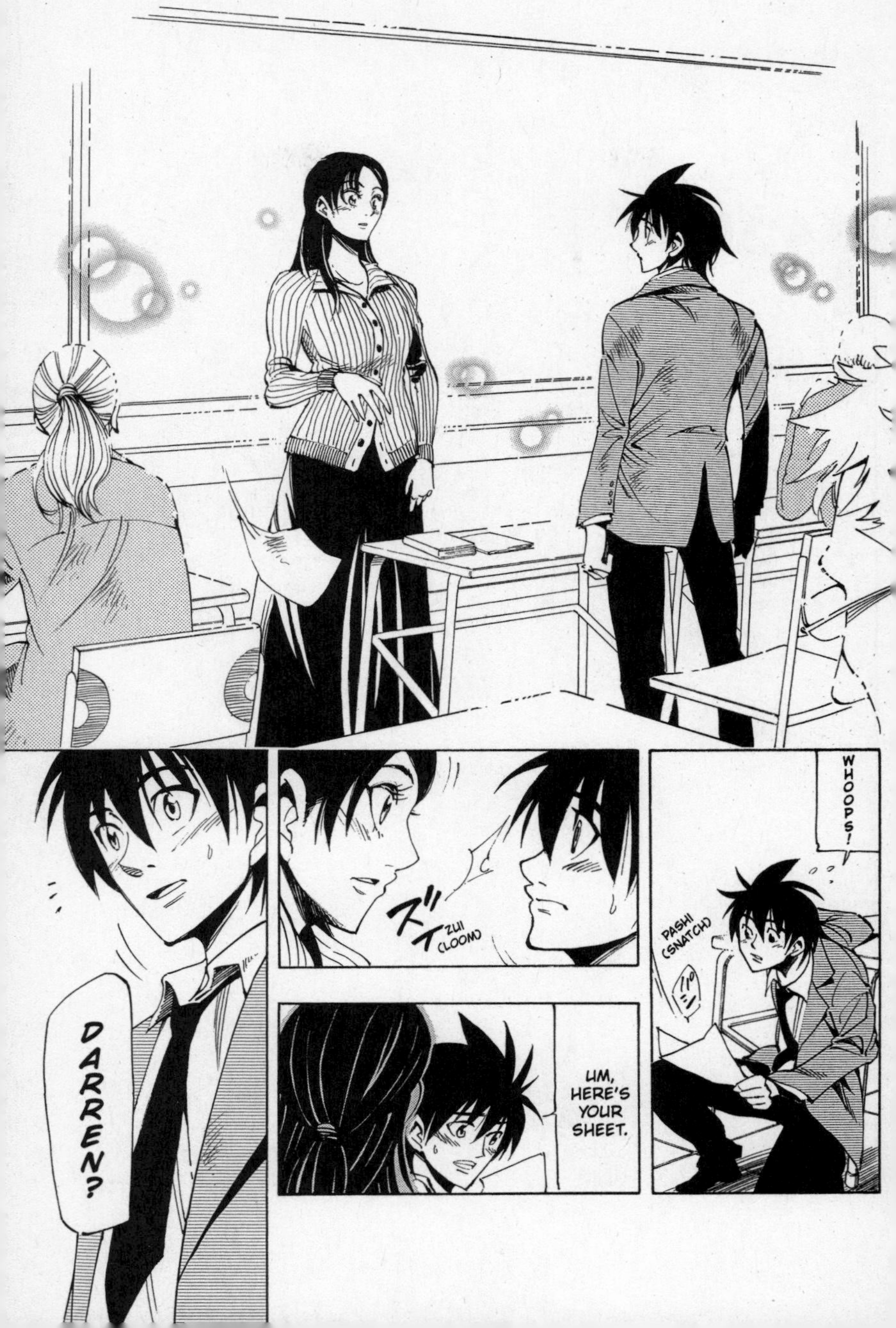
WHOOPS!
PASHI (SNATCH)
ZUI (LOOM)
UM, HERE'S YOUR SHEET.
DARREN?

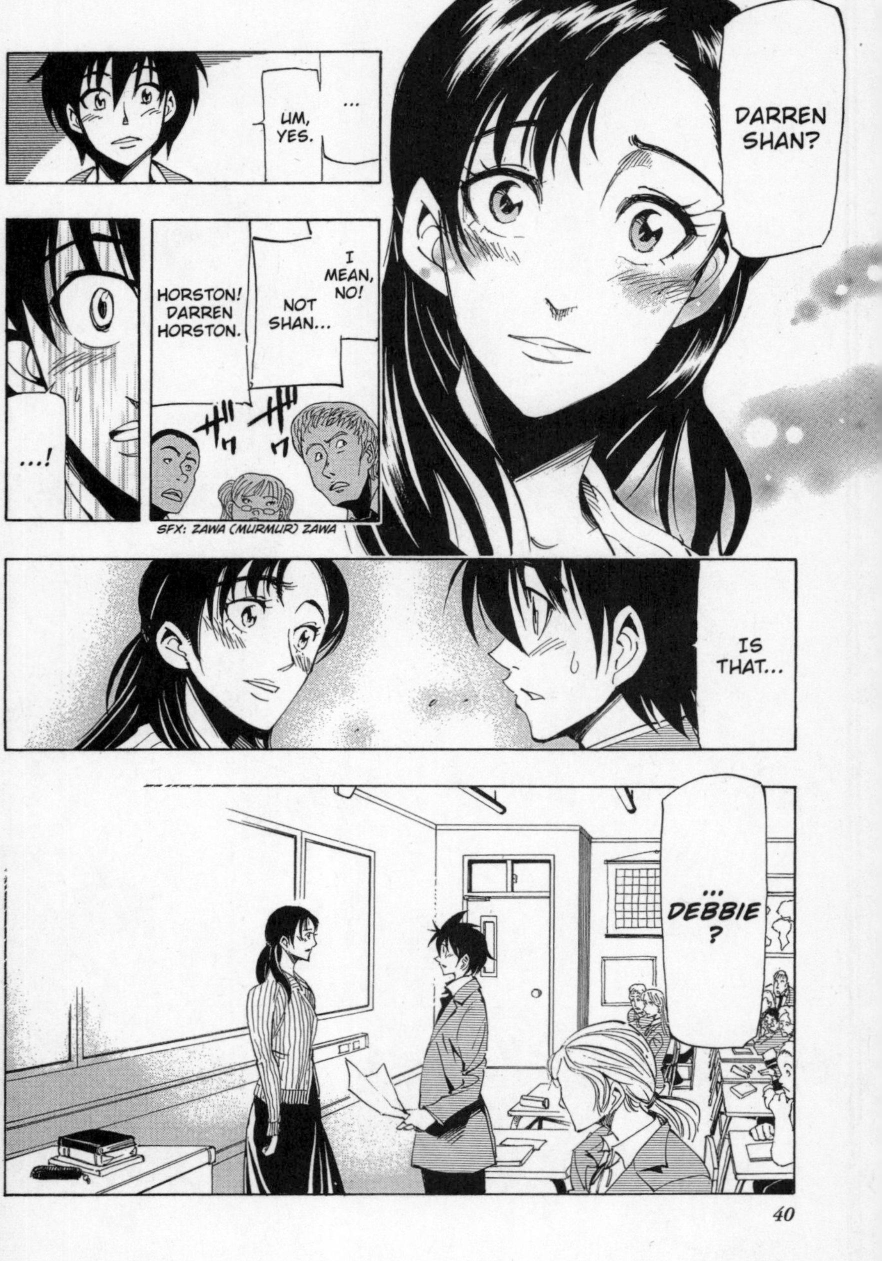
DARREN SHAN?
...
UM, YES.
I MEAN, NO!
NOT SHAN...
HORSTON! DARREN HORSTON.
SFX: ZAWA (MURMUR) ZAWA
...!
IS THAT...
... DEBBIE ?

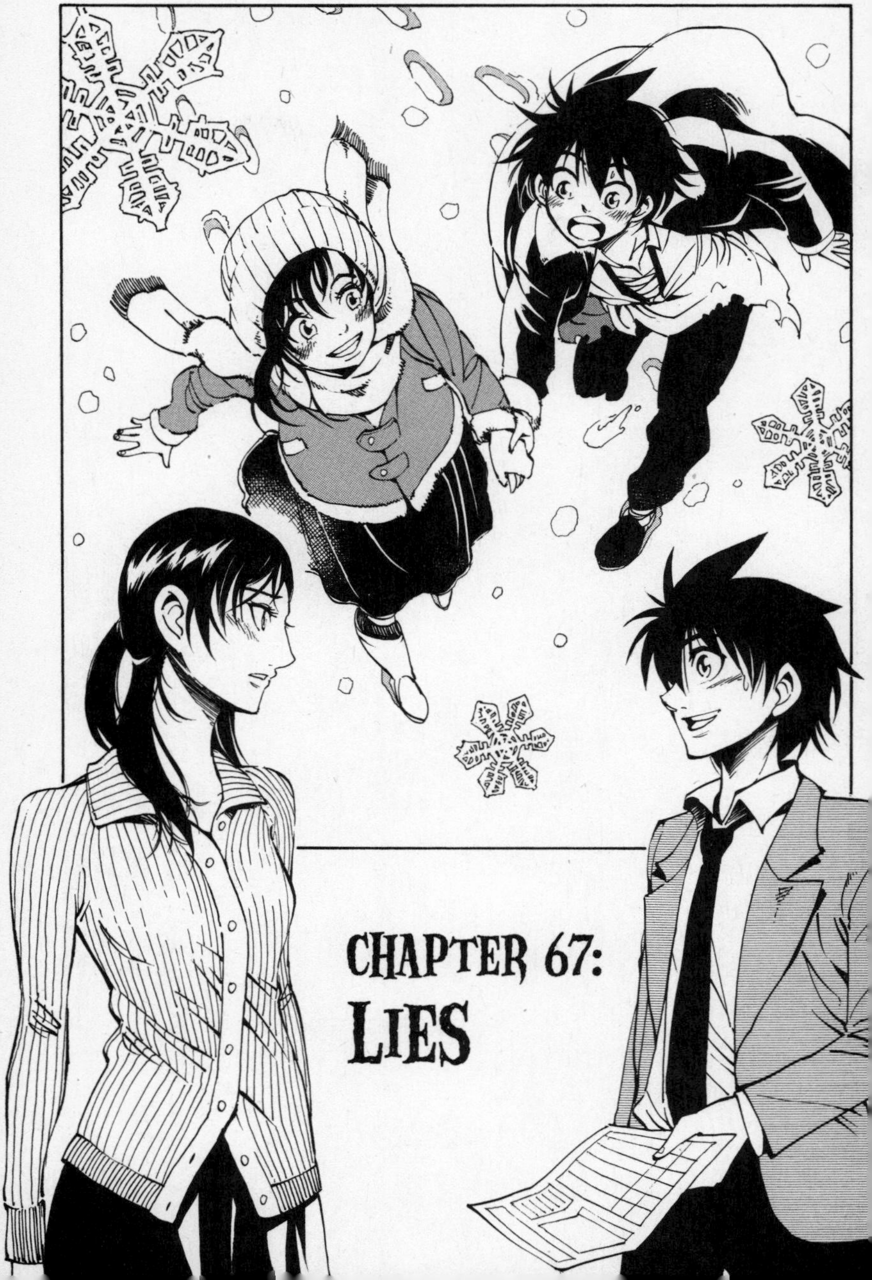
CHAPTER 67:
LIES

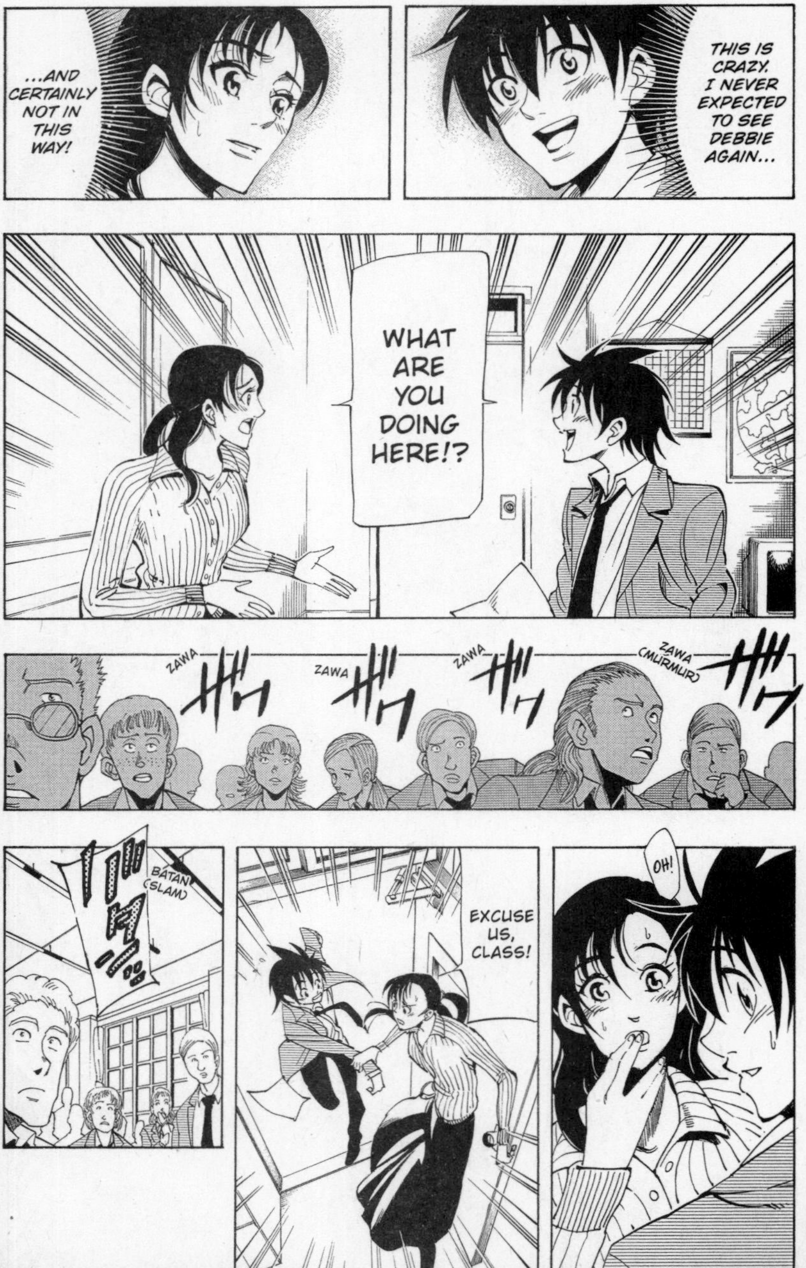
THIS IS CRAZY. I NEVER EXPECTED TO SEE DEBBIE AGAIN...
...AND CERTAINLY NOT IN THIS WAY!
WHAT ARE YOU DOING HERE!?
ZAWA (MURMUR)
ZAWA
ZAWA
ZAWA
OH!
EXCUSE US, CLASS!
BATAN (SLAM)

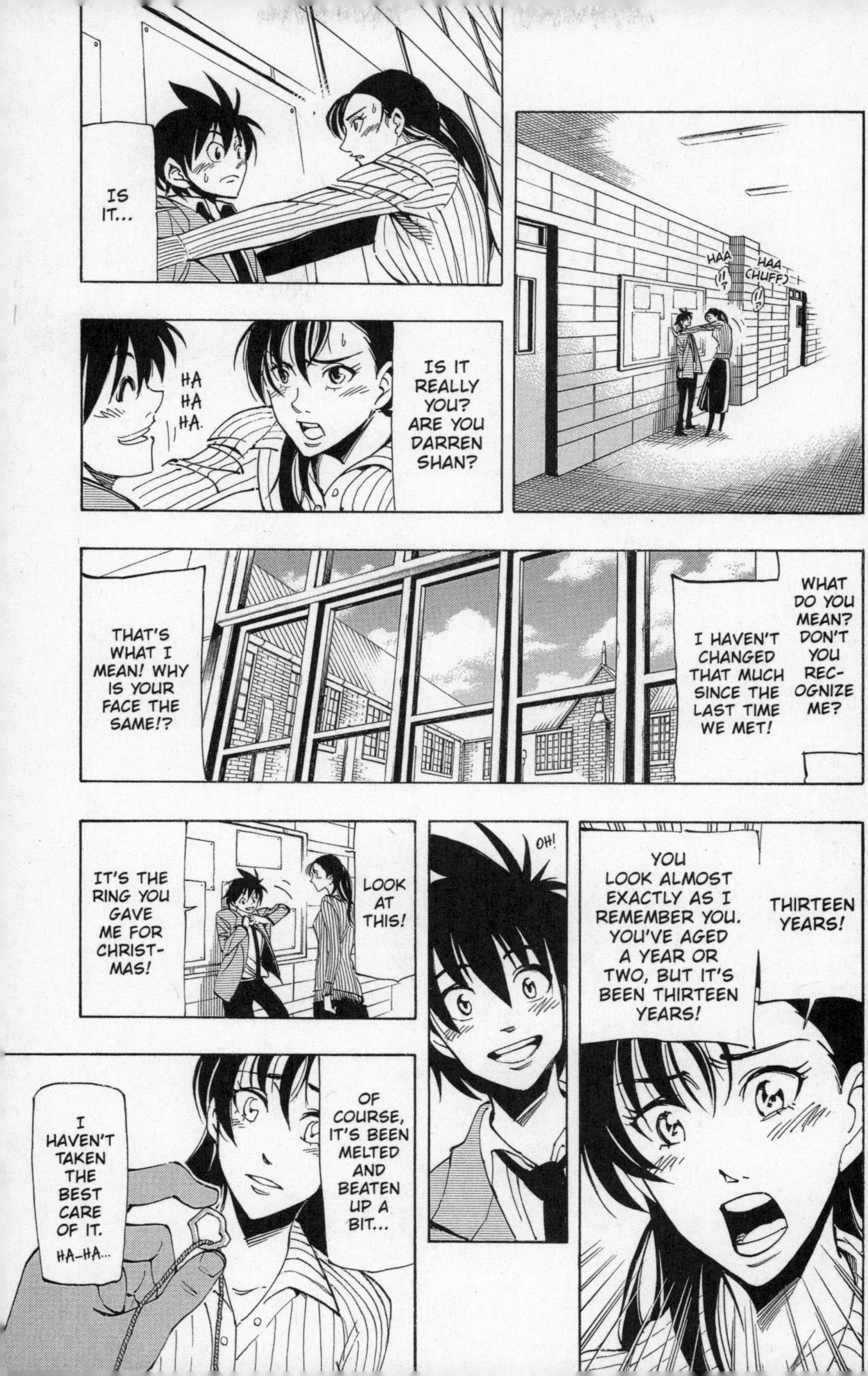
HAA
HAA (HUFF)
IS IT...
IS IT REALLY YOU? ARE YOU DARREN SHAN?
HA HA HA.
WHAT DO YOU MEAN? DON'T YOU RECOGNIZE ME?
I HAVEN'T CHANGED THAT MUCH SINCE THE LAST TIME WE MET!
THAT'S WHAT I MEAN! WHY IS YOUR FACE THE SAME!?
THIRTEEN YEARS!
YOU LOOK ALMOST EXACTLY AS I REMEMBER YOU. YOU'VE AGED A YEAR OR TWO, BUT IT'S BEEN THIRTEEN YEARS!
OH!
LOOK AT THIS!
IT'S THE RING YOU GAVE ME FOR CHRISTMAS!
OF COURSE, IT'S BEEN MELTED AND BEATEN UP A BIT...
I HAVEN'T TAKEN THE BEST CARE OF IT.
HA-HA...

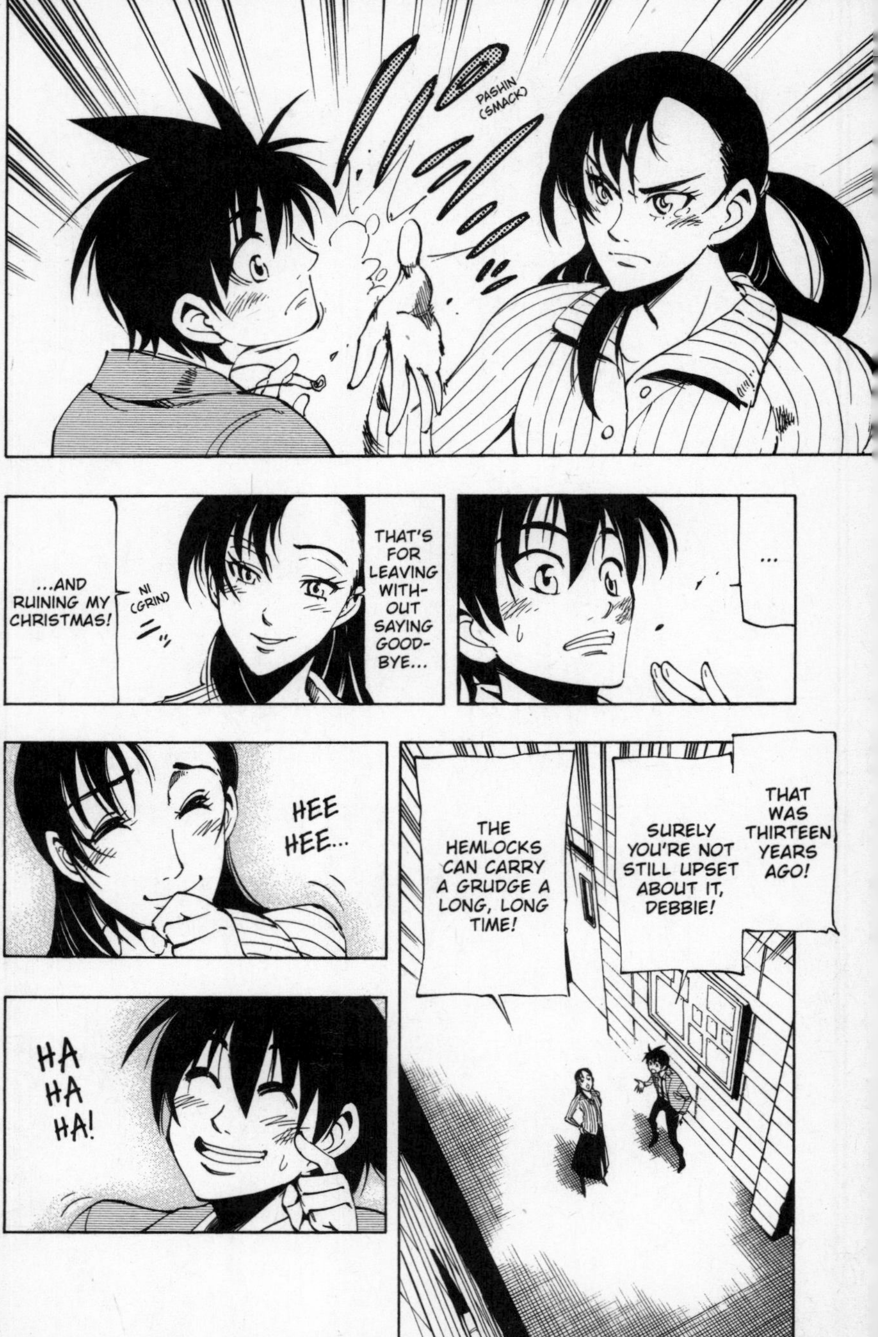
PASHIN (SMACK)
...
THAT'S FOR LEAVING WITH-OUT SAYING GOOD-BYE...
NI (GRIN)
...AND RUINING MY CHRISTMAS!
THAT WAS THIRTEEN YEARS AGO!
SURELY YOU'RE NOT STILL UPSET ABOUT IT, DEBBIE!
THE HEMLOCKS CAN CARRY A GRUDGE A LONG, LONG TIME!
HEE HEE...
HA HA HA!

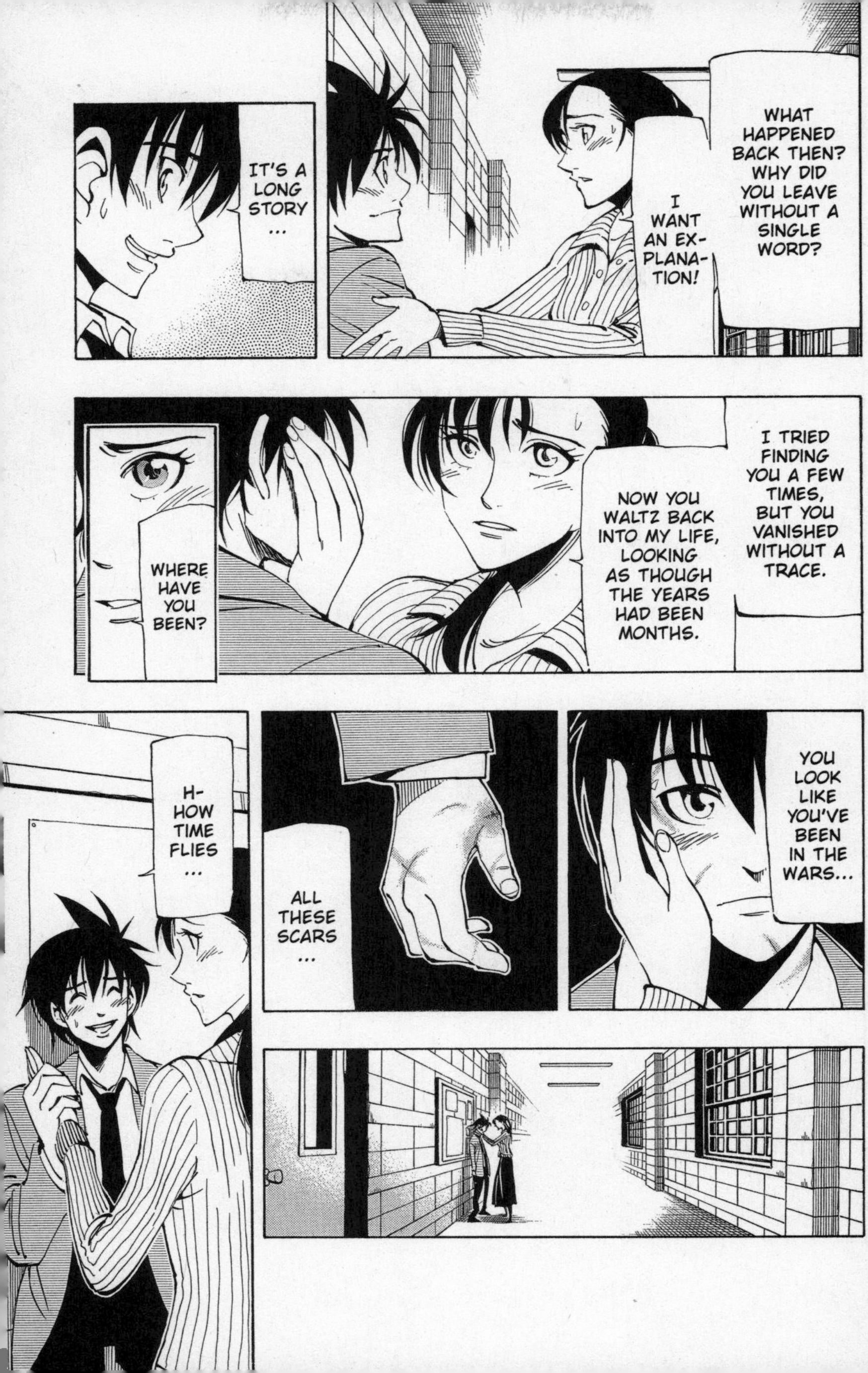
WHAT HAPPENED BACK THEN? WHY DID YOU LEAVE WITHOUT A SINGLE WORD?
I WANT AN EX-PLANA-TION!
IT'S A LONG STORY ...
I TRIED FINDING YOU A FEW TIMES, BUT YOU VANISHED WITHOUT A TRACE.
NOW YOU WALTZ BACK INTO MY LIFE, LOOKING AS THOUGH THE YEARS HAD BEEN MONTHS.
WHERE HAVE YOU BEEN?
YOU LOOK LIKE YOU'VE BEEN IN THE WARS...
ALL THESE SCARS ...
H-HOW TIME FLIES ...

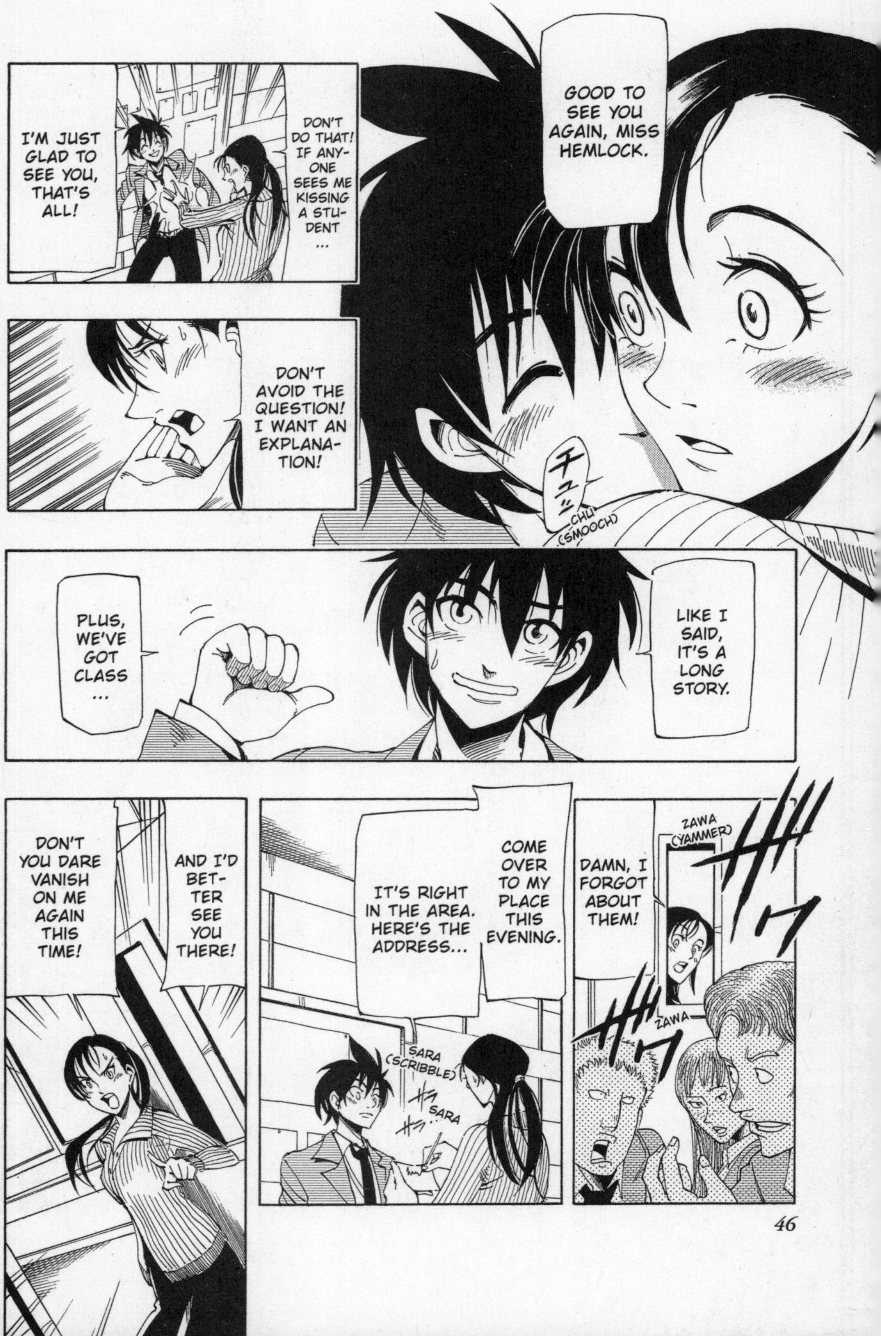
GOOD TO SEE YOU AGAIN, MISS HEMLOCK.
チュッ
CHU (SMOOCH)
DON'T DO THAT! IF ANYONE SEES ME KISSING A STUDENT ...
I'M JUST GLAD TO SEE YOU, THAT'S ALL!
DON'T AVOID THE QUESTION! I WANT AN EXPLANATION!
LIKE I SAID, IT'S A LONG STORY.
PLUS, WE'VE GOT CLASS ...
ZAWA (YAMMER)
DAMN, I FORGOT ABOUT THEM!
ZAWA
COME OVER TO MY PLACE THIS EVENING.
IT'S RIGHT IN THE AREA. HERE'S THE ADDRESS...
SARA (SCRIBBLE)
SARA
AND I'D BETTER SEE YOU THERE!
DON'T YOU DARE VANISH ON ME AGAIN THIS TIME!

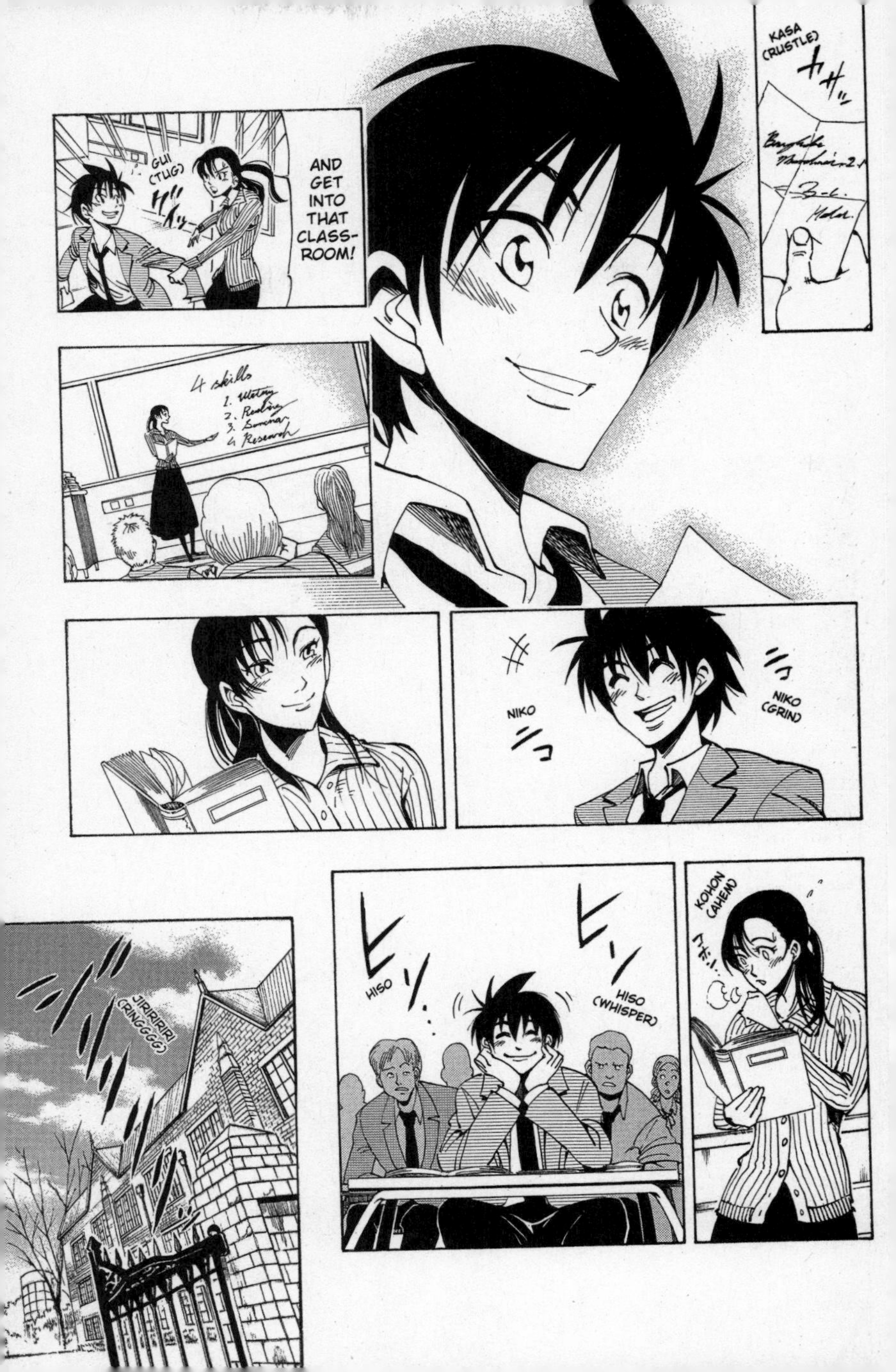
KASA (RUSTLE)
GUI (TUG)
AND GET INTO THAT CLASSROOM!
4 skills
3. Seminar
4. Research
NIKO (GRIN)
NIKO
KOHON (AHEM)
HISO (WHISPER)
HISO
JIRIRIRIRI (RINGGGG)

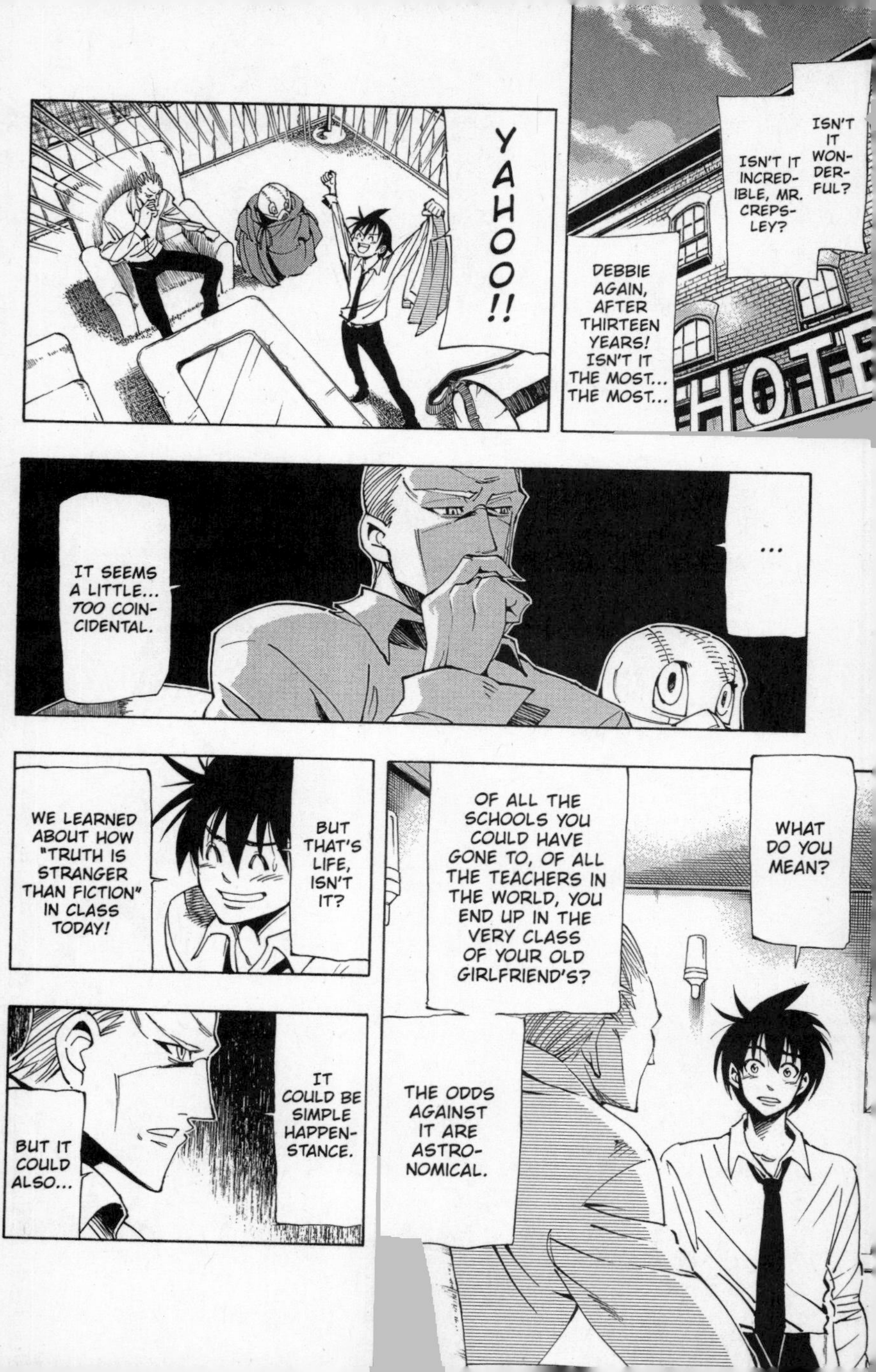
ISN'T IT WONDERFUL?
ISN'T IT INCREDIBLE, MR. CREPSLEY?
DEBBIE AGAIN, AFTER THIRTEEN YEARS! ISN'T IT THE MOST... THE MOST...
HOTE
YAHOO!!
...
IT SEEMS A LITTLE... *TOO* COINCIDENTAL.
WHAT DO YOU MEAN?
OF ALL THE SCHOOLS YOU COULD HAVE GONE TO, OF ALL THE TEACHERS IN THE WORLD, YOU END UP IN THE VERY CLASS OF YOUR OLD GIRLFRIEND'S?
THE ODDS AGAINST IT ARE ASTRONOMICAL.
BUT THAT'S LIFE, ISN'T IT?
WE LEARNED ABOUT HOW "TRUTH IS STRANGER THAN FICTION" IN CLASS TODAY!
IT COULD BE SIMPLE HAPPENSTANCE.
BUT IT COULD ALSO...

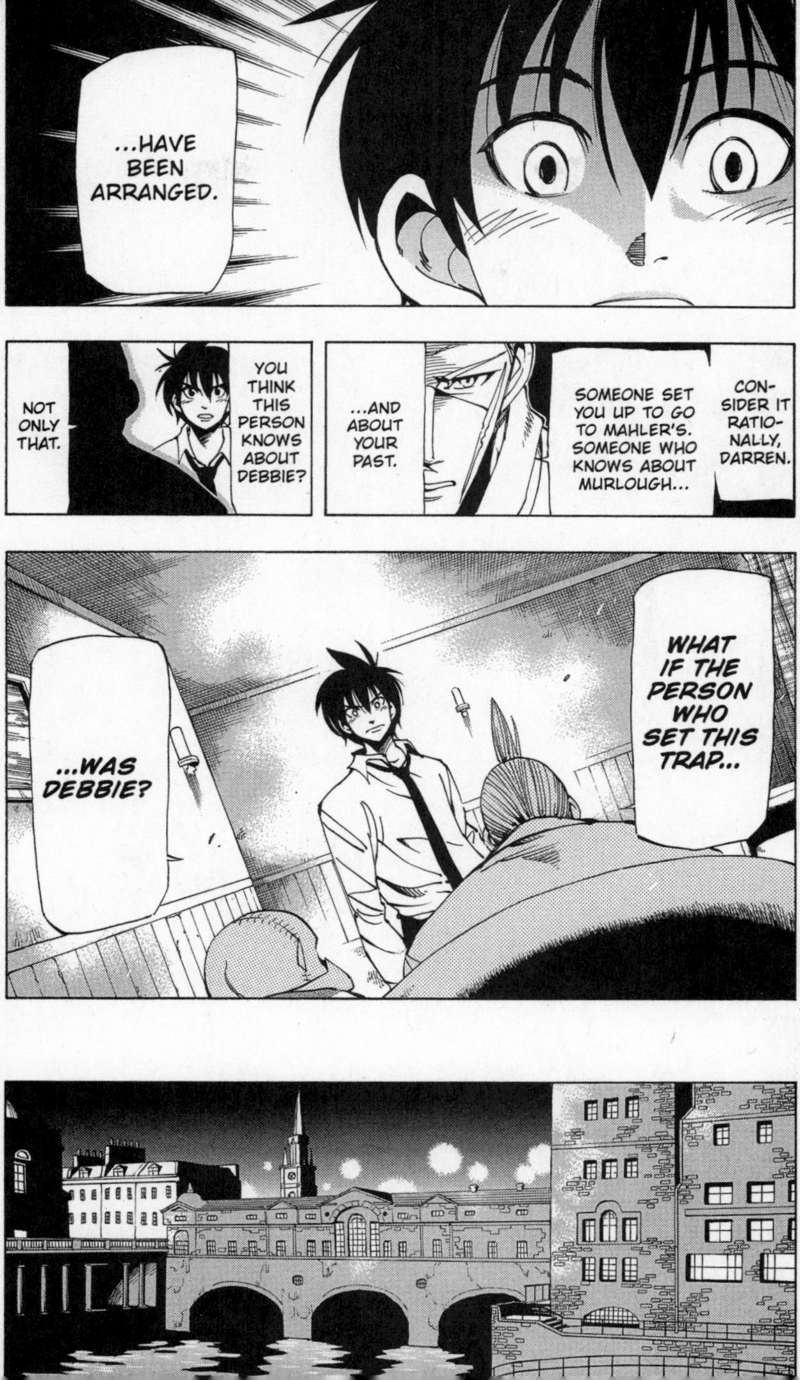
...HAVE BEEN ARRANGED.
CON-SIDER IT RATIO-NALLY, DARREN.
SOMEONE SET YOU UP TO GO TO MAHLER'S. SOMEONE WHO KNOWS ABOUT MURLOUGH...
...AND ABOUT YOUR PAST.
YOU THINK THIS PERSON KNOWS ABOUT DEBBIE?
NOT ONLY THAT.
WHAT IF THE PERSON WHO SET THIS TRAP...
...WAS DEBBIE?

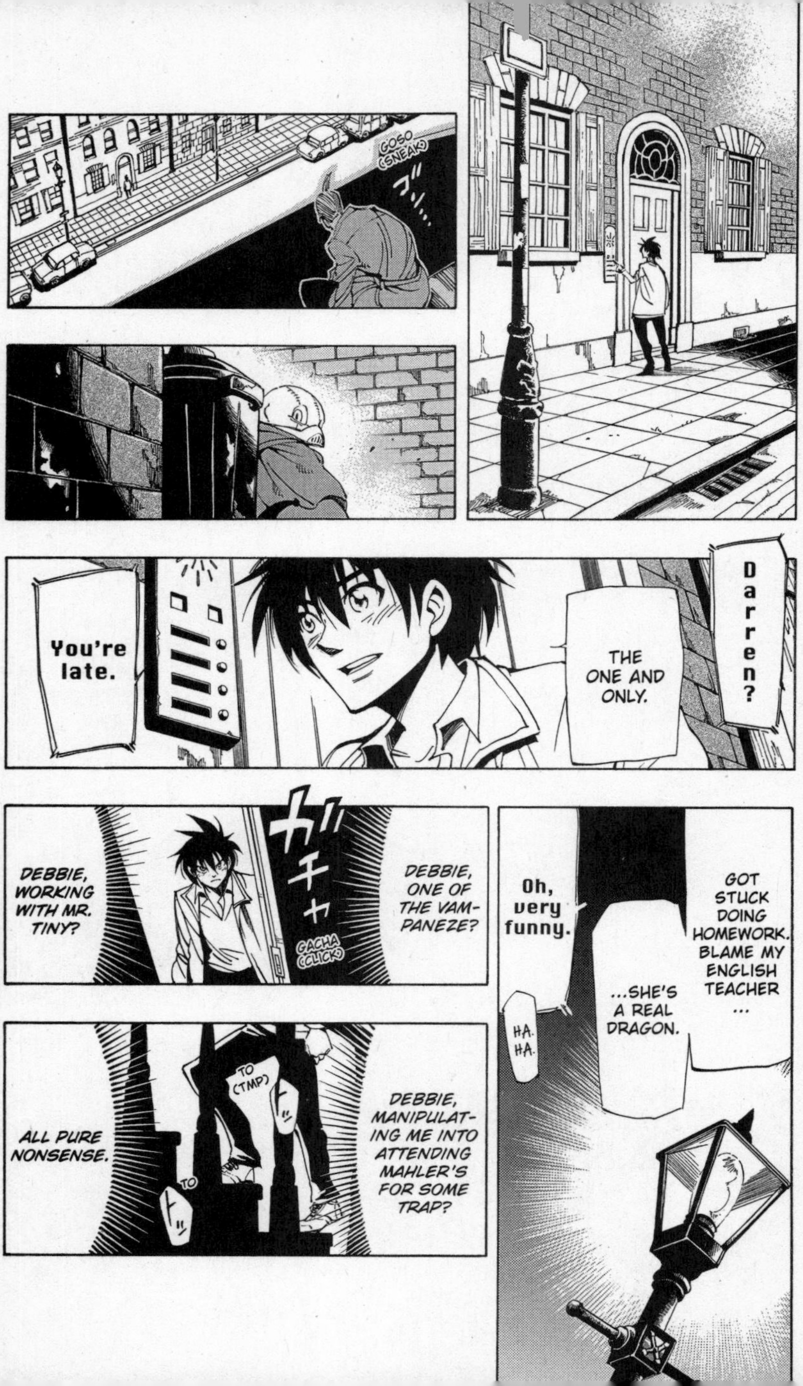

GOSO (SNEAK)
ゴソ…
Darren?
THE ONE AND ONLY.
You're late.
GOT STUCK DOING HOMEWORK. BLAME MY ENGLISH TEACHER ...
...SHE'S A REAL DRAGON.
Oh, very funny.
HA. HA.
DEBBIE, ONE OF THE VAM-PANEZE?
ガチャ
GACHA (CLICK)
DEBBIE, WORKING WITH MR. TINY?
DEBBIE, MANIPULAT-ING ME INTO ATTENDING MAHLER'S FOR SOME TRAP?
TO (TMP)
トッ
TO
トッ
ALL PURE NONSENSE.

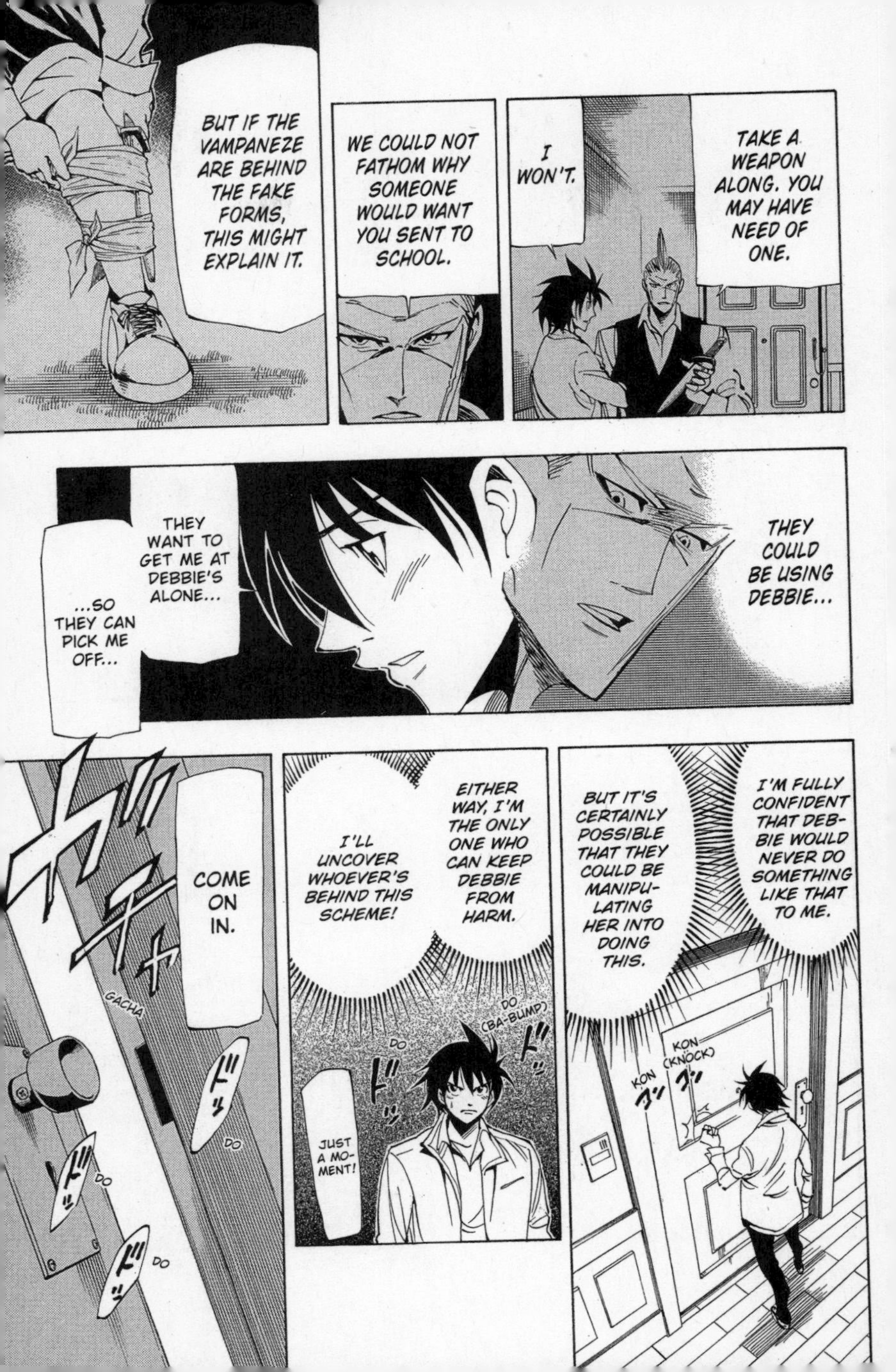
TAKE A WEAPON ALONG. YOU MAY HAVE NEED OF ONE.
I WON'T.
WE COULD NOT FATHOM WHY SOMEONE WOULD WANT YOU SENT TO SCHOOL.
BUT IF THE VAMPANEZE ARE BEHIND THE FAKE FORMS, THIS MIGHT EXPLAIN IT.
THEY COULD BE USING DEBBIE...
THEY WANT TO GET ME AT DEBBIE'S ALONE...
...SO THEY CAN PICK ME OFF...
I'M FULLY CONFIDENT THAT DEB-BIE WOULD NEVER DO SOMETHING LIKE THAT TO ME.
BUT IT'S CERTAINLY POSSIBLE THAT THEY COULD BE MANIPU-LATING HER INTO DOING THIS.
KON KON (KNOCK)
EITHER WAY, I'M THE ONLY ONE WHO CAN KEEP DEBBIE FROM HARM.
I'LL UNCOVER WHOEVER'S BEHIND THIS SCHEME!
DO DO (BA-BUMP)
JUST A MO-MENT!
COME ON IN.
GACHA
DO
DO
DO

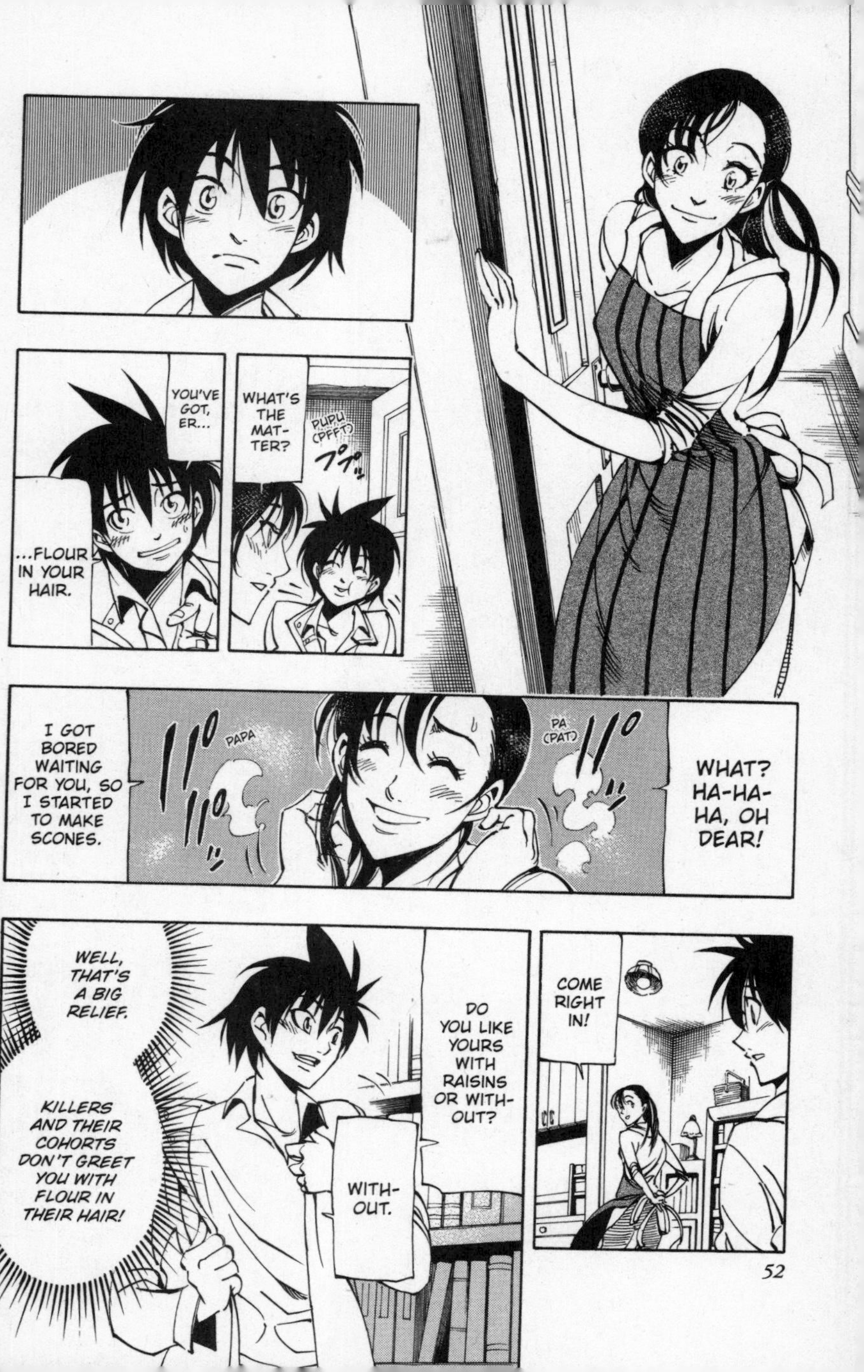
WHAT'S THE MATTER?
PUPU (PFFT)
YOU'VE GOT, ER...
...FLOUR IN YOUR HAIR.
WHAT? HA-HA-HA, OH DEAR!
PA (PAT)
PAPA
I GOT BORED WAITING FOR YOU, SO I STARTED TO MAKE SCONES.
COME RIGHT IN!
DO YOU LIKE YOURS WITH RAISINS OR WITHOUT?
WITHOUT.
WELL, THAT'S A BIG RELIEF.
KILLERS AND THEIR COHORTS DON'T GREET YOU WITH FLOUR IN THEIR HAIR!

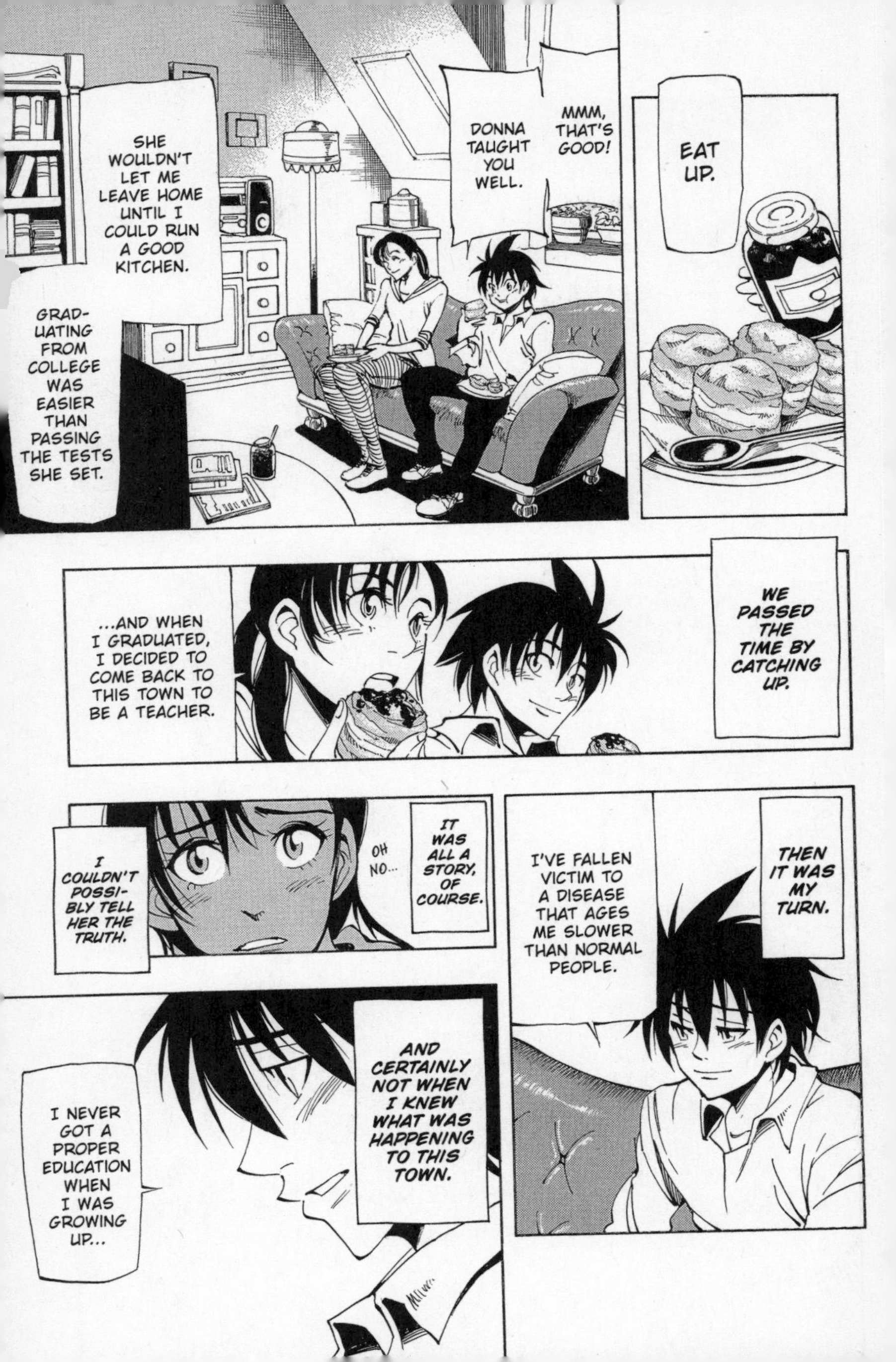
EAT UP.
MMM, THAT'S GOOD!
DONNA TAUGHT YOU WELL.
SHE WOULDN'T LET ME LEAVE HOME UNTIL I COULD RUN A GOOD KITCHEN.
GRAD-UATING FROM COLLEGE WAS EASIER THAN PASSING THE TESTS SHE SET.
WE PASSED THE TIME BY CATCHING UP.
...AND WHEN I GRADUATED, I DECIDED TO COME BACK TO THIS TOWN TO BE A TEACHER.
THEN IT WAS MY TURN.
I'VE FALLEN VICTIM TO A DISEASE THAT AGES ME SLOWER THAN NORMAL PEOPLE.
IT WAS ALL A STORY, OF COURSE.
OH NO...
I COULDN'T POSSI-BLY TELL HER THE TRUTH.
AND CERTAINLY NOT WHEN I KNEW WHAT WAS HAPPENING TO THIS TOWN.
I NEVER GOT A PROPER EDUCATION WHEN I WAS GROWING UP...

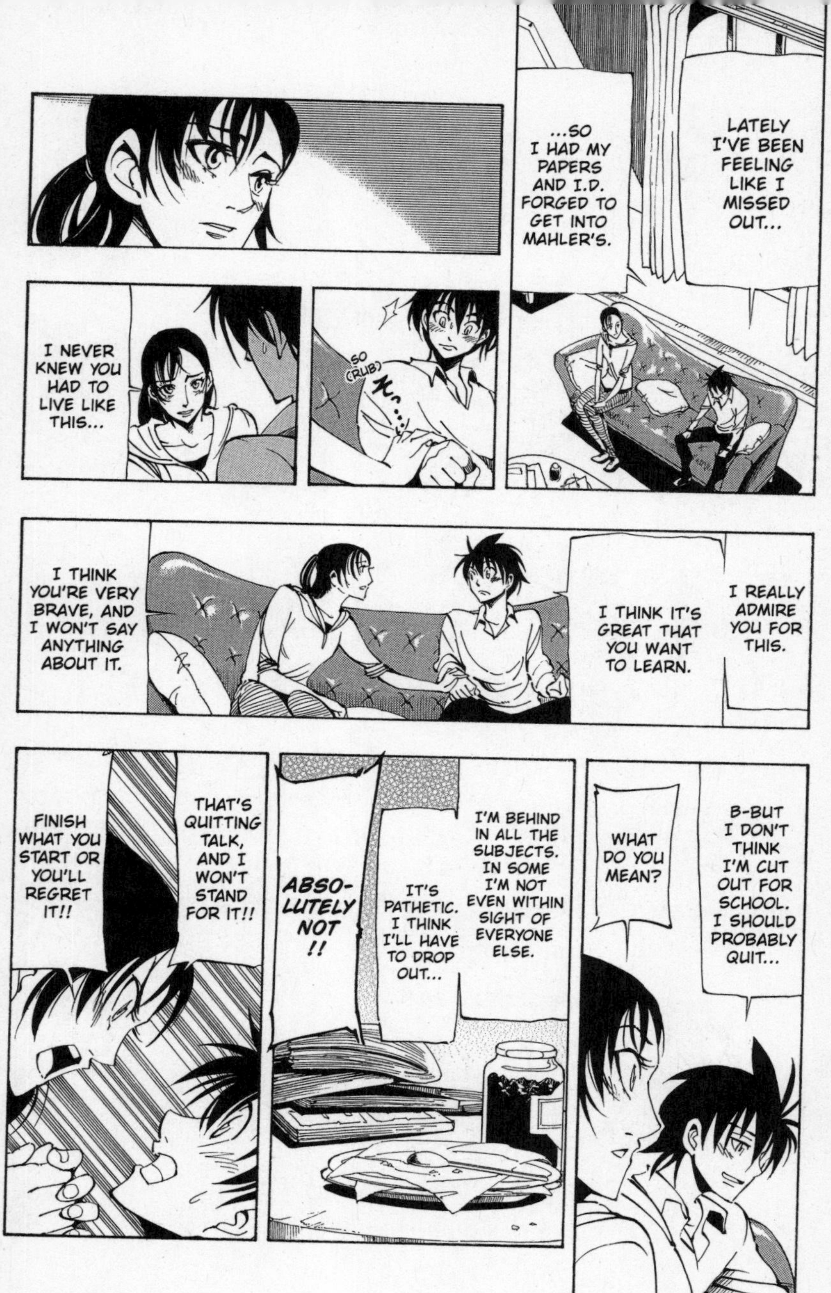
LATELY I'VE BEEN FEELING LIKE I MISSED OUT...
...SO I HAD MY PAPERS AND I.D. FORGED TO GET INTO MAHLER'S.
SO (RUB)
I NEVER KNEW YOU HAD TO LIVE LIKE THIS...
I REALLY ADMIRE YOU FOR THIS.
I THINK IT'S GREAT THAT YOU WANT TO LEARN.
I THINK YOU'RE VERY BRAVE, AND I WON'T SAY ANYTHING ABOUT IT.
B-BUT I DON'T THINK I'M CUT OUT FOR SCHOOL. I SHOULD PROBABLY QUIT...
WHAT DO YOU MEAN?
I'M BEHIND IN ALL THE SUBJECTS. IN SOME I'M NOT EVEN WITHIN SIGHT OF EVERYONE ELSE.
IT'S PATHETIC. I THINK I'LL HAVE TO DROP OUT...
ABSOLUTELY NOT!!
THAT'S QUITTING TALK, AND I WON'T STAND FOR IT!!
FINISH WHAT YOU START OR YOU'LL REGRET IT!!

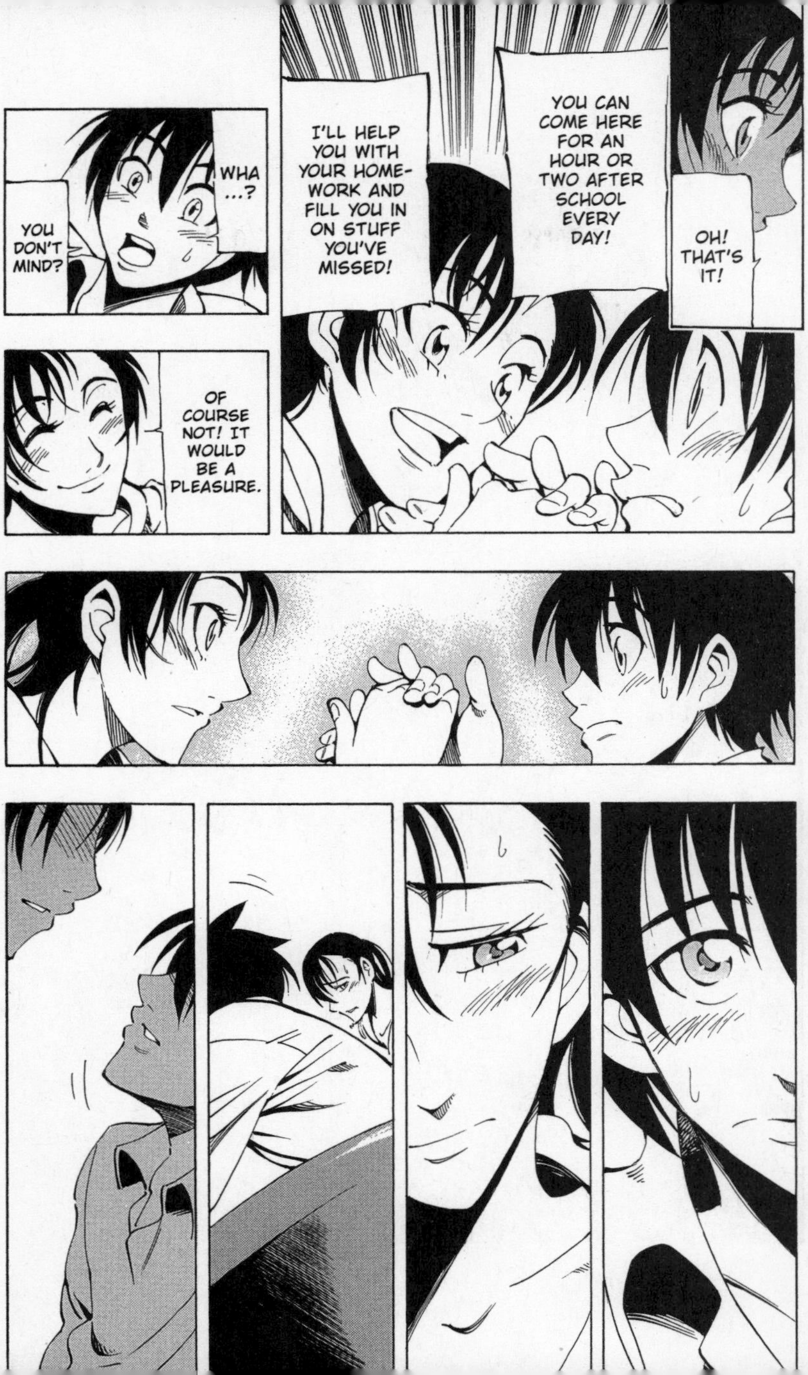
OH! THAT'S IT!
YOU CAN COME HERE FOR AN HOUR OR TWO AFTER SCHOOL EVERY DAY!
I'LL HELP YOU WITH YOUR HOME-WORK AND FILL YOU IN ON STUFF YOU'VE MISSED!
WHA ...?
YOU DON'T MIND?
OF COURSE NOT! IT WOULD BE A PLEASURE.

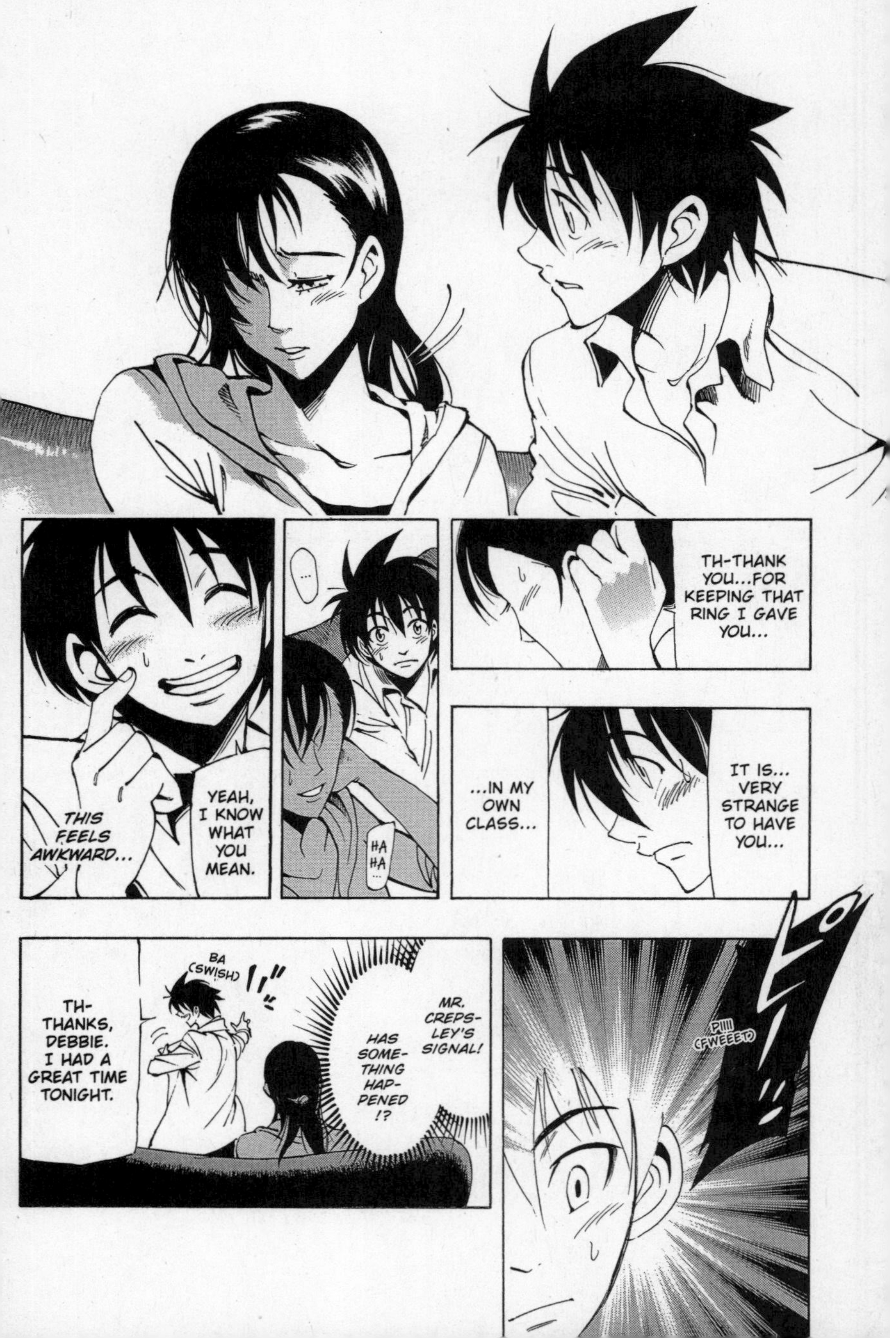
TH-THANK YOU...FOR KEEPING THAT RING I GAVE YOU...
IT IS... VERY STRANGE TO HAVE YOU...
...IN MY OWN CLASS...
...
HA HA ...
YEAH, I KNOW WHAT YOU MEAN.
THIS FEELS AWKWARD...
PIIII (FWEEET)
MR. CREPSLEY'S SIGNAL!
HAS SOMETHING HAPPENED !?
BA (SWISH)
TH-THANKS, DEBBIE. I HAD A GREAT TIME TONIGHT.

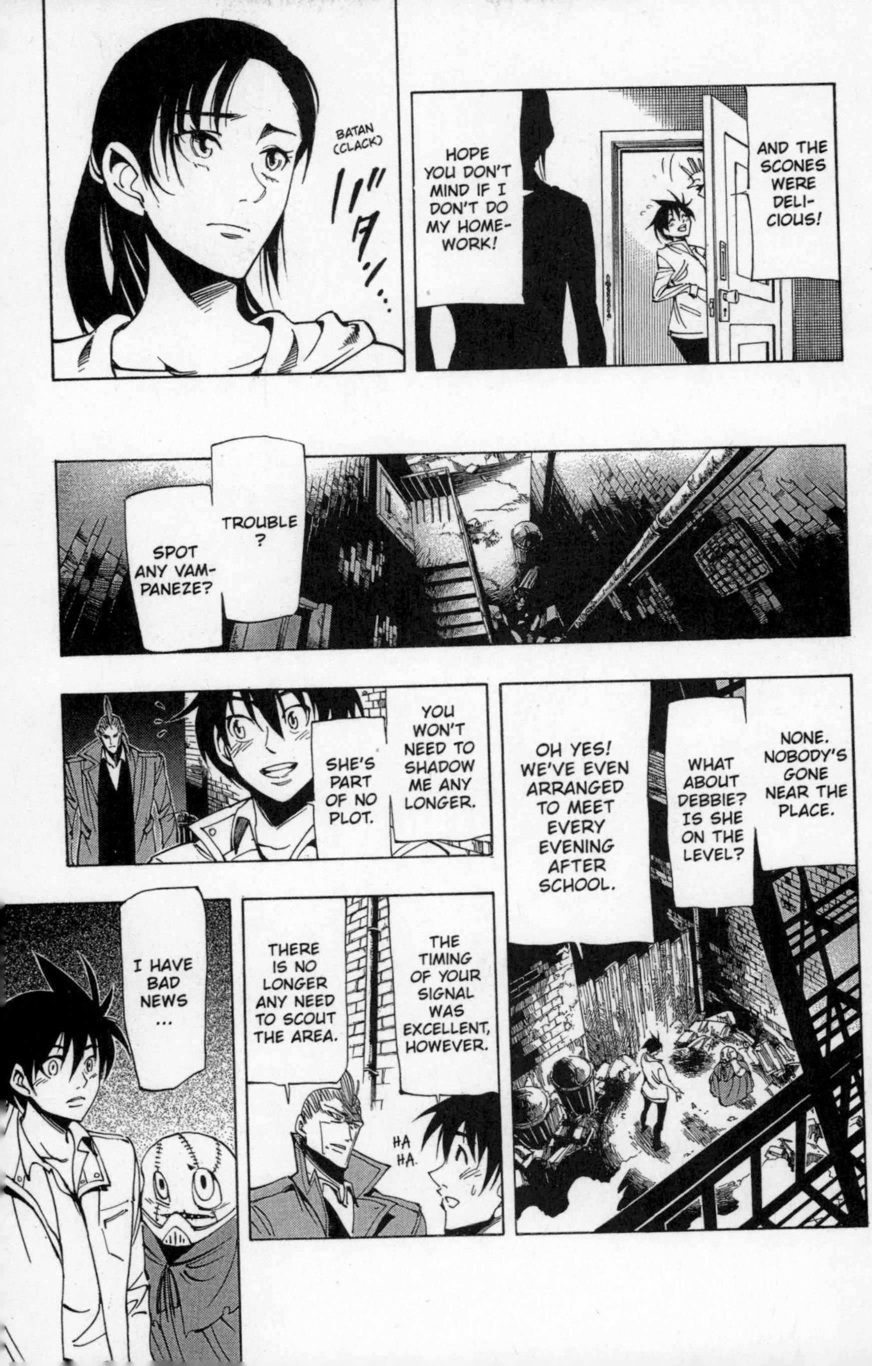

AND THE SCONES WERE DELICIOUS!
HOPE YOU DON'T MIND IF I DON'T DO MY HOME-WORK!
BATAN (CLACK)
TROUBLE?
SPOT ANY VAM-PANEZE?
NONE. NOBODY'S GONE NEAR THE PLACE.
WHAT ABOUT DEBBIE? IS SHE ON THE LEVEL?
OH YES! WE'VE EVEN ARRANGED TO MEET EVERY EVENING AFTER SCHOOL.
YOU WON'T NEED TO SHADOW ME ANY LONGER.
SHE'S PART OF NO PLOT.
THE TIMING OF YOUR SIGNAL WAS EXCELLENT, HOWEVER.
THERE IS NO LONGER ANY NEED TO SCOUT THE AREA.
HA HA.
I HAVE BAD NEWS ...

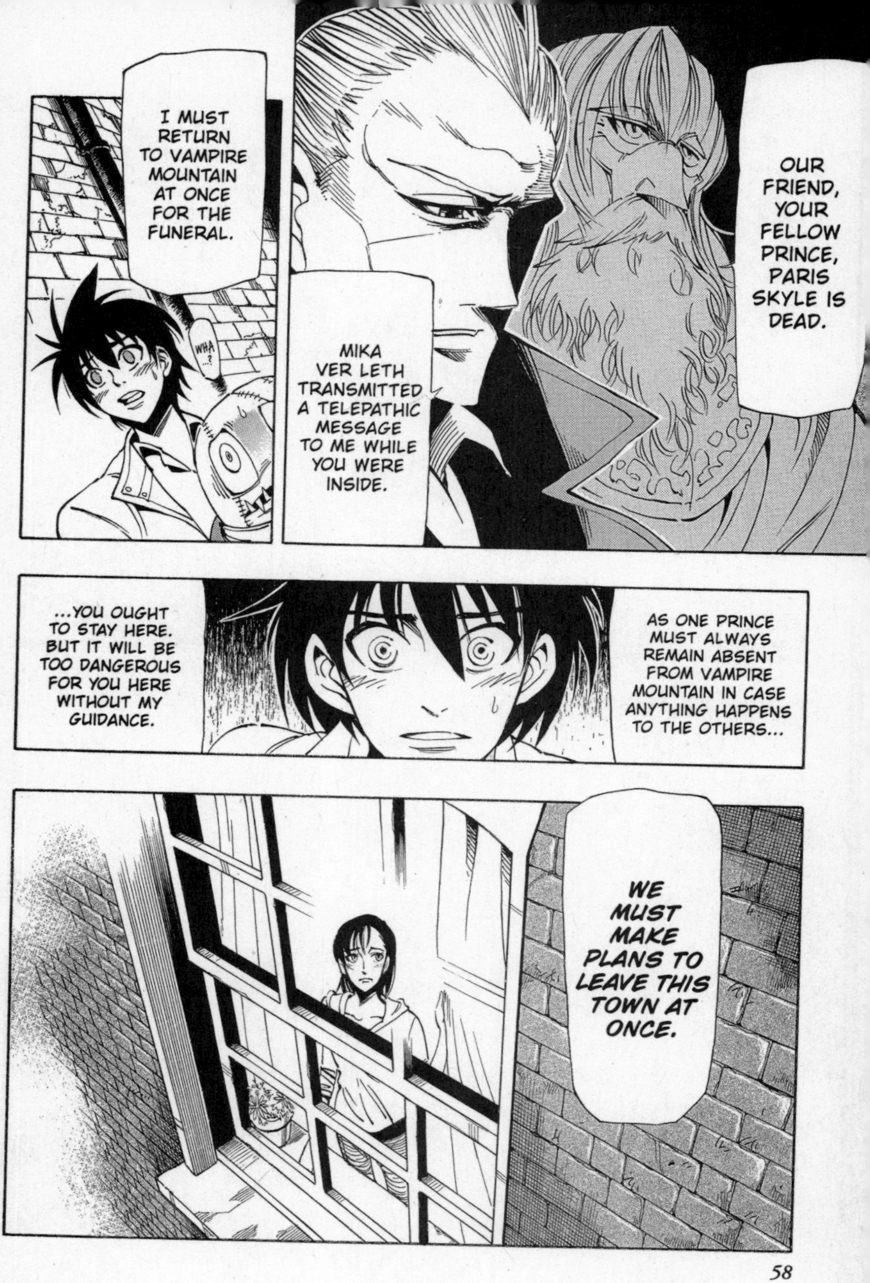
OUR FRIEND, YOUR FELLOW PRINCE, PARIS SKYLE IS DEAD.
MIKA VER LETH TRANSMITTED A TELEPATHIC MESSAGE TO ME WHILE YOU WERE INSIDE.
I MUST RETURN TO VAMPIRE MOUNTAIN AT ONCE FOR THE FUNERAL.
WHA ...?
AS ONE PRINCE MUST ALWAYS REMAIN ABSENT FROM VAMPIRE MOUNTAIN IN CASE ANYTHING HAPPENS TO THE OTHERS...
...YOU OUGHT TO STAY HERE. BUT IT WILL BE TOO DANGEROUS FOR YOU HERE WITHOUT MY GUIDANCE.
WE MUST MAKE PLANS TO LEAVE THIS TOWN AT ONCE.

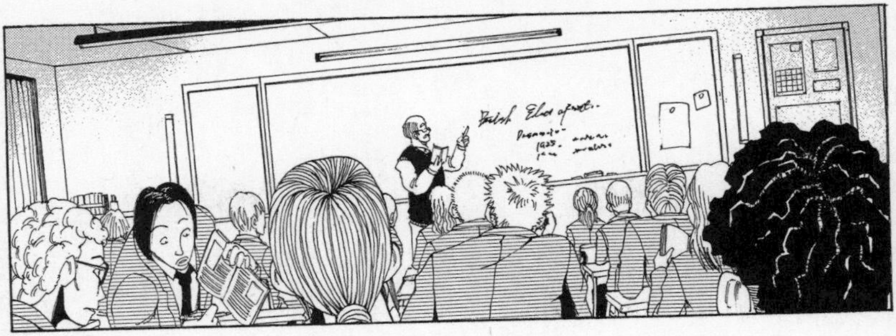

CHAPTER 68: FRIEND AND LOVER

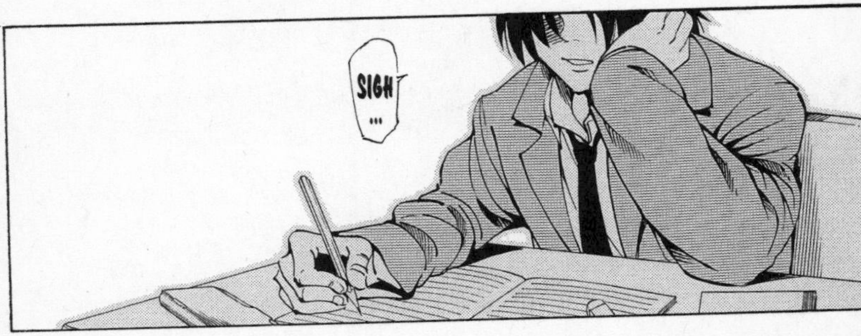
SIGH ...

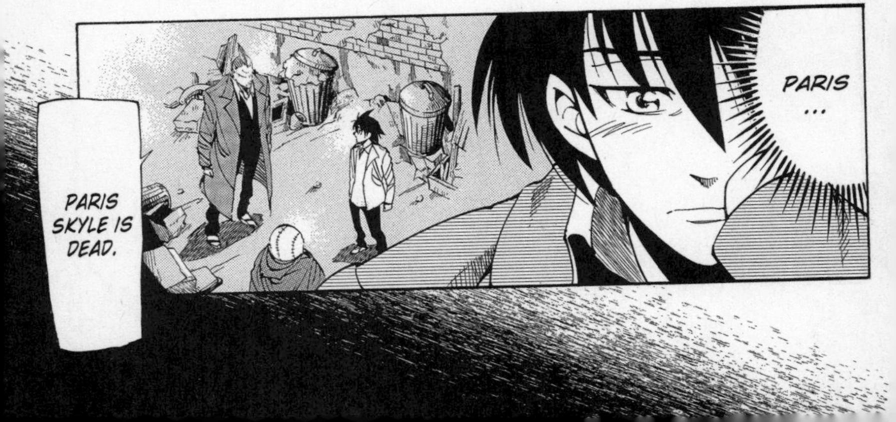
PARIS ...
PARIS SKYLE IS DEAD.

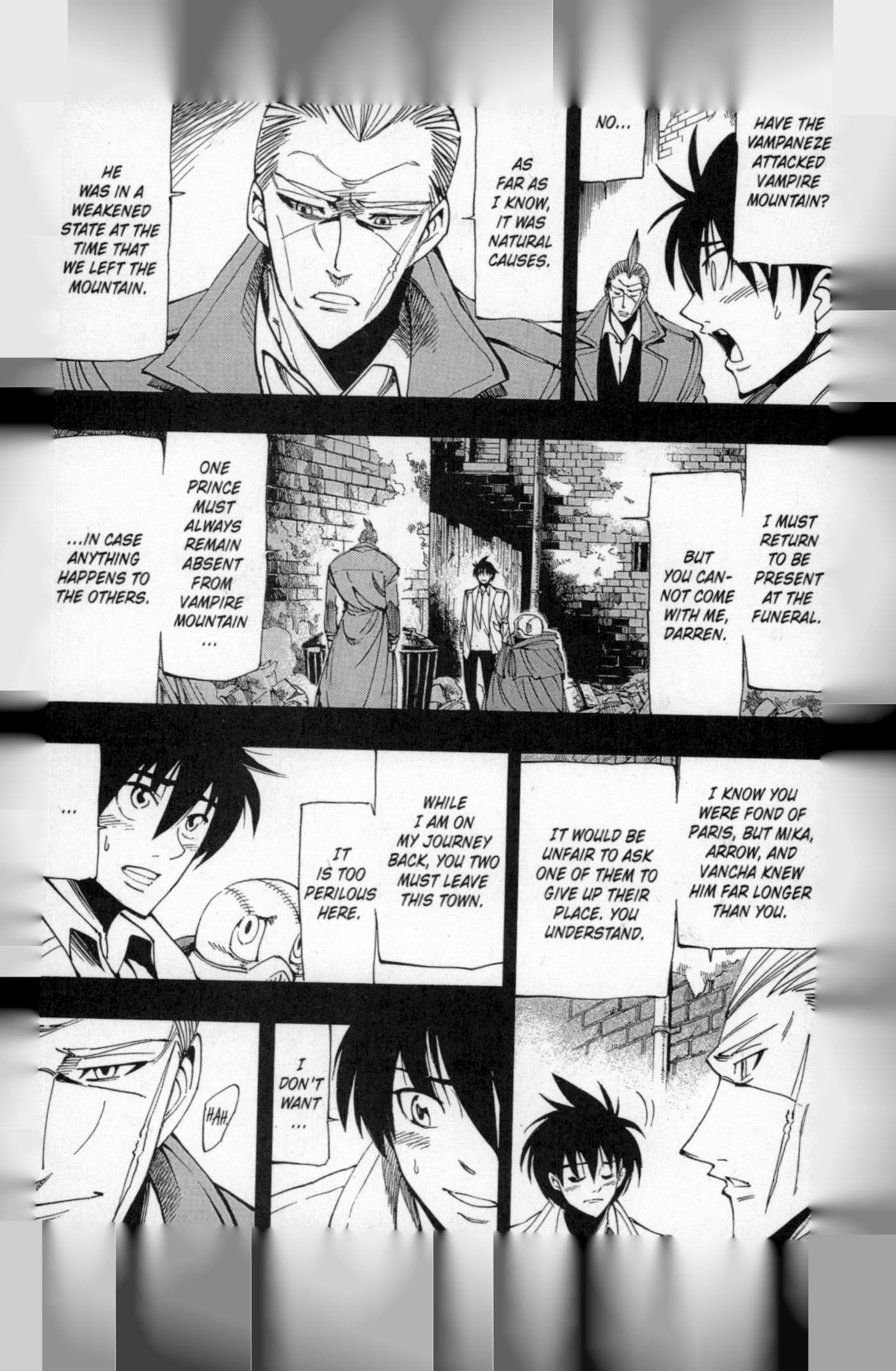
HAVE THE VAMPANEZE ATTACKED VAMPIRE MOUNTAIN?
NO...
AS FAR AS I KNOW, IT WAS NATURAL CAUSES.
HE WAS IN A WEAKENED STATE AT THE TIME THAT WE LEFT THE MOUNTAIN.
I MUST RETURN TO BE PRESENT AT THE FUNERAL.
BUT YOU CAN-NOT COME WITH ME, DARREN.
ONE PRINCE MUST ALWAYS REMAIN ABSENT FROM VAMPIRE MOUNTAIN...
...IN CASE ANYTHING HAPPENS TO THE OTHERS.
I KNOW YOU WERE FOND OF PARIS, BUT MIKA, ARROW, AND VANCHA KNEW HIM FAR LONGER THAN YOU.
IT WOULD BE UNFAIR TO ASK ONE OF THEM TO GIVE UP THEIR PLACE. YOU UNDERSTAND.
WHILE I AM ON MY JOURNEY BACK, YOU TWO MUST LEAVE THIS TOWN.
IT IS TOO PERILOUS HERE.
...
I DON'T WANT...
HAH.

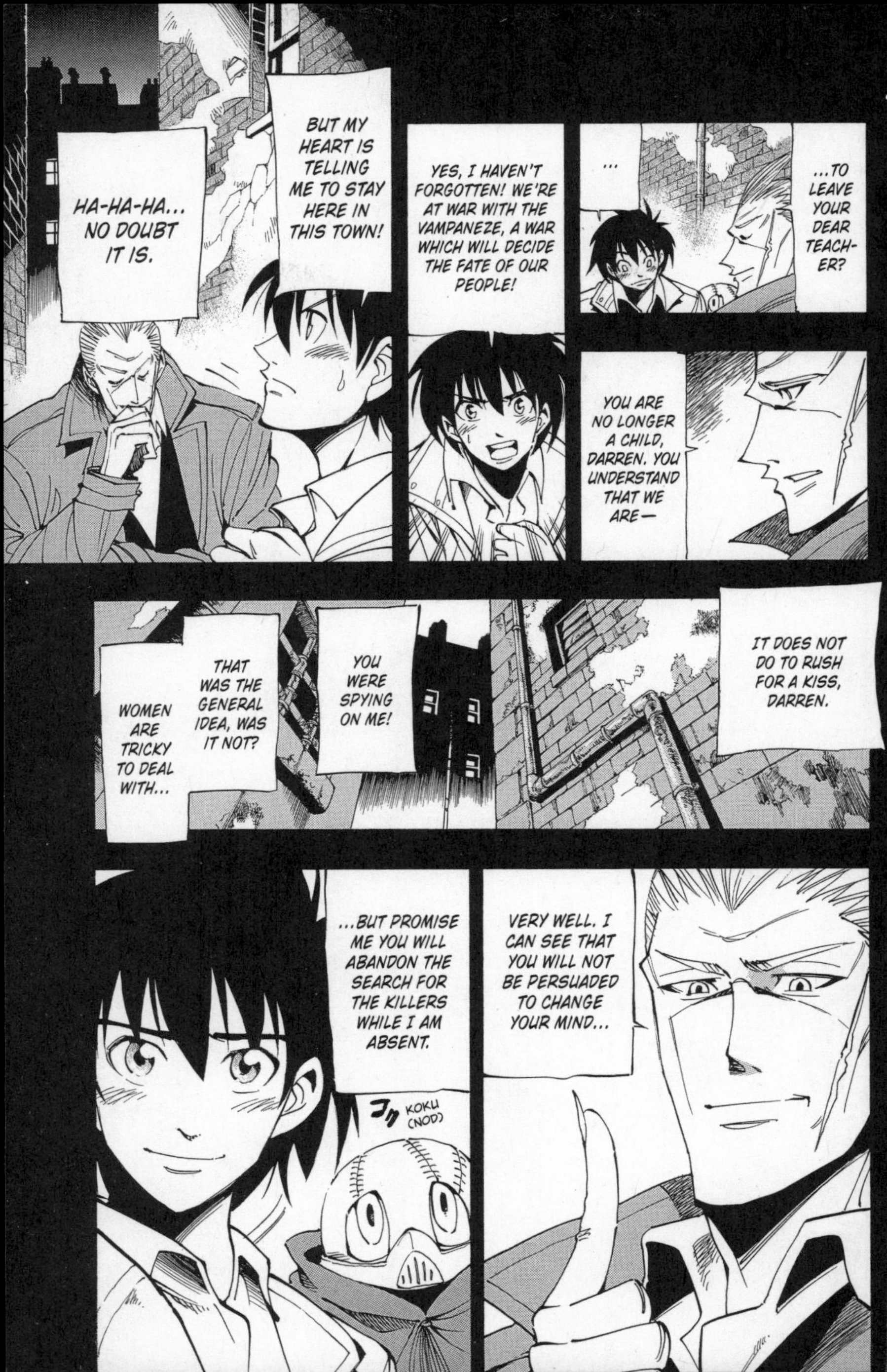
...TO LEAVE YOUR DEAR TEACHER?
...
YOU ARE NO LONGER A CHILD, DARREN. YOU UNDERSTAND THAT WE ARE—
YES, I HAVEN'T FORGOTTEN! WE'RE AT WAR WITH THE VAMPANEZE, A WAR WHICH WILL DECIDE THE FATE OF OUR PEOPLE!
BUT MY HEART IS TELLING ME TO STAY HERE IN THIS TOWN!
HA-HA-HA... NO DOUBT IT IS.
IT DOES NOT DO TO RUSH FOR A KISS, DARREN.
YOU WERE SPYING ON ME!
THAT WAS THE GENERAL IDEA, WAS IT NOT?
WOMEN ARE TRICKY TO DEAL WITH...
VERY WELL. I CAN SEE THAT YOU WILL NOT BE PERSUADED TO CHANGE YOUR MIND...
...BUT PROMISE ME YOU WILL ABANDON THE SEARCH FOR THE KILLERS WHILE I AM ABSENT.
KOKU (NOD)

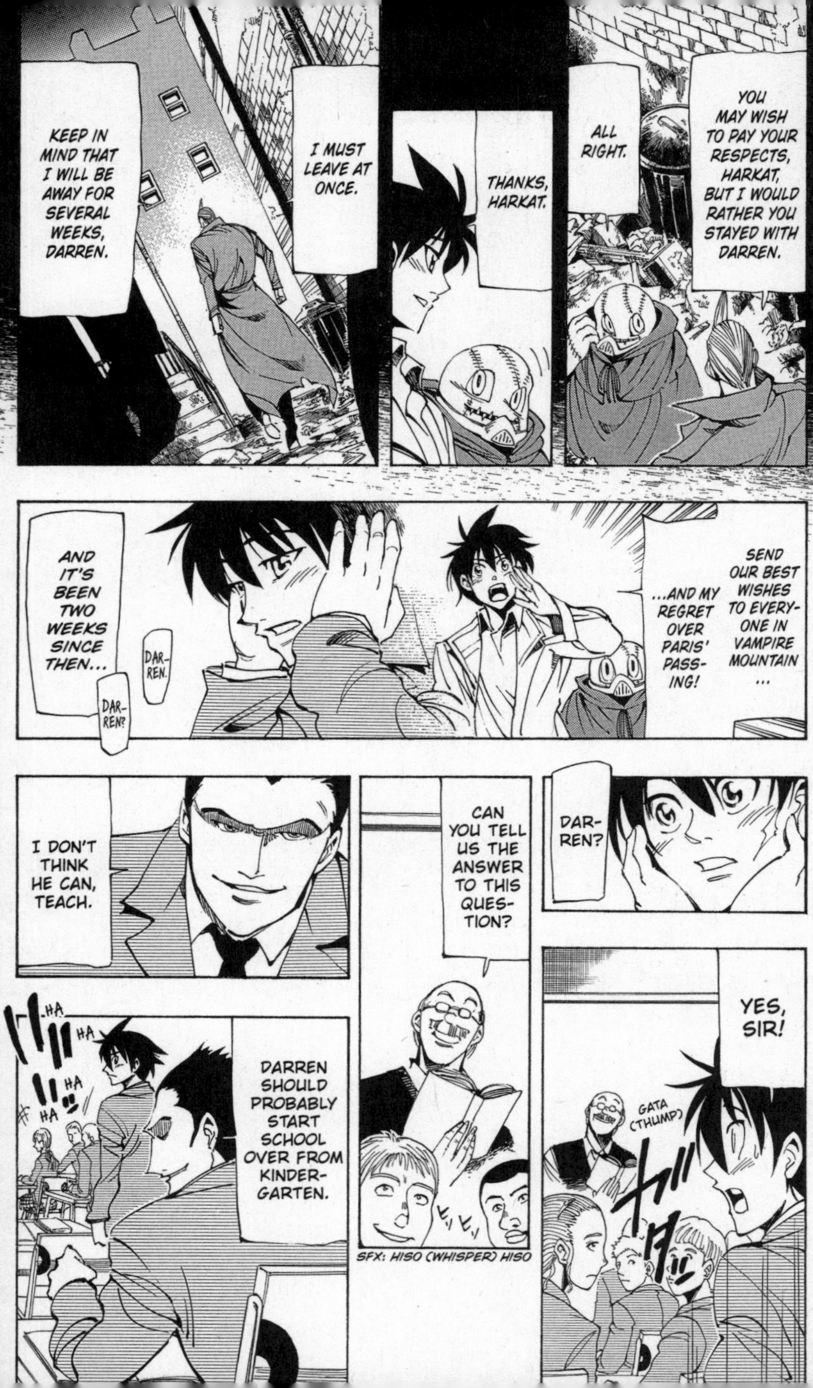

YOU MAY WISH TO PAY YOUR RESPECTS, HARKAT, BUT I WOULD RATHER YOU STAYED WITH DARREN.
ALL RIGHT.
THANKS, HARKAT.
I MUST LEAVE AT ONCE.
KEEP IN MIND THAT I WILL BE AWAY FOR SEVERAL WEEKS, DARREN.
SEND OUR BEST WISHES TO EVERYONE IN VAMPIRE MOUNTAIN...
...AND MY REGRET OVER PARIS' PASSING!
AND IT'S BEEN TWO WEEKS SINCE THEN...
DARREN.
DARREN?
DARREN?
YES, SIR!
GATA (THUMP)
CAN YOU TELL US THE ANSWER TO THIS QUESTION?
SFX: HISO (WHISPER) HISO
I DON'T THINK HE CAN, TEACH.
DARREN SHOULD PROBABLY START SCHOOL OVER FROM KINDERGARTEN.
HA
HA
HA
HA

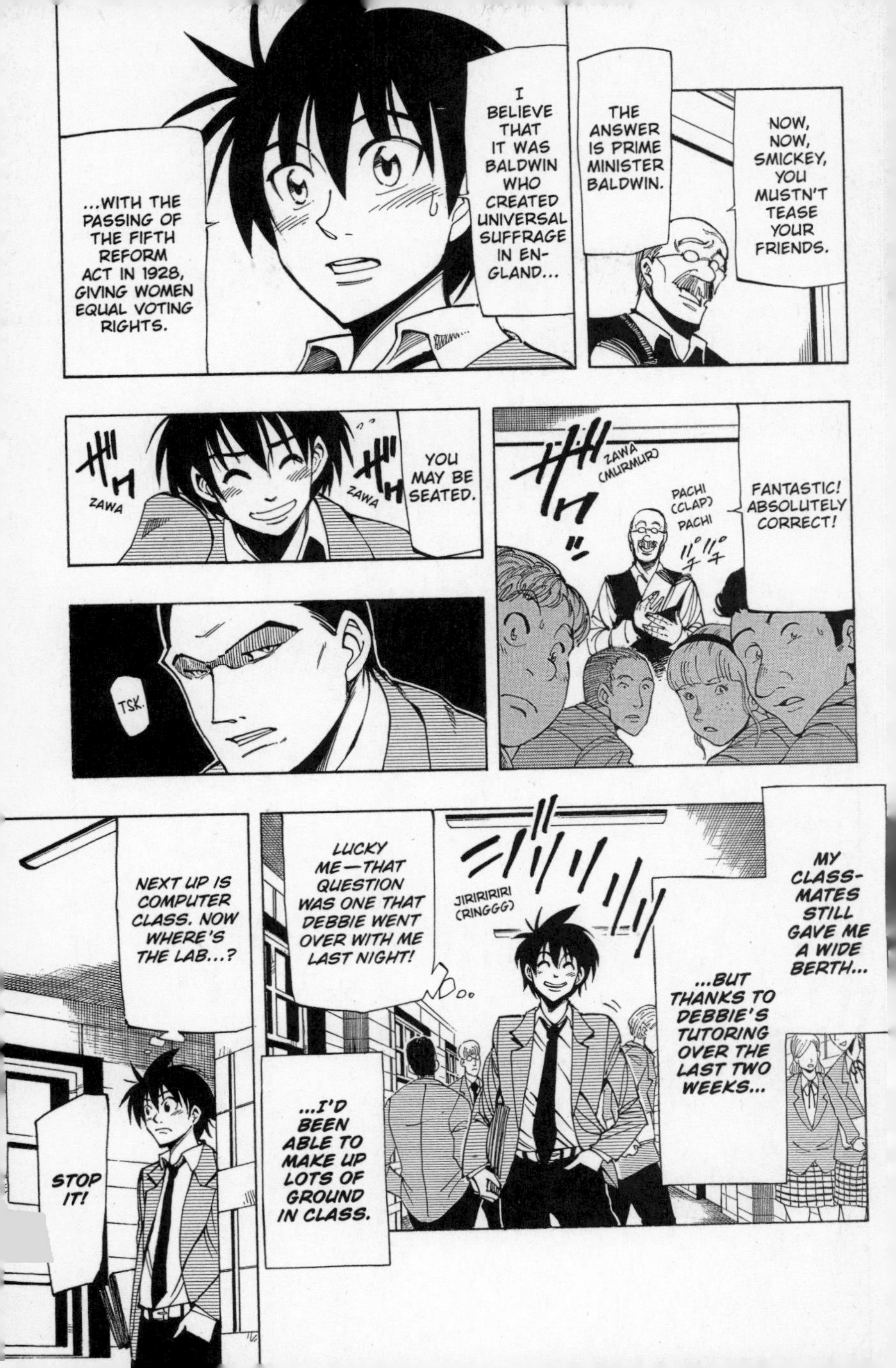
NOW, NOW, SMICKEY, YOU MUSTN'T TEASE YOUR FRIENDS.
THE ANSWER IS PRIME MINISTER BALDWIN.
I BELIEVE THAT IT WAS BALDWIN WHO CREATED UNIVERSAL SUFFRAGE IN ENGLAND...
...WITH THE PASSING OF THE FIFTH REFORM ACT IN 1928, GIVING WOMEN EQUAL VOTING RIGHTS.
FANTASTIC! ABSOLUTELY CORRECT!
PACHI (CLAP) PACHI
ZAWA (MURMUR)
YOU MAY BE SEATED.
ZAWA
ZAWA
TSK.
MY CLASSMATES STILL GAVE ME A WIDE BERTH...
...BUT THANKS TO DEBBIE'S TUTORING OVER THE LAST TWO WEEKS...
JIRIRIRIRI (RINGGG)
LUCKY ME—THAT QUESTION WAS ONE THAT DEBBIE WENT OVER WITH ME LAST NIGHT!
...I'D BEEN ABLE TO MAKE UP LOTS OF GROUND IN CLASS.
NEXT UP IS COMPUTER CLASS. NOW WHERE'S THE LAB...?
STOP IT!

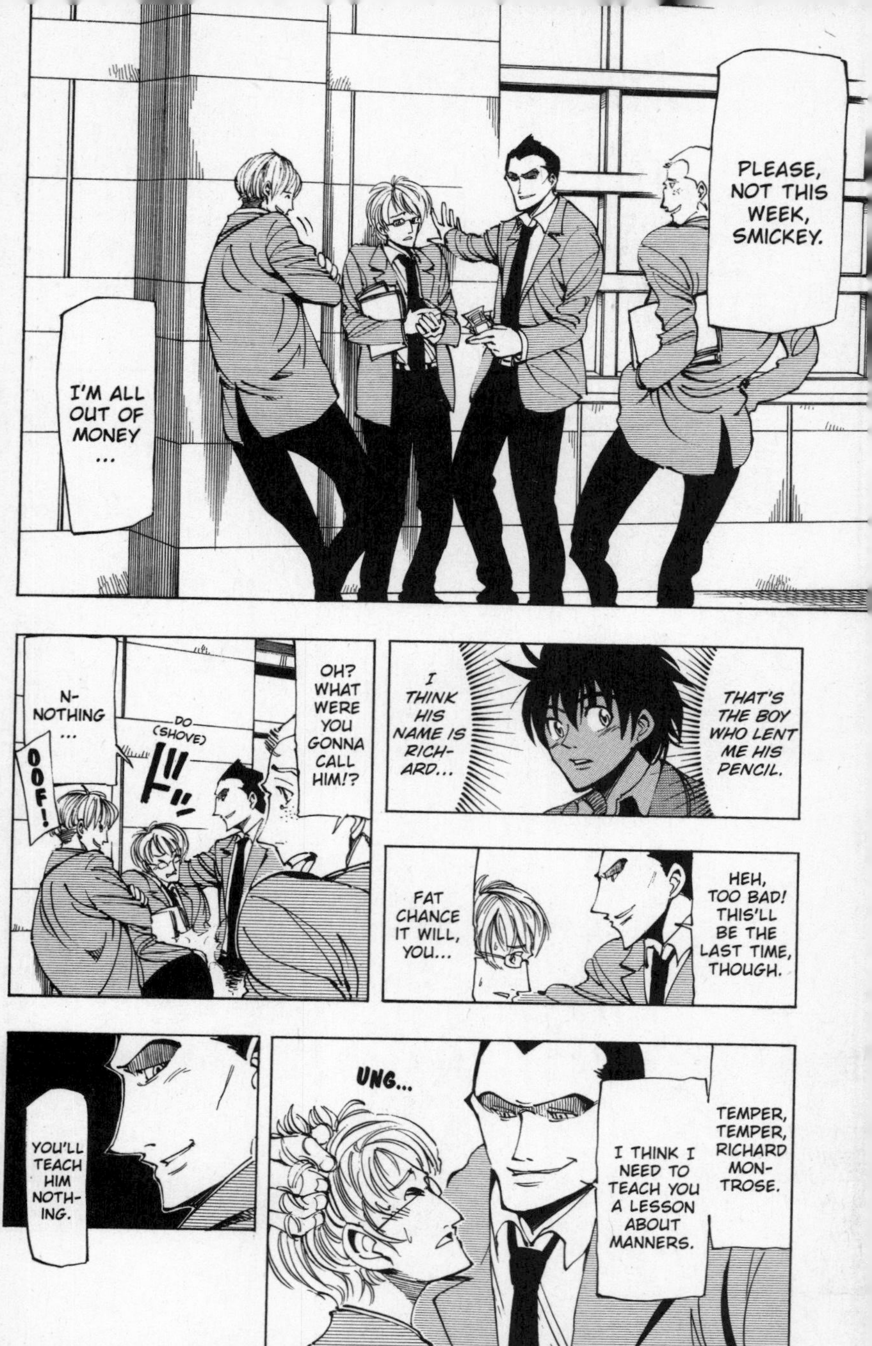
PLEASE, NOT THIS WEEK, SMICKEY.
I'M ALL OUT OF MONEY ...
THAT'S THE BOY WHO LENT ME HIS PENCIL.
I THINK HIS NAME IS RICH-ARD...
HEH, TOO BAD! THIS'LL BE THE LAST TIME, THOUGH.
FAT CHANCE IT WILL, YOU...
OH? WHAT WERE YOU GONNA CALL HIM!?
N-NOTHING ...
DO (SHOVE)
OOF!
TEMPER, TEMPER, RICHARD MON-TROSE.
I THINK I NEED TO TEACH YOU A LESSON ABOUT MANNERS.
UNG...
YOU'LL TEACH HIM NOTH-ING.

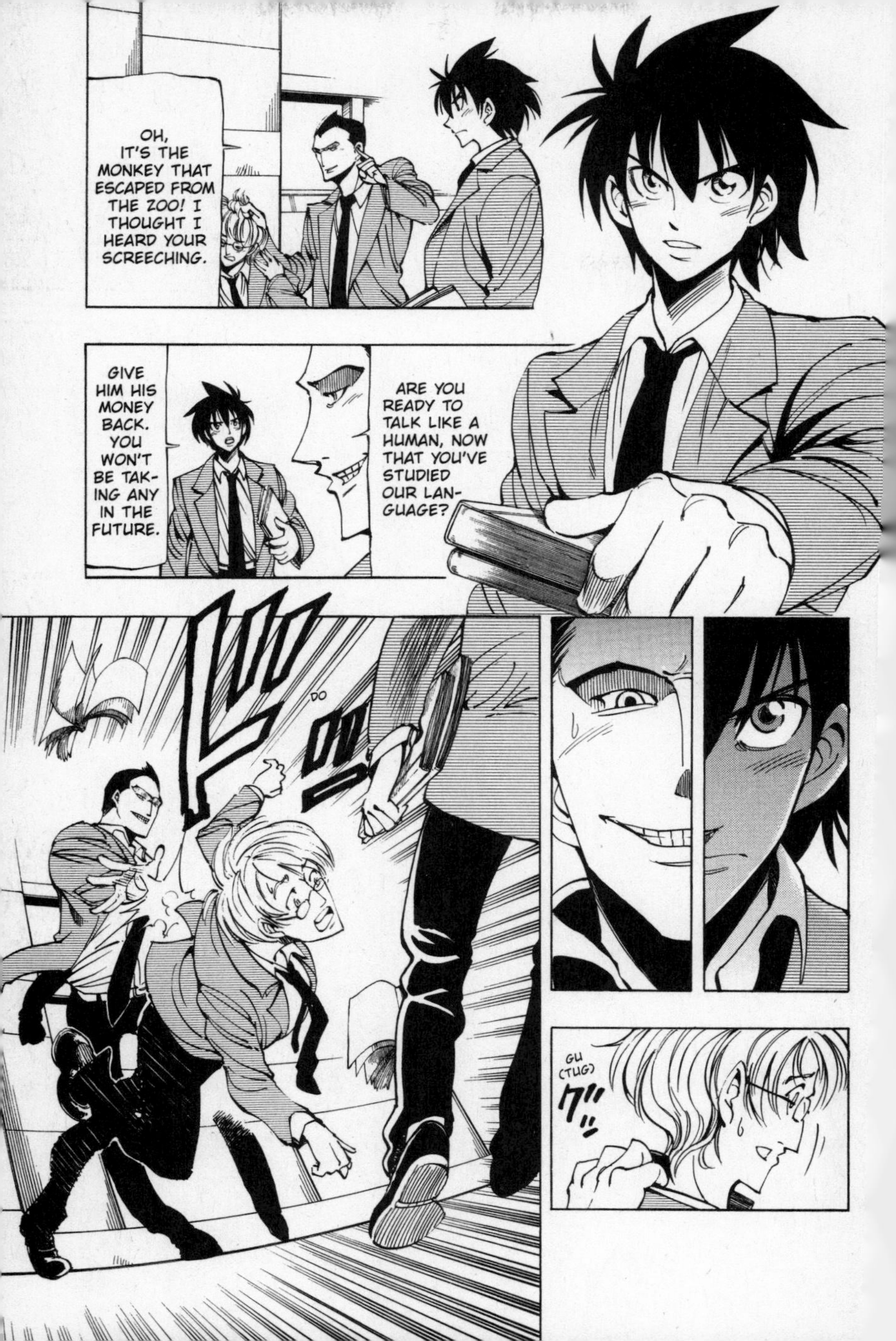
OH, IT'S THE MONKEY THAT ESCAPED FROM THE ZOO! I THOUGHT I HEARD YOUR SCREECHING.
ARE YOU READY TO TALK LIKE A HUMAN, NOW THAT YOU'VE STUDIED OUR LANGUAGE?
GIVE HIM HIS MONEY BACK. YOU WON'T BE TAKING ANY IN THE FUTURE.
GU (TUG)
DO

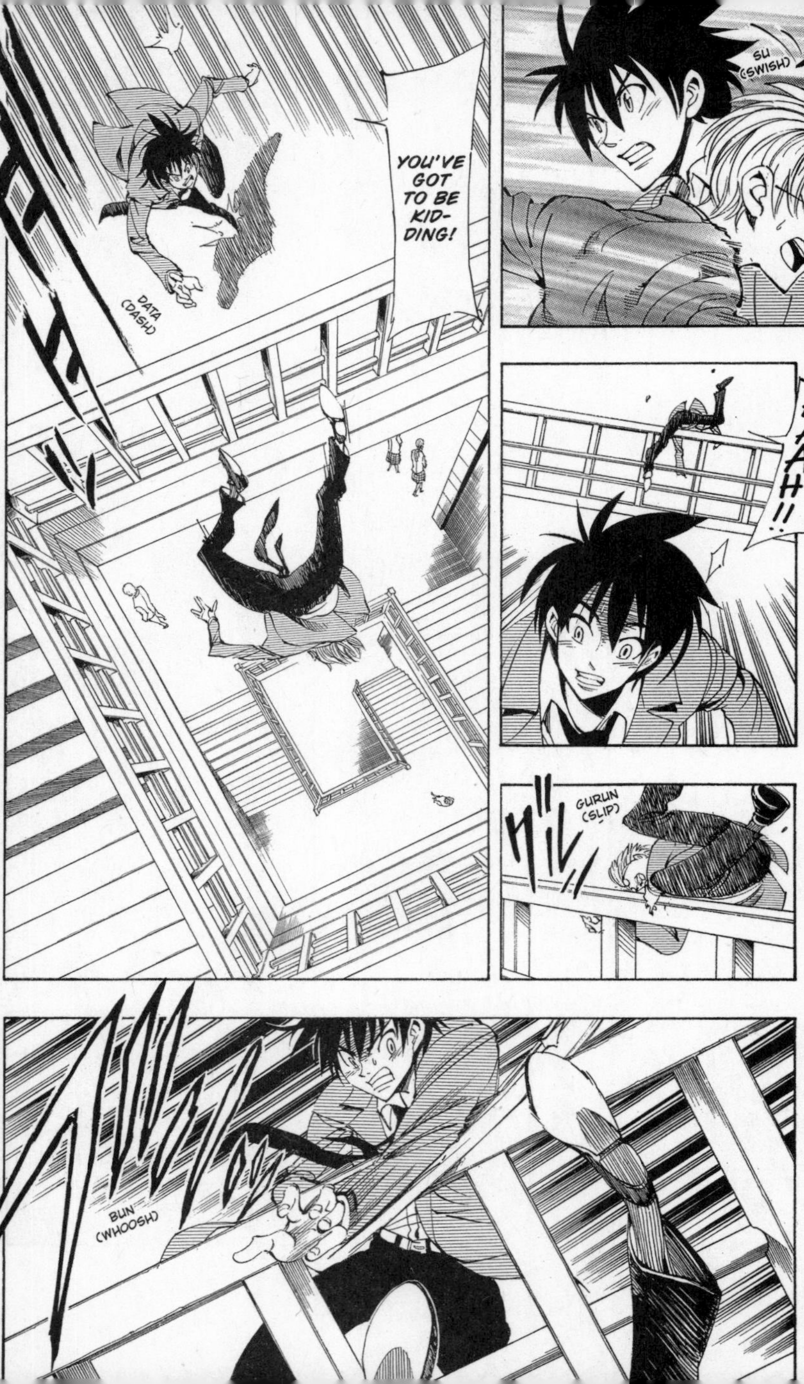
SU (SWISH)
AAAAH!!
GURUN (SLIP)
YOU'VE GOT TO BE KID-DING!
DATA (DASH)
BUN (WHOOSH)

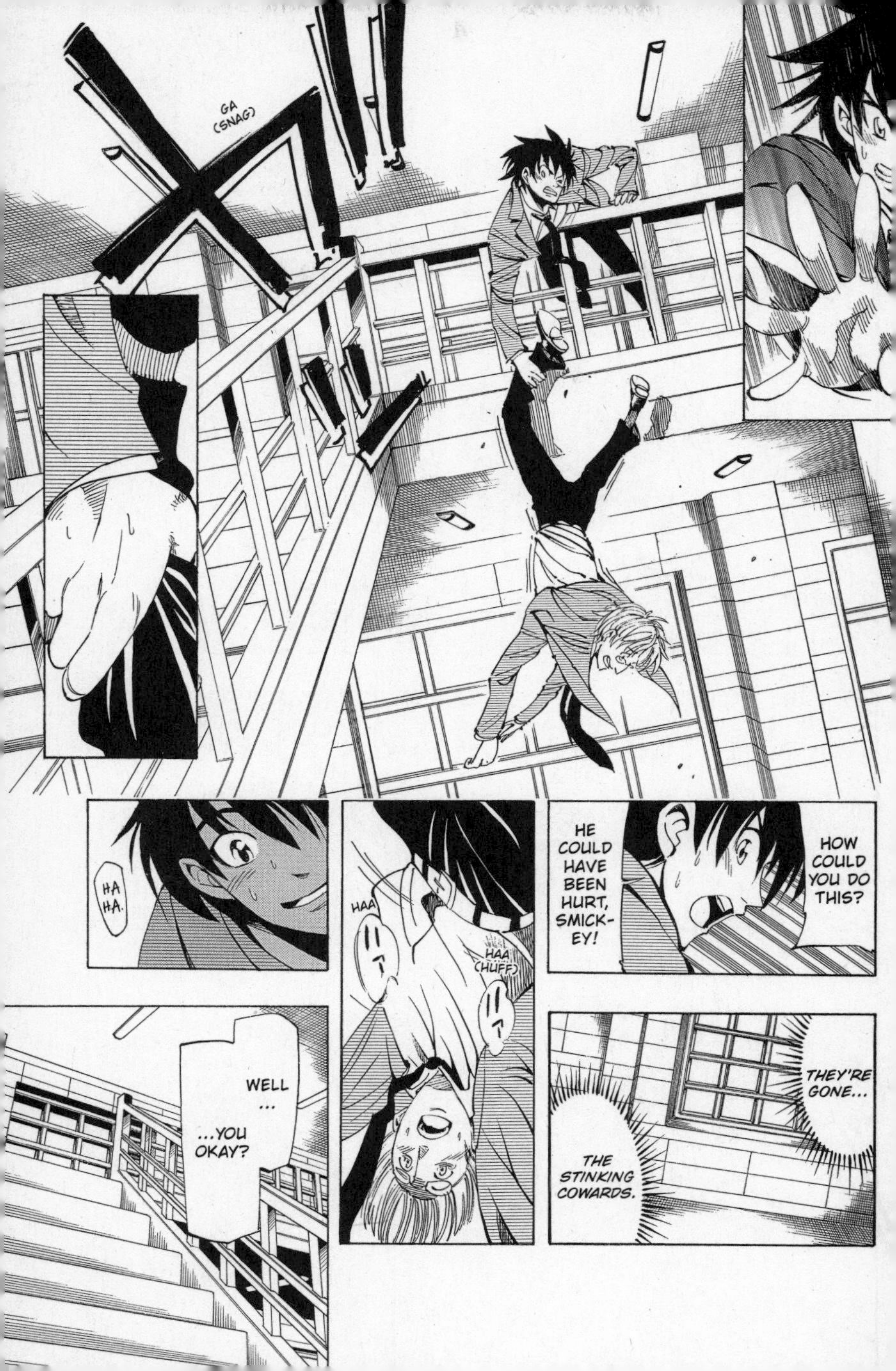
GA (SNAG)
HOW COULD YOU DO THIS?
HE COULD HAVE BEEN HURT, SMICKEY!
HAA HAA (CHUFF)
HA HA.
THEY'RE GONE...
THE STINKING COWARDS.
WELL ...
...YOU OKAY?

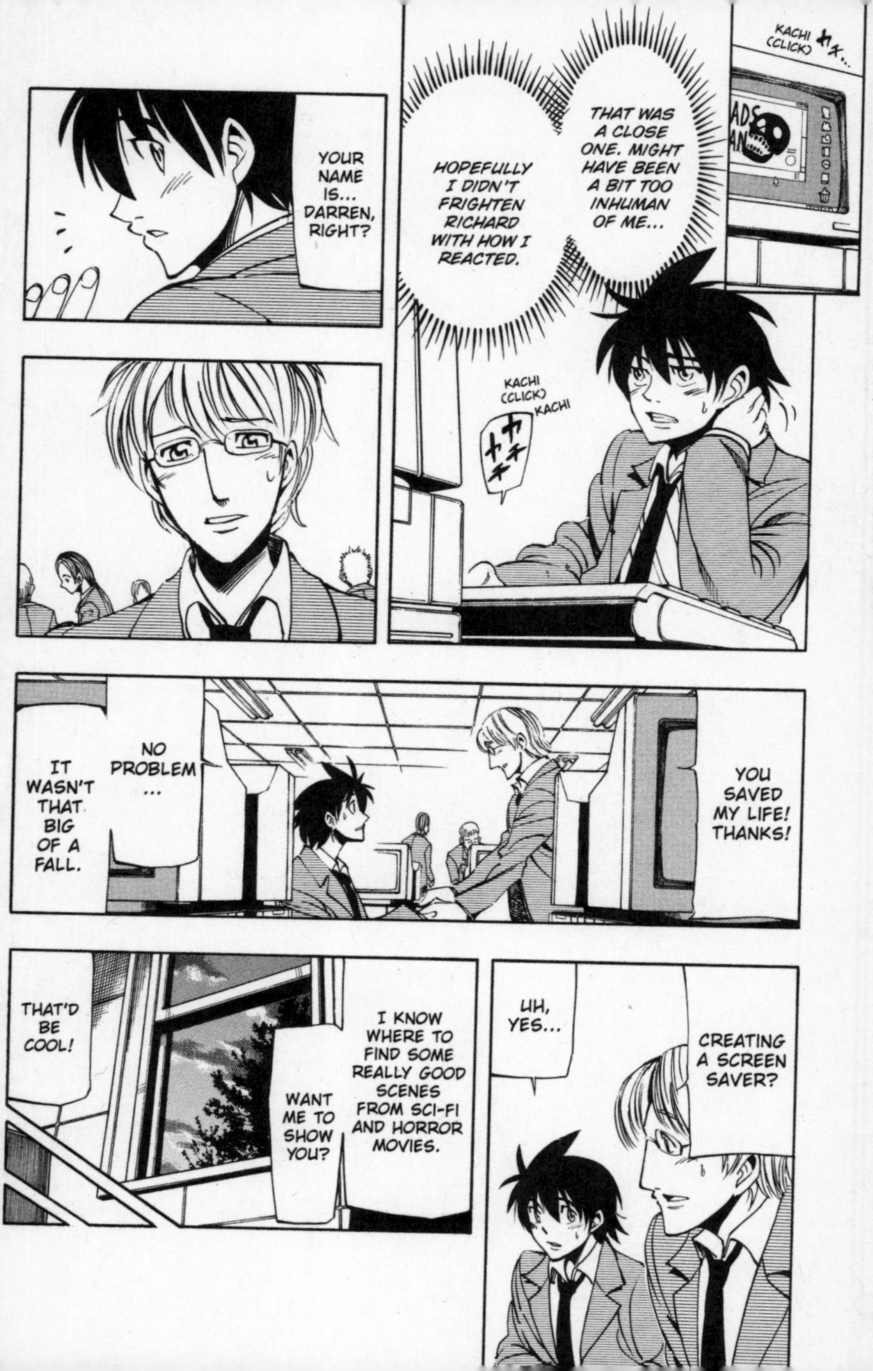
KACHI (CLICK)
THAT WAS A CLOSE ONE. MIGHT HAVE BEEN A BIT TOO INHUMAN OF ME...
HOPEFULLY I DIDN'T FRIGHTEN RICHARD WITH HOW I REACTED.
KACHI (CLICK) KACHI
YOUR NAME IS... DARREN, RIGHT?
YOU SAVED MY LIFE! THANKS!
NO PROBLEM...
IT WASN'T THAT BIG OF A FALL.
CREATING A SCREEN SAVER?
UH, YES...
I KNOW WHERE TO FIND SOME REALLY GOOD SCENES FROM SCI-FI AND HORROR MOVIES.
WANT ME TO SHOW YOU?
THAT'D BE COOL!

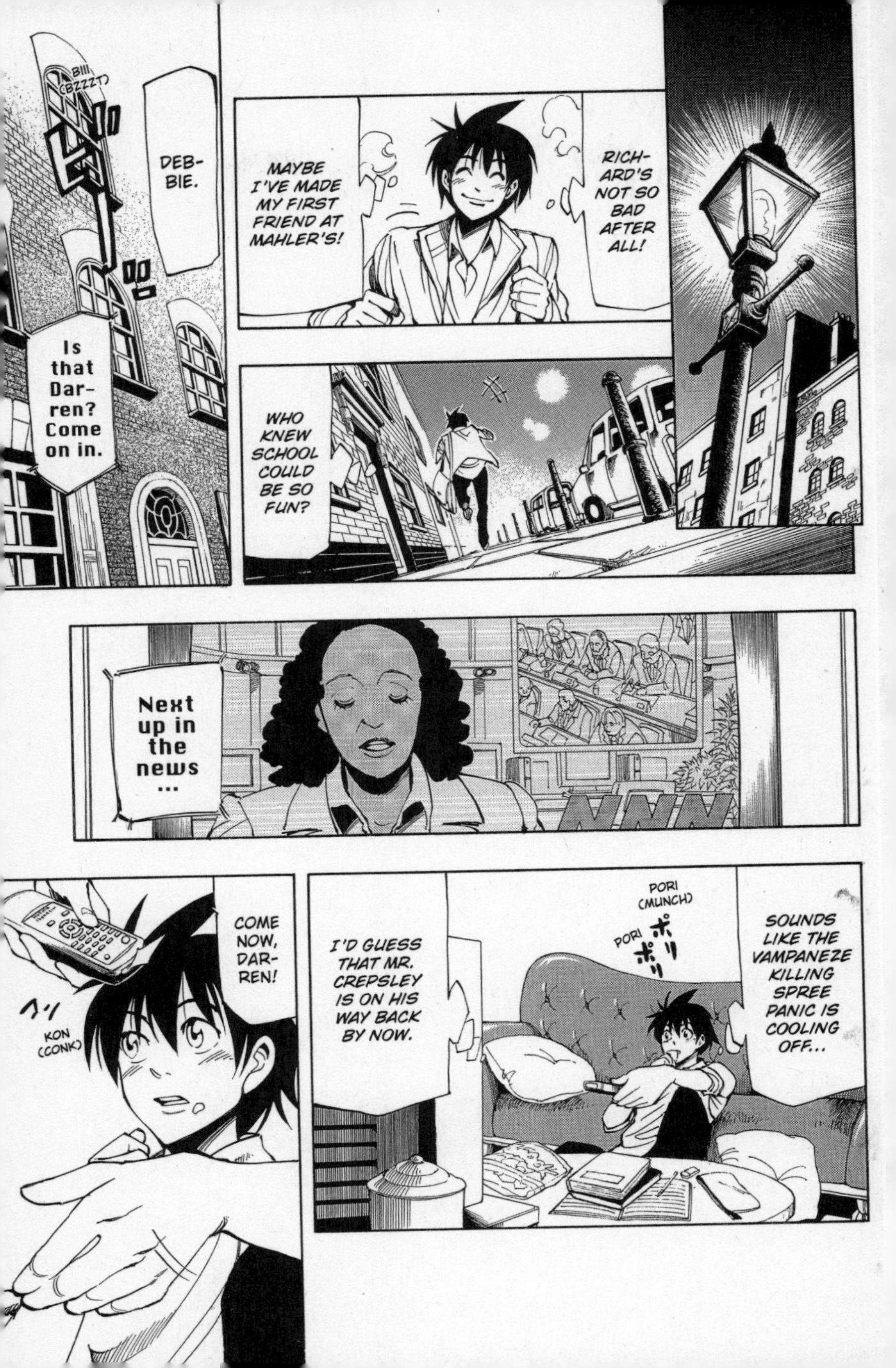
RICHARD'S NOT SO BAD AFTER ALL!
MAYBE I'VE MADE MY FIRST FRIEND AT MAHLER'S!
WHO KNEW SCHOOL COULD BE SO FUN?
BIII (BZZZT)
DEBBIE.
Is that Darren? Come on in.
Next up in the news...
SOUNDS LIKE THE VAMPANEZE KILLING SPREE PANIC IS COOLING OFF...
PORI (MUNCH)
PORI
I'D GUESS THAT MR. CREPSLEY IS ON HIS WAY BACK BY NOW.
COME NOW, DARREN!
KON (CONK)

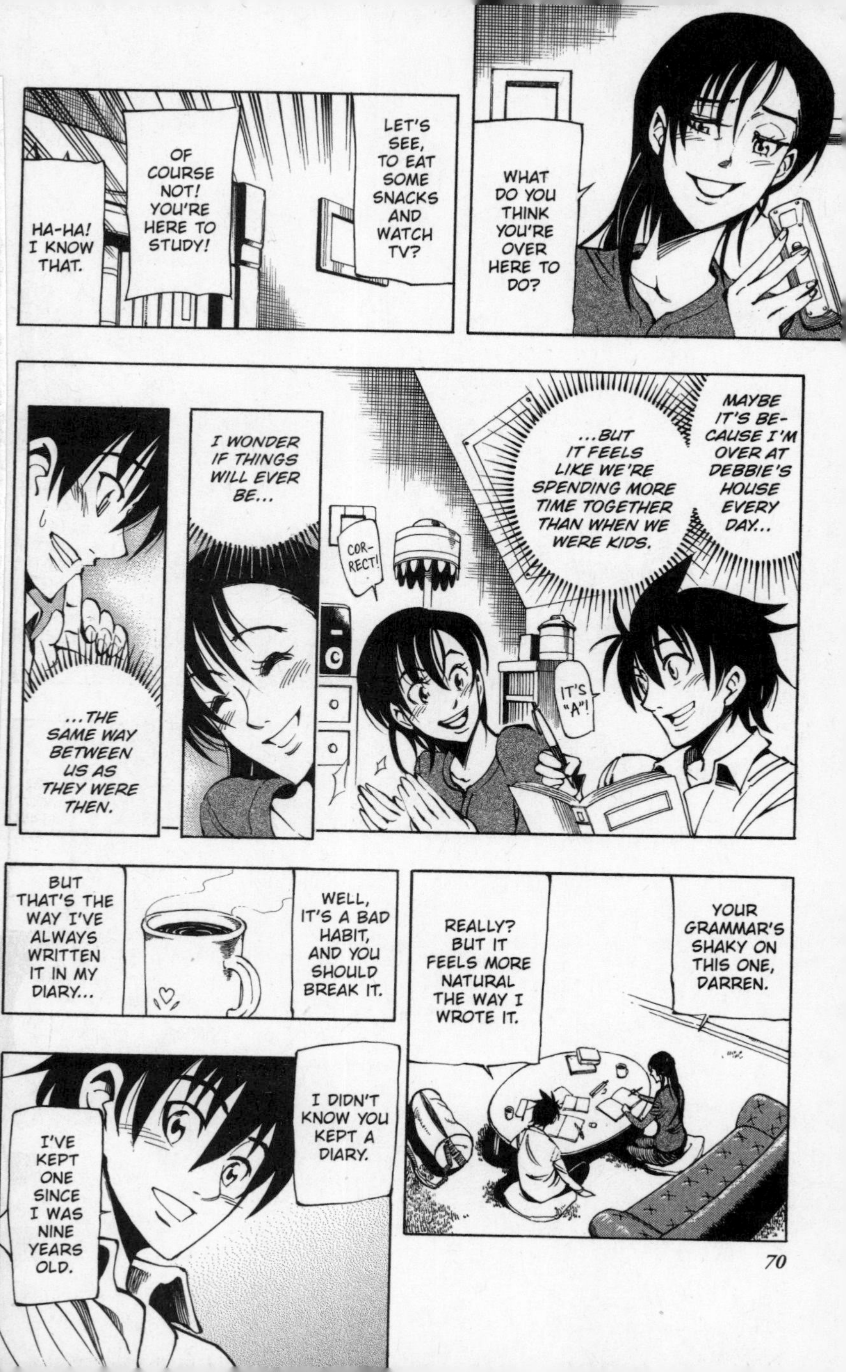

WHAT DO YOU THINK YOU'RE OVER HERE TO DO?
LET'S SEE, TO EAT SOME SNACKS AND WATCH TV?
OF COURSE NOT! YOU'RE HERE TO STUDY!
HA-HA! I KNOW THAT.
MAYBE IT'S BE-CAUSE I'M OVER AT DEBBIE'S HOUSE EVERY DAY...
...BUT IT FEELS LIKE WE'RE SPENDING MORE TIME TOGETHER THAN WHEN WE WERE KIDS.
IT'S "A"!
COR-RECT!
I WONDER IF THINGS WILL EVER BE...
...THE SAME WAY BETWEEN US AS THEY WERE THEN.
YOUR GRAMMAR'S SHAKY ON THIS ONE, DARREN.
REALLY? BUT IT FEELS MORE NATURAL THE WAY I WROTE IT.
WELL, IT'S A BAD HABIT, AND YOU SHOULD BREAK IT.
BUT THAT'S THE WAY I'VE ALWAYS WRITTEN IT IN MY DIARY...
I DIDN'T KNOW YOU KEPT A DIARY.
I'VE KEPT ONE SINCE I WAS NINE YEARS OLD.

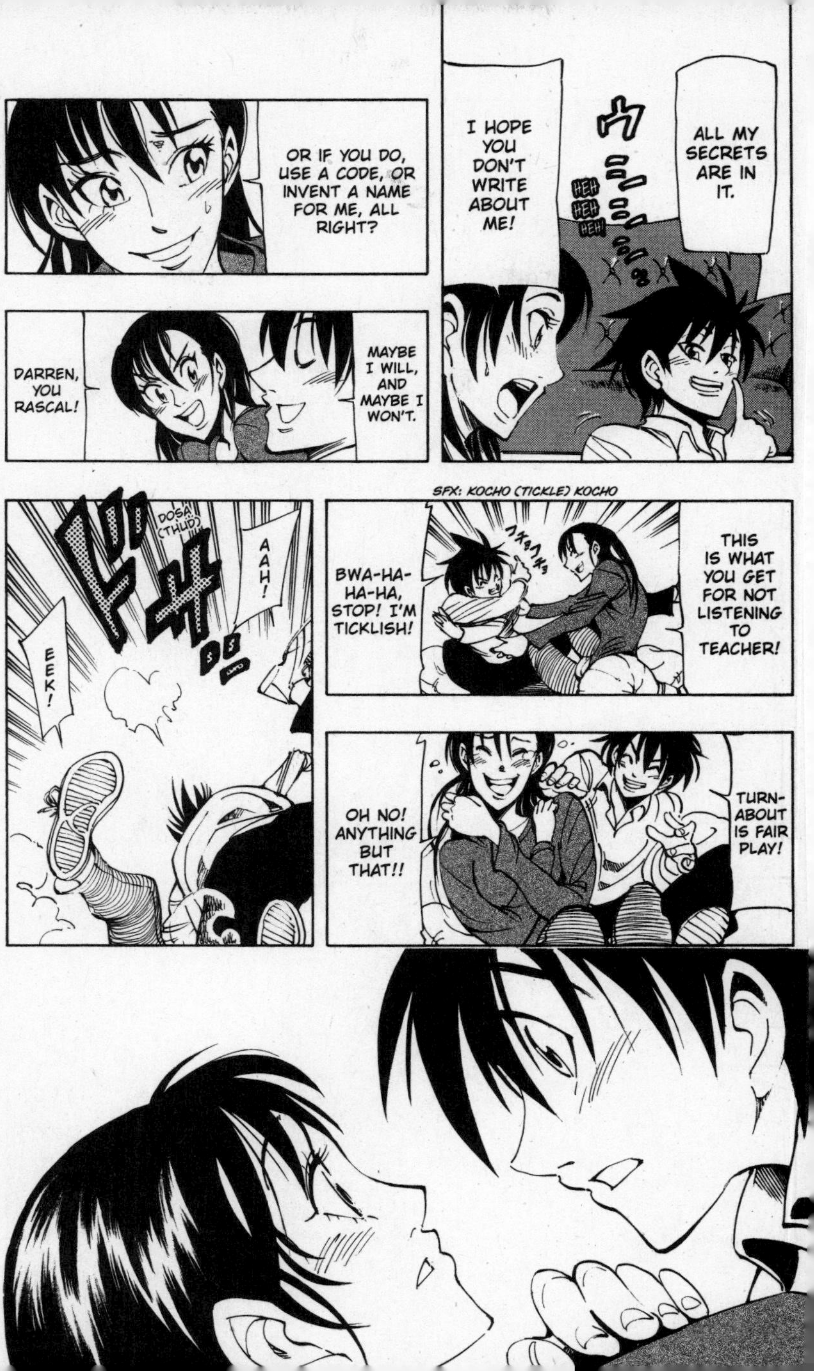
ALL MY SECRETS ARE IN IT.
HEH HEH HEH!
I HOPE YOU DON'T WRITE ABOUT ME!
OR IF YOU DO, USE A CODE, OR INVENT A NAME FOR ME, ALL RIGHT?
MAYBE I WILL, AND MAYBE I WON'T.
DARREN, YOU RASCAL!
SFX: KOCHO (TICKLE) KOCHO
THIS IS WHAT YOU GET FOR NOT LISTENING TO TEACHER!
BWA-HA-HA-HA, STOP! I'M TICKLISH!
TURN-ABOUT IS FAIR PLAY!
OH NO! ANYTHING BUT THAT!!
AAH!
DOSA (THUD)
EEK!

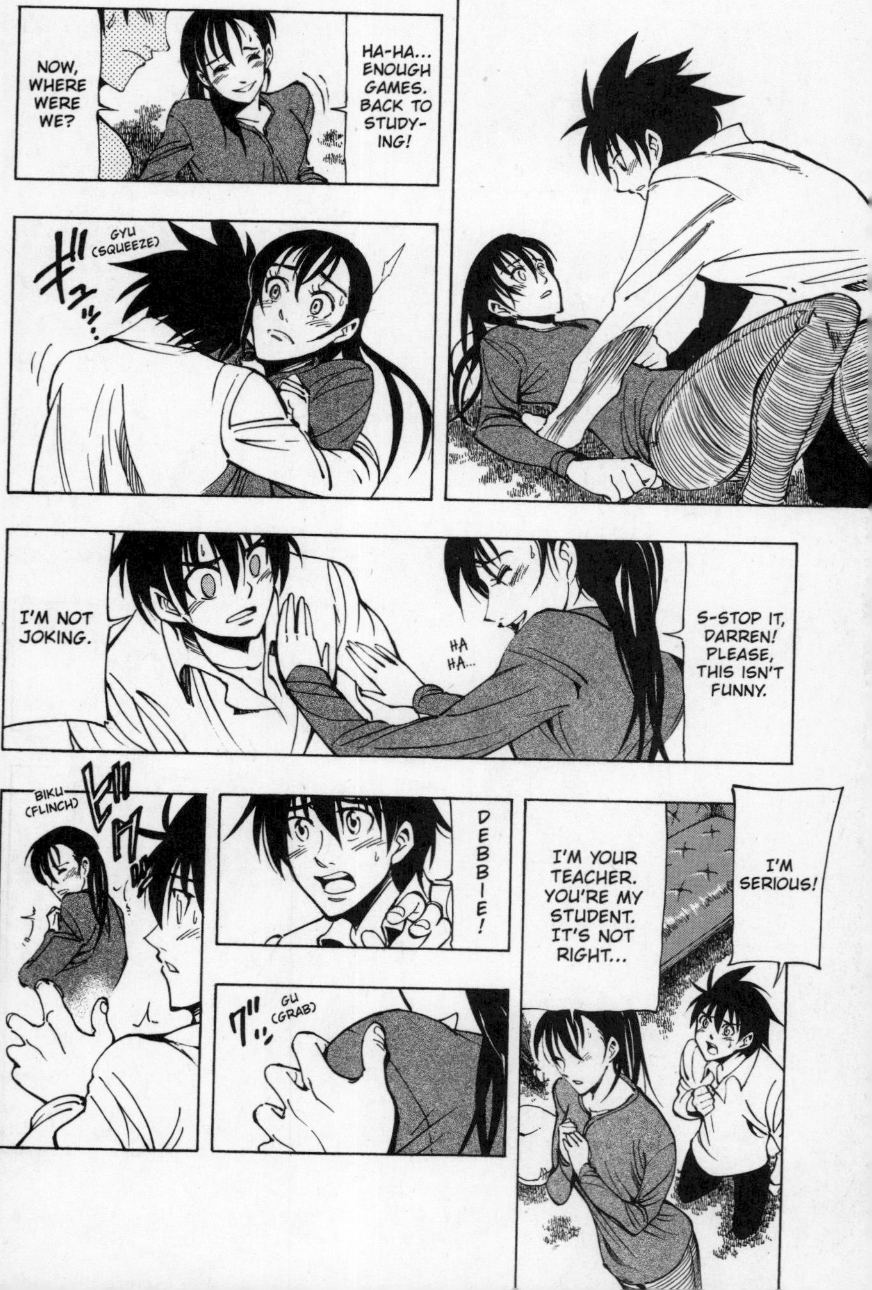
HA-HA... ENOUGH GAMES. BACK TO STUDY-ING!
NOW, WHERE WERE WE?
GYU (SQUEEZE)
S-STOP IT, DARREN! PLEASE, THIS ISN'T FUNNY.
HA HA...
I'M NOT JOKING.
I'M SERIOUS!
I'M YOUR TEACHER. YOU'RE MY STUDENT. IT'S NOT RIGHT...
DEBBIE!
GU (GRAB)
BIKU (FLINCH)

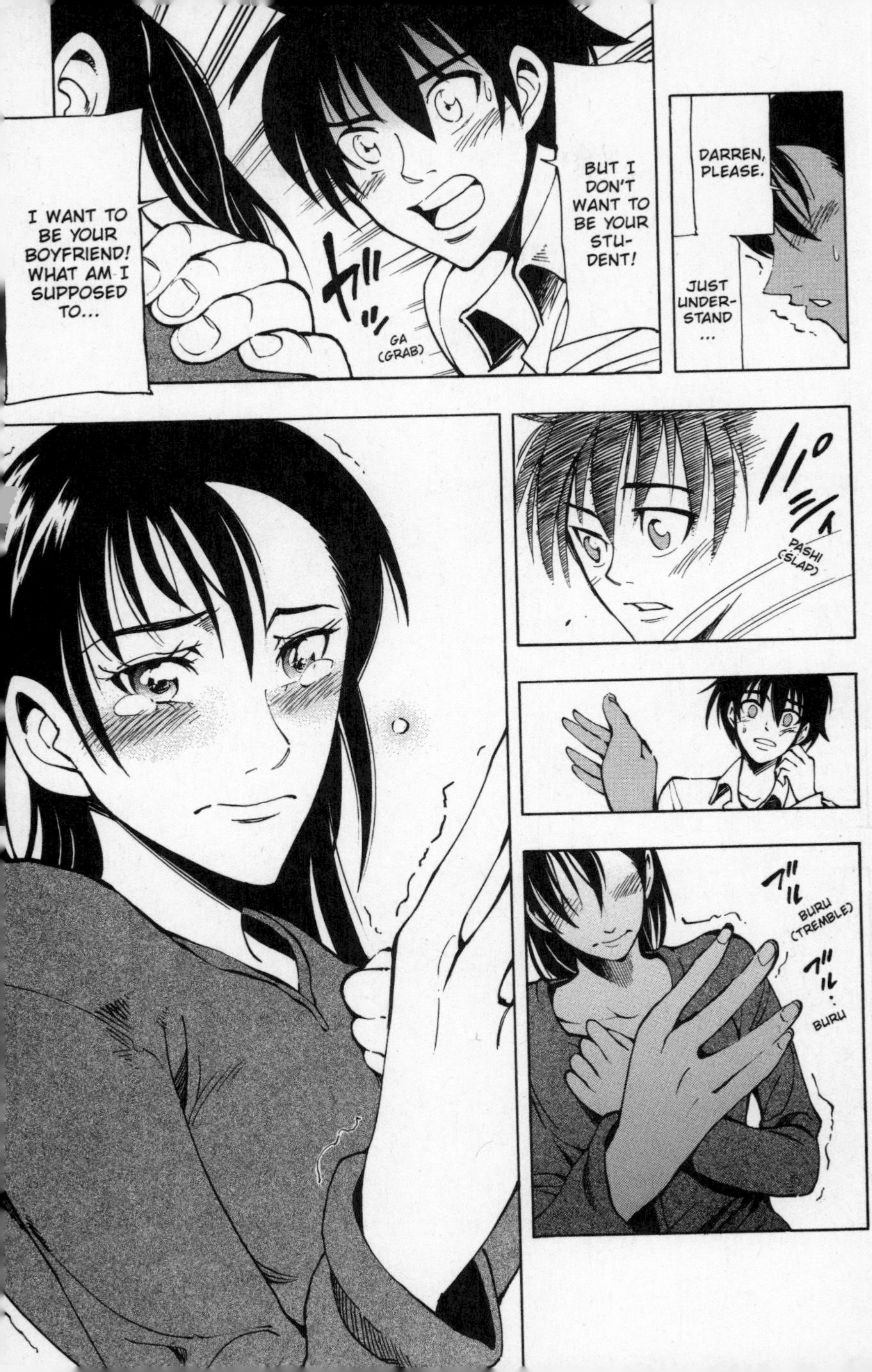
DARREN, PLEASE.
JUST UNDERSTAND...
BUT I DON'T WANT TO BE YOUR STU-DENT!
I WANT TO BE YOUR BOYFRIEND! WHAT AM I SUPPOSED TO...
GA (GRAB)
PASHI (SLAP)
BURU (TREMBLE)
BURU

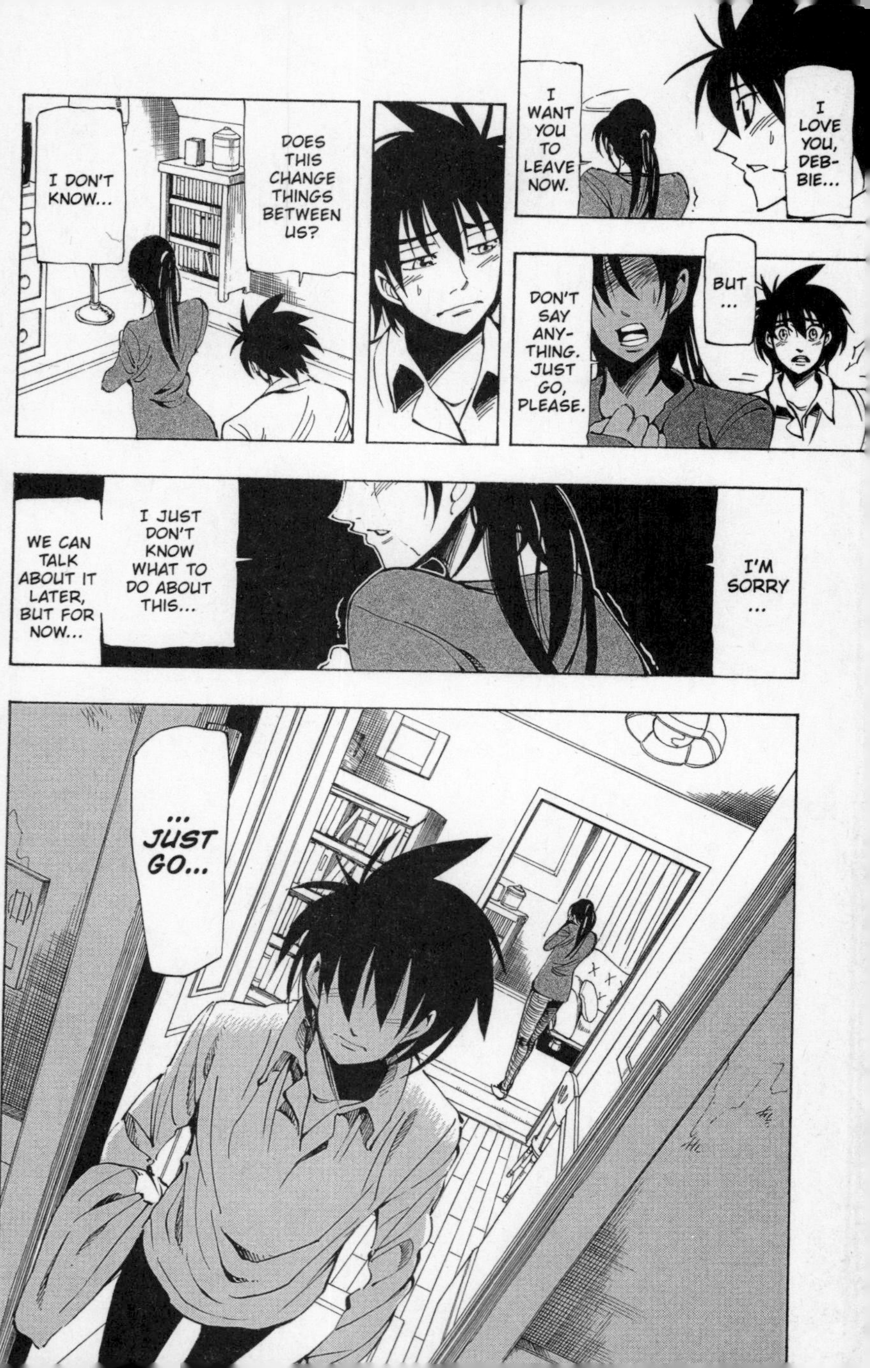

I LOVE YOU, DEBBIE...
I WANT YOU TO LEAVE NOW.
BUT ...
DON'T SAY ANYTHING. JUST GO, PLEASE.
DOES THIS CHANGE THINGS BETWEEN US?
I DON'T KNOW...
I'M SORRY ...
I JUST DON'T KNOW WHAT TO DO ABOUT THIS...
WE CAN TALK ABOUT IT LATER, BUT FOR NOW...
... JUST GO...

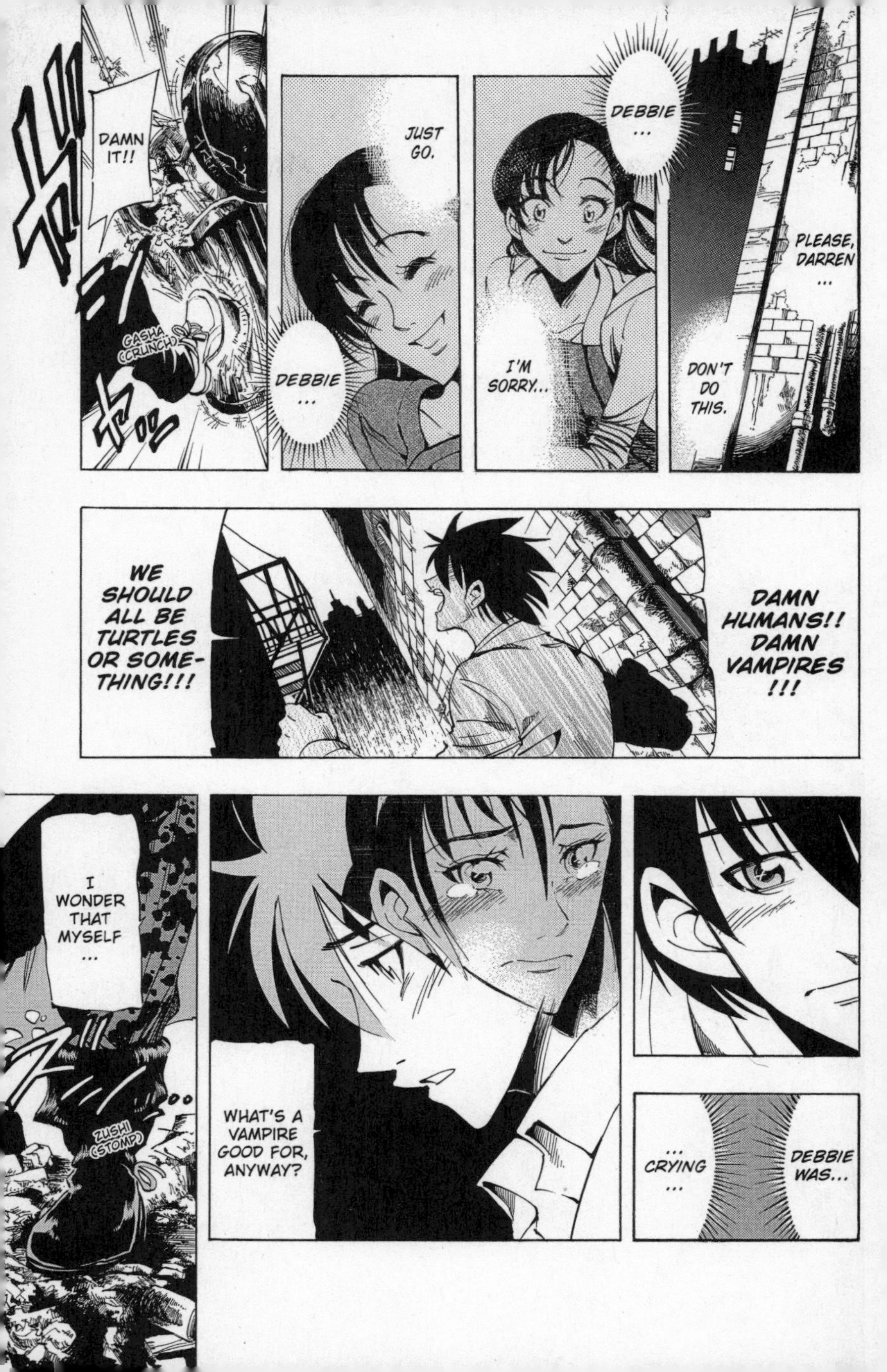
PLEASE, DARREN ...
DON'T DO THIS.
DEBBIE ...
I'M SORRY...
JUST GO.
DEBBIE ...
DAMN IT!!
GASHA (CRUNCH)
DAMN HUMANS!! DAMN VAMPIRES !!!
WE SHOULD ALL BE TURTLES OR SOMETHING!!!
DEBBIE WAS...
... CRYING ...
WHAT'S A VAMPIRE GOOD FOR, ANYWAY?
I WONDER THAT MYSELF ...
ZUSHI (STOMP)

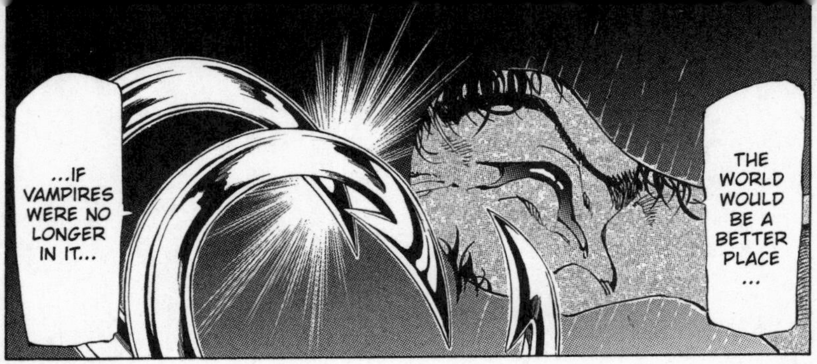
THE WORLD WOULD BE A BETTER PLACE ...
...IF VAMPIRES WERE NO LONGER IN IT...
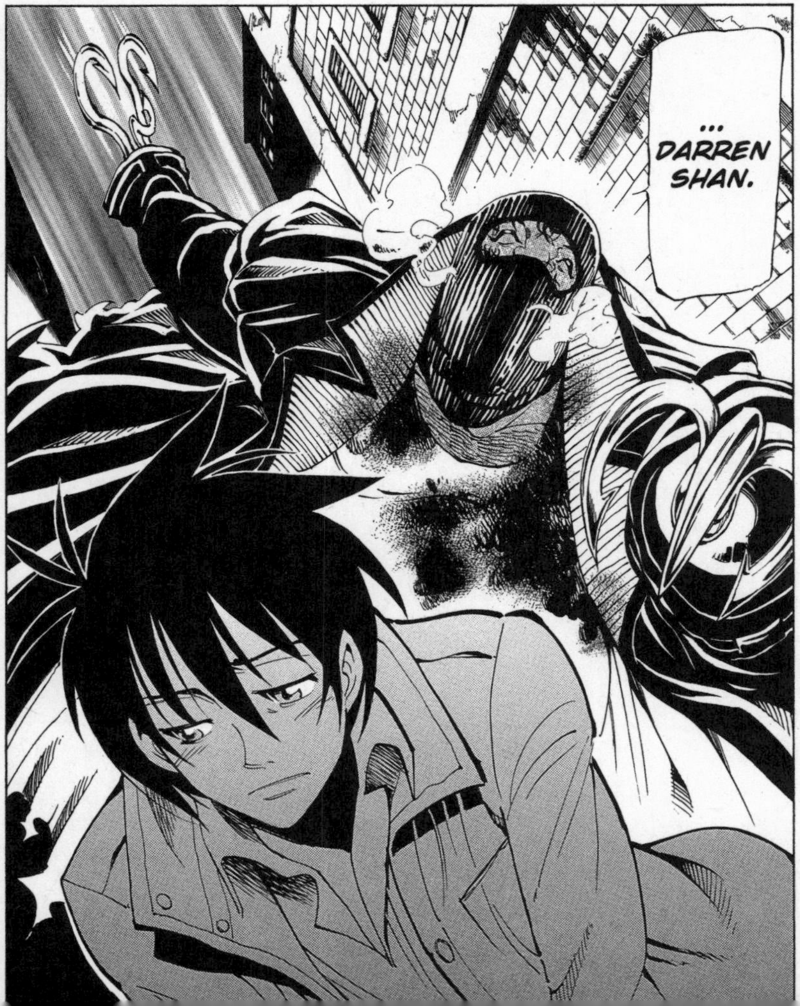
... DARREN SHAN.

CHAPTER 69: IN A DARK ALLEY

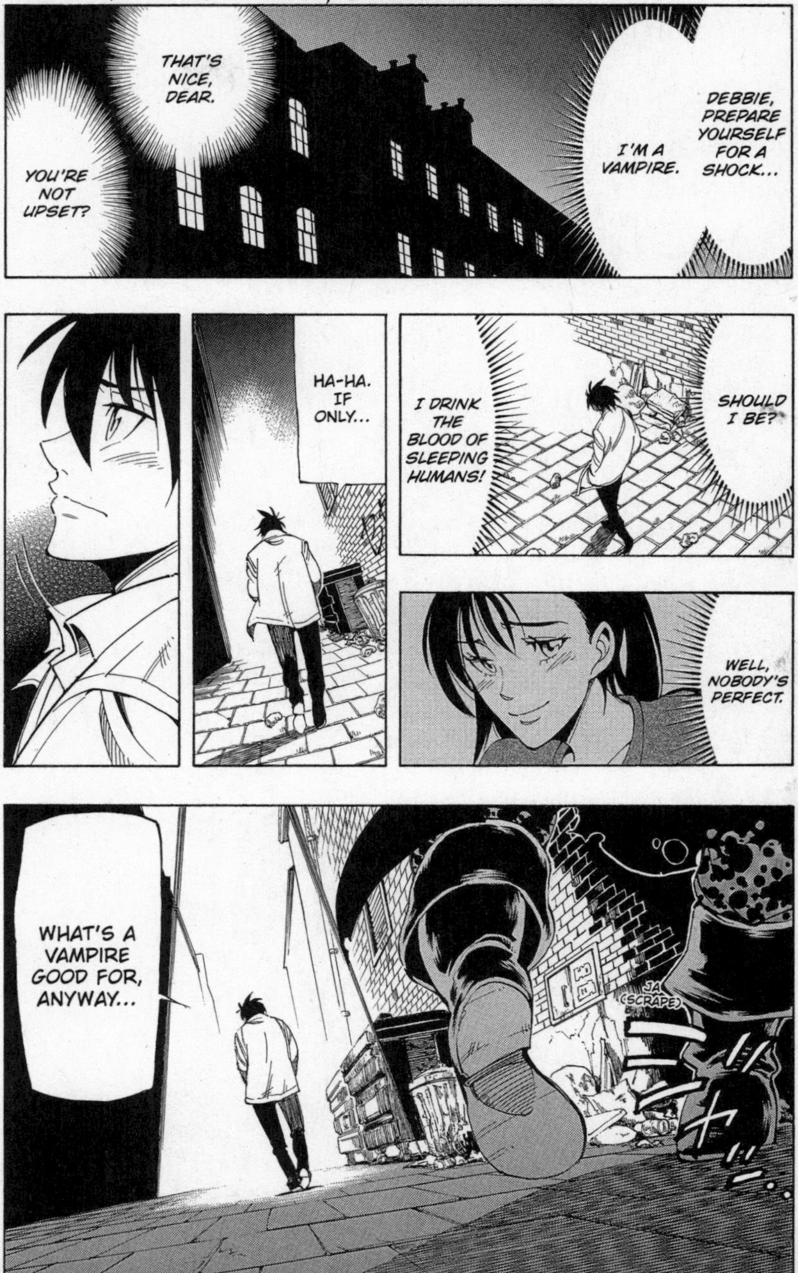
DEBBIE, PREPARE YOURSELF FOR A SHOCK...
I'M A VAMPIRE.
THAT'S NICE, DEAR.
YOU'RE NOT UPSET?
SHOULD I BE?
I DRINK THE BLOOD OF SLEEPING HUMANS!
WELL, NOBODY'S PERFECT.
HA-HA. IF ONLY...
WHAT'S A VAMPIRE GOOD FOR, ANYWAY...
JA (SCRAPE)

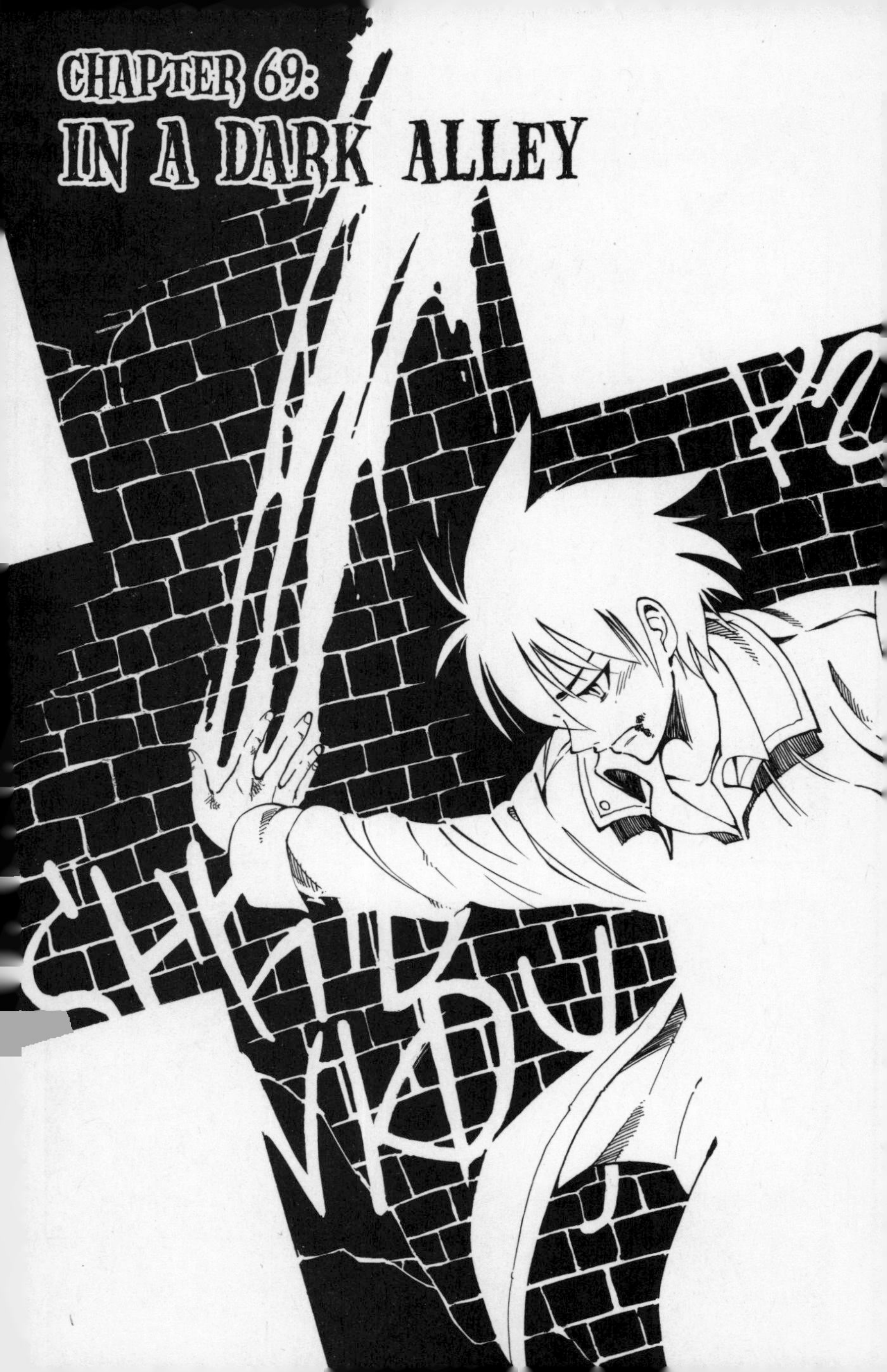
CHAPTER 69:
IN A DARK ALLEY

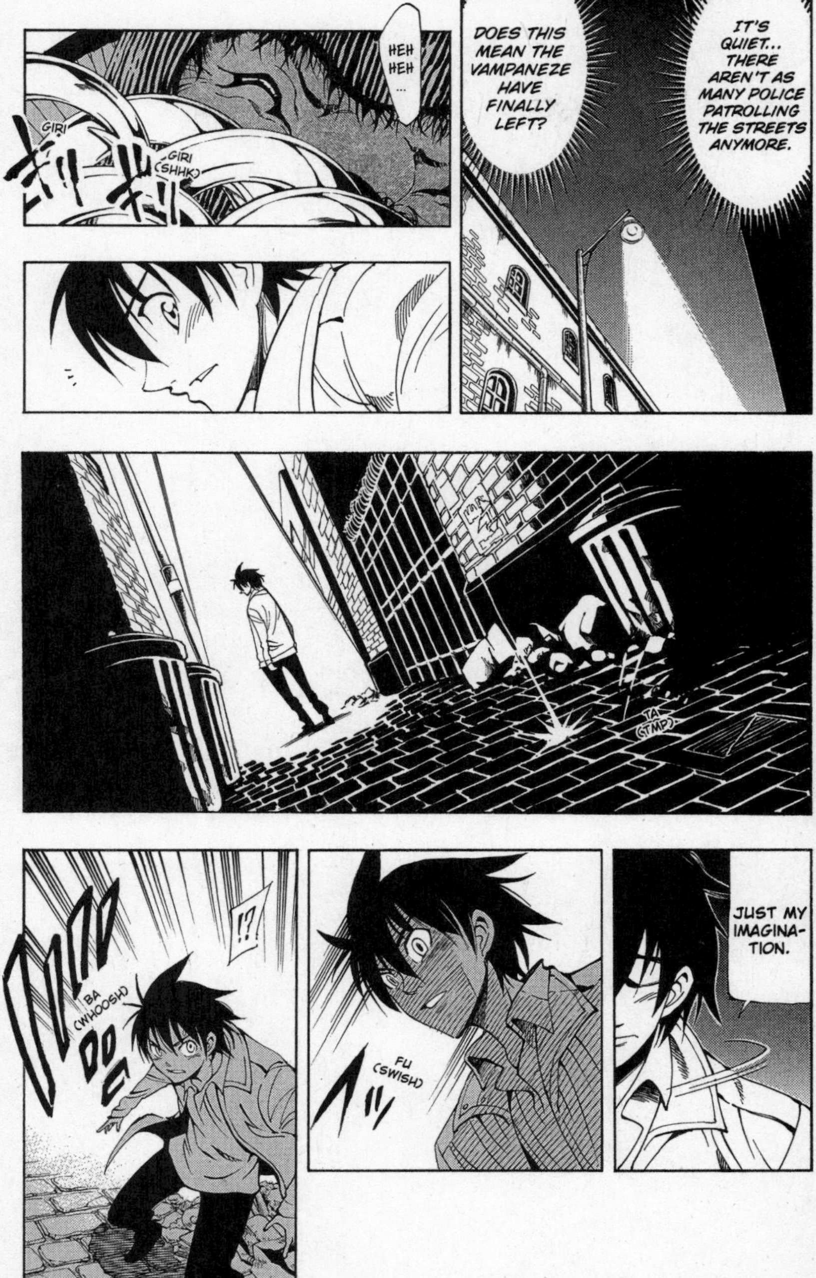
IT'S QUIET... THERE AREN'T AS MANY POLICE PATROLLING THE STREETS ANYMORE.
DOES THIS MEAN THE VAMPANEZE HAVE FINALLY LEFT?
HEH HEH ...
GIRI
GIRI (SHHK)
TA (TMP)
JUST MY IMAGINA-TION.
FU (SWISH)
!?
BA (WHOOSH)

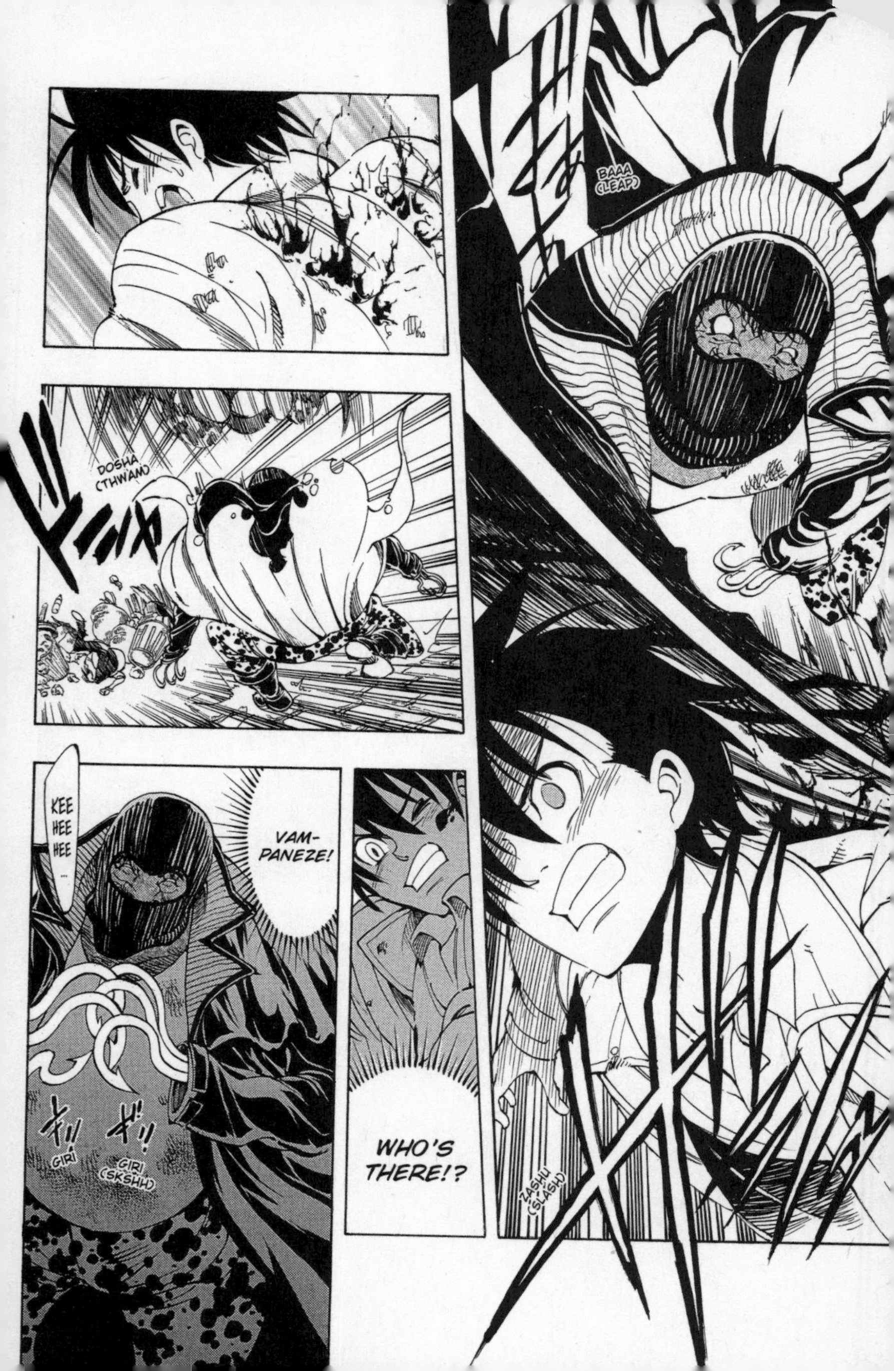
BAAA (LEAP)
ZASHU (SLASH)
DOSHA (THWAM)
VAM-PANEZE!
WHO'S THERE!?
KEE HEE HEE ...
GIRI
GIRI (SKSHH)

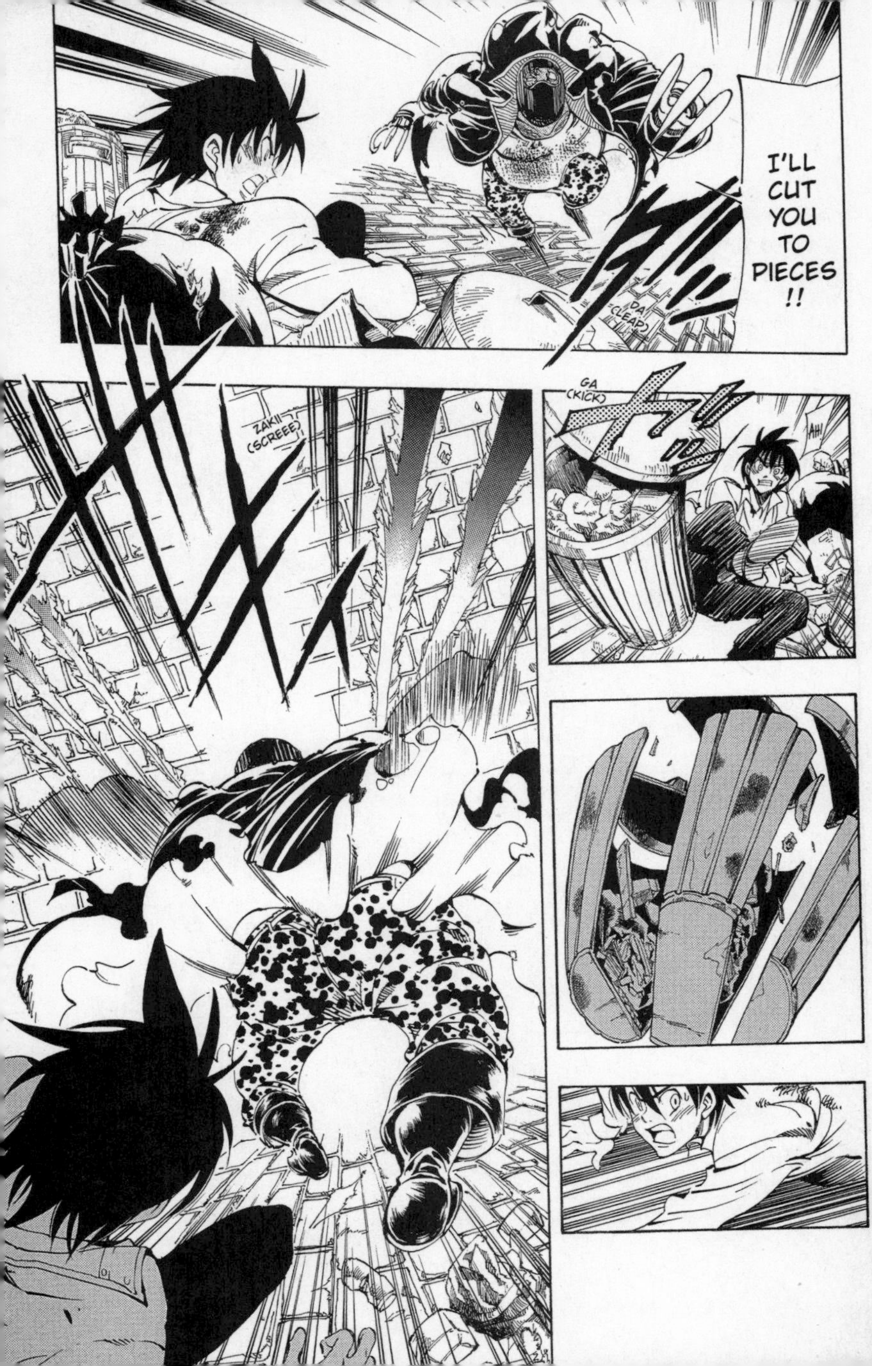
I'LL CUT YOU TO PIECES !!
DA (LEAP)
GA (KICK)
AH!
ZAKII (SCREEE)

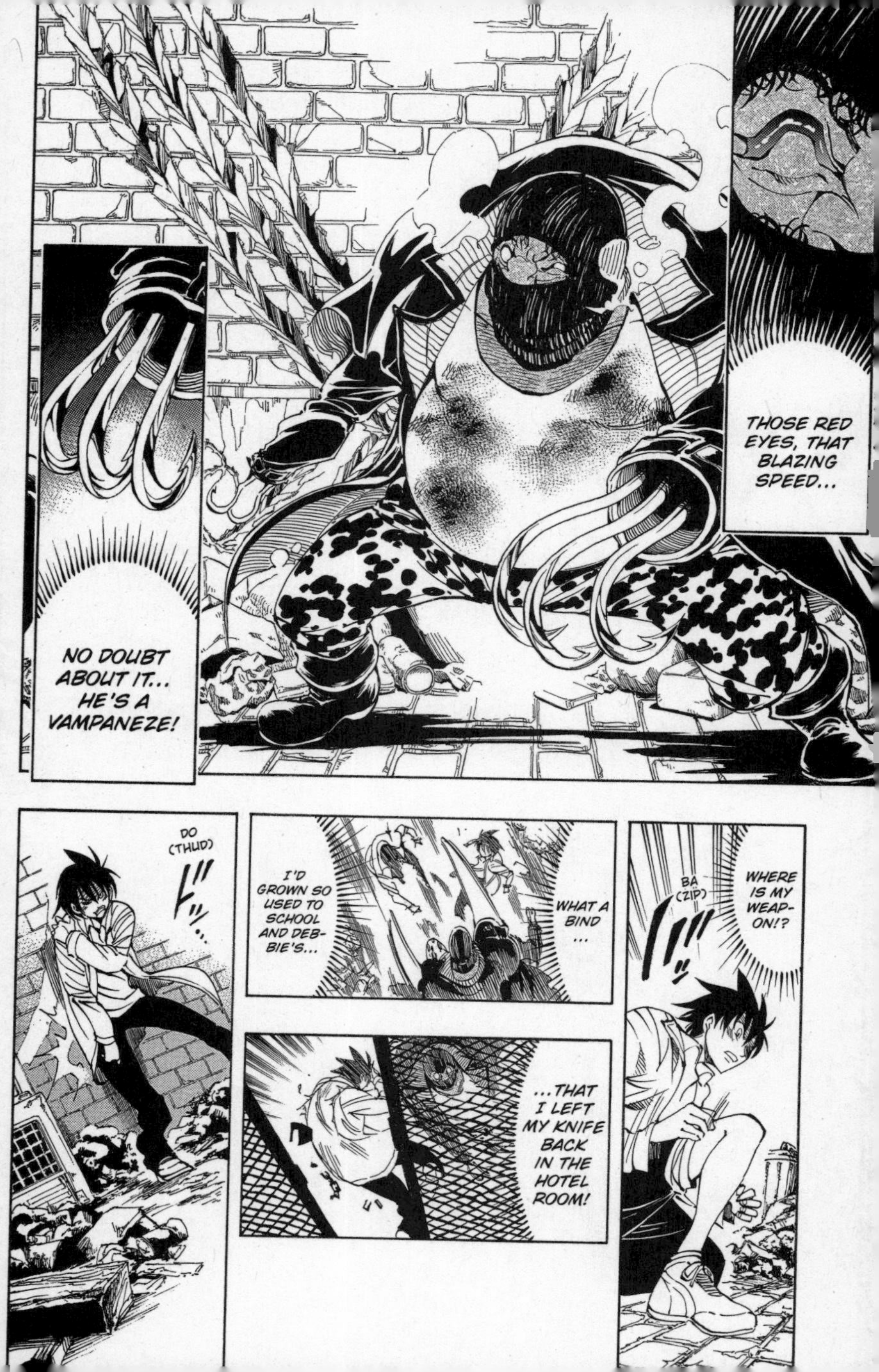
THOSE RED EYES, THAT BLAZING SPEED...
NO DOUBT ABOUT IT... HE'S A VAMPANEZE!
WHERE IS MY WEAP-ON!?
BA (ZIP)
WHAT A BIND ...
I'D GROWN SO USED TO SCHOOL AND DEB-BIE'S...
...THAT I LEFT MY KNIFE BACK IN THE HOTEL ROOM!
DO (THUD)

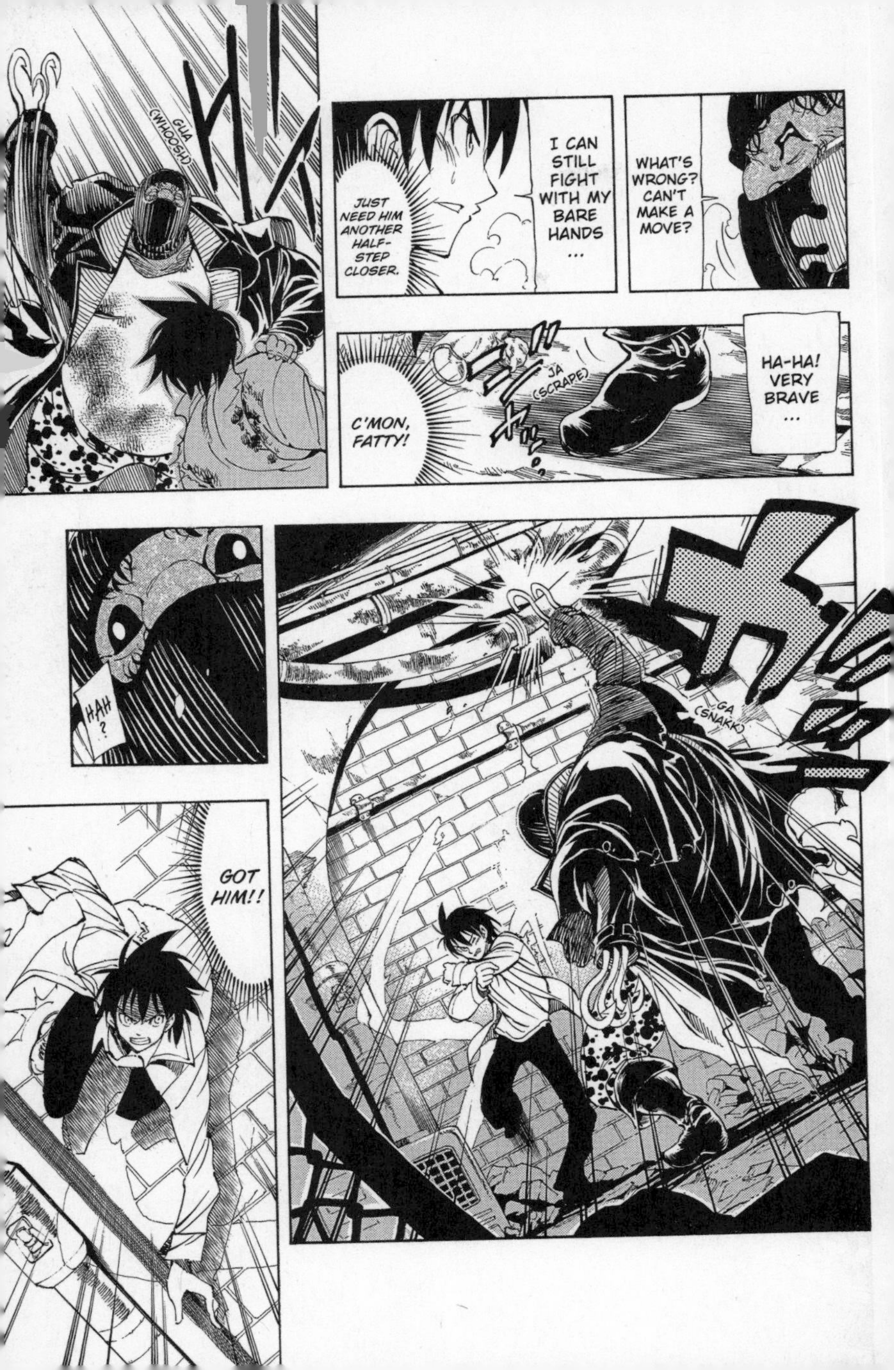
WHAT'S WRONG? CAN'T MAKE A MOVE?
I CAN STILL FIGHT WITH MY BARE HANDS ...
JUST NEED HIM ANOTHER HALF-STEP CLOSER.
HA-HA! VERY BRAVE ...
JA (SCRAPE)
C'MON, FATTY!
GUA (WHOOSH)
GA (SNAKK)
HAH ?
GOT HIM!!

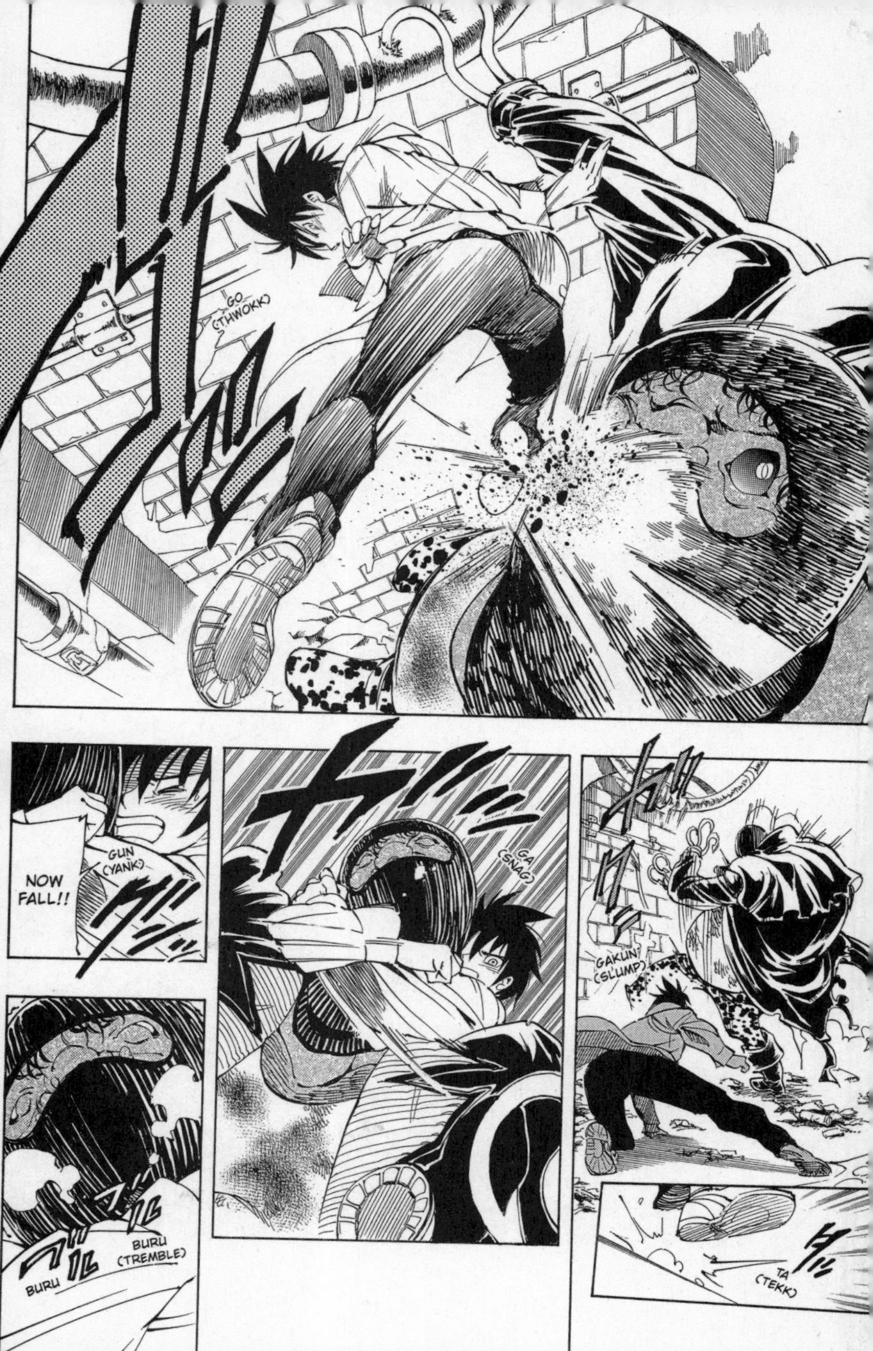
GO
(THWOKK)
GAKUN
(SLUMP)
TA
(TEKK)
GA
(SNAG)
GUN
(YANK)
NOW FALL!!
BURU
(TREMBLE)
BURU

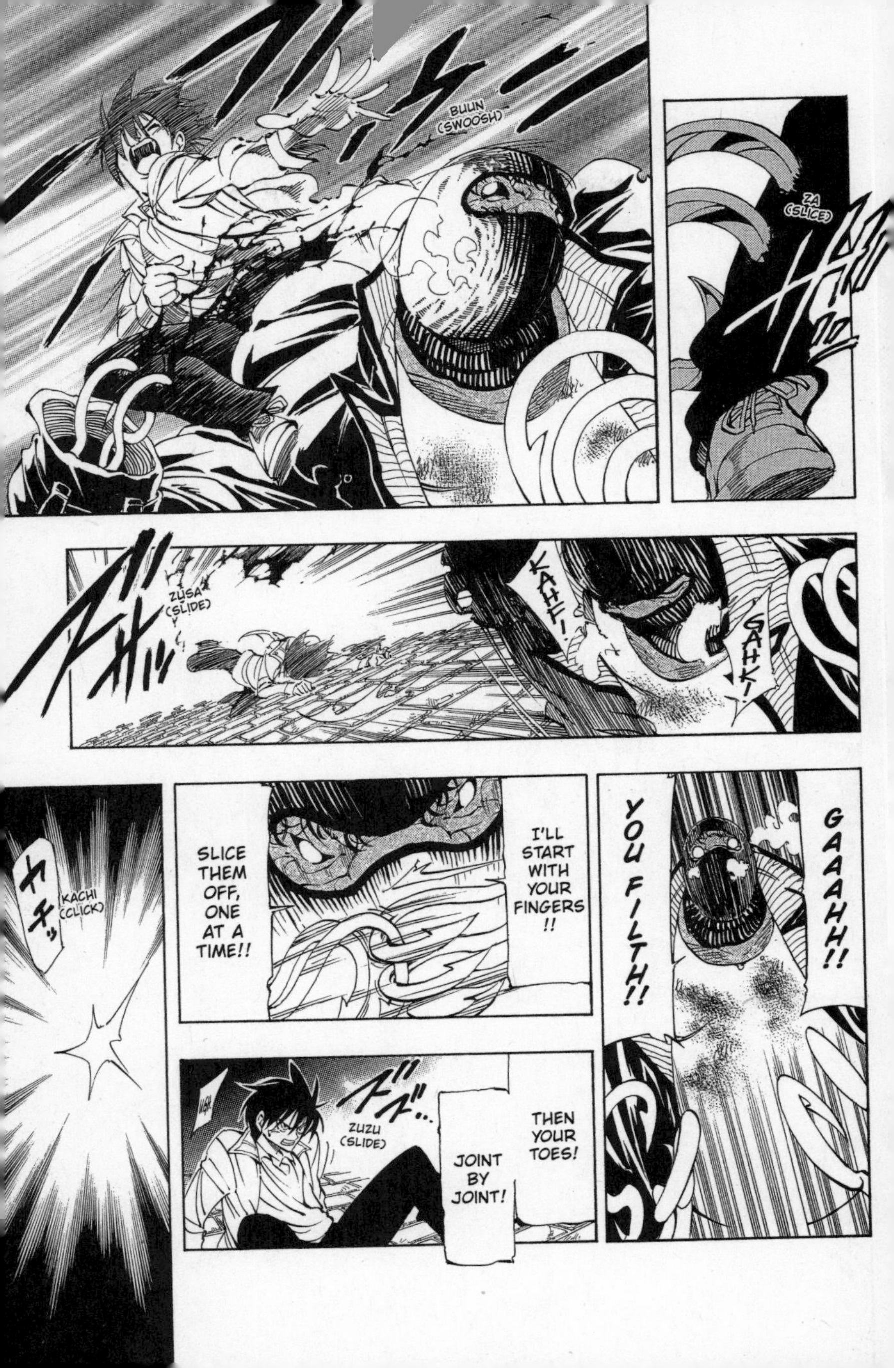
ZA
(SLICE)
BUUN
(SWOOSH)
GAHK!
KAHF!
ZUSA
(SLIDE)
GAAAAHH!!
YOU FILTH!!
I'LL START WITH YOUR FINGERS!!
SLICE THEM OFF, ONE AT A TIME!!
THEN YOUR TOES!
JOINT BY JOINT!
ZUZU
(SLIDE)
UGH.
カチッ
KACHI
(CLICK)

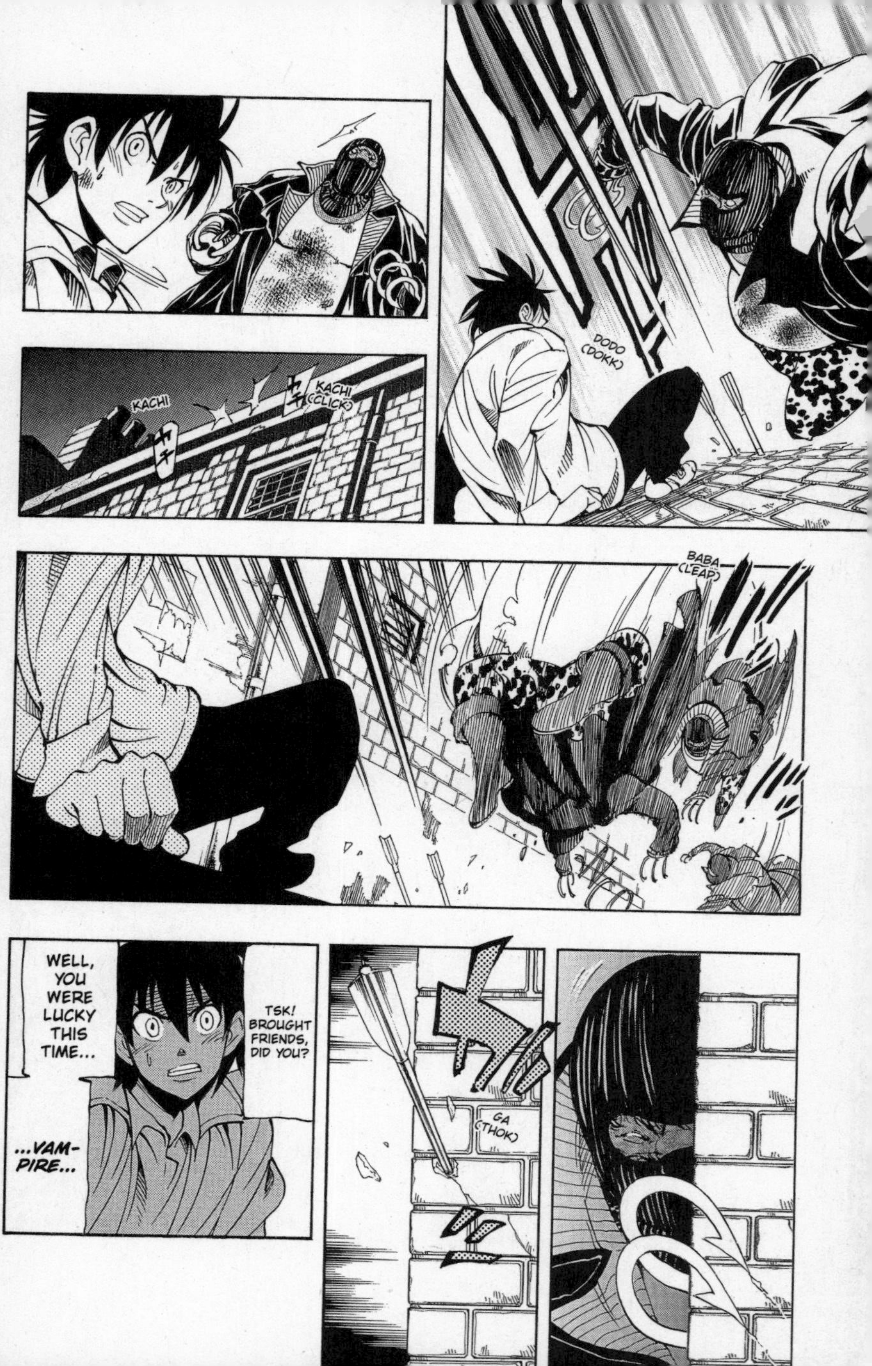
DODO (DOKK)
KACHI (CLICK)
KACHI
BABA (LEAP)
GA (THOK)
TSK! BROUGHT FRIENDS, DID YOU?
WELL, YOU WERE LUCKY THIS TIME...
...VAMPIRE...

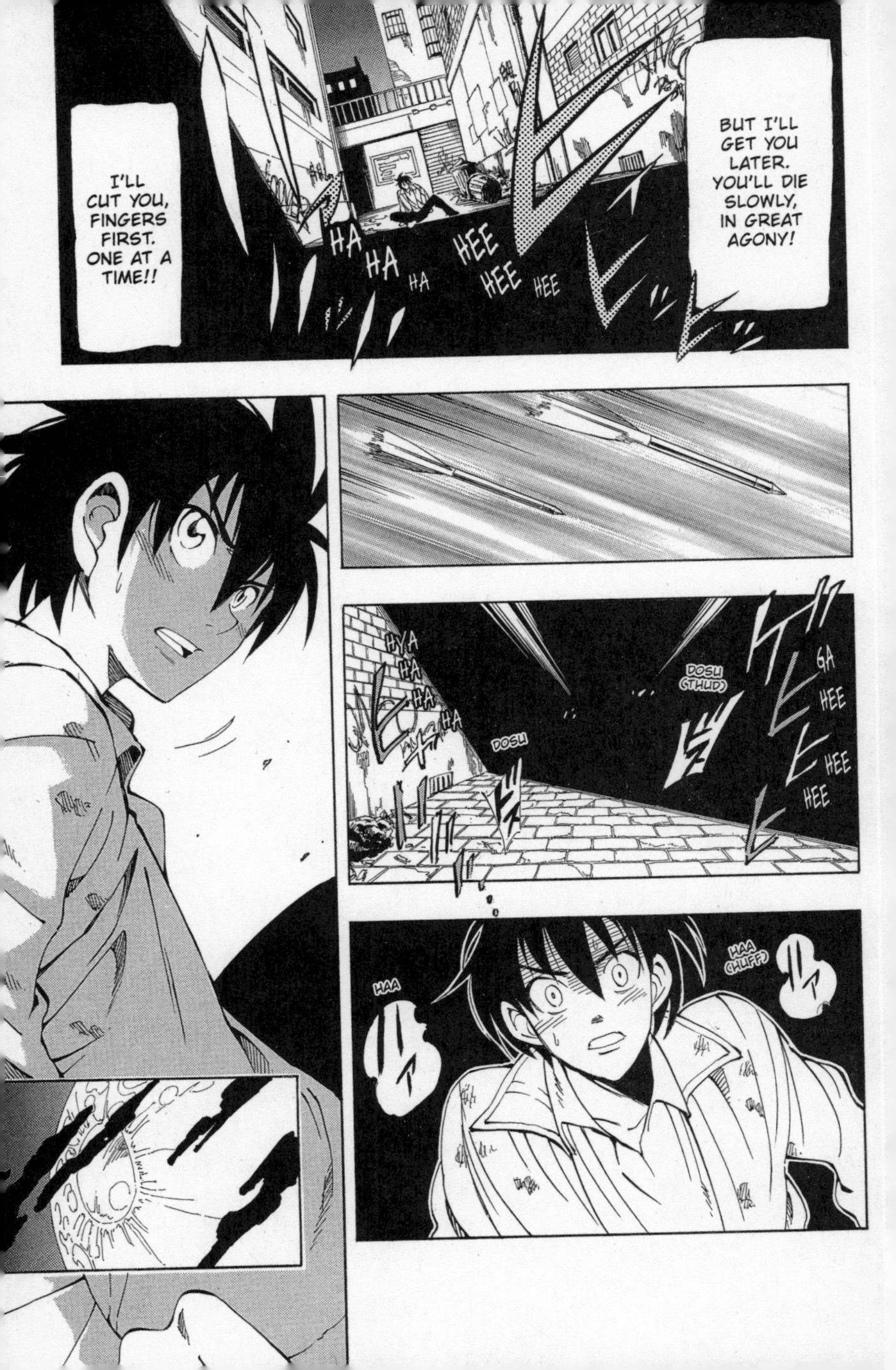
BUT I'LL GET YOU LATER. YOU'LL DIE SLOWLY, IN GREAT AGONY!
HEE HEE HEE
HA HA HA
I'LL CUT YOU, FINGERS FIRST. ONE AT A TIME!!
GA HEE HEE HEE
DOSU (THUD)
DOSU
HYA HA HA HA
HAA (HUFF)
HAA

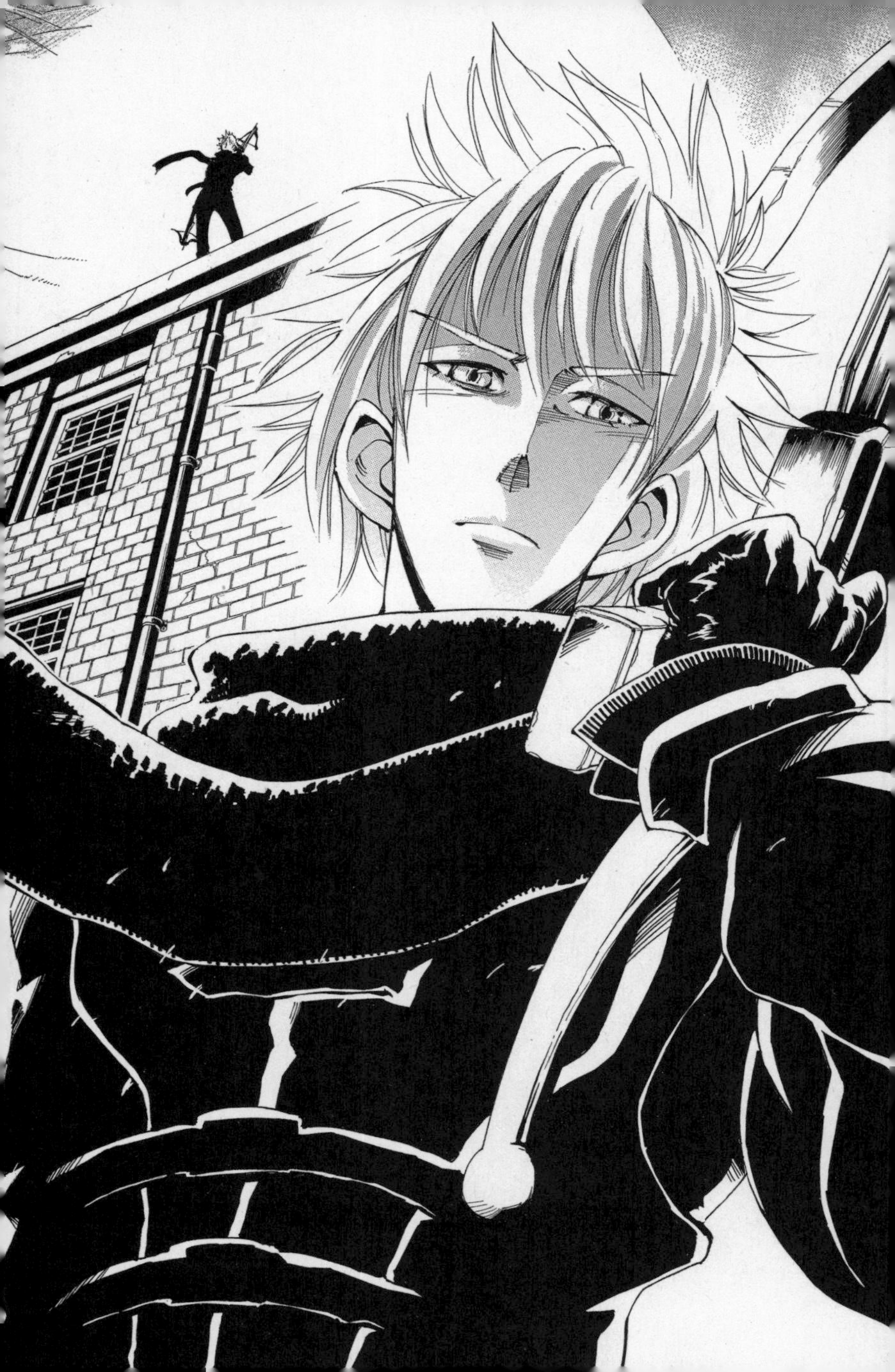

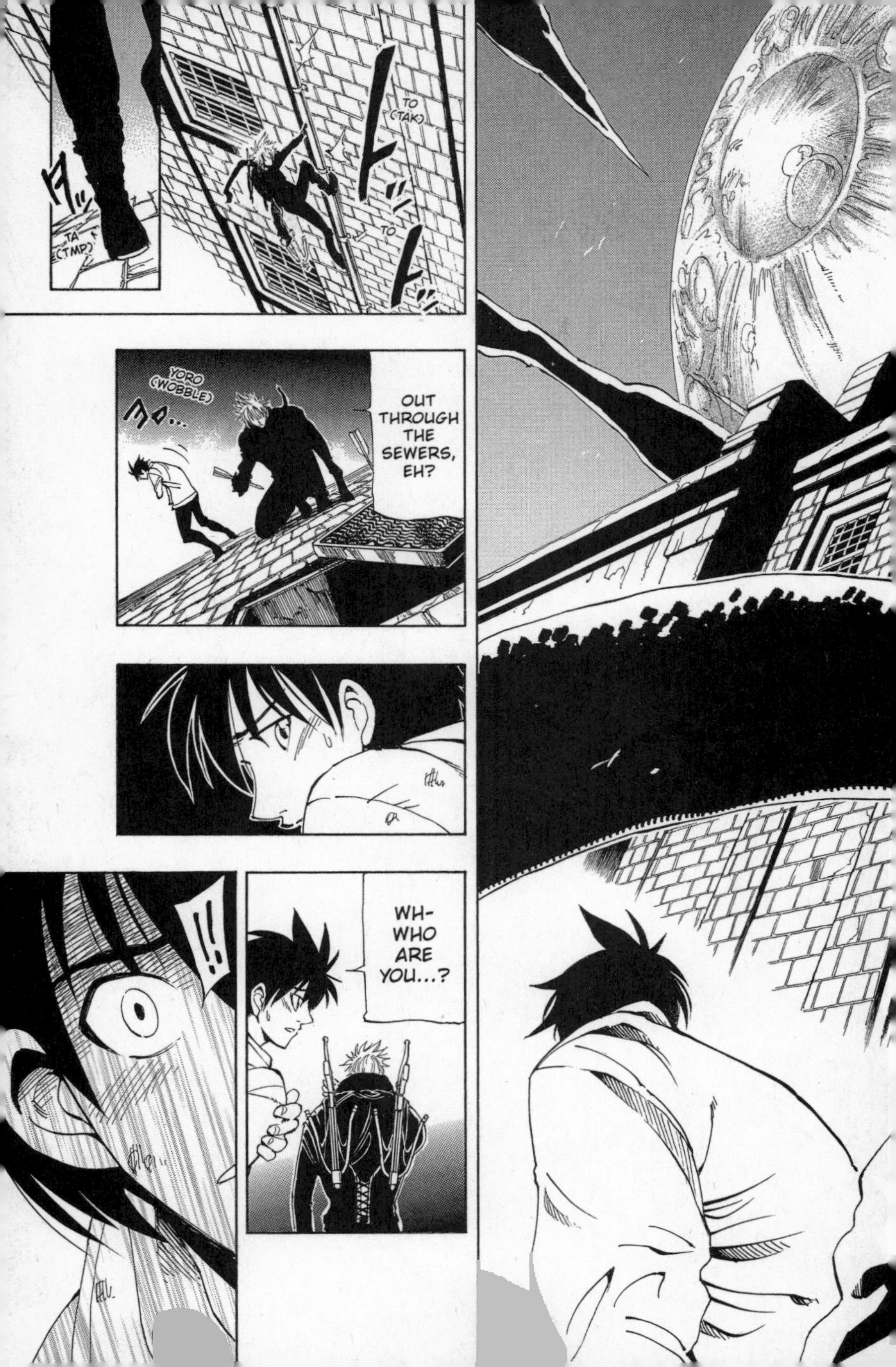
TO (TAK)
TO
TA (TMP)
YORO (WOBBLE)
OUT THROUGH THE SEWERS, EH?
WH-WHO ARE YOU...?

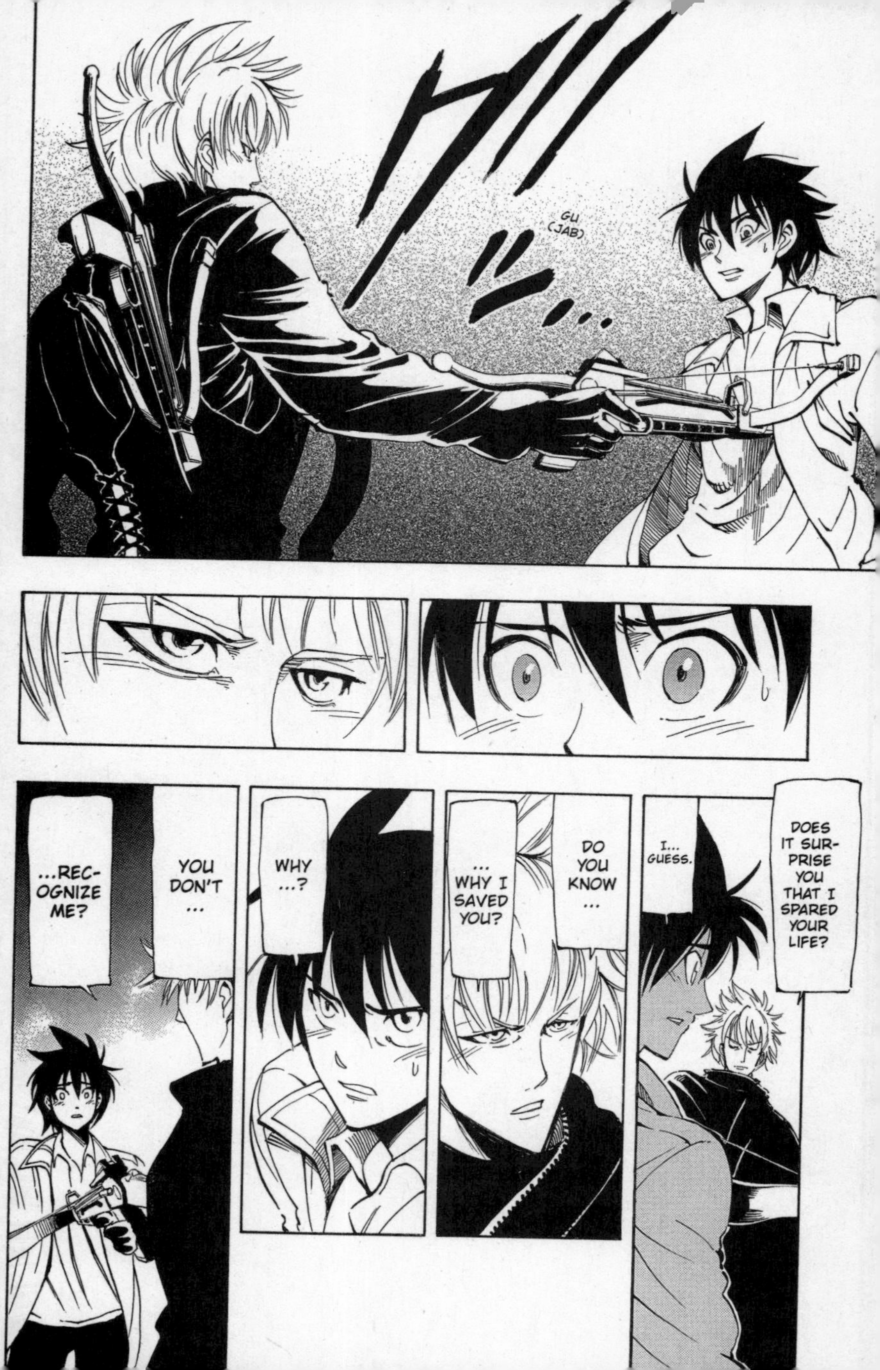
GU (JAB)
DOES IT SURPRISE YOU THAT I SPARED YOUR LIFE?
I... GUESS.
DO YOU KNOW ...
... WHY I SAVED YOU?
WHY ...?
YOU DON'T ...
...RECOGNIZE ME?

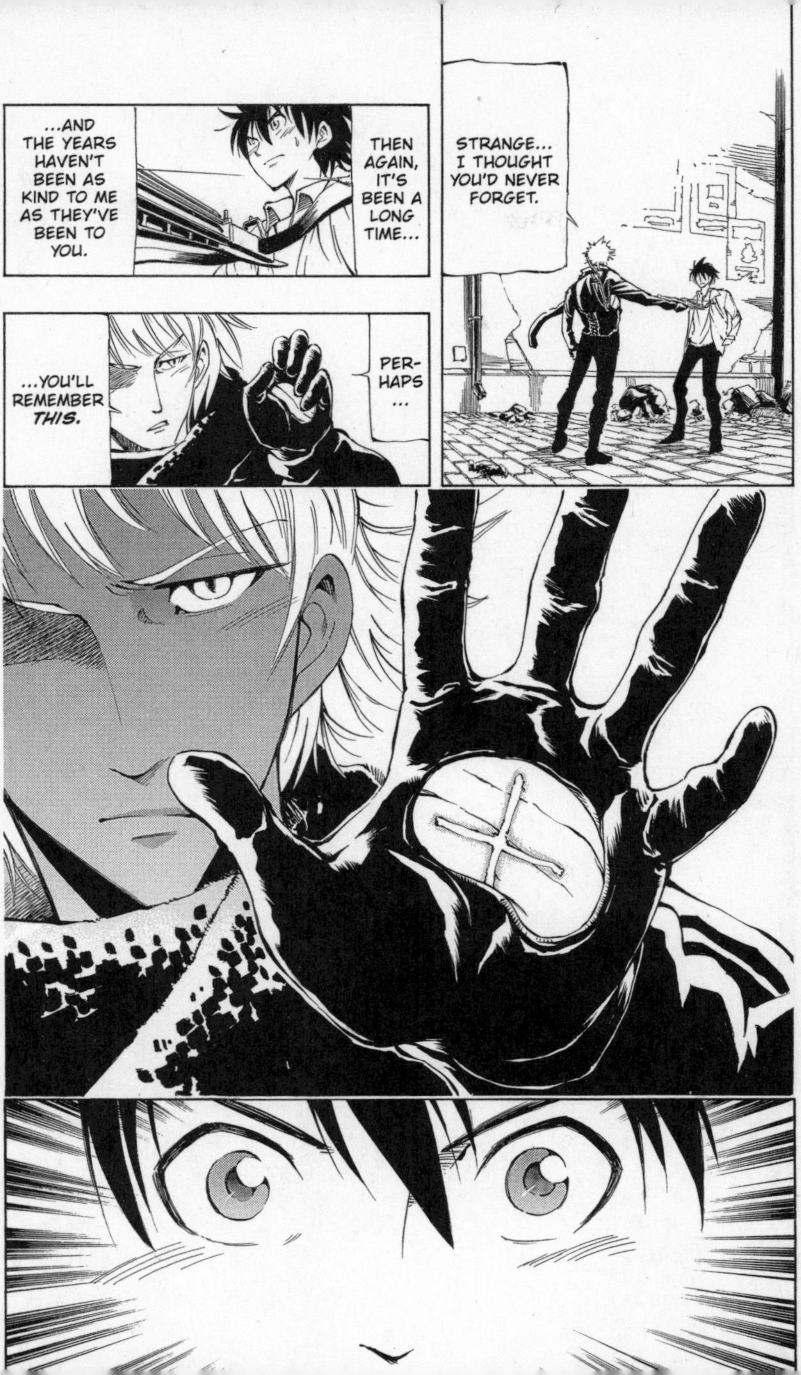
STRANGE... I THOUGHT YOU'D NEVER FORGET.
THEN AGAIN, IT'S BEEN A LONG TIME...
...AND THE YEARS HAVEN'T BEEN AS KIND TO ME AS THEY'VE BEEN TO YOU.
PER-HAPS...
...YOU'LL REMEMBER *THIS.*

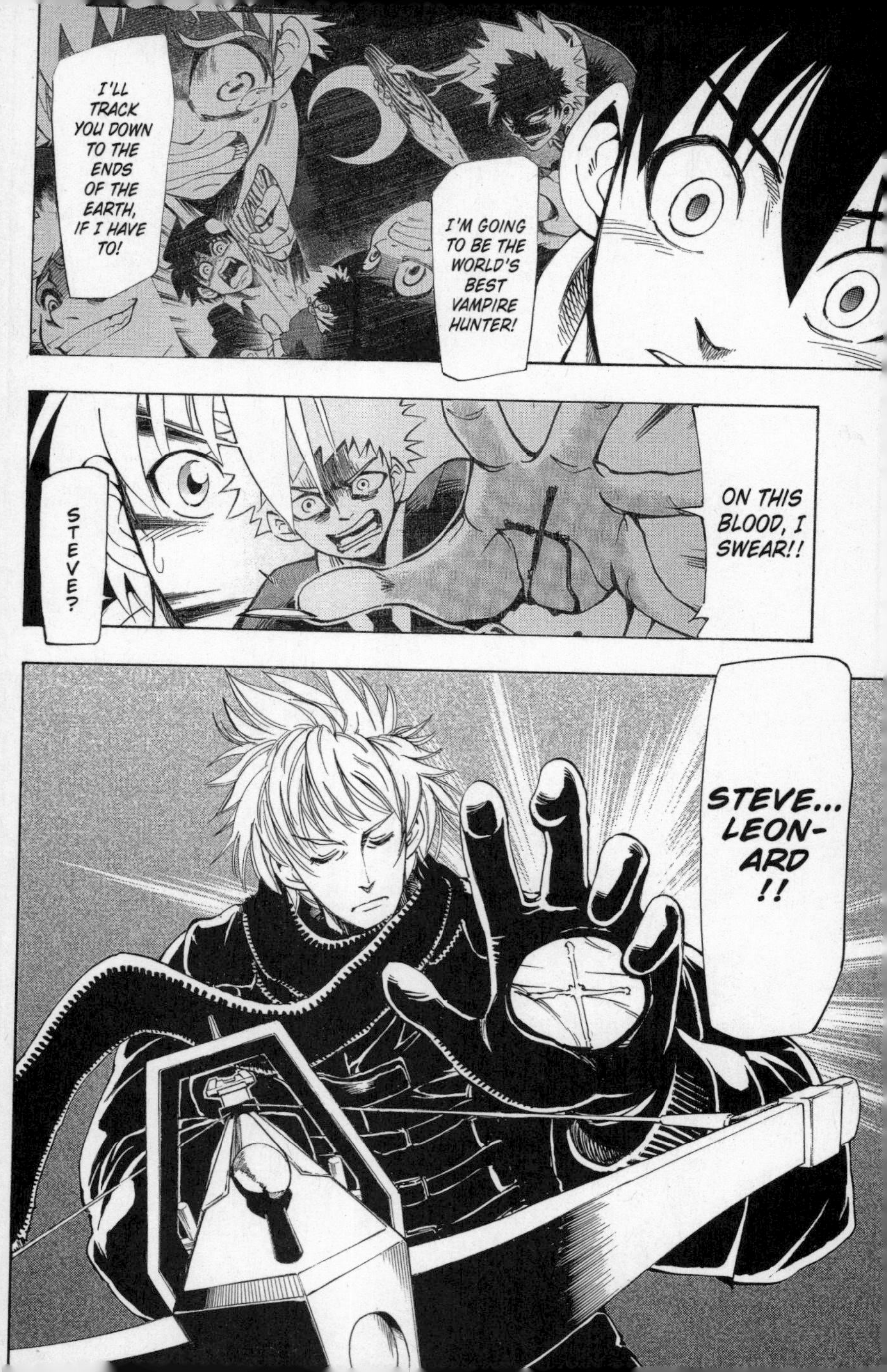
I'M GOING TO BE THE WORLD'S BEST VAMPIRE HUNTER!
I'LL TRACK YOU DOWN TO THE ENDS OF THE EARTH, IF I HAVE TO!
ON THIS BLOOD, I SWEAR!!
STEVE?
STEVE... LEON-ARD!!

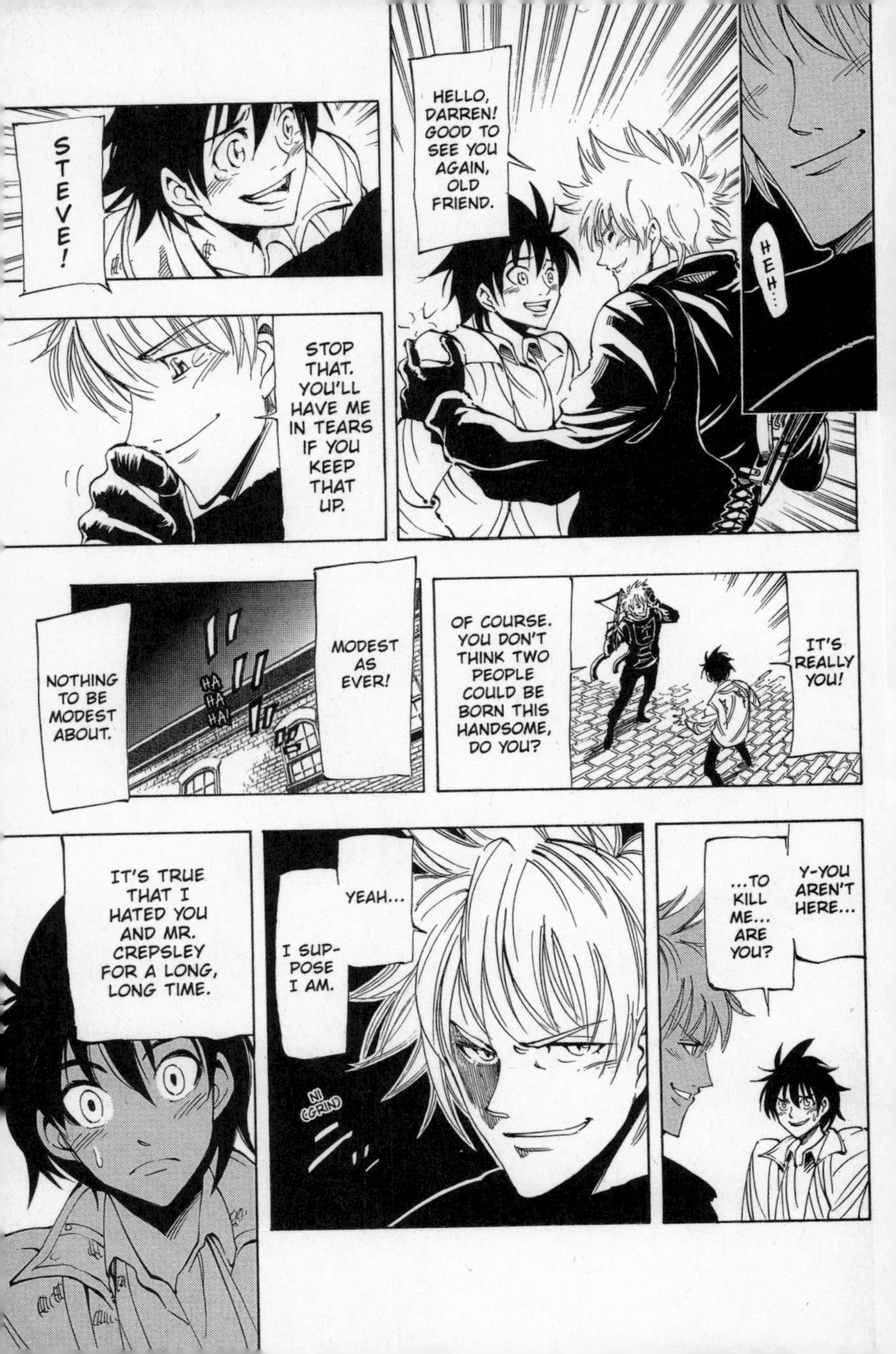
HEH...
HELLO, DARREN! GOOD TO SEE YOU AGAIN, OLD FRIEND.
STEVE!
STOP THAT. YOU'LL HAVE ME IN TEARS IF YOU KEEP THAT UP.
IT'S REALLY YOU!
OF COURSE. YOU DON'T THINK TWO PEOPLE COULD BE BORN THIS HANDSOME, DO YOU?
MODEST AS EVER!
HA HA HA!
NOTHING TO BE MODEST ABOUT.
Y-YOU AREN'T HERE...
...TO KILL ME... ARE YOU?
YEAH...
I SUP-POSE I AM.
NI (GRIN)
IT'S TRUE THAT I HATED YOU AND MR. CREPSLEY FOR A LONG, LONG TIME.

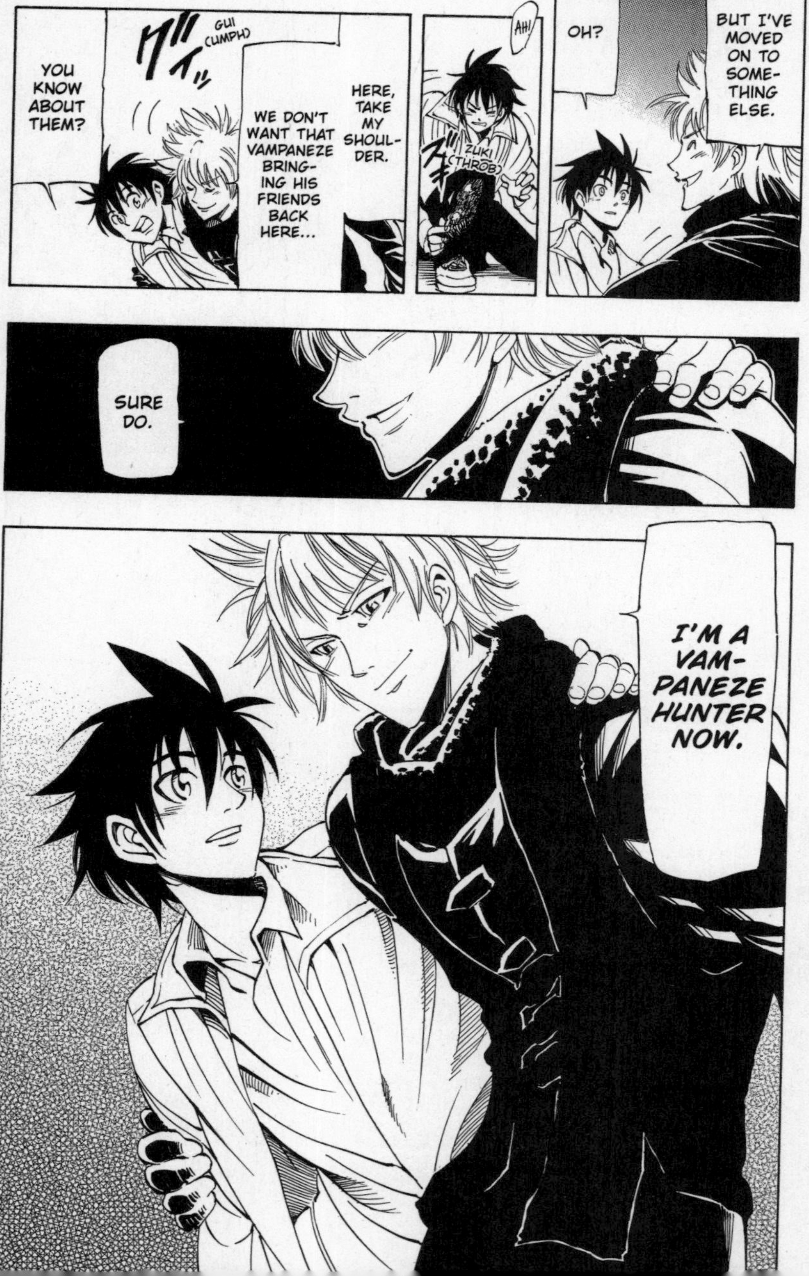
BUT I'VE MOVED ON TO SOMETHING ELSE.
OH?
AH!
ZUKI (THROB)
HERE, TAKE MY SHOULDER.
WE DON'T WANT THAT VAMPANEZE BRINGING HIS FRIENDS BACK HERE...
GUI (UMPH)
YOU KNOW ABOUT THEM?
SURE DO.
I'M A VAMPANEZE HUNTER NOW.

CHAPTER 70: KINDRED SPIRIT

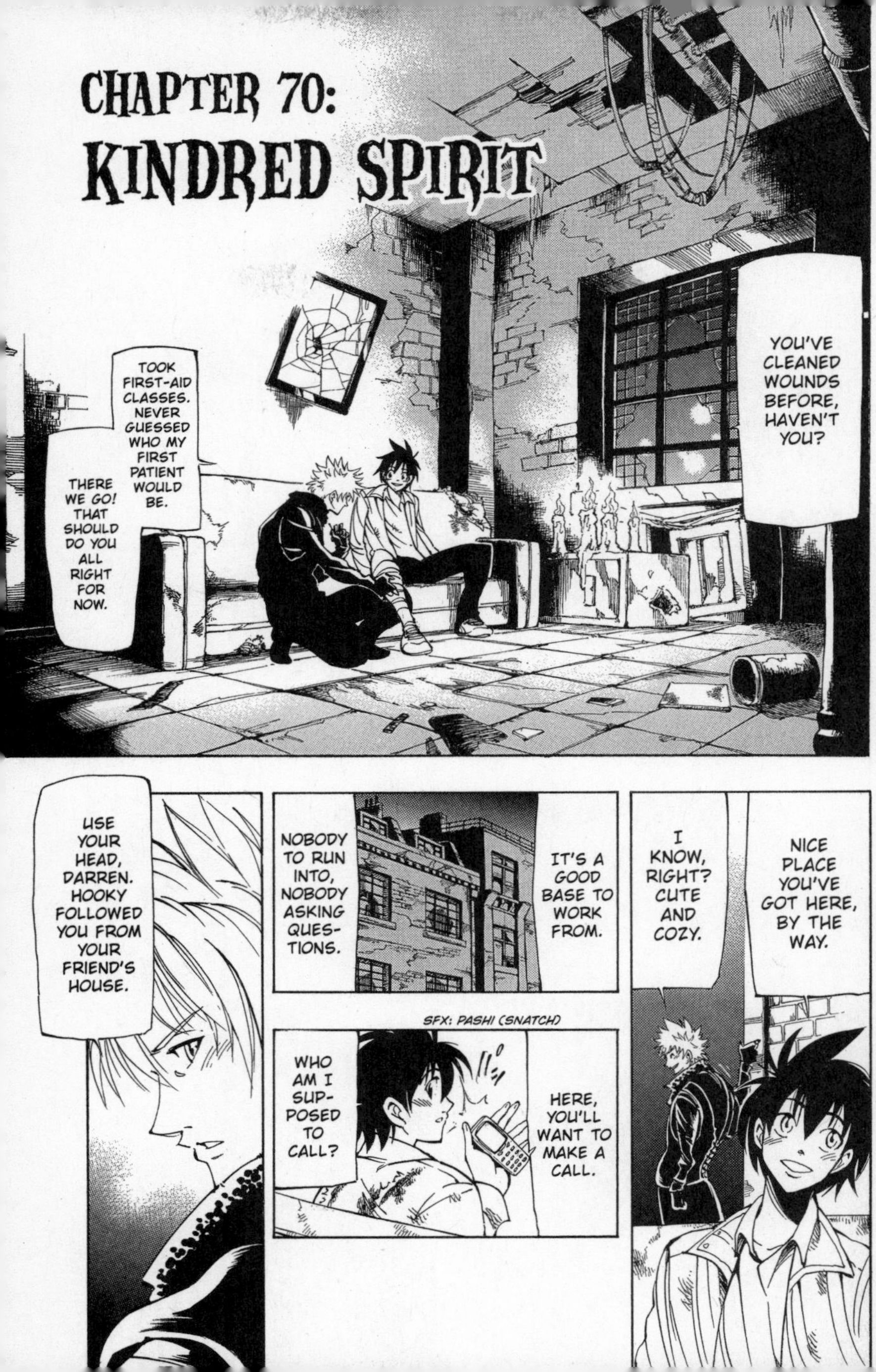
YOU'VE CLEANED WOUNDS BEFORE, HAVEN'T YOU?
TOOK FIRST-AID CLASSES. NEVER GUESSED WHO MY FIRST PATIENT WOULD BE.
THERE WE GO! THAT SHOULD DO YOU ALL RIGHT FOR NOW.
NICE PLACE YOU'VE GOT HERE, BY THE WAY.
I KNOW, RIGHT? CUTE AND COZY.
IT'S A GOOD BASE TO WORK FROM.
NOBODY TO RUN INTO, NOBODY ASKING QUES-TIONS.
SFX: PASHI (SNATCH)
HERE, YOU'LL WANT TO MAKE A CALL.
WHO AM I SUP-POSED TO CALL?
USE YOUR HEAD, DARREN. HOOKY FOLLOWED YOU FROM YOUR FRIEND'S HOUSE.

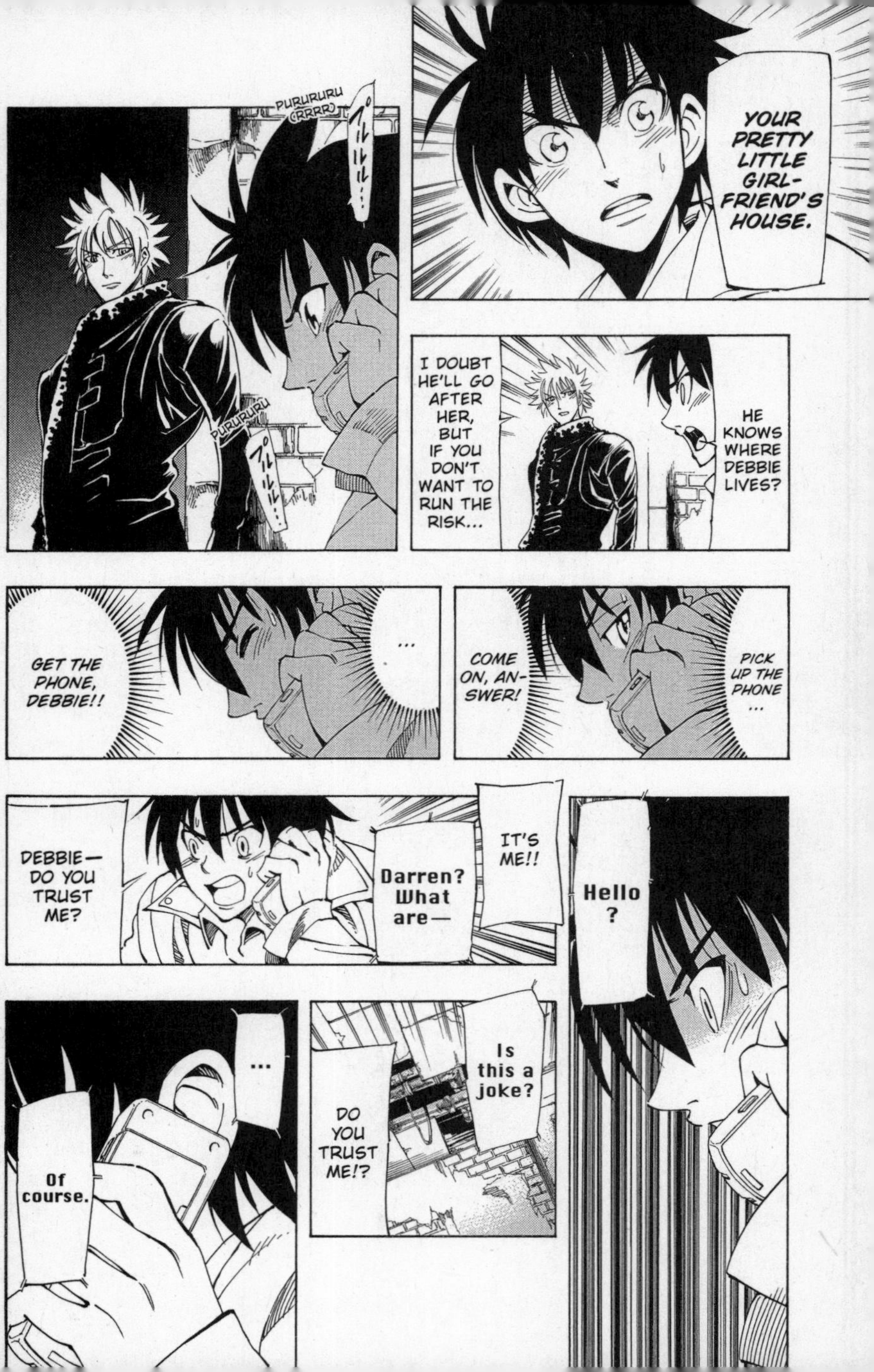

YOUR PRETTY LITTLE GIRL-FRIEND'S HOUSE.
HE KNOWS WHERE DEBBIE LIVES?
I DOUBT HE'LL GO AFTER HER, BUT IF YOU DON'T WANT TO RUN THE RISK...
PURURURU (RRRR)
プルルル…
PURURURU
プルルル…
PICK UP THE PHONE ...
COME ON, AN-SWER!
...
GET THE PHONE, DEBBIE!!
Hello ?
IT'S ME!!
Darren? What are—
DEBBIE—DO YOU TRUST ME?
Is this a joke?
DO YOU TRUST ME!?
...
Of course.

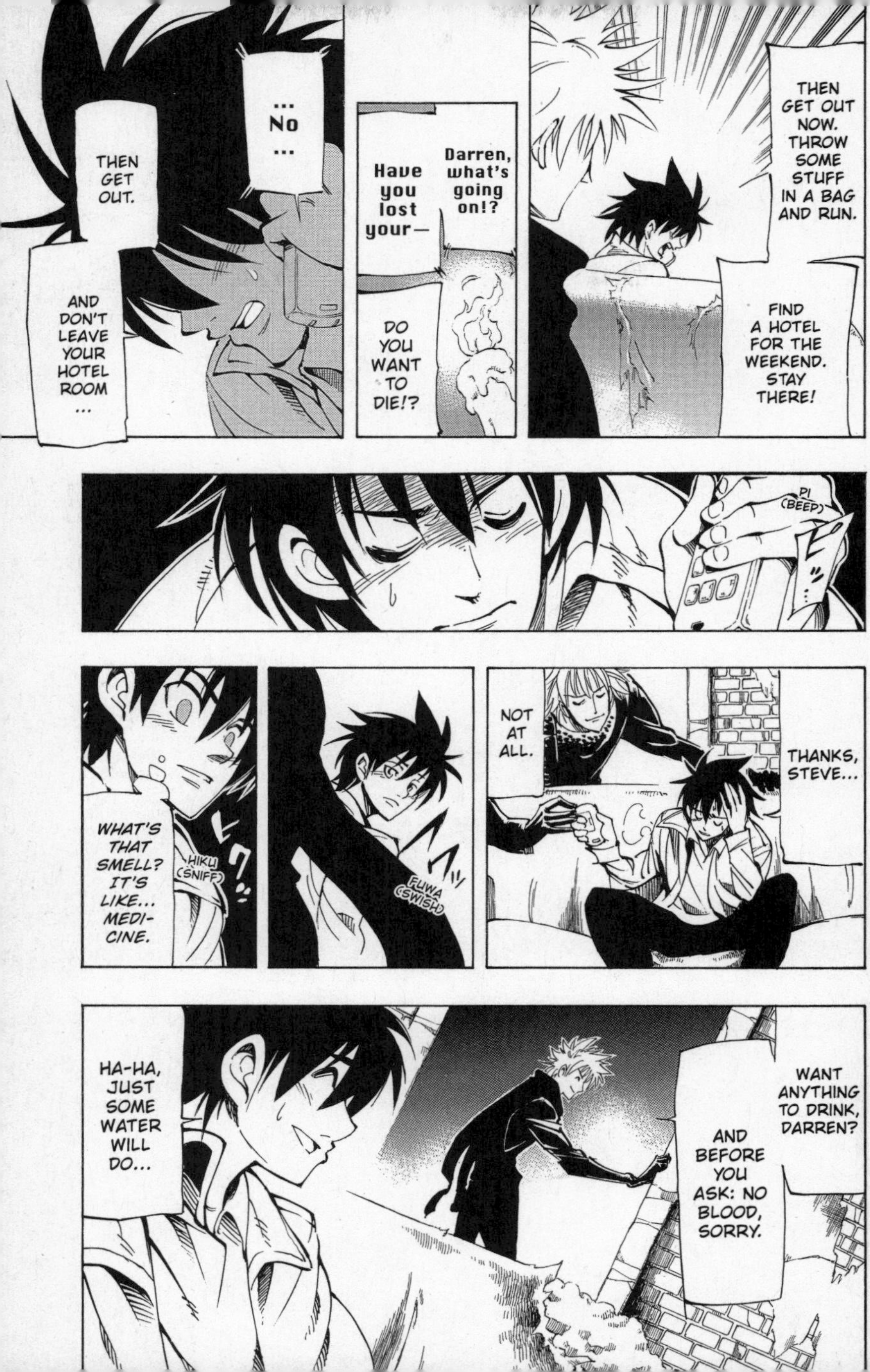
THEN GET OUT NOW. THROW SOME STUFF IN A BAG AND RUN.
FIND A HOTEL FOR THE WEEKEND. STAY THERE!
Darren, what's going on!?
Have you lost your—
DO YOU WANT TO DIE!?
... No ...
THEN GET OUT.
AND DON'T LEAVE YOUR HOTEL ROOM ...
PI (BEEP)
THANKS, STEVE...
NOT AT ALL.
FUWA (SWISH)
HIKU (SNIFF)
WHAT'S THAT SMELL? IT'S LIKE... MEDICINE.
WANT ANYTHING TO DRINK, DARREN?
AND BEFORE YOU ASK: NO BLOOD, SORRY.
HA-HA, JUST SOME WATER WILL DO...

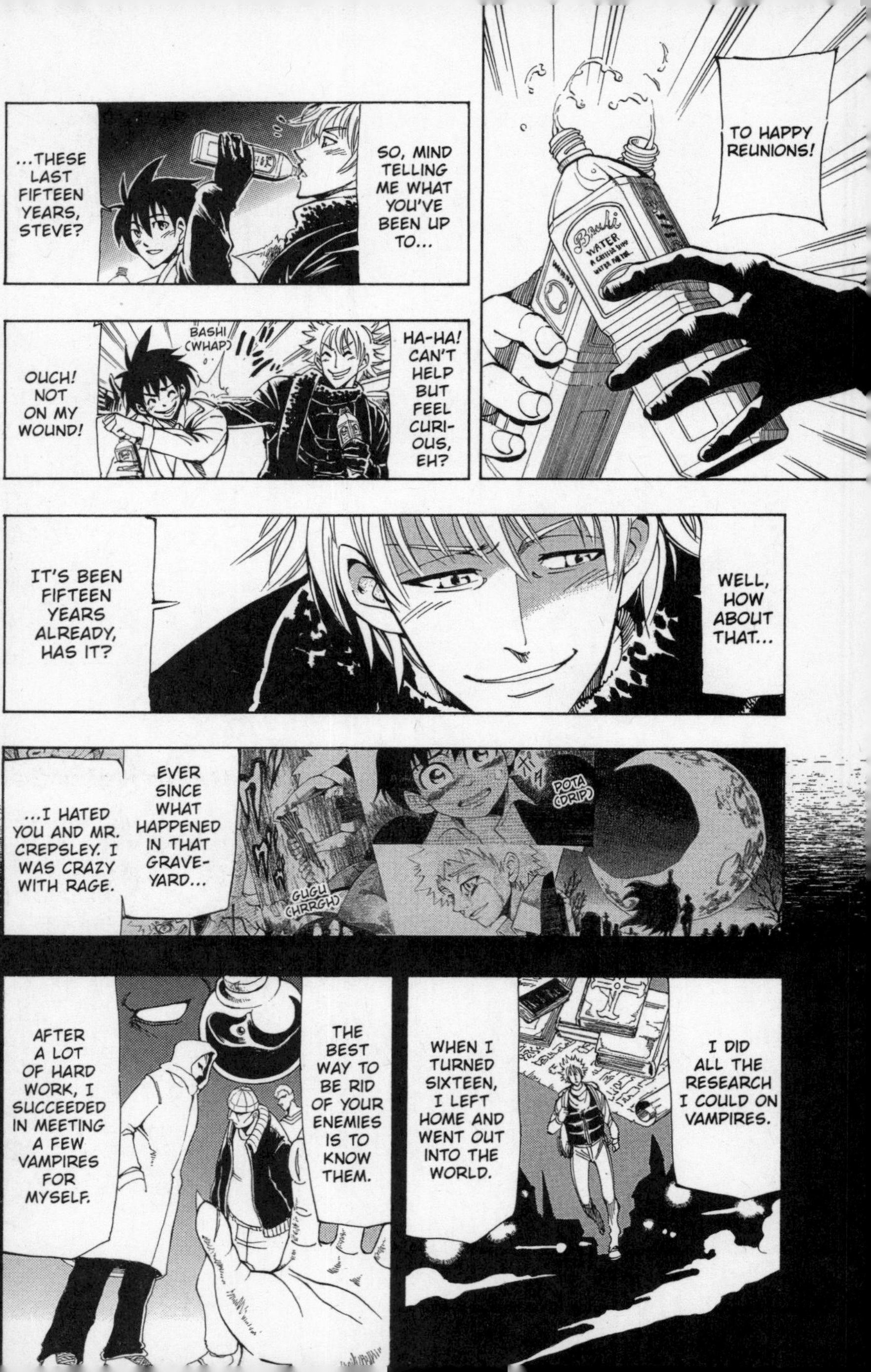
TO HAPPY REUNIONS!
SO, MIND TELLING ME WHAT YOU'VE BEEN UP TO...
...THESE LAST FIFTEEN YEARS, STEVE?
HA-HA! CAN'T HELP BUT FEEL CURIOUS, EH?
BASHI (WHAP)
OUCH! NOT ON MY WOUND!
WELL, HOW ABOUT THAT...
IT'S BEEN FIFTEEN YEARS ALREADY, HAS IT?
POTA (DRIP)
EVER SINCE WHAT HAPPENED IN THAT GRAVEYARD...
...I HATED YOU AND MR. CREPSLEY. I WAS CRAZY WITH RAGE.
GUGU (HRRGH)
I DID ALL THE RESEARCH I COULD ON VAMPIRES.
WHEN I TURNED SIXTEEN, I LEFT HOME AND WENT OUT INTO THE WORLD.
THE BEST WAY TO BE RID OF YOUR ENEMIES IS TO KNOW THEM.
AFTER A LOT OF HARD WORK, I SUCCEEDED IN MEETING A FEW VAMPIRES FOR MYSELF.

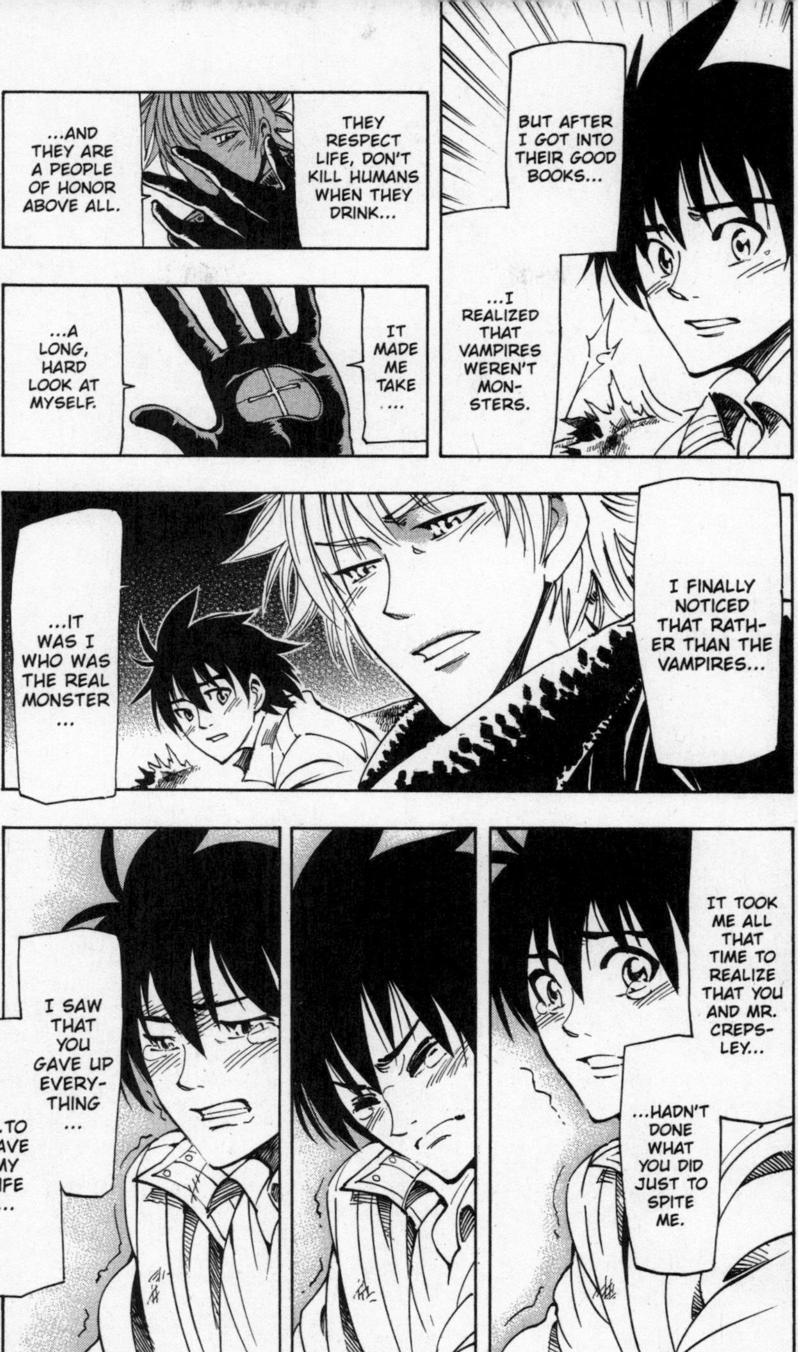
BUT AFTER I GOT INTO THEIR GOOD BOOKS...
...I REALIZED THAT VAMPIRES WEREN'T MON-STERS.
THEY RESPECT LIFE, DON'T KILL HUMANS WHEN THEY DRINK...
...AND THEY ARE A PEOPLE OF HONOR ABOVE ALL.
IT MADE ME TAKE...
...A LONG, HARD LOOK AT MYSELF.
I FINALLY NOTICED THAT RATH-ER THAN THE VAMPIRES...
...IT WAS I WHO WAS THE REAL MONSTER...
IT TOOK ME ALL THAT TIME TO REALIZE THAT YOU AND MR. CREPS-LEY...
...HADN'T DONE WHAT YOU DID JUST TO SPITE ME.
I SAW THAT YOU GAVE UP EVERY-THING...
...TO SAVE MY LIFE...

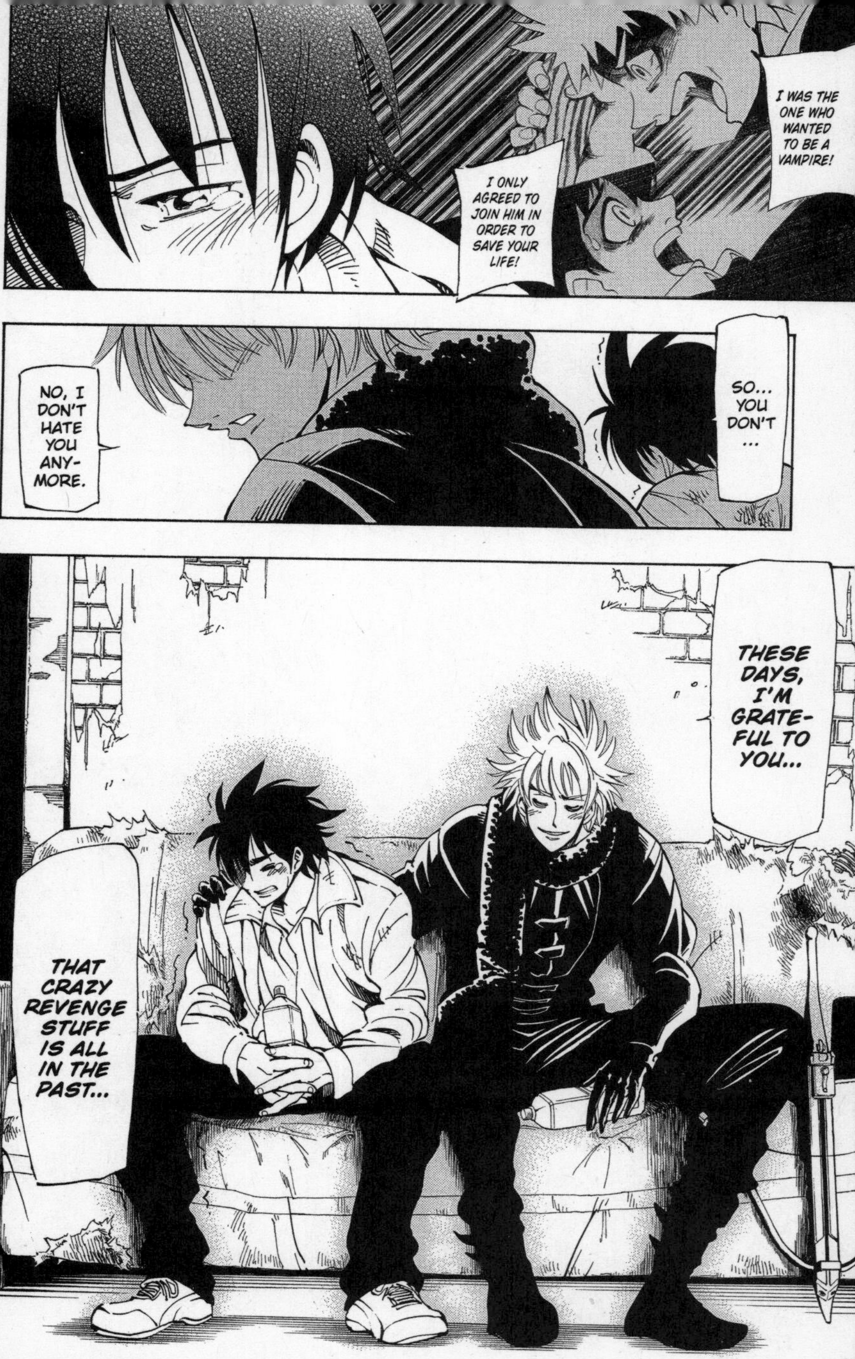
I WAS THE ONE WHO WANTED TO BE A VAMPIRE!
I ONLY AGREED TO JOIN HIM IN ORDER TO SAVE YOUR LIFE!
SO... YOU DON'T ...
NO, I DON'T HATE YOU ANY-MORE.
THESE DAYS, I'M GRATE-FUL TO YOU...
THAT CRAZY REVENGE STUFF IS ALL IN THE PAST...

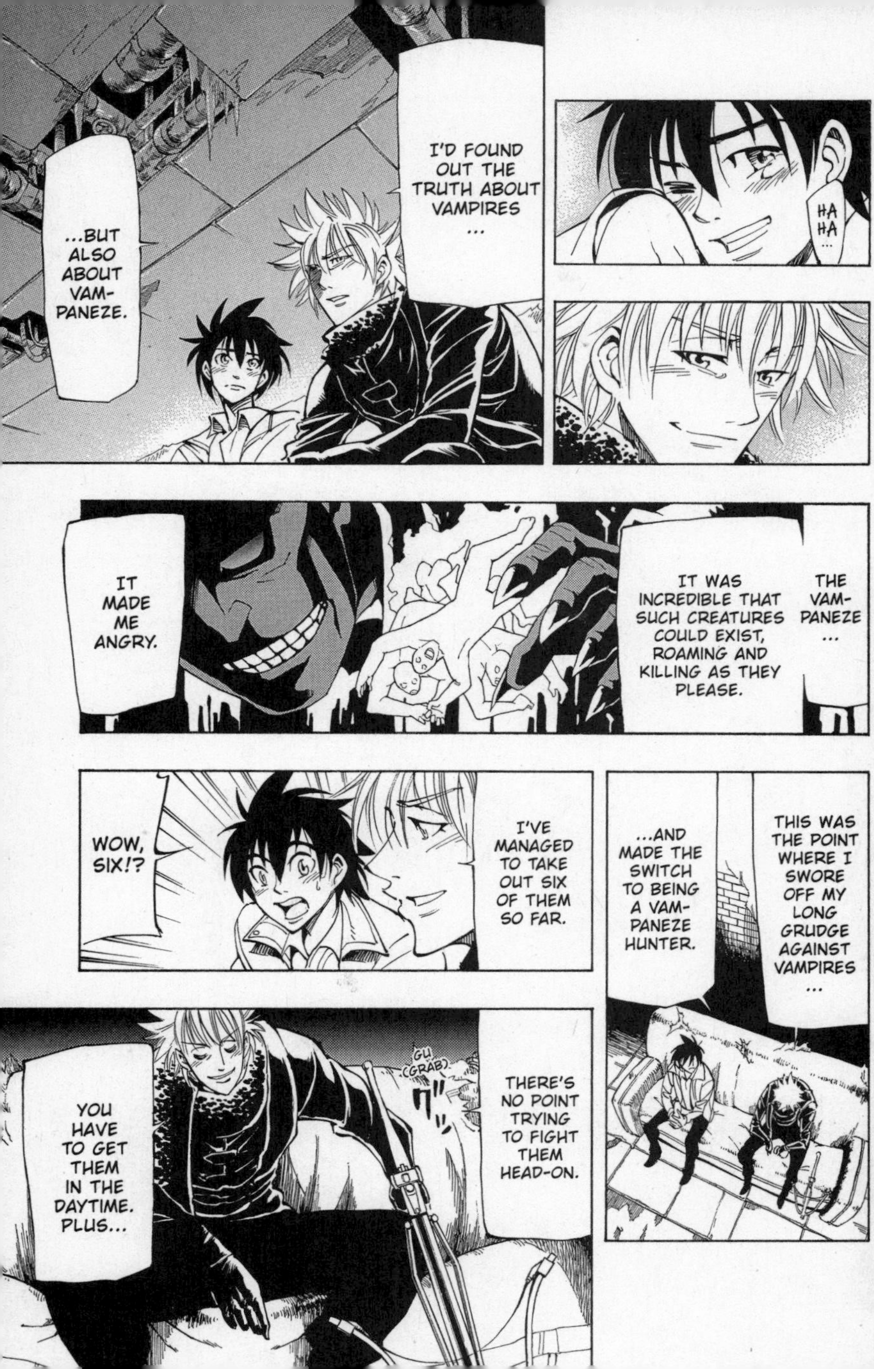
HA HA ...
I'D FOUND OUT THE TRUTH ABOUT VAMPIRES ...
...BUT ALSO ABOUT VAM-PANEZE.
THE VAM-PANEZE ...
IT WAS INCREDIBLE THAT SUCH CREATURES COULD EXIST, ROAMING AND KILLING AS THEY PLEASE.
IT MADE ME ANGRY.
THIS WAS THE POINT WHERE I SWORE OFF MY LONG GRUDGE AGAINST VAMPIRES ...
...AND MADE THE SWITCH TO BEING A VAM-PANEZE HUNTER.
I'VE MANAGED TO TAKE OUT SIX OF THEM SO FAR.
WOW, SIX!?
THERE'S NO POINT TRYING TO FIGHT THEM HEAD-ON.
GU (GRAB)
YOU HAVE TO GET THEM IN THE DAYTIME. PLUS...

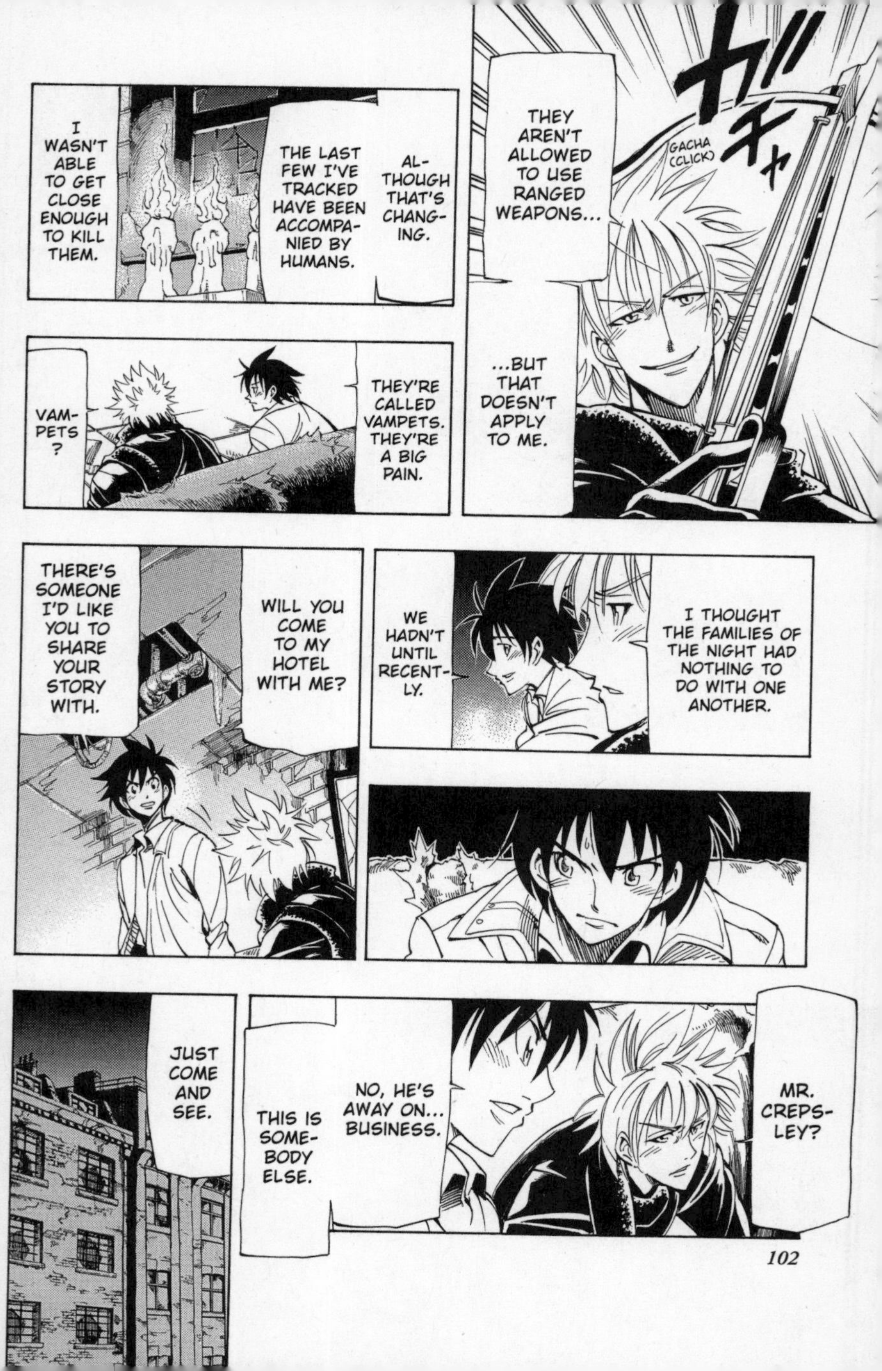
THEY AREN'T ALLOWED TO USE RANGED WEAPONS...
GACHA (CLICK)
...BUT THAT DOESN'T APPLY TO ME.
AL-THOUGH THAT'S CHANG-ING.
THE LAST FEW I'VE TRACKED HAVE BEEN ACCOMPA-NIED BY HUMANS.
I WASN'T ABLE TO GET CLOSE ENOUGH TO KILL THEM.
THEY'RE CALLED VAMPETS. THEY'RE A BIG PAIN.
VAM-PETS?
I THOUGHT THE FAMILIES OF THE NIGHT HAD NOTHING TO DO WITH ONE ANOTHER.
WE HADN'T UNTIL RECENT-LY.
WILL YOU COME TO MY HOTEL WITH ME?
THERE'S SOMEONE I'D LIKE YOU TO SHARE YOUR STORY WITH.
MR. CREPS-LEY?
NO, HE'S AWAY ON... BUSINESS.
THIS IS SOME-BODY ELSE.
JUST COME AND SEE.

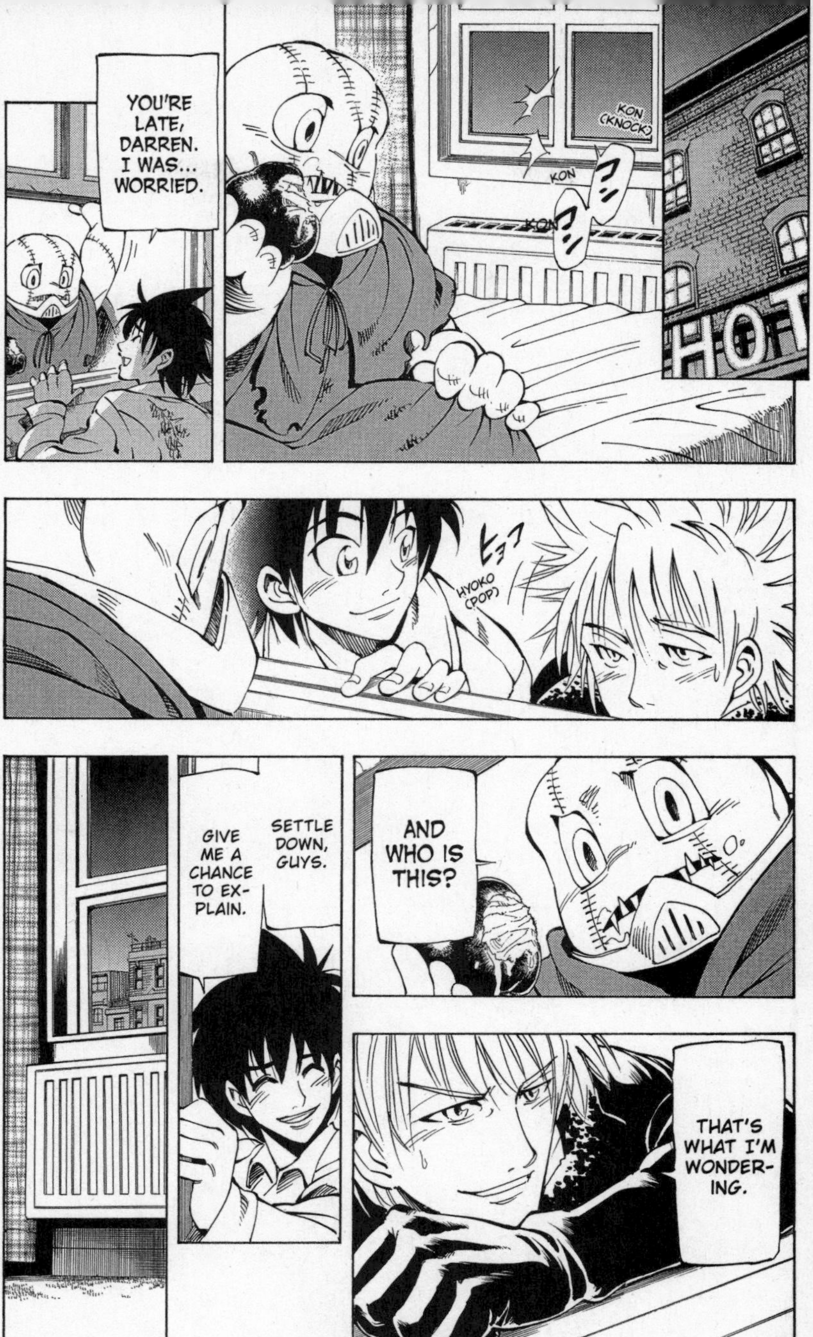
HOT
KON (KNOCK)
KON
KON
YOU'RE LATE, DARREN. I WAS... WORRIED.
HYOKO (POP)
AND WHO IS THIS?
THAT'S WHAT I'M WONDERING.
SETTLE DOWN, GUYS.
GIVE ME A CHANCE TO EX-PLAIN.

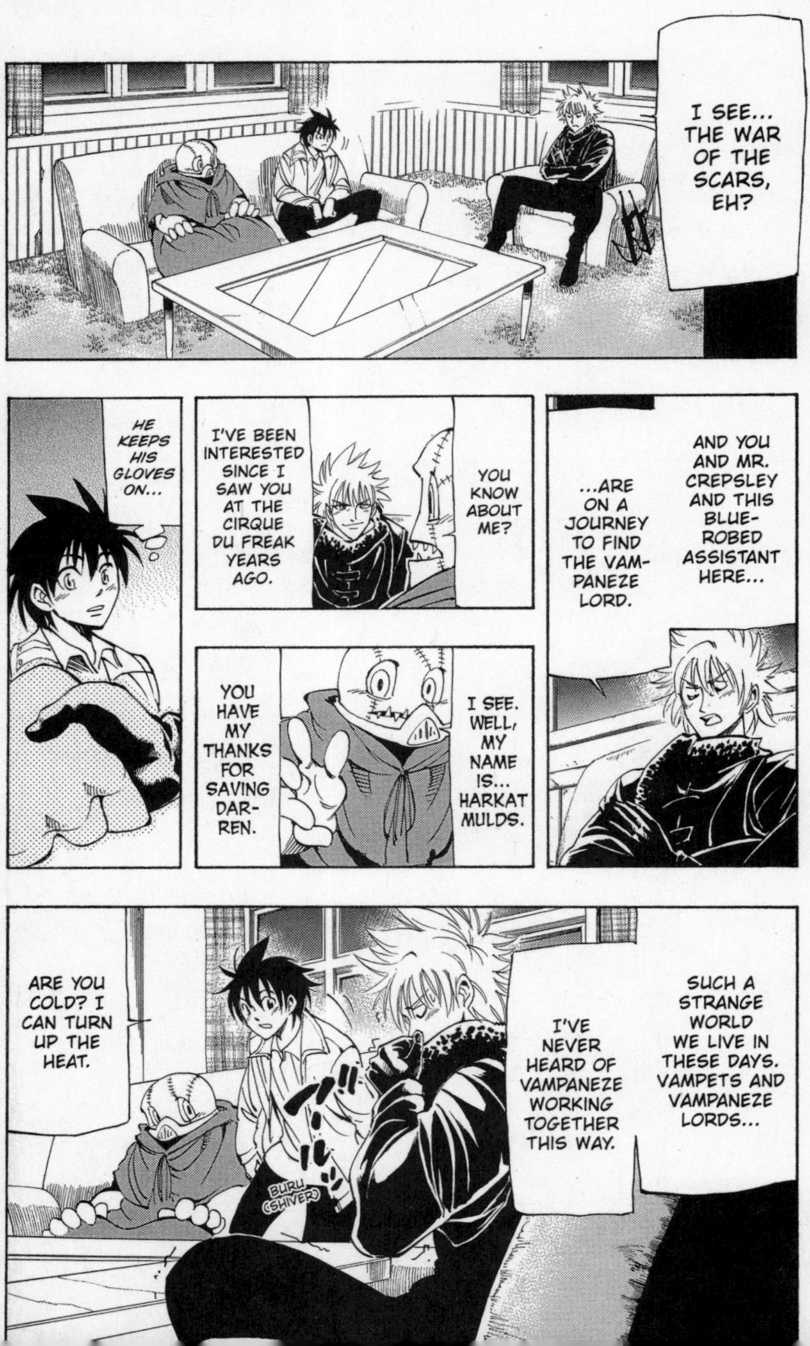
I SEE... THE WAR OF THE SCARS, EH?
AND YOU AND MR. CREPSLEY AND THIS BLUE-ROBED ASSISTANT HERE...
...ARE ON A JOURNEY TO FIND THE VAMPANEZE LORD.
YOU KNOW ABOUT ME?
I'VE BEEN INTERESTED SINCE I SAW YOU AT THE CIRQUE DU FREAK YEARS AGO.
I SEE. WELL, MY NAME IS... HARKAT MULDS.
YOU HAVE MY THANKS FOR SAVING DARREN.
HE KEEPS HIS GLOVES ON...
SUCH A STRANGE WORLD WE LIVE IN THESE DAYS. VAMPETS AND VAMPANEZE LORDS...
I'VE NEVER HEARD OF VAMPANEZE WORKING TOGETHER THIS WAY.
!!
BURU (SHIVER)
ARE YOU COLD? I CAN TURN UP THE HEAT.

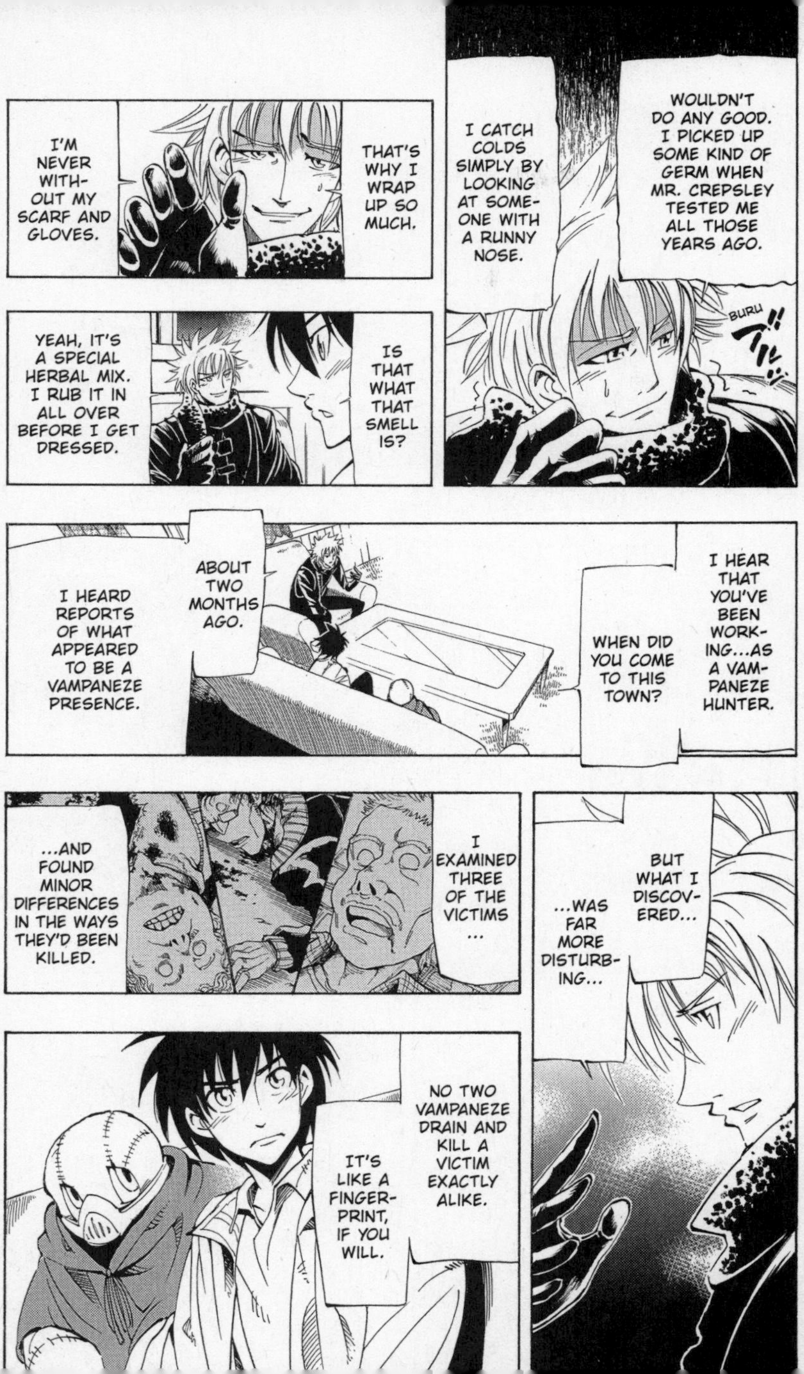
WOULDN'T DO ANY GOOD. I PICKED UP SOME KIND OF GERM WHEN MR. CREPSLEY TESTED ME ALL THOSE YEARS AGO.
I CATCH COLDS SIMPLY BY LOOKING AT SOME-ONE WITH A RUNNY NOSE.
BURU
THAT'S WHY I WRAP UP SO MUCH.
I'M NEVER WITH-OUT MY SCARF AND GLOVES.
IS THAT WHAT THAT SMELL IS?
YEAH, IT'S A SPECIAL HERBAL MIX. I RUB IT IN ALL OVER BEFORE I GET DRESSED.
I HEAR THAT YOU'VE BEEN WORK-ING...AS A VAM-PANEZE HUNTER.
WHEN DID YOU COME TO THIS TOWN?
ABOUT TWO MONTHS AGO.
I HEARD REPORTS OF WHAT APPEARED TO BE A VAMPANEZE PRESENCE.
BUT WHAT I DISCOV-ERED...
...WAS FAR MORE DISTURB-ING...
I EXAMINED THREE OF THE VICTIMS ...
...AND FOUND MINOR DIFFERENCES IN THE WAYS THEY'D BEEN KILLED.
NO TWO VAMPANEZE DRAIN AND KILL A VICTIM EXACTLY ALIKE.
IT'S LIKE A FINGER-PRINT, IF YOU WILL.

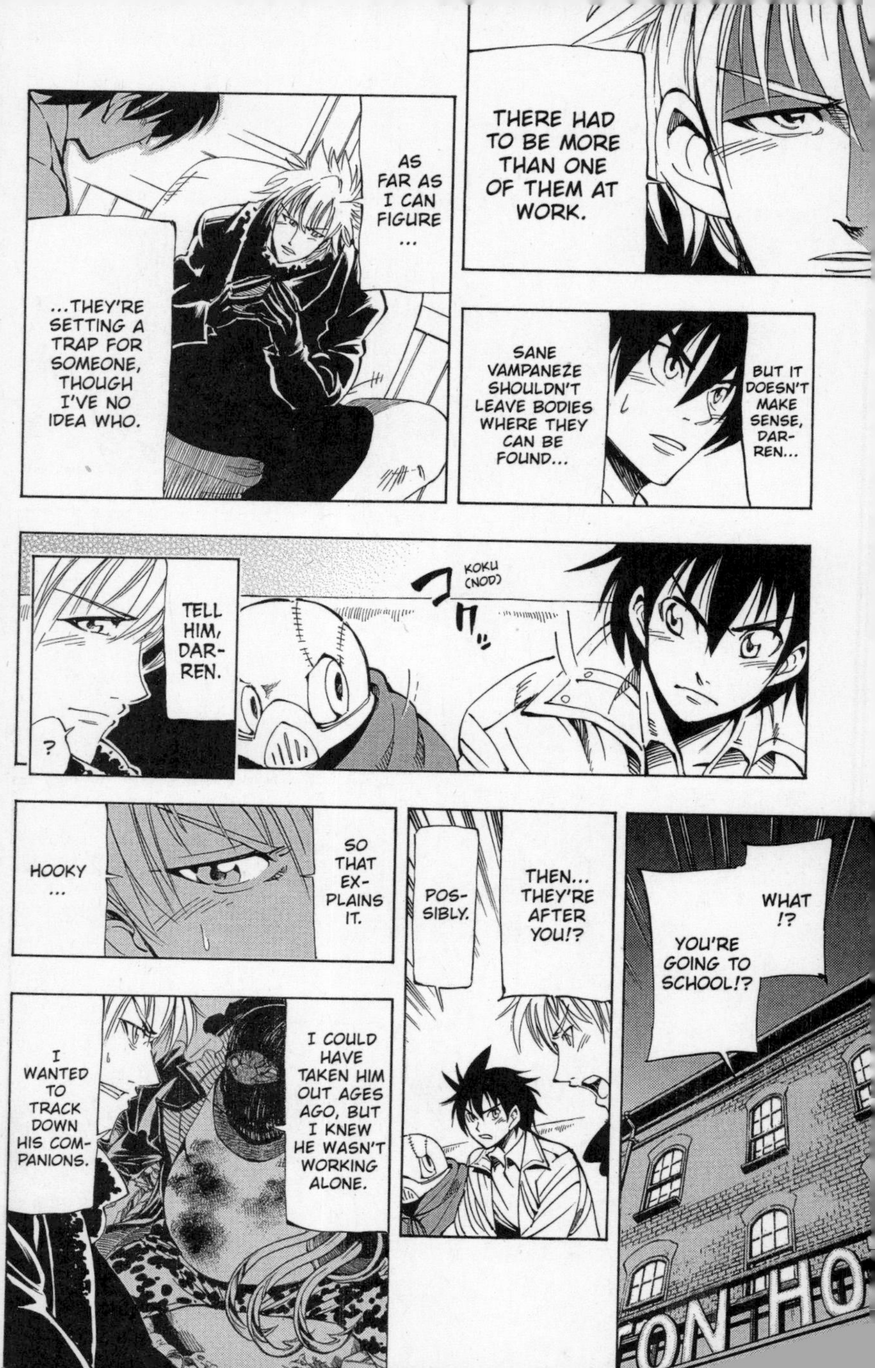
THERE HAD TO BE MORE THAN ONE OF THEM AT WORK.
BUT IT DOESN'T MAKE SENSE, DARREN...
SANE VAMPANEZE SHOULDN'T LEAVE BODIES WHERE THEY CAN BE FOUND...
AS FAR AS I CAN FIGURE...
...THEY'RE SETTING A TRAP FOR SOMEONE, THOUGH I'VE NO IDEA WHO.
KOKU (NOD)
TELL HIM, DARREN.
?
WHAT!?
YOU'RE GOING TO SCHOOL!?
ON HO
THEN... THEY'RE AFTER YOU!?
POSSIBLY.
SO THAT EXPLAINS IT.
HOOKY...
I COULD HAVE TAKEN HIM OUT AGES AGO, BUT I KNEW HE WASN'T WORKING ALONE.
I WANTED TO TRACK DOWN HIS COMPANIONS.

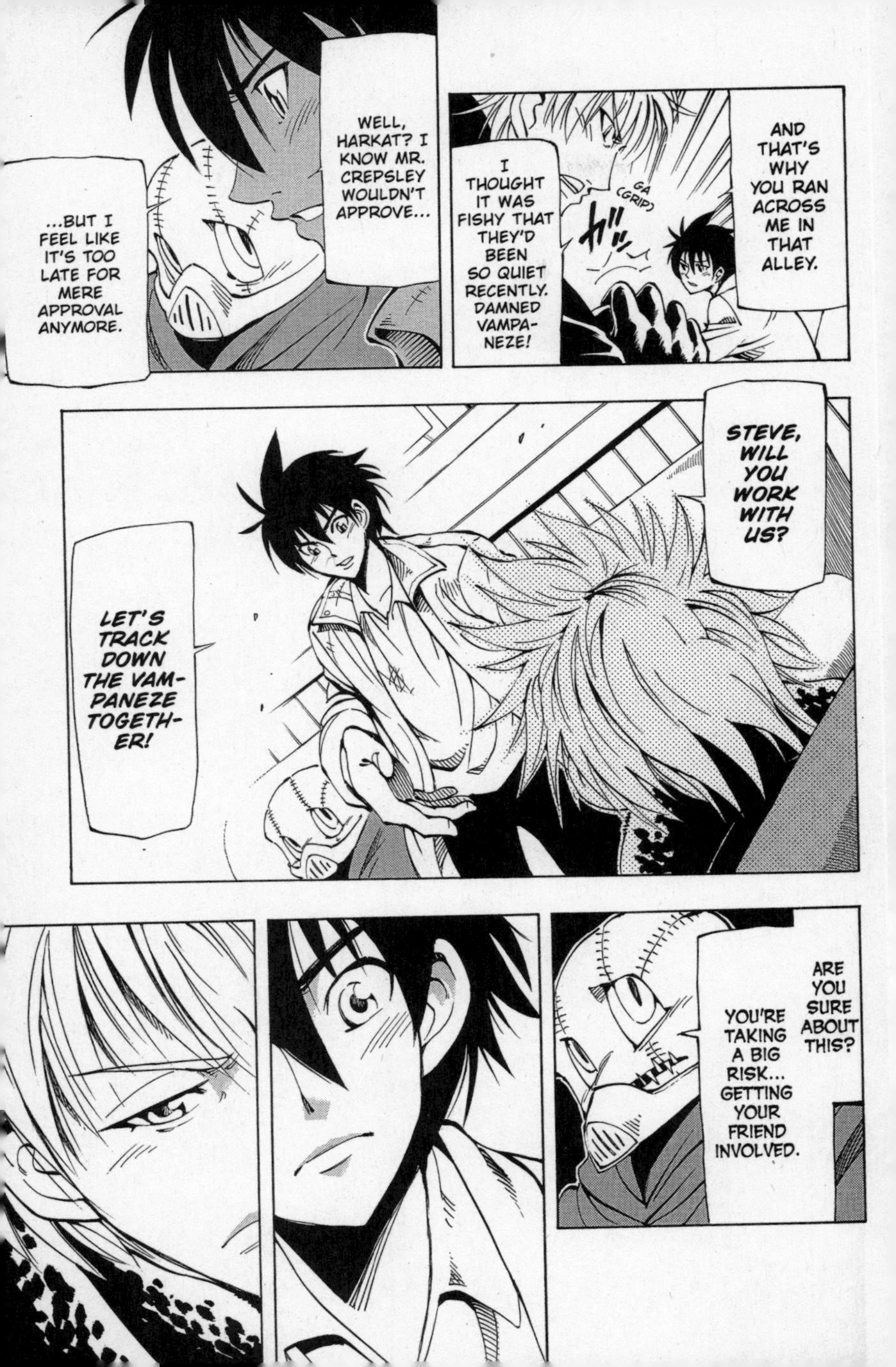
AND THAT'S WHY YOU RAN ACROSS ME IN THAT ALLEY.
GA (GRIP)
I THOUGHT IT WAS FISHY THAT THEY'D BEEN SO QUIET RECENTLY. DAMNED VAMPANEZE!
WELL, HARKAT? I KNOW MR. CREPSLEY WOULDN'T APPROVE...
...BUT I FEEL LIKE IT'S TOO LATE FOR MERE APPROVAL ANYMORE.
STEVE, WILL YOU WORK WITH US?
LET'S TRACK DOWN THE VAMPANEZE TOGETHER!
ARE YOU SURE ABOUT THIS?
YOU'RE TAKING A BIG RISK... GETTING YOUR FRIEND INVOLVED.

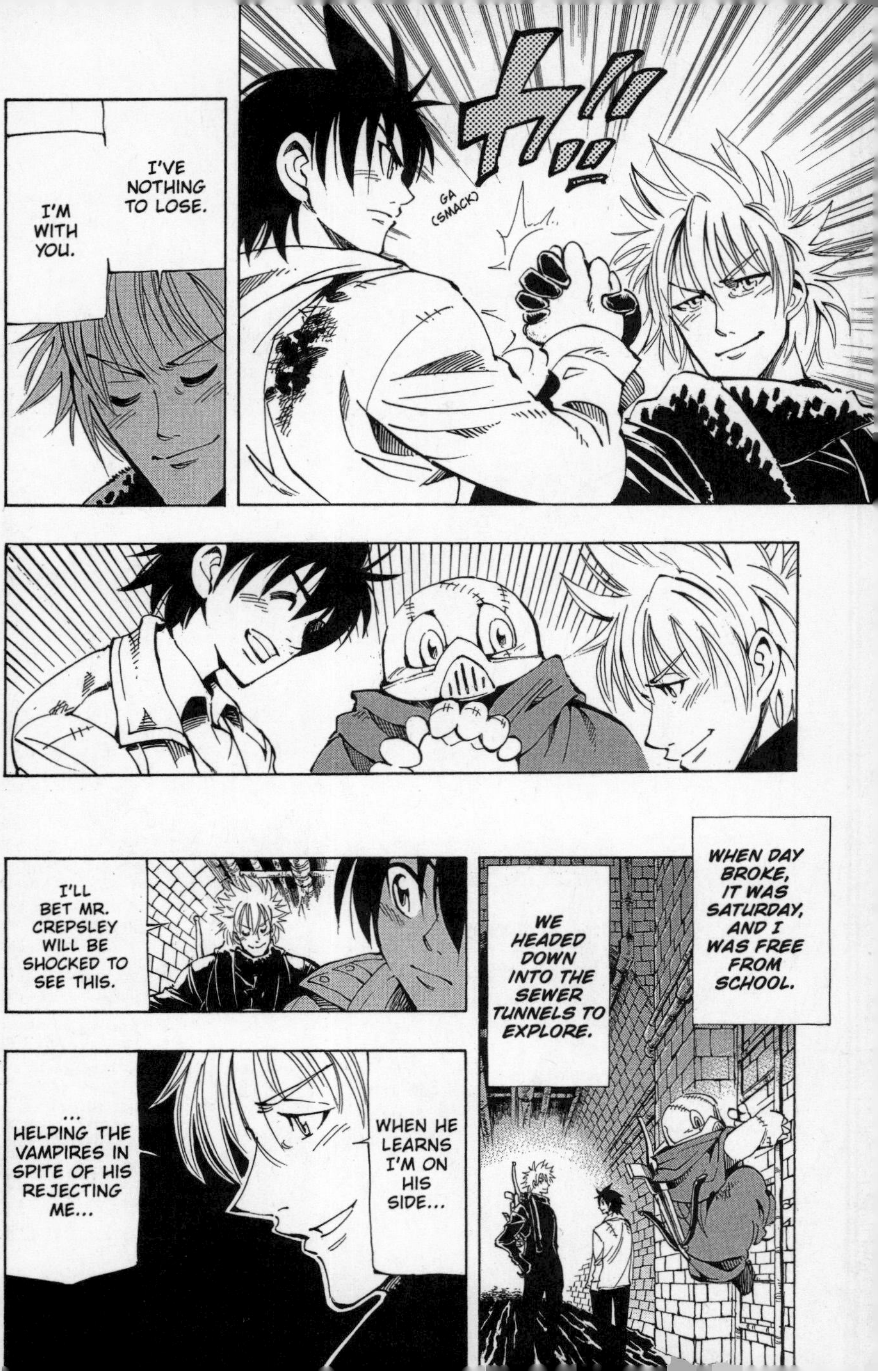
GA (SMACK)
I'VE NOTHING TO LOSE.
I'M WITH YOU.
WHEN DAY BROKE, IT WAS SATURDAY, AND I WAS FREE FROM SCHOOL.
WE HEADED DOWN INTO THE SEWER TUNNELS TO EXPLORE.
I'LL BET MR. CREPSLEY WILL BE SHOCKED TO SEE THIS.
WHEN HE LEARNS I'M ON HIS SIDE...
...HELPING THE VAMPIRES IN SPITE OF HIS REJECTING ME...

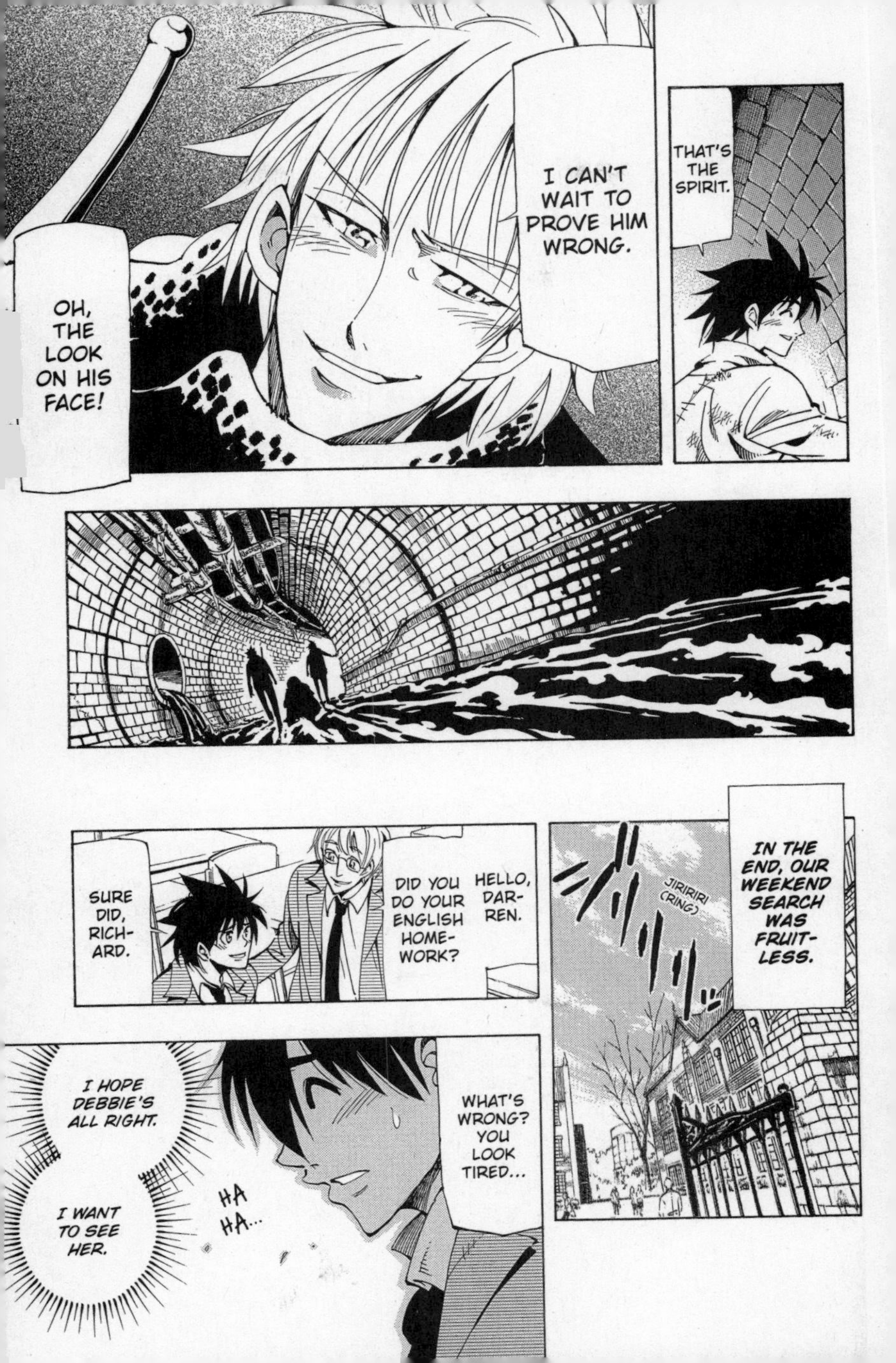
THAT'S THE SPIRIT.
I CAN'T WAIT TO PROVE HIM WRONG.
OH, THE LOOK ON HIS FACE!
IN THE END, OUR WEEKEND SEARCH WAS FRUITLESS.
JIRIRIRI (RING)
HELLO, DARREN.
DID YOU DO YOUR ENGLISH HOMEWORK?
SURE DID, RICHARD.
WHAT'S WRONG? YOU LOOK TIRED...
HA HA...
I HOPE DEBBIE'S ALL RIGHT.
I WANT TO SEE HER.

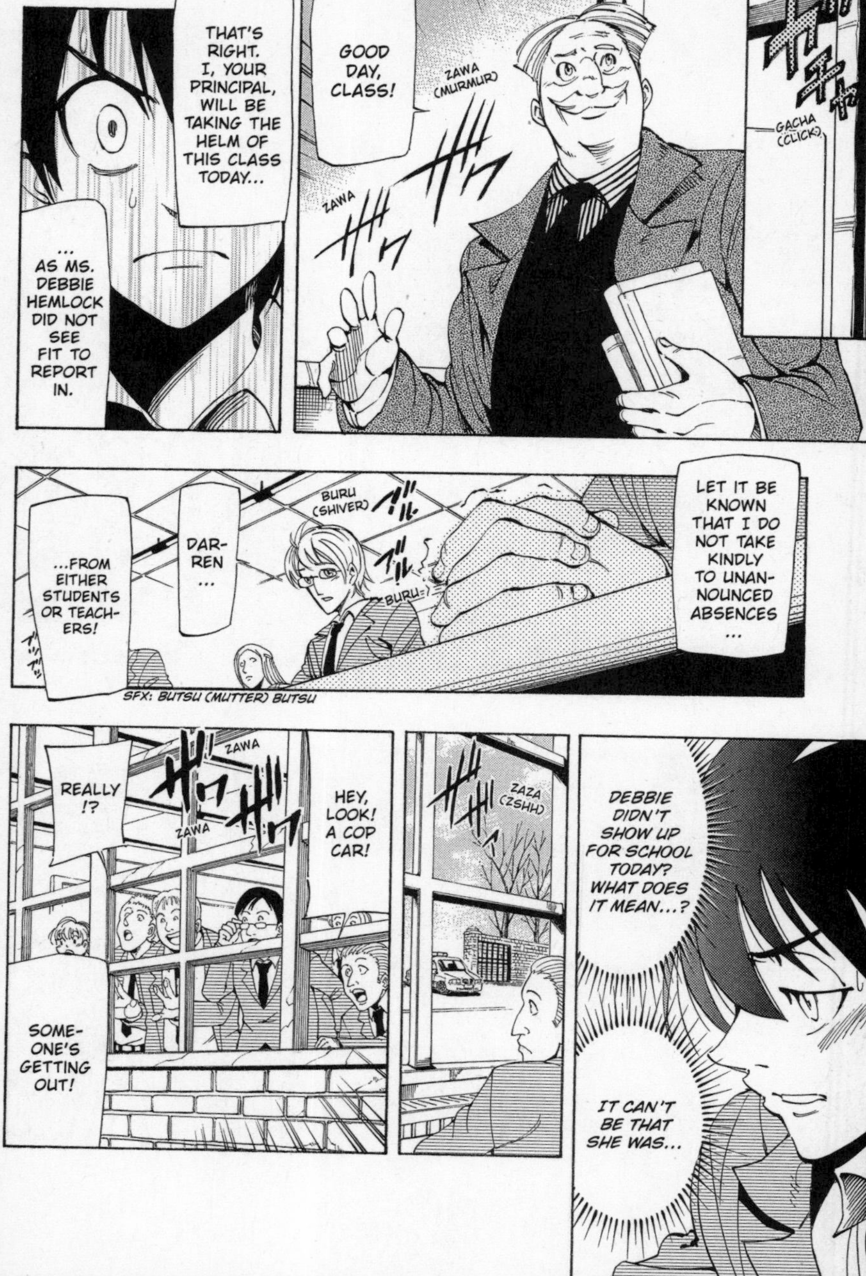
GACHA (CLICK)
GOOD DAY, CLASS!
ZAWA (MURMUR)
ZAWA
THAT'S RIGHT. I, YOUR PRINCIPAL, WILL BE TAKING THE HELM OF THIS CLASS TODAY...
...AS MS. DEBBIE HEMLOCK DID NOT SEE FIT TO REPORT IN.
LET IT BE KNOWN THAT I DO NOT TAKE KINDLY TO UNANNOUNCED ABSENCES...
BURU (SHIVER)
BURU
DARREN...
...FROM EITHER STUDENTS OR TEACHERS!
SFX: BUTSU (MUTTER) BUTSU
DEBBIE DIDN'T SHOW UP FOR SCHOOL TODAY? WHAT DOES IT MEAN...?
IT CAN'T BE THAT SHE WAS...
ZAZA (ZSHH)
HEY, LOOK! A COP CAR!
ZAWA
ZAWA
REALLY!?
SOME-ONE'S GETTING OUT!

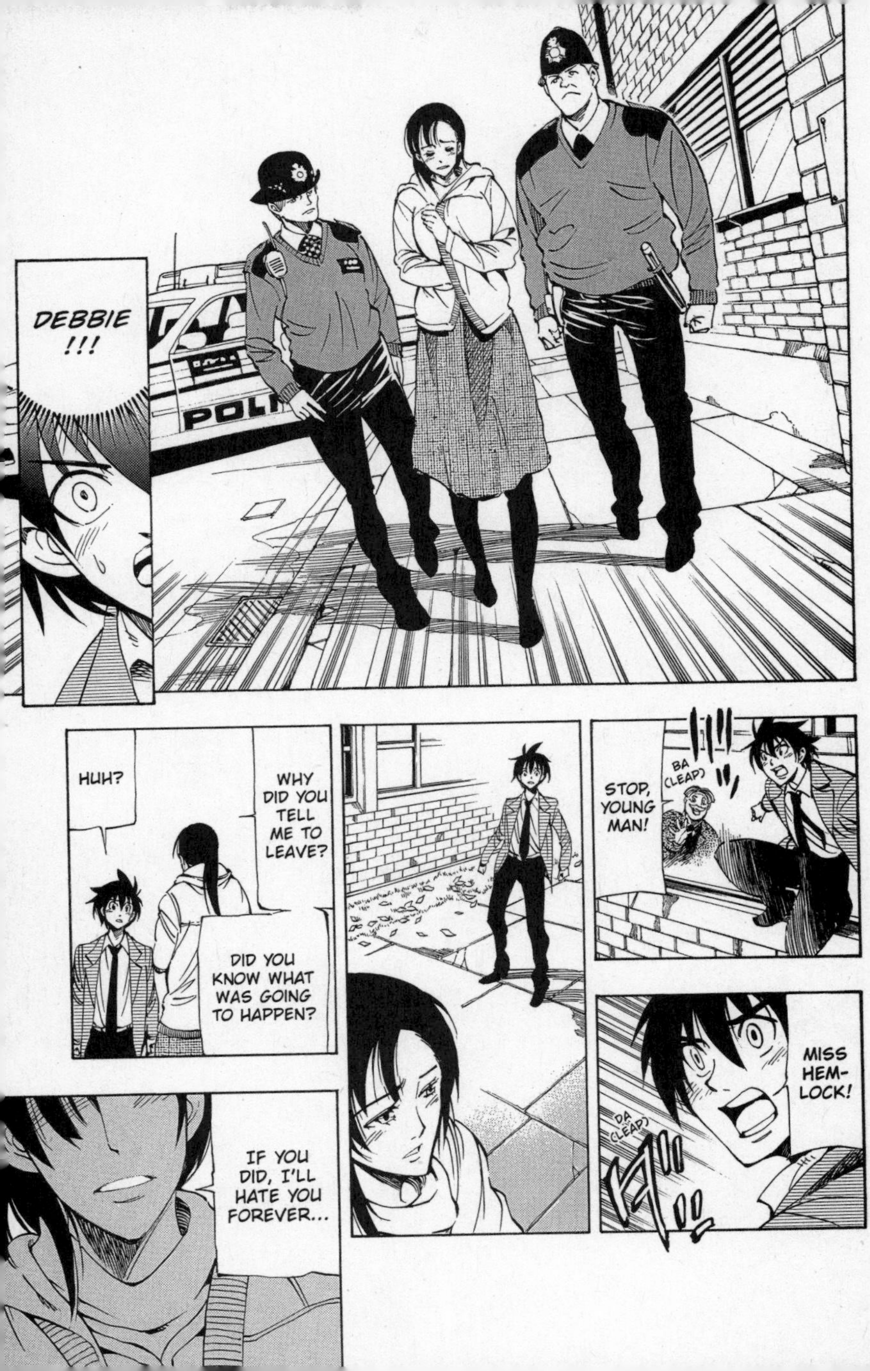
POLI
DEBBIE!!!
BA (LEAP)
STOP, YOUNG MAN!
HUH?
WHY DID YOU TELL ME TO LEAVE?
DID YOU KNOW WHAT WAS GOING TO HAPPEN?
MISS HEMLOCK!
DA (LEAP)
IF YOU DID, I'LL HATE YOU FOREVER...

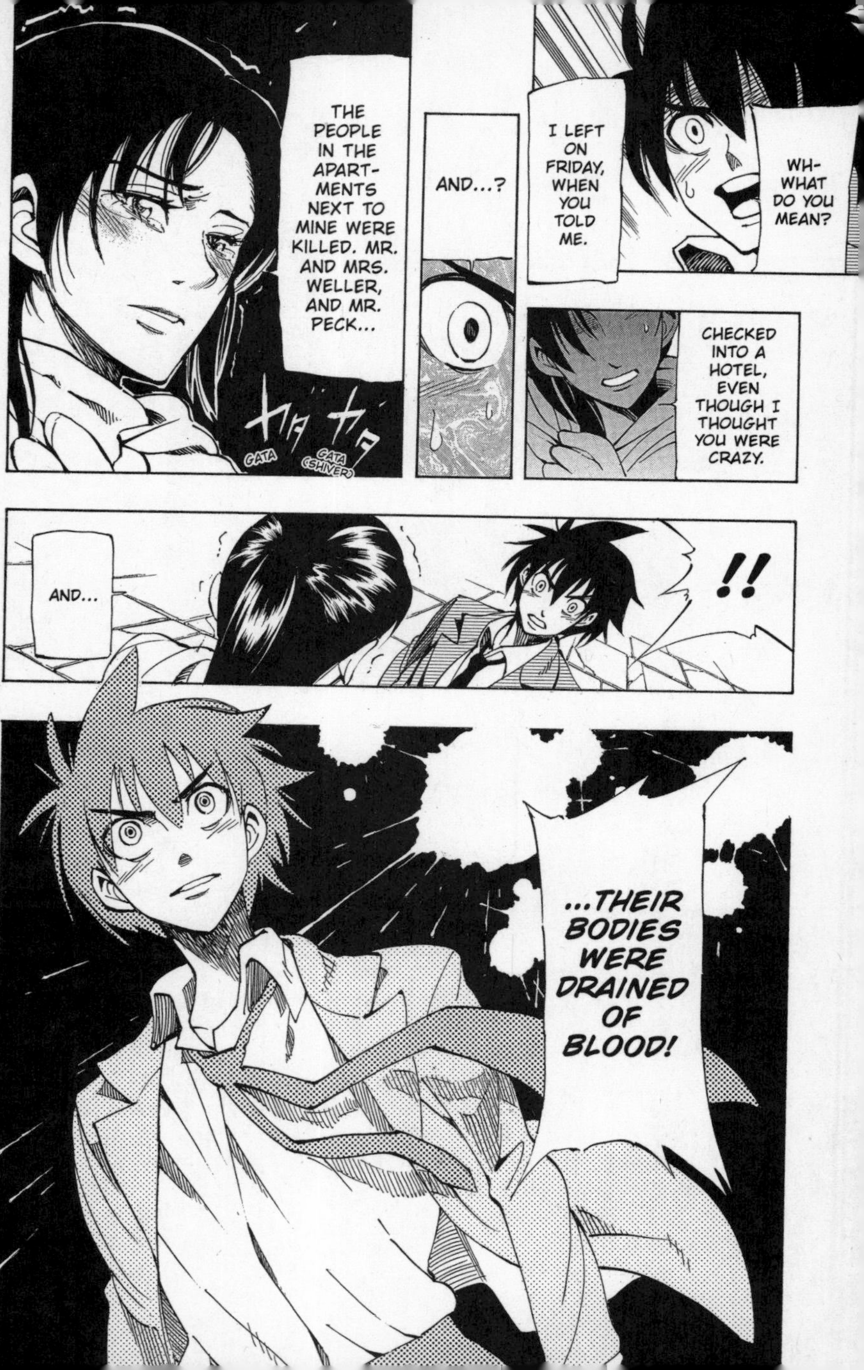
WH- WHAT DO YOU MEAN?
I LEFT ON FRIDAY, WHEN YOU TOLD ME.
CHECKED INTO A HOTEL, EVEN THOUGH I THOUGHT YOU WERE CRAZY.
AND...?
THE PEOPLE IN THE APART-MENTS NEXT TO MINE WERE KILLED. MR. AND MRS. WELLER, AND MR. PECK...
GATA GATA (SHIVER)
!!
AND...
...THEIR BODIES WERE DRAINED OF BLOOD!

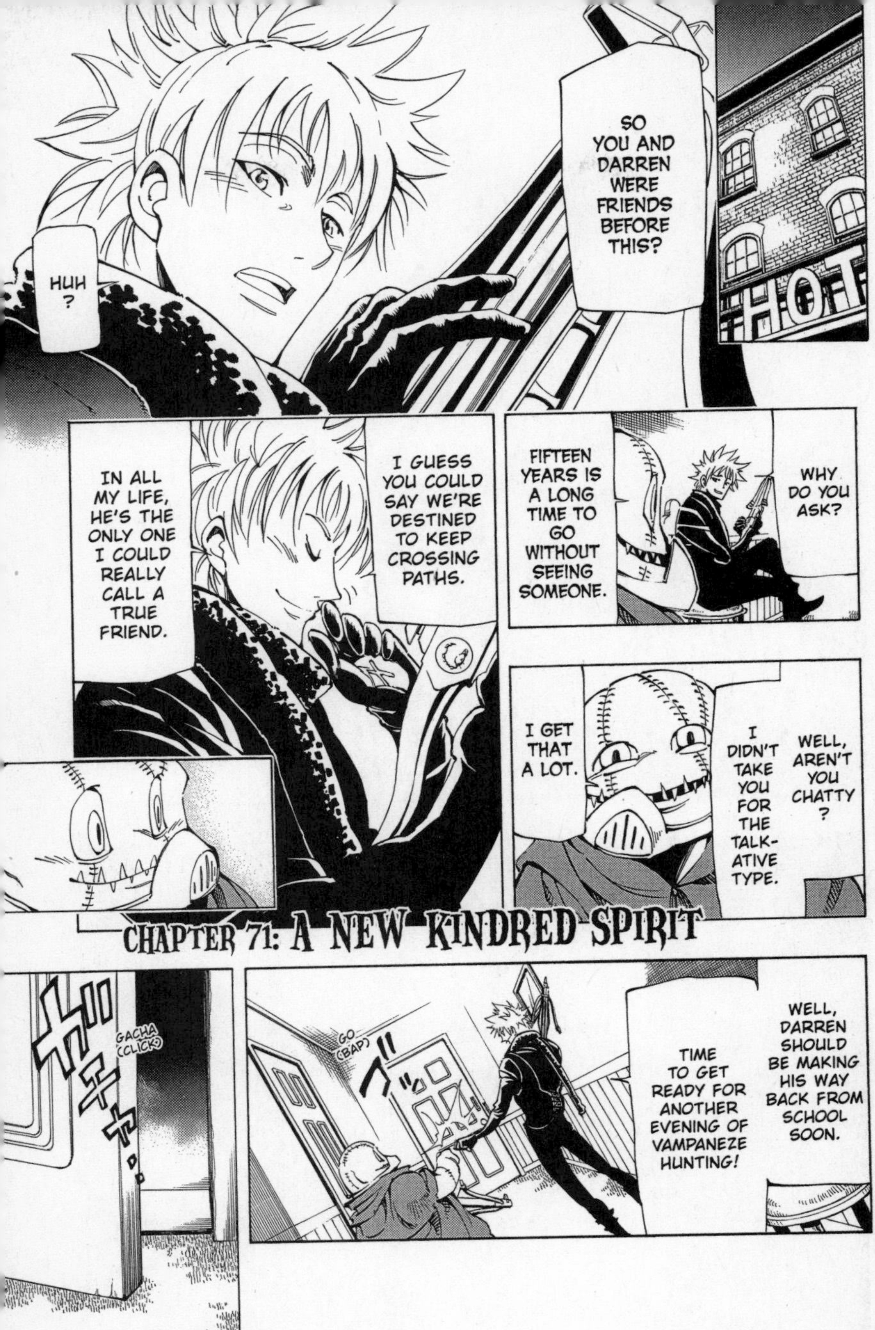
SO YOU AND DARREN WERE FRIENDS BEFORE THIS?
HUH?
WHY DO YOU ASK?
FIFTEEN YEARS IS A LONG TIME TO GO WITHOUT SEEING SOMEONE.
WELL, AREN'T YOU CHATTY?
I DIDN'T TAKE YOU FOR THE TALK-ATIVE TYPE.
I GET THAT A LOT.
I GUESS YOU COULD SAY WE'RE DESTINED TO KEEP CROSSING PATHS.
IN ALL MY LIFE, HE'S THE ONLY ONE I COULD REALLY CALL A TRUE FRIEND.
CHAPTER 71: A NEW KINDRED SPIRIT
WELL, DARREN SHOULD BE MAKING HIS WAY BACK FROM SCHOOL SOON.
TIME TO GET READY FOR ANOTHER EVENING OF VAMPANEZE HUNTING!
GO (BAP)
GACHA (CLICK)

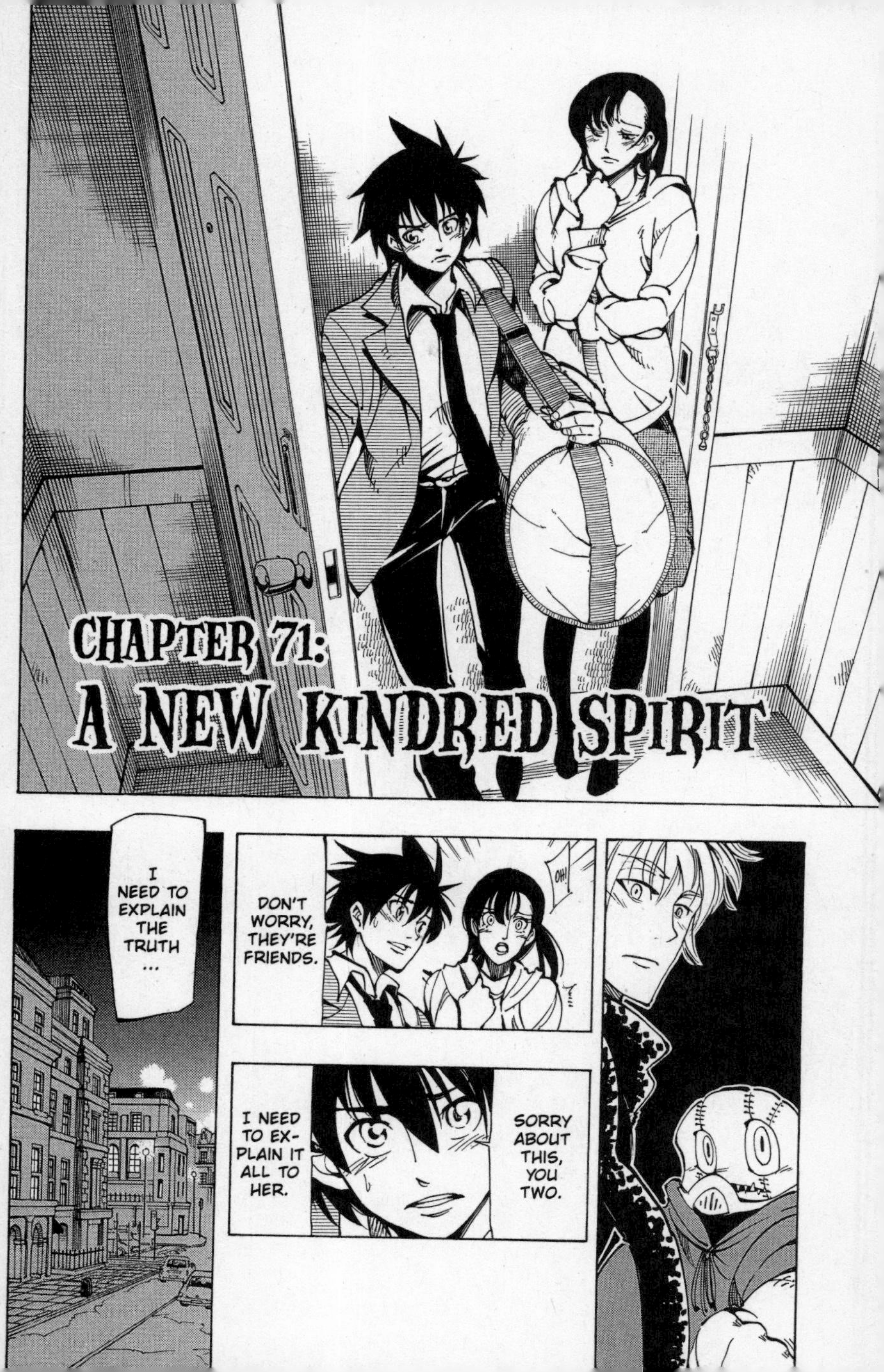
CHAPTER 71:
A NEW KINDRED SPIRIT
OH!
DON'T WORRY, THEY'RE FRIENDS.
SORRY ABOUT THIS, YOU TWO.
I NEED TO EXPLAIN IT ALL TO HER.
I NEED TO EXPLAIN THE TRUTH ...

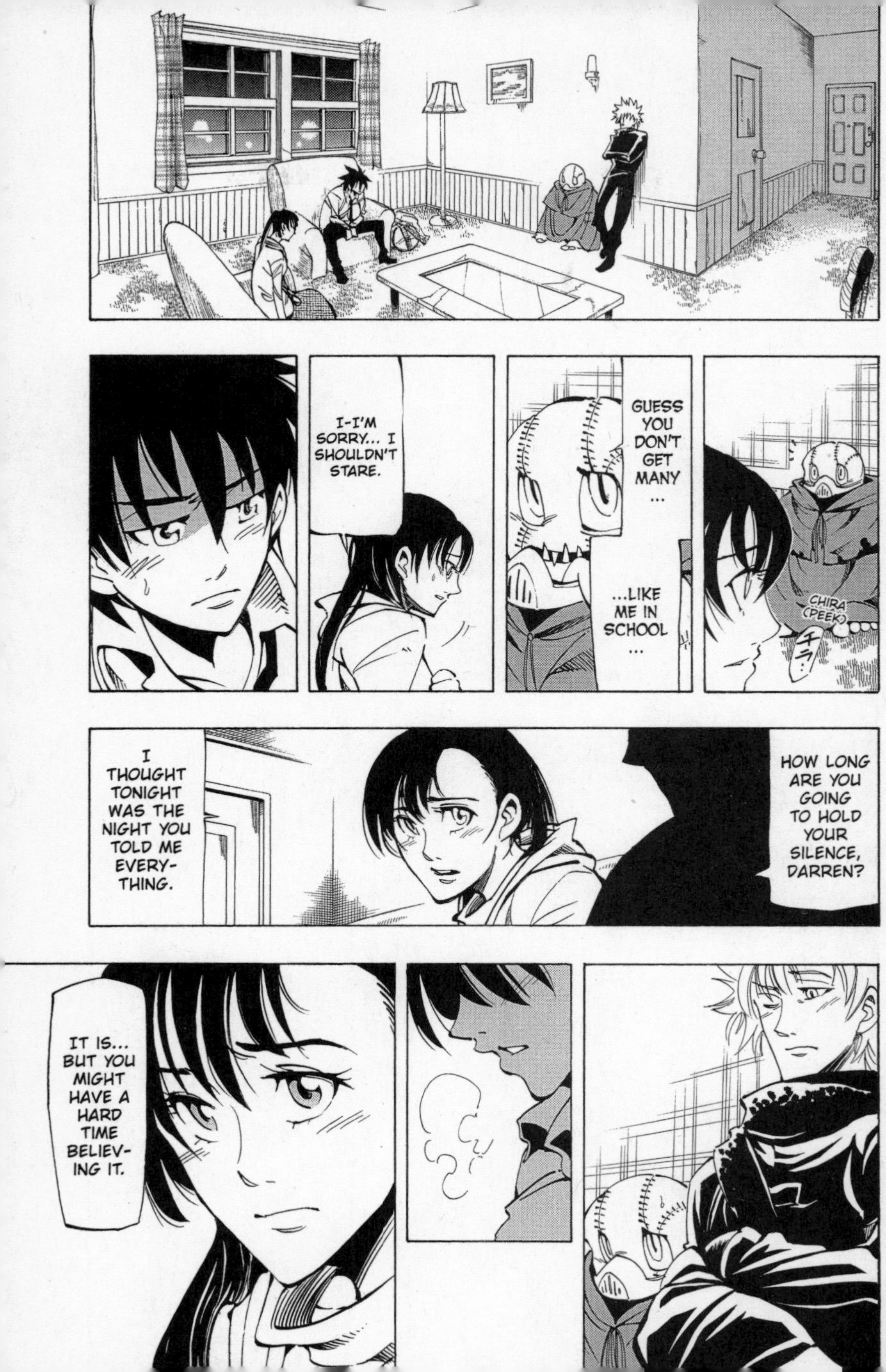
CHIRA (PEEK)
チラ
GUESS YOU DON'T GET MANY ...
...LIKE ME IN SCHOOL ...
I-I'M SORRY... I SHOULDN'T STARE.
HOW LONG ARE YOU GOING TO HOLD YOUR SILENCE, DARREN?
I THOUGHT TONIGHT WAS THE NIGHT YOU TOLD ME EVERY-THING.
IT IS... BUT YOU MIGHT HAVE A HARD TIME BELIEV-ING IT.

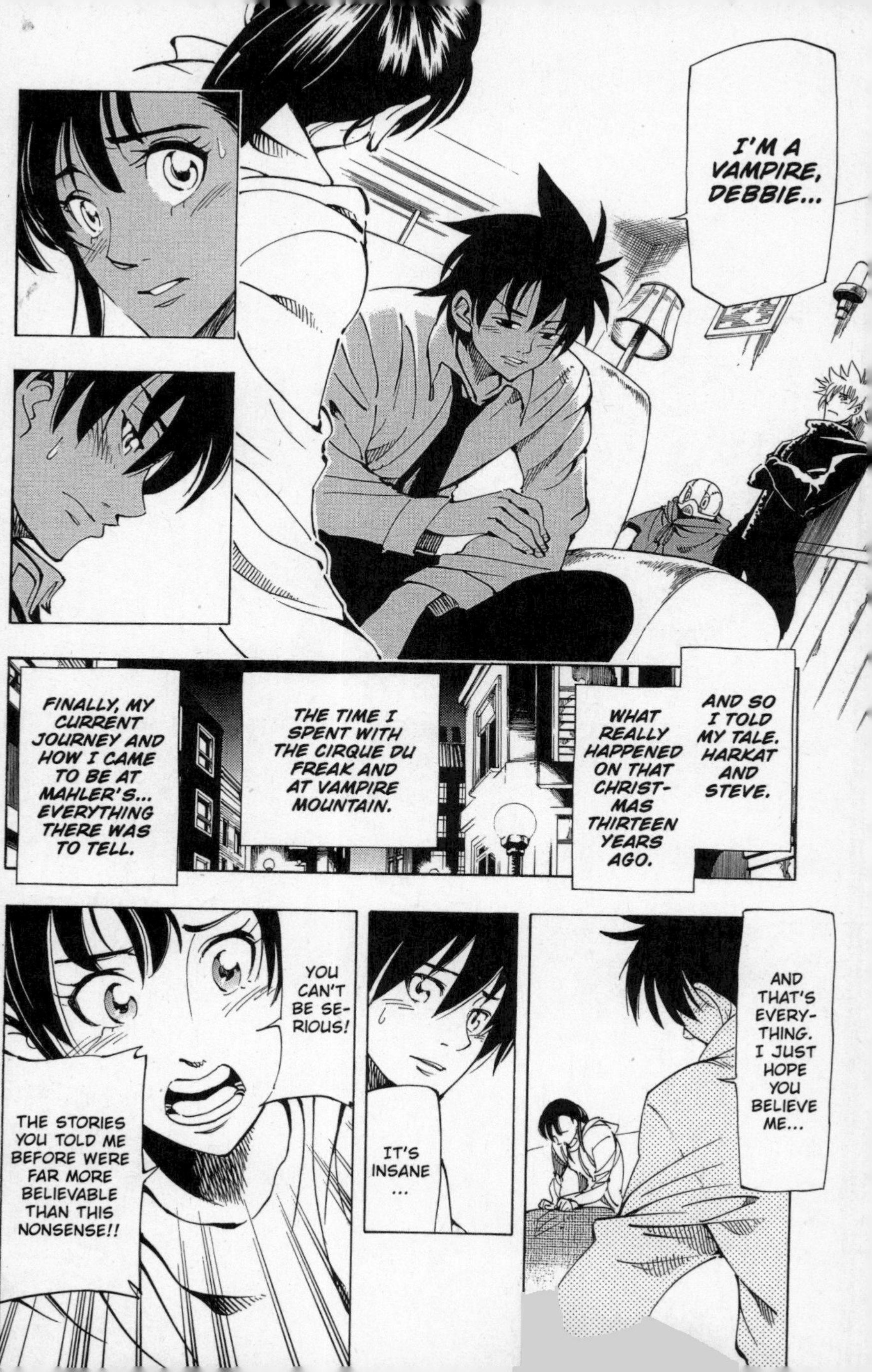
I'M A VAMPIRE, DEBBIE...
AND SO I TOLD MY TALE. HARKAT AND STEVE.
WHAT REALLY HAPPENED ON THAT CHRIST-MAS THIRTEEN YEARS AGO.
THE TIME I SPENT WITH THE CIRQUE DU FREAK AND AT VAMPIRE MOUNTAIN.
FINALLY, MY CURRENT JOURNEY AND HOW I CAME TO BE AT MAHLER'S... EVERYTHING THERE WAS TO TELL.
AND THAT'S EVERY-THING. I JUST HOPE YOU BELIEVE ME...
IT'S INSANE ...
YOU CAN'T BE SE-RIOUS!
THE STORIES YOU TOLD ME BEFORE WERE FAR MORE BELIEVABLE THAN THIS NONSENSE!!

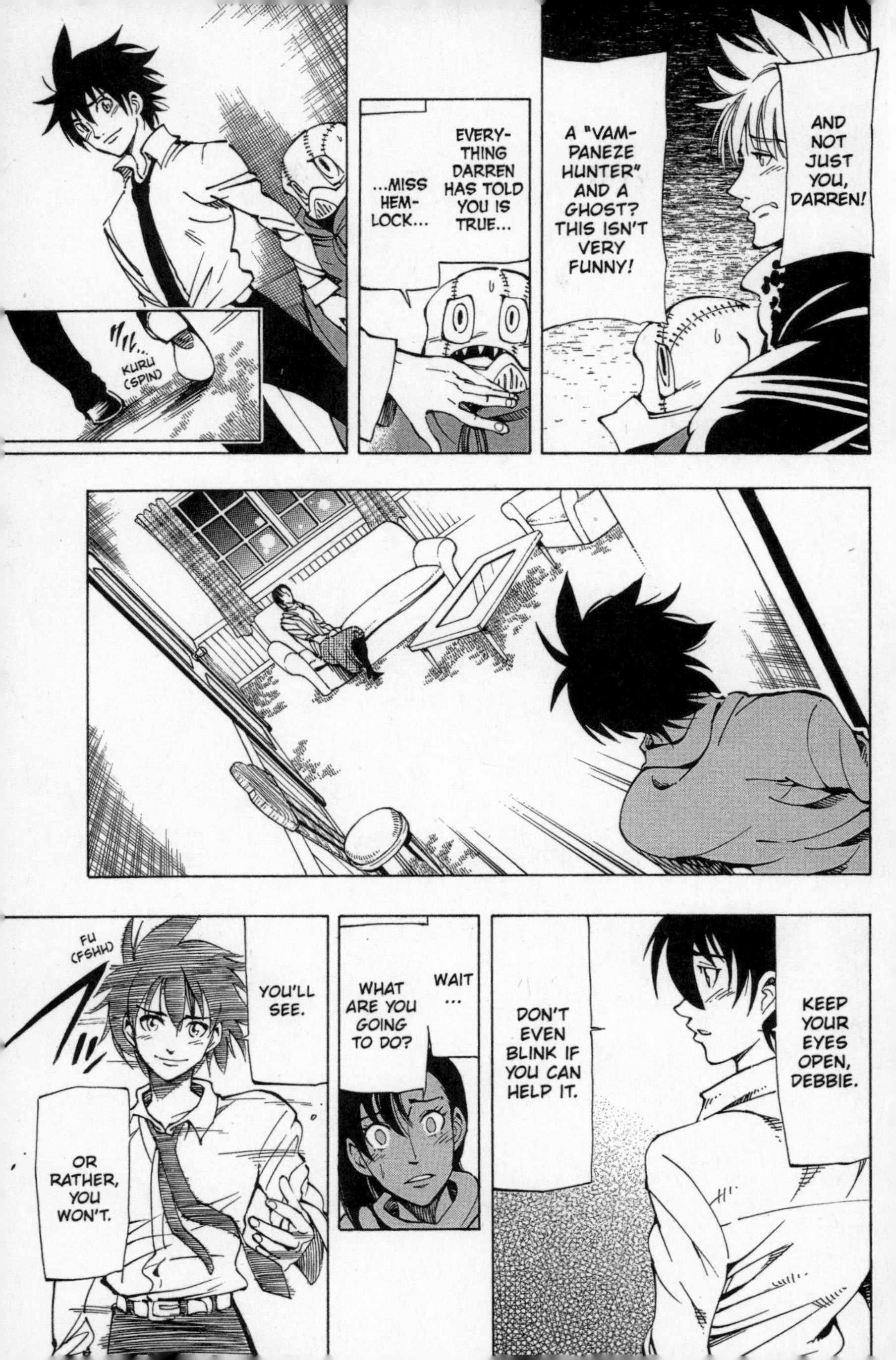
AND NOT JUST YOU, DARREN!
A "VAMPANEZE HUNTER" AND A GHOST? THIS ISN'T VERY FUNNY!
EVERYTHING DARREN HAS TOLD YOU IS TRUE...
...MISS HEMLOCK...
KURU (SPIN)
KEEP YOUR EYES OPEN, DEBBIE.
DON'T EVEN BLINK IF YOU CAN HELP IT.
WAIT ...
WHAT ARE YOU GOING TO DO?
YOU'LL SEE.
FU (FSHH)
OR RATHER, YOU WON'T.

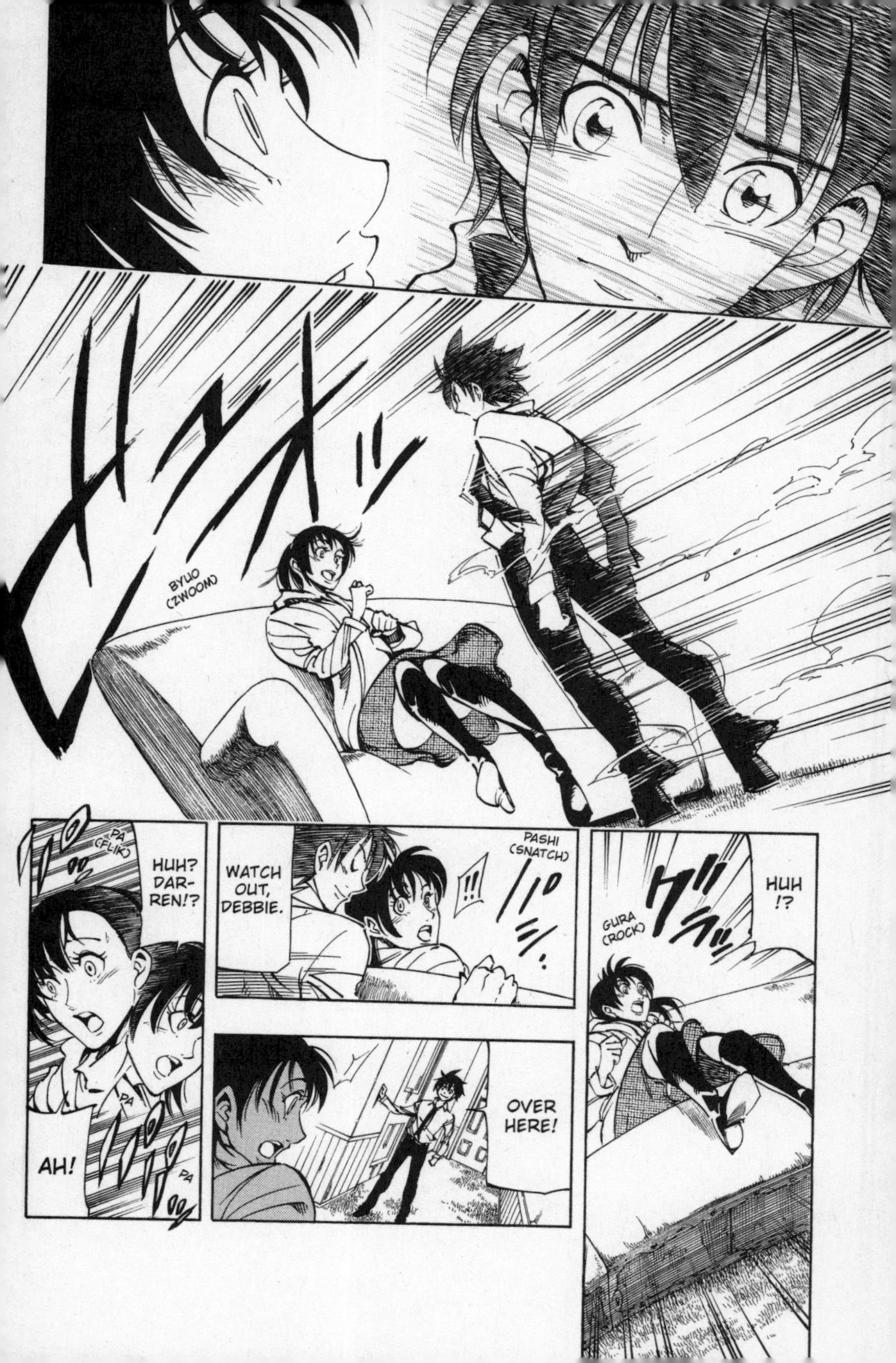
BYUO
(ZWOOM)
HUH
!?
GURA
(ROCK)
PASHI
(SNATCH)
WATCH
OUT,
DEBBIE.
!!!
OVER
HERE!
PA
(FLIK)
HUH?
DAR-
REN!?
PA
AH!
PA

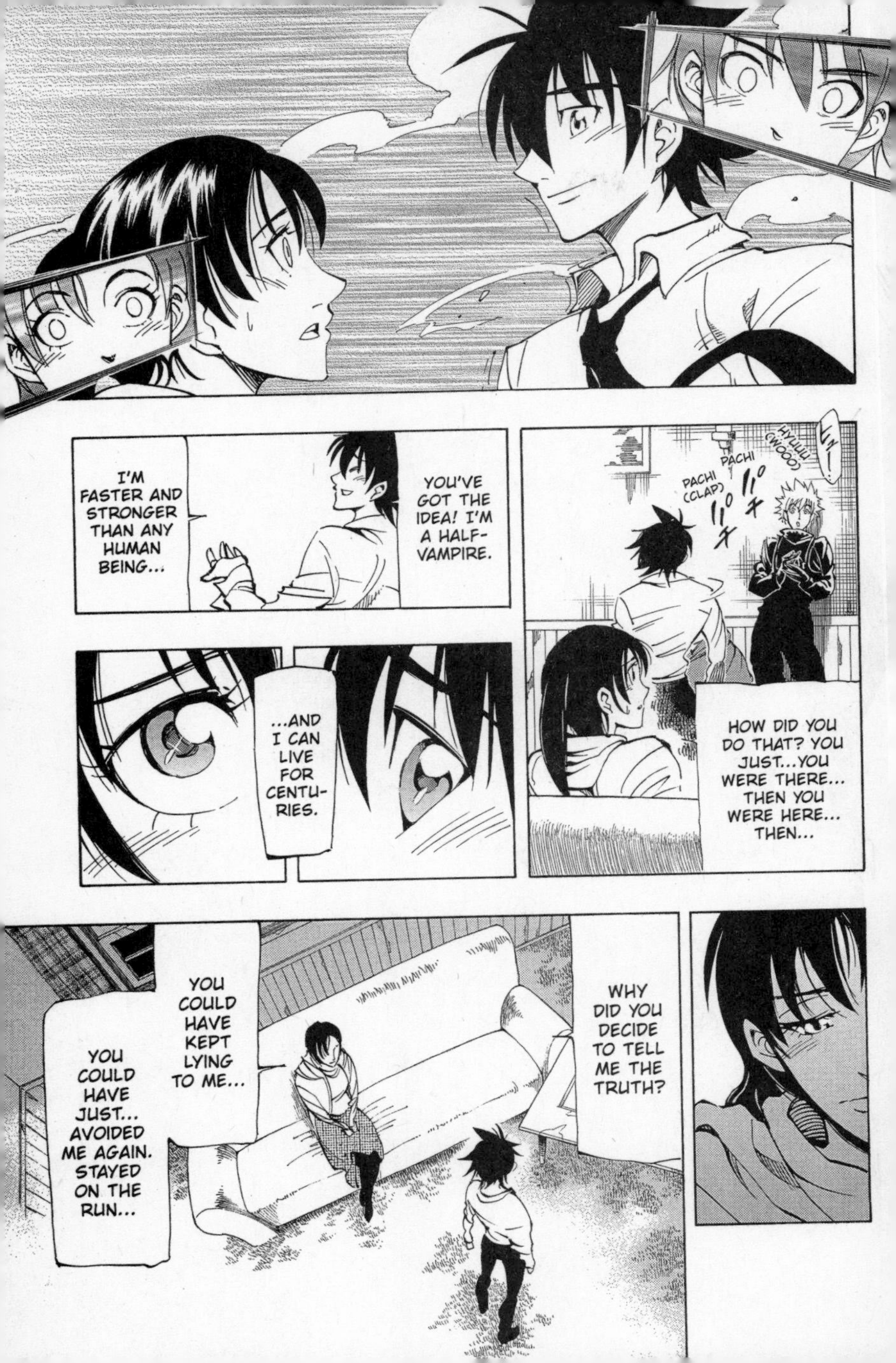
HYUUU (WOOO)
PACHI
PACHI (CLAP)
HOW DID YOU DO THAT? YOU JUST...YOU WERE THERE... THEN YOU WERE HERE... THEN...
YOU'VE GOT THE IDEA! I'M A HALF-VAMPIRE.
I'M FASTER AND STRONGER THAN ANY HUMAN BEING...
...AND I CAN LIVE FOR CENTURIES.
WHY DID YOU DECIDE TO TELL ME THE TRUTH?
YOU COULD HAVE KEPT LYING TO ME...
YOU COULD HAVE JUST... AVOIDED ME AGAIN. STAYED ON THE RUN...

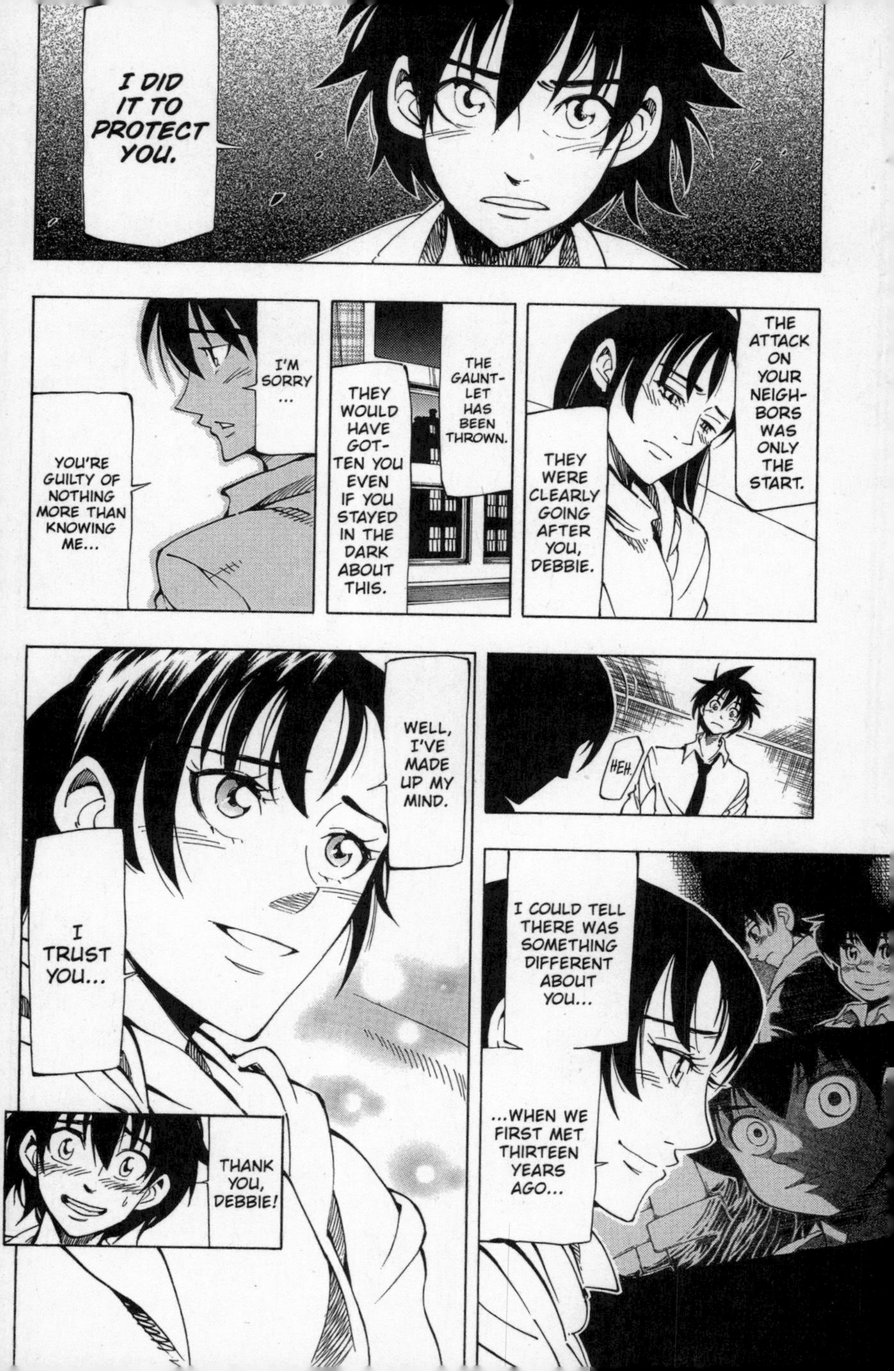
I DID IT TO PROTECT YOU.
THE ATTACK ON YOUR NEIGHBORS WAS ONLY THE START.
THEY WERE CLEARLY GOING AFTER YOU, DEBBIE.
THE GAUNTLET HAS BEEN THROWN.
THEY WOULD HAVE GOTTEN YOU EVEN IF YOU STAYED IN THE DARK ABOUT THIS.
I'M SORRY...
YOU'RE GUILTY OF NOTHING MORE THAN KNOWING ME...
HEH.
I COULD TELL THERE WAS SOMETHING DIFFERENT ABOUT YOU...
...WHEN WE FIRST MET THIRTEEN YEARS AGO...
WELL, I'VE MADE UP MY MIND.
I TRUST YOU...
THANK YOU, DEBBIE!

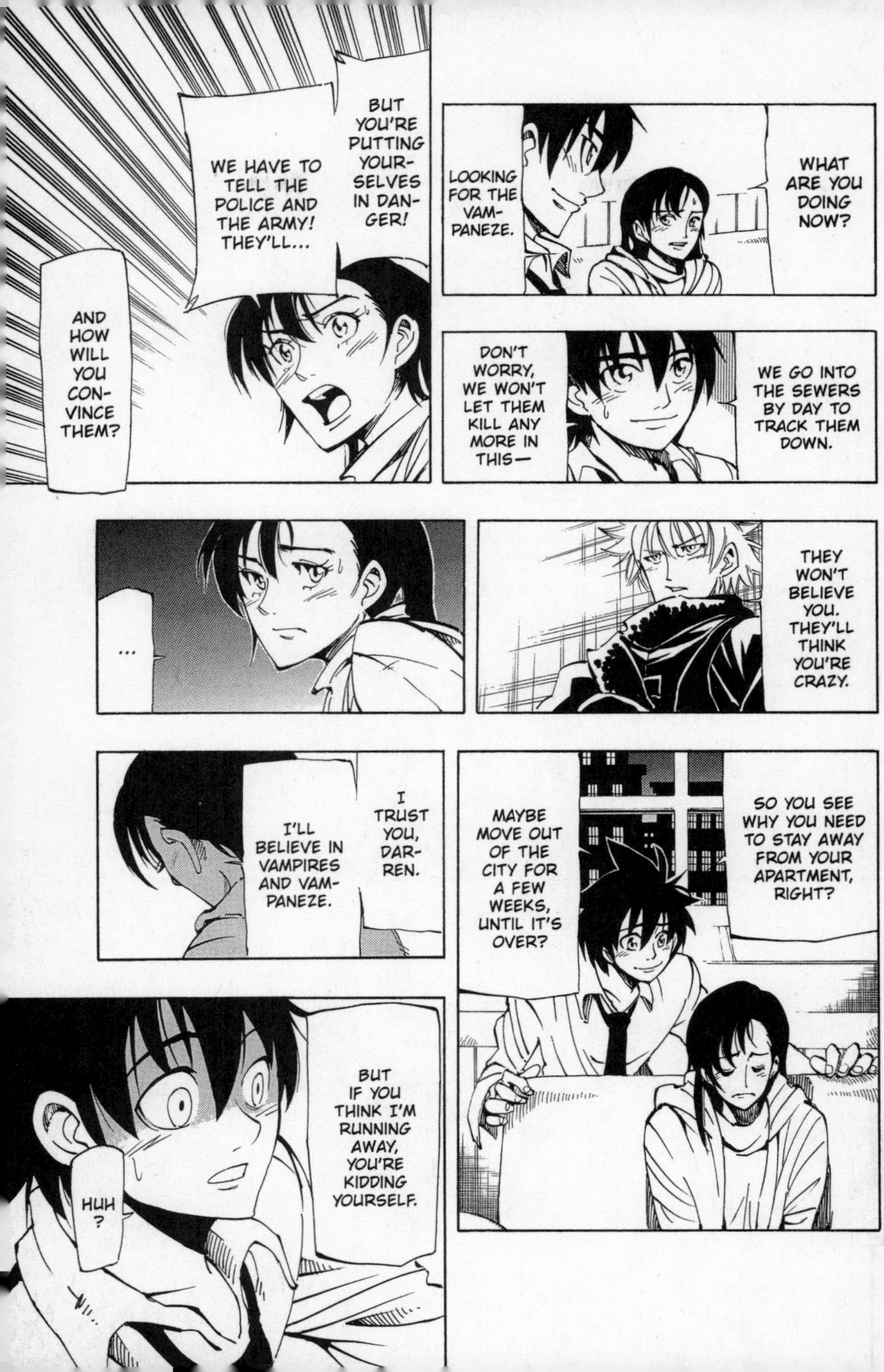
WHAT ARE YOU DOING NOW?
LOOKING FOR THE VAMPANEZE.
WE GO INTO THE SEWERS BY DAY TO TRACK THEM DOWN.
DON'T WORRY, WE WON'T LET THEM KILL ANY MORE IN THIS—
BUT YOU'RE PUTTING YOURSELVES IN DANGER!
WE HAVE TO TELL THE POLICE AND THE ARMY! THEY'LL...
AND HOW WILL YOU CONVINCE THEM?
THEY WON'T BELIEVE YOU. THEY'LL THINK YOU'RE CRAZY.
...
SO YOU SEE WHY YOU NEED TO STAY AWAY FROM YOUR APARTMENT, RIGHT?
MAYBE MOVE OUT OF THE CITY FOR A FEW WEEKS, UNTIL IT'S OVER?
I TRUST YOU, DARREN.
I'LL BELIEVE IN VAMPIRES AND VAMPANEZE.
BUT IF YOU THINK I'M RUNNING AWAY, YOU'RE KIDDING YOURSELF.
HUH?

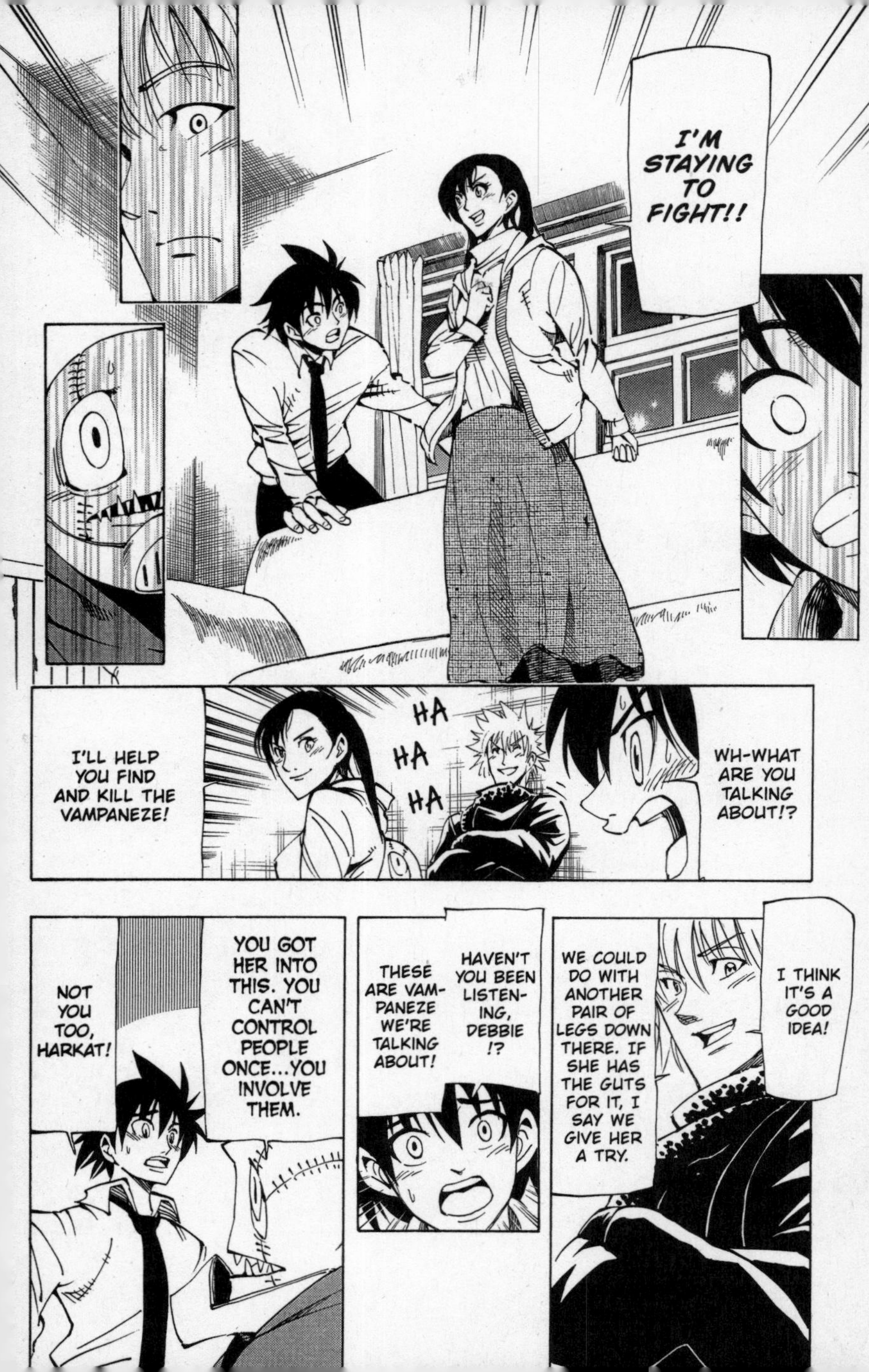
I'M STAYING TO FIGHT!!
WH-WHAT ARE YOU TALKING ABOUT!?
HA HA HA
I'LL HELP YOU FIND AND KILL THE VAMPANEZE!
I THINK IT'S A GOOD IDEA!
WE COULD DO WITH ANOTHER PAIR OF LEGS DOWN THERE. IF SHE HAS THE GUTS FOR IT, I SAY WE GIVE HER A TRY.
HAVEN'T YOU BEEN LISTEN-ING, DEBBIE!?
THESE ARE VAM-PANEZE WE'RE TALKING ABOUT!
YOU GOT HER INTO THIS. YOU CAN'T CONTROL PEOPLE ONCE...YOU INVOLVE THEM.
NOT YOU TOO, HARKAT!

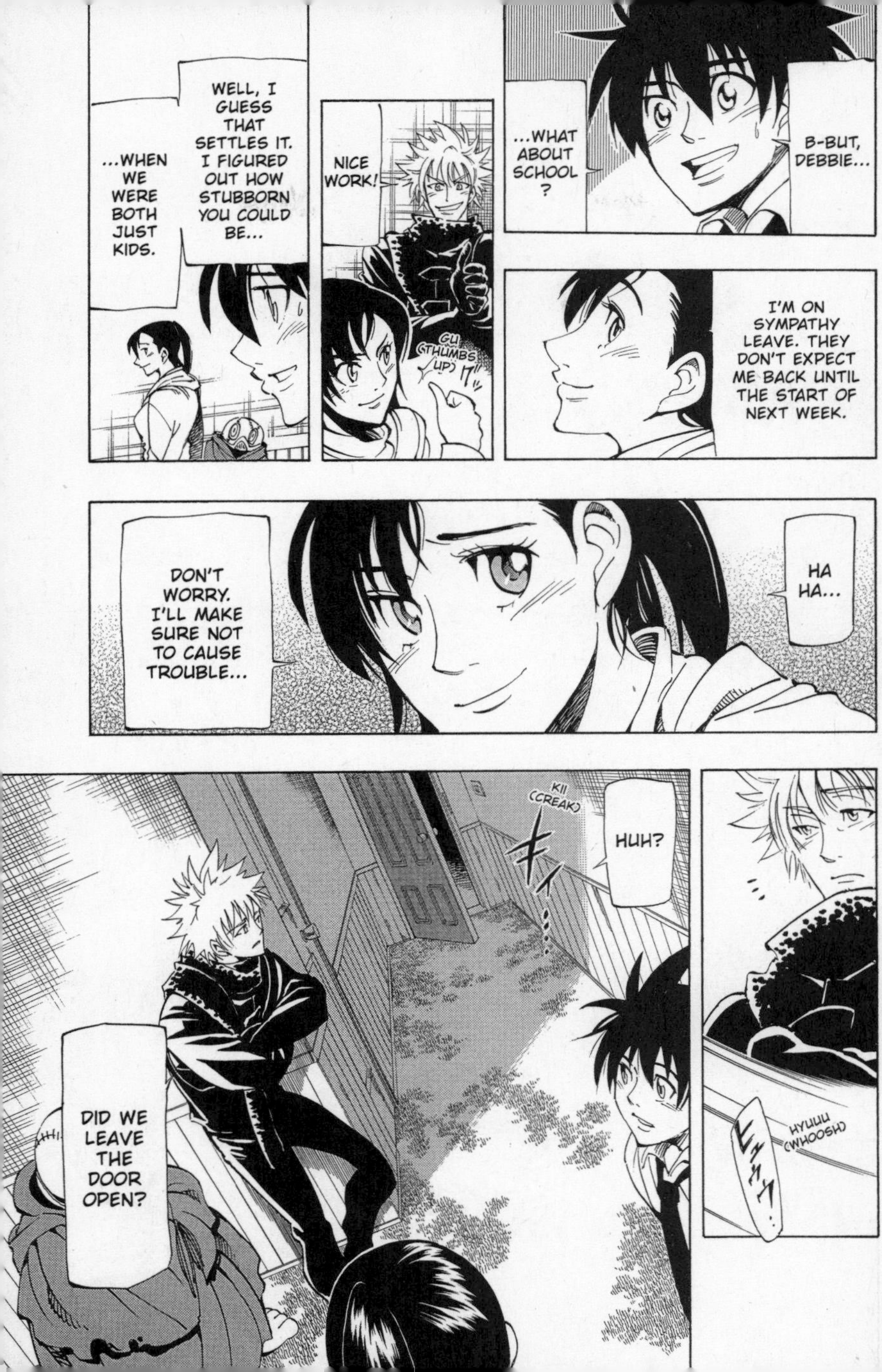
B-BUT, DEBBIE...
...WHAT ABOUT SCHOOL?
I'M ON SYMPATHY LEAVE. THEY DON'T EXPECT ME BACK UNTIL THE START OF NEXT WEEK.
NICE WORK!
GU (THUMBS UP)
WELL, I GUESS THAT SETTLES IT. I FIGURED OUT HOW STUBBORN YOU COULD BE...
...WHEN WE WERE BOTH JUST KIDS.
HA HA...
DON'T WORRY. I'LL MAKE SURE NOT TO CAUSE TROUBLE...
HYUUU (WHOOSH)
KII (CREAK)
HUH?
DID WE LEAVE THE DOOR OPEN?

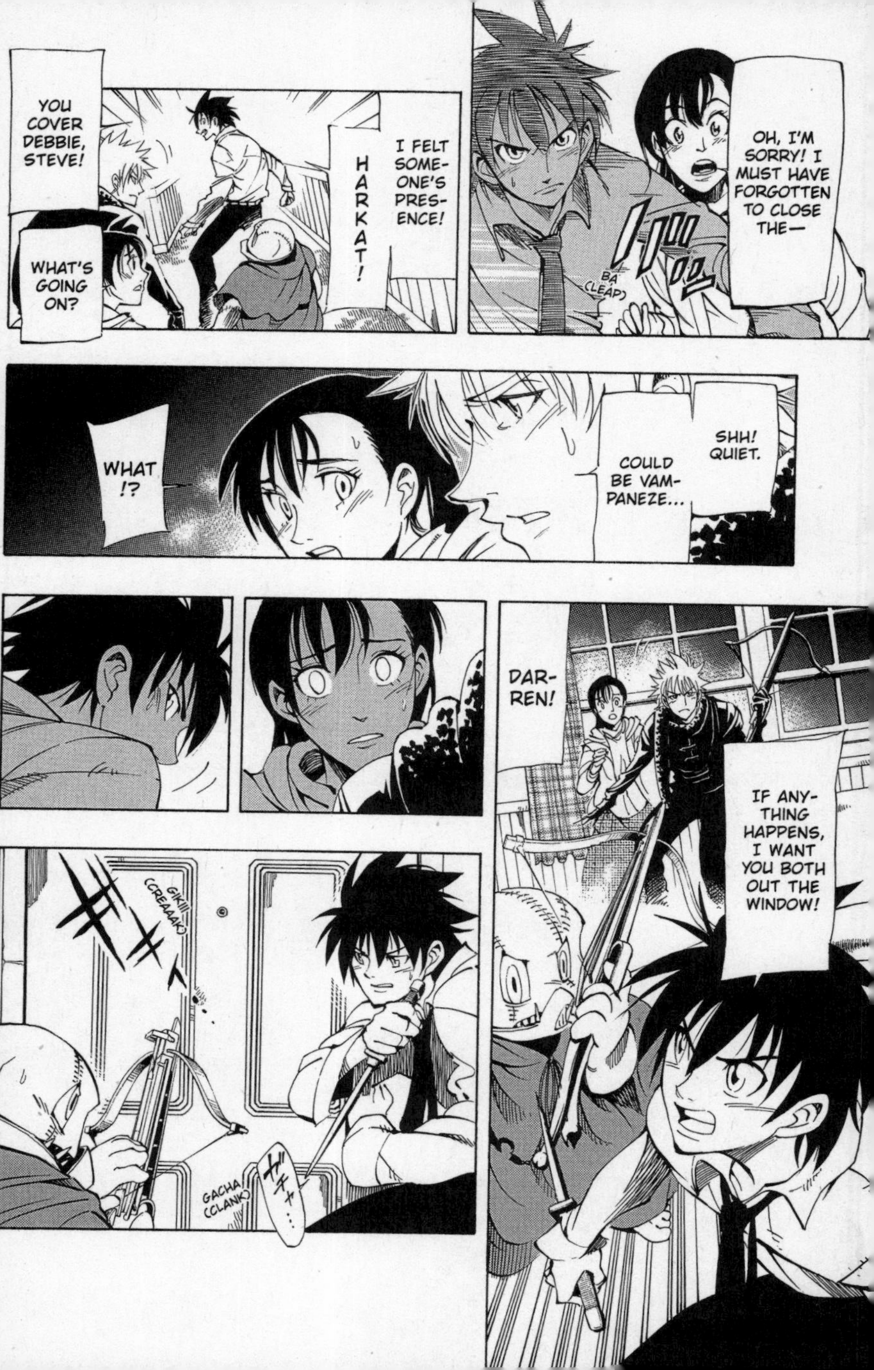
OH, I'M SORRY! I MUST HAVE FORGOTTEN TO CLOSE THE—
BA (LEAP)
I FELT SOME-ONE'S PRES-ENCE!
HARKAT!
YOU COVER DEBBIE, STEVE!
WHAT'S GOING ON?
SHH! QUIET.
COULD BE VAM-PANEZE...
WHAT !?
DAR-REN!
IF ANY-THING HAPPENS, I WANT YOU BOTH OUT THE WINDOW!
GIKIII (CREAAAK)
GACHA (CLANK)

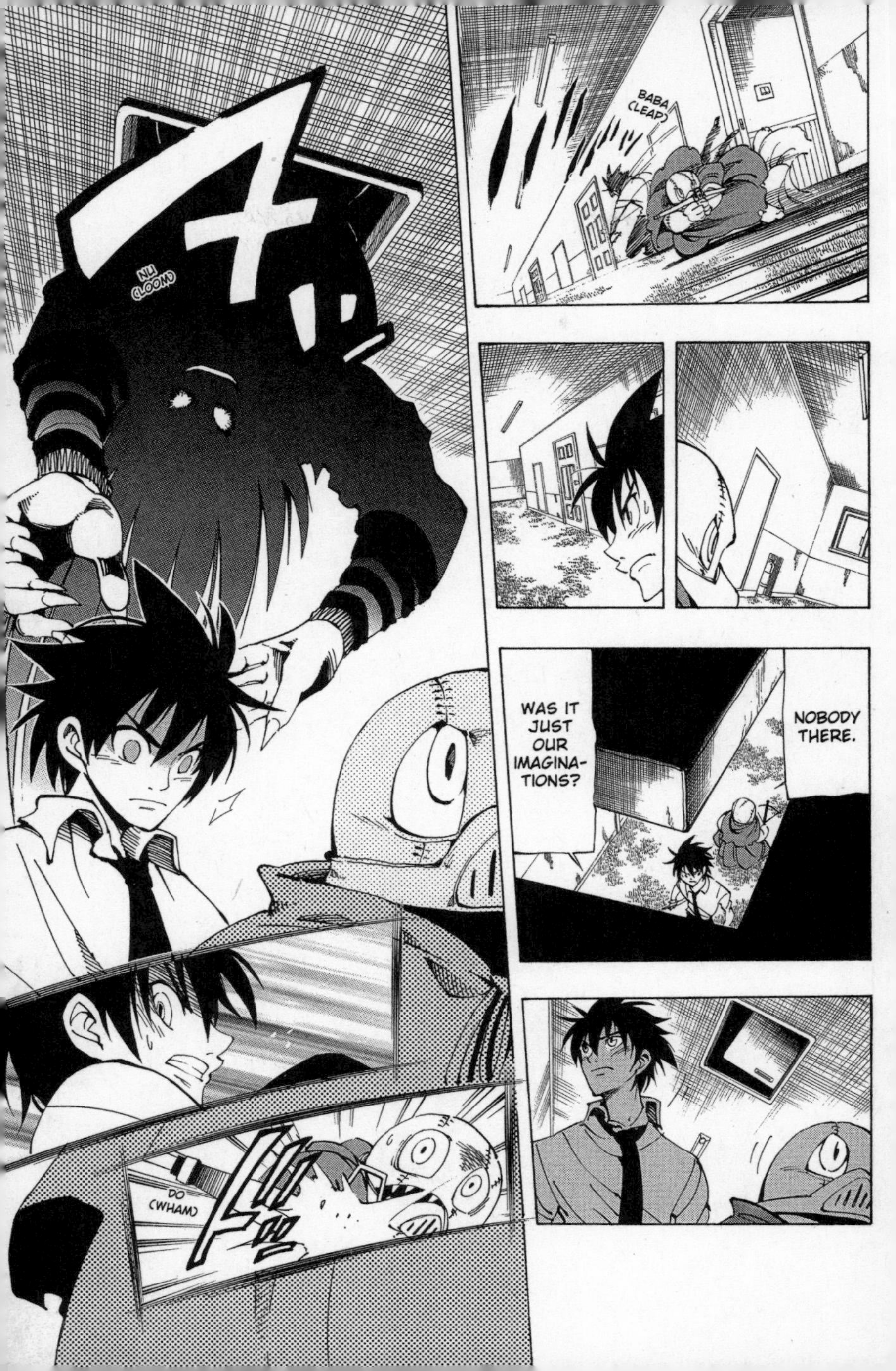
BABA (LEAP)
NOBODY THERE.
WAS IT JUST OUR IMAGINATIONS?
NU (LOOM)
DO (WHAM)

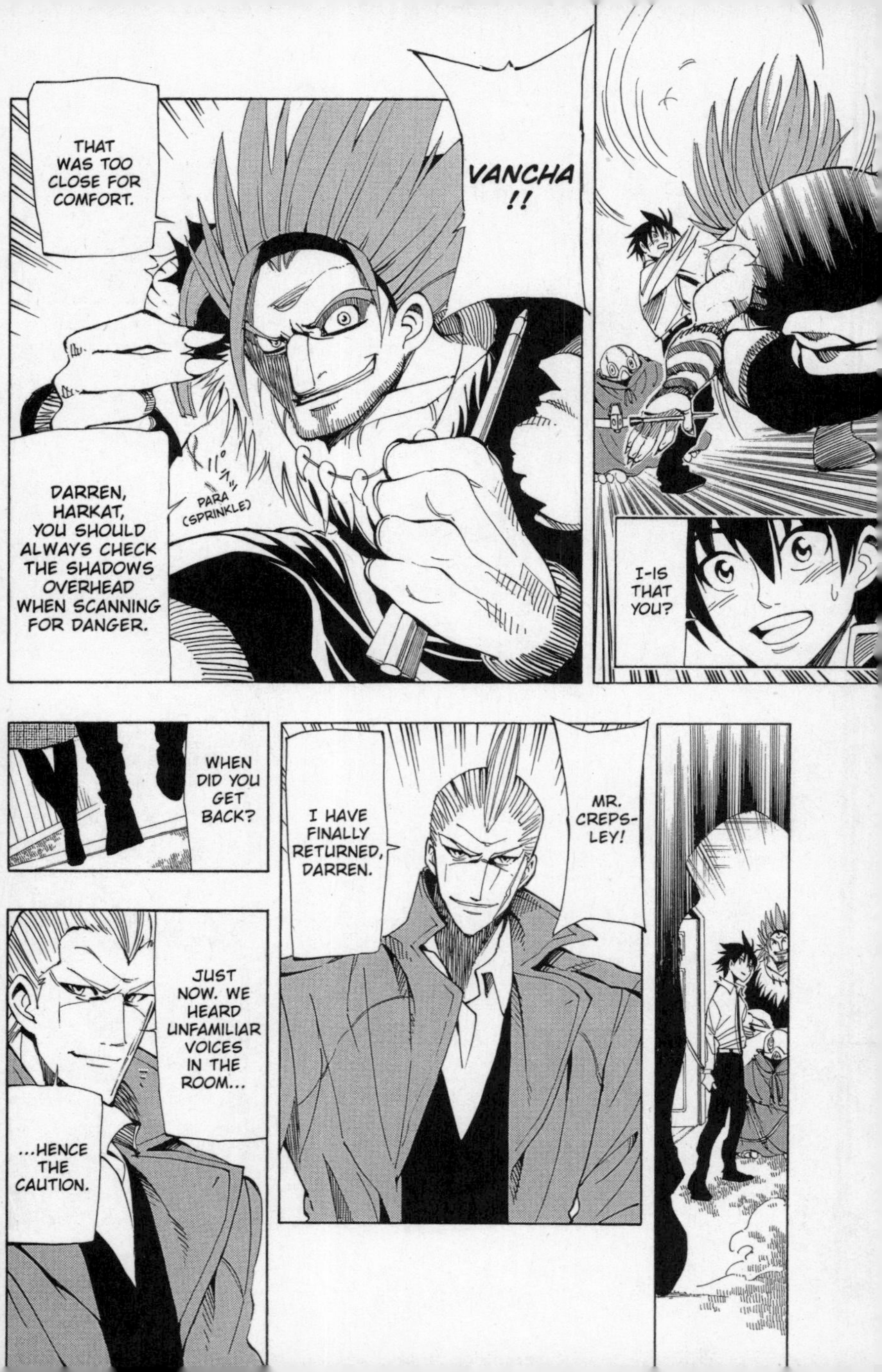
VANCHA!!
I-IS THAT YOU?
THAT WAS TOO CLOSE FOR COMFORT.
PARA (SPRINKLE)
DARREN, HARKAT, YOU SHOULD ALWAYS CHECK THE SHADOWS OVERHEAD WHEN SCANNING FOR DANGER.
MR. CREPSLEY!
I HAVE FINALLY RETURNED, DARREN.
WHEN DID YOU GET BACK?
JUST NOW. WE HEARD UNFAMILIAR VOICES IN THE ROOM...
...HENCE THE CAUTION.

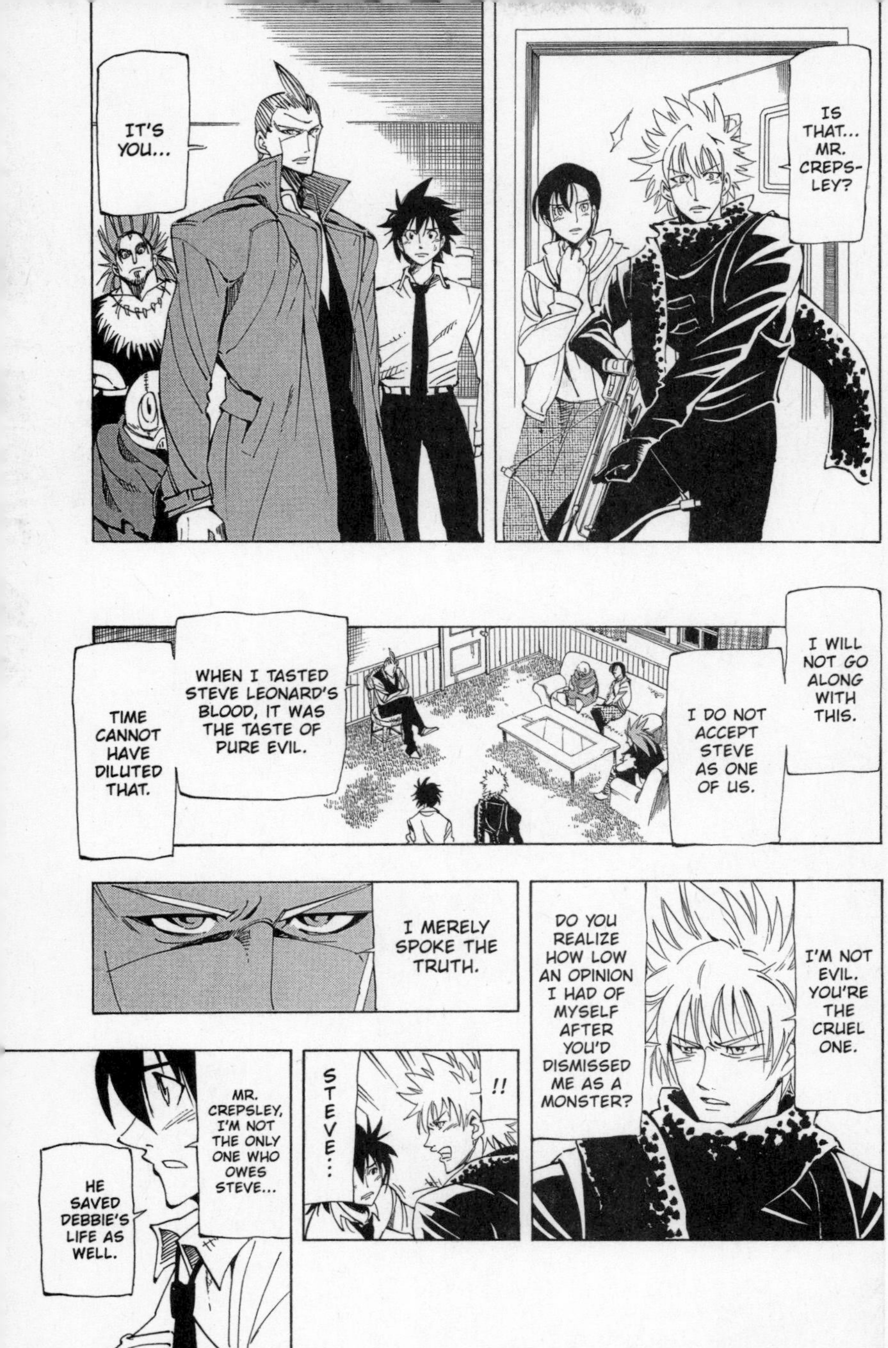
IS THAT... MR. CREPSLEY?
IT'S YOU...
I WILL NOT GO ALONG WITH THIS.
I DO NOT ACCEPT STEVE AS ONE OF US.
WHEN I TASTED STEVE LEONARD'S BLOOD, IT WAS THE TASTE OF PURE EVIL.
TIME CANNOT HAVE DILUTED THAT.
I'M NOT EVIL. YOU'RE THE CRUEL ONE.
DO YOU REALIZE HOW LOW AN OPINION I HAD OF MYSELF AFTER YOU'D DISMISSED ME AS A MONSTER?
I MERELY SPOKE THE TRUTH.
!!
STEVE...
MR. CREPSLEY, I'M NOT THE ONLY ONE WHO OWES STEVE...
HE SAVED DEBBIE'S LIFE AS WELL.

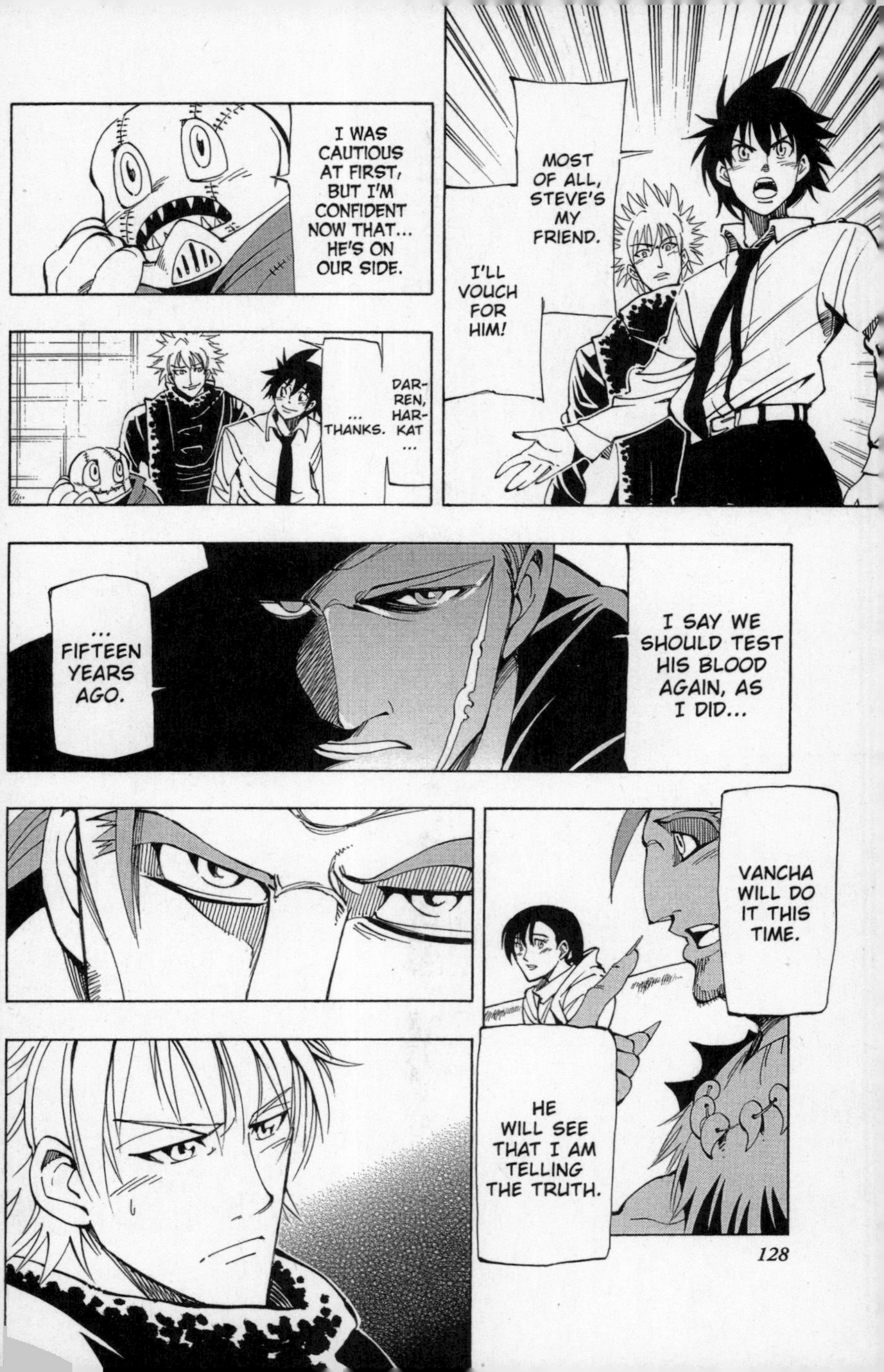
MOST OF ALL, STEVE'S MY FRIEND.
I'LL VOUCH FOR HIM!
I WAS CAUTIOUS AT FIRST, BUT I'M CONFIDENT NOW THAT... HE'S ON OUR SIDE.
DARREN, HARKAT...
...THANKS.
I SAY WE SHOULD TEST HIS BLOOD AGAIN, AS I DID...
...FIFTEEN YEARS AGO.
VANCHA WILL DO IT THIS TIME.
HE WILL SEE THAT I AM TELLING THE TRUTH.

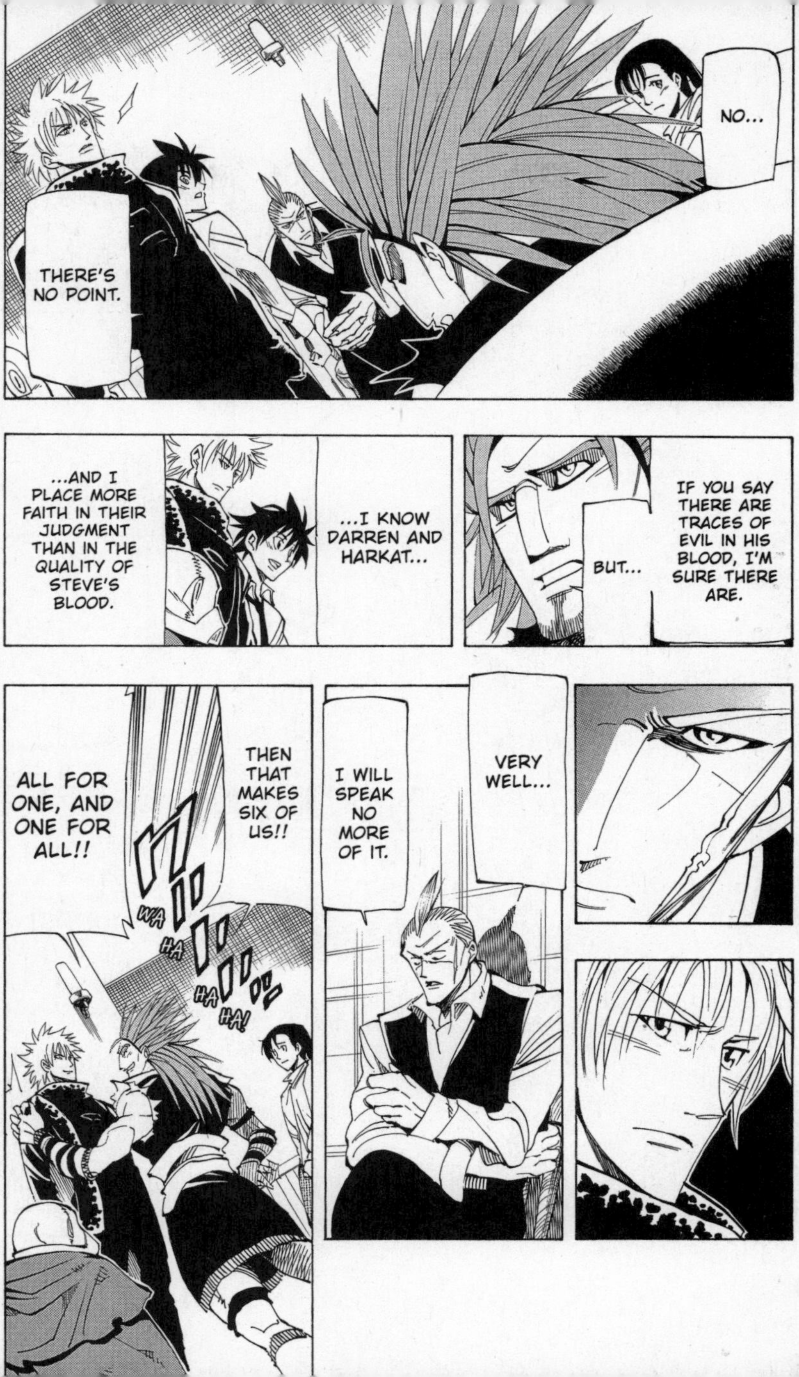
NO...
THERE'S NO POINT.
IF YOU SAY THERE ARE TRACES OF EVIL IN HIS BLOOD, I'M SURE THERE ARE.
BUT...
...I KNOW DARREN AND HARKAT...
...AND I PLACE MORE FAITH IN THEIR JUDGMENT THAN IN THE QUALITY OF STEVE'S BLOOD.
VERY WELL...
I WILL SPEAK NO MORE OF IT.
THEN THAT MAKES SIX OF US!!
ALL FOR ONE, AND ONE FOR ALL!!
WA HA HA HA!

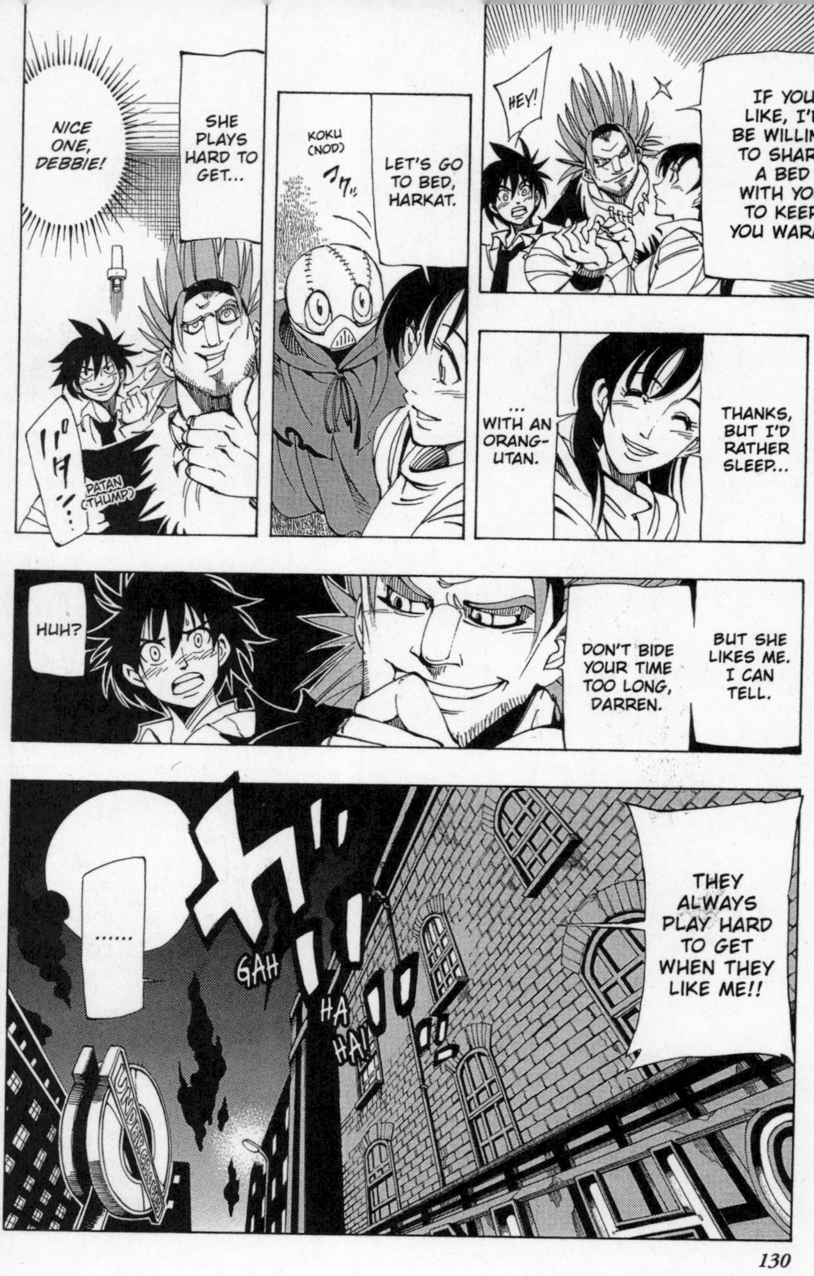
IF YOU LIKE, I'D BE WILLING TO SHARE A BED WITH YOU TO KEEP YOU WARM!
HEY!
THANKS, BUT I'D RATHER SLEEP...
... WITH AN ORANG-UTAN.
LET'S GO TO BED, HARKAT.
KOKU (NOD)
SHE PLAYS HARD TO GET...
NICE ONE, DEBBIE!
PATAN (THUMP)
BUT SHE LIKES ME. I CAN TELL.
DON'T BIDE YOUR TIME TOO LONG, DARREN.
HUH?
THEY ALWAYS PLAY HARD TO GET WHEN THEY LIKE ME!!
GAH HA HA!
......

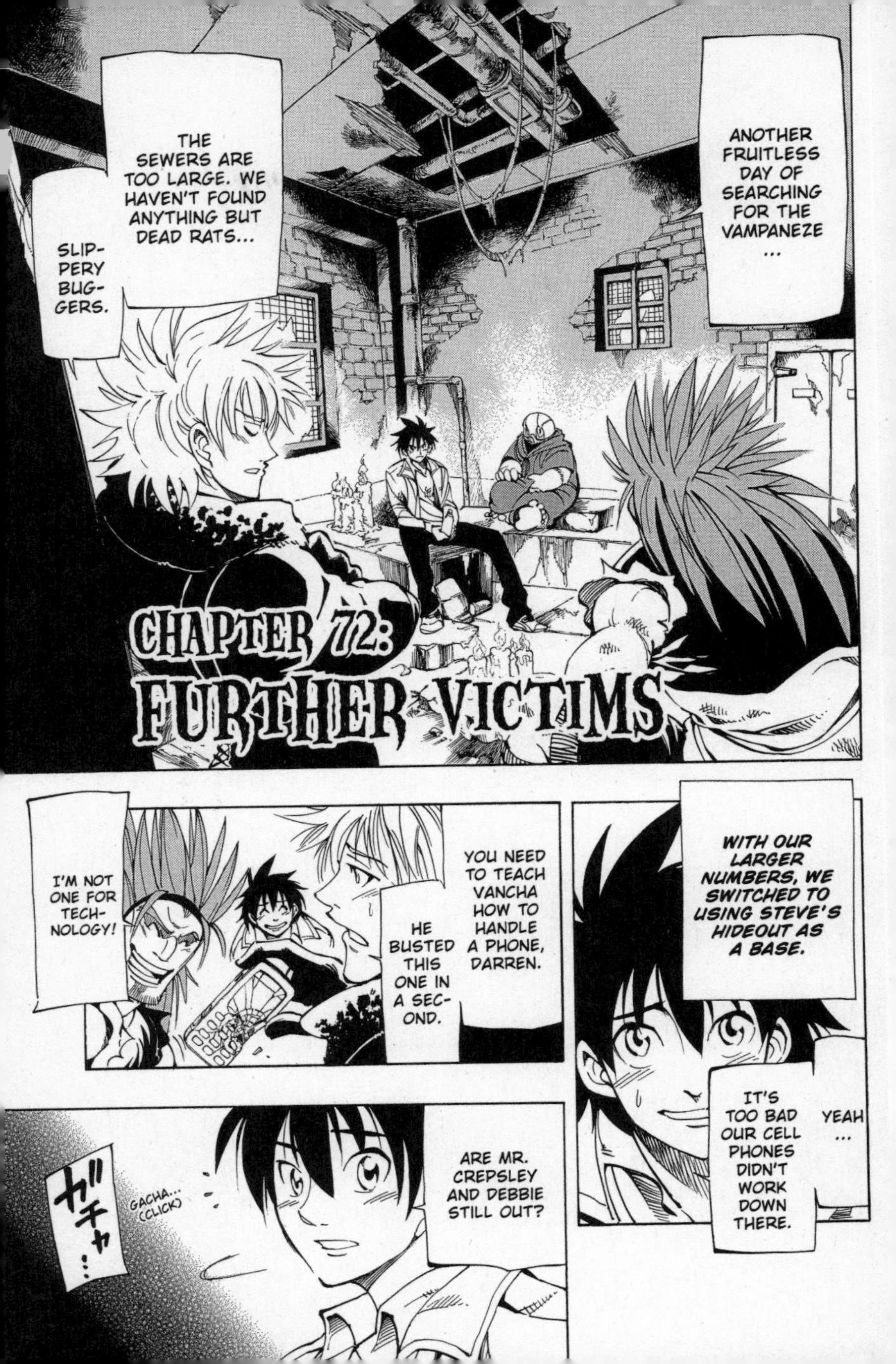
ANOTHER FRUITLESS DAY OF SEARCHING FOR THE VAMPANEZE …
THE SEWERS ARE TOO LARGE. WE HAVEN'T FOUND ANYTHING BUT DEAD RATS…
SLIPPERY BUGGERS.
CHAPTER 72: FURTHER VICTIMS
WITH OUR LARGER NUMBERS, WE SWITCHED TO USING STEVE'S HIDEOUT AS A BASE.
YEAH …
IT'S TOO BAD OUR CELL PHONES DIDN'T WORK DOWN THERE.
YOU NEED TO TEACH VANCHA HOW TO HANDLE A PHONE, DARREN.
HE BUSTED THIS ONE IN A SECOND.
I'M NOT ONE FOR TECHNOLOGY!
ARE MR. CREPSLEY AND DEBBIE STILL OUT?
GACHA… (CLICK)
ガチャ…

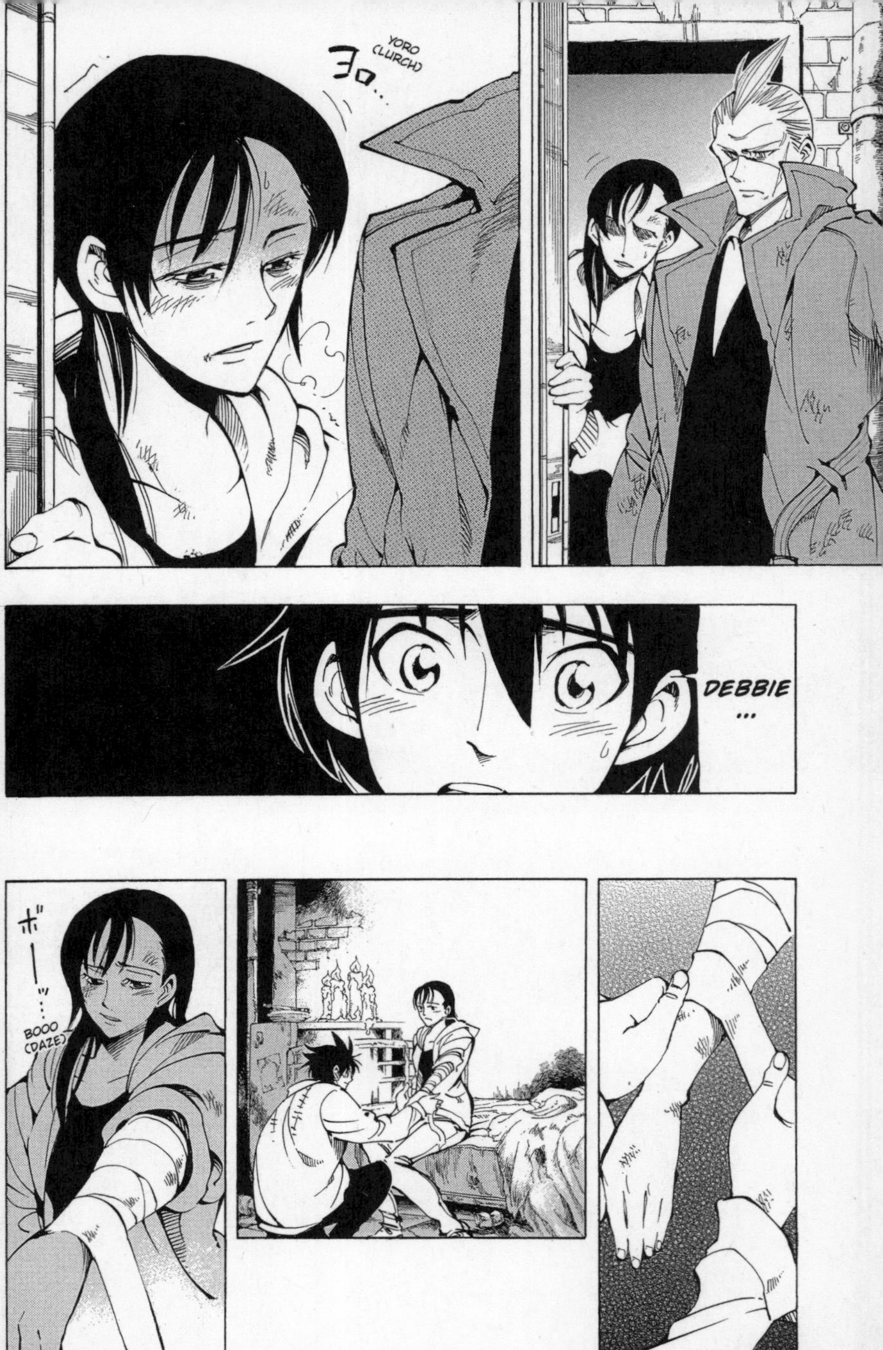
YORO (LURCH)
ヨロ…
DEBBIE ...
ボーッ…
BOOO (DAZE)

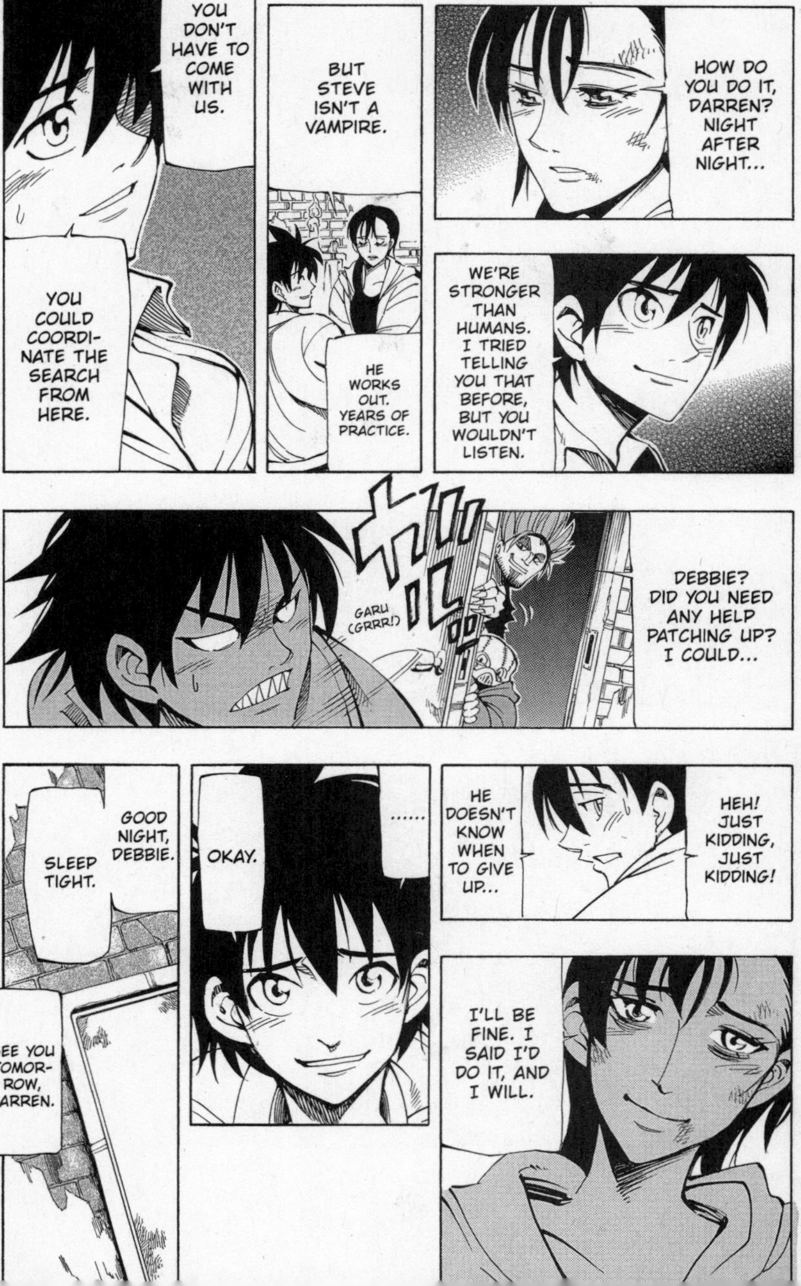
HOW DO YOU DO IT, DARREN? NIGHT AFTER NIGHT...
WE'RE STRONGER THAN HUMANS. I TRIED TELLING YOU THAT BEFORE, BUT YOU WOULDN'T LISTEN.
BUT STEVE ISN'T A VAMPIRE.
HE WORKS OUT. YEARS OF PRACTICE.
YOU DON'T HAVE TO COME WITH US.
YOU COULD COORDINATE THE SEARCH FROM HERE.
DEBBIE? DID YOU NEED ANY HELP PATCHING UP? I COULD...
GARU (GRRR!)
HEH! JUST KIDDING, JUST KIDDING!
HE DOESN'T KNOW WHEN TO GIVE UP...
I'LL BE FINE. I SAID I'D DO IT, AND I WILL.
......
OKAY.
GOOD NIGHT, DEBBIE.
SLEEP TIGHT.
SEE YOU TOMORROW, DARREN.

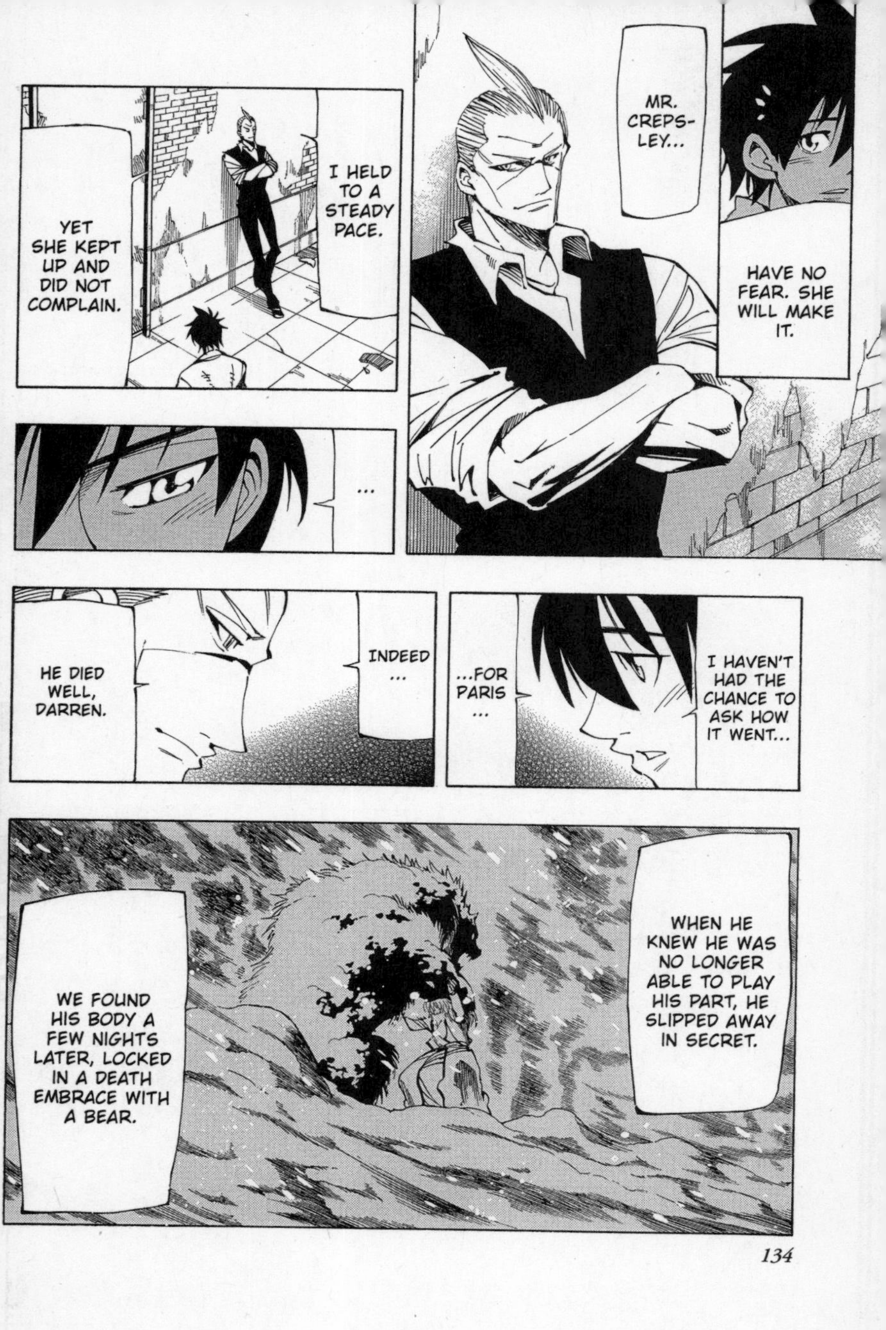
MR. CREPSLEY...
HAVE NO FEAR. SHE WILL MAKE IT.
I HELD TO A STEADY PACE.
YET SHE KEPT UP AND DID NOT COMPLAIN.
...
I HAVEN'T HAD THE CHANCE TO ASK HOW IT WENT...
...FOR PARIS...
INDEED...
HE DIED WELL, DARREN.
WHEN HE KNEW HE WAS NO LONGER ABLE TO PLAY HIS PART, HE SLIPPED AWAY IN SECRET.
WE FOUND HIS BODY A FEW NIGHTS LATER, LOCKED IN A DEATH EMBRACE WITH A BEAR.

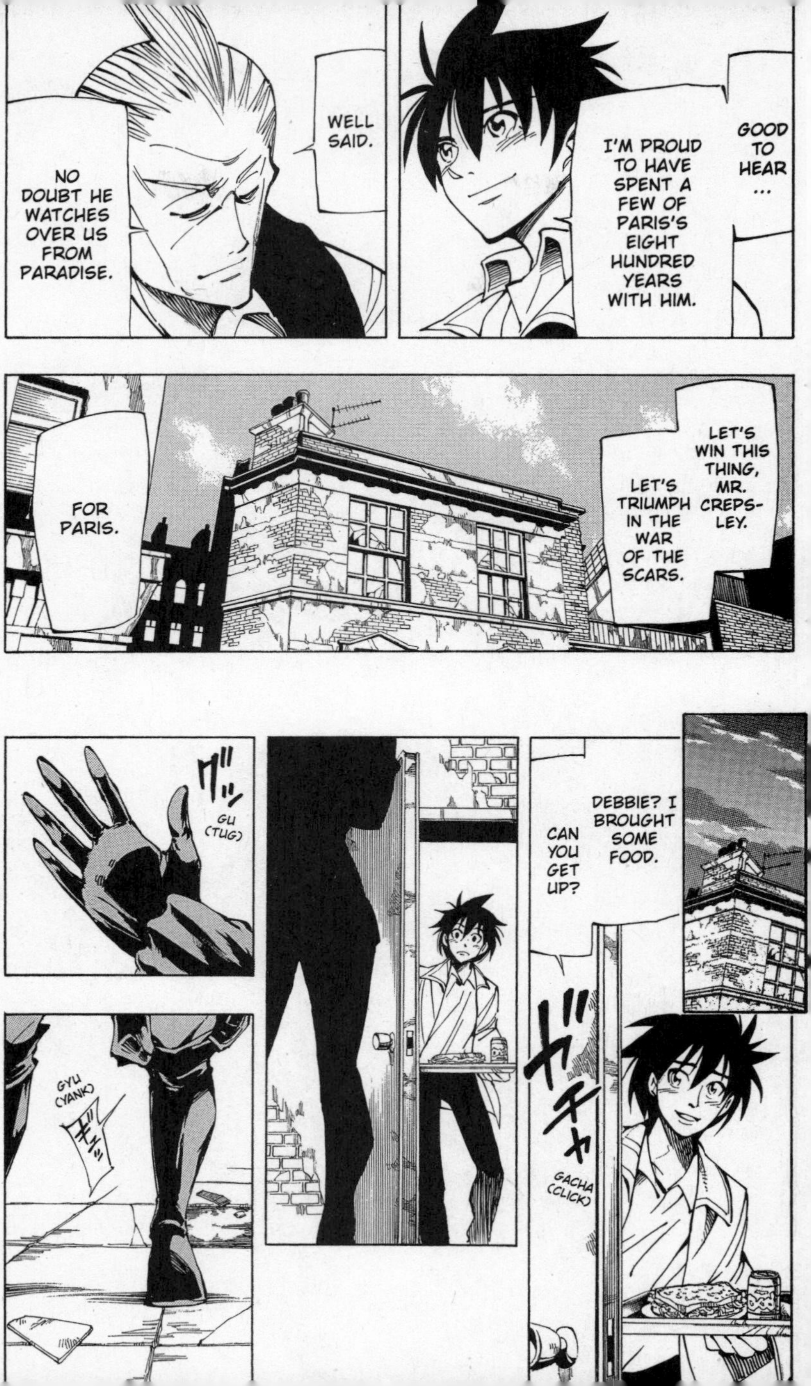
GOOD TO HEAR ...
I'M PROUD TO HAVE SPENT A FEW OF PARIS'S EIGHT HUNDRED YEARS WITH HIM.
WELL SAID.
NO DOUBT HE WATCHES OVER US FROM PARADISE.
LET'S WIN THIS THING, MR. CREPS-LEY.
LET'S TRIUMPH IN THE WAR OF THE SCARS.
FOR PARIS.
DEBBIE? I BROUGHT SOME FOOD.
CAN YOU GET UP?
ガチャ
GACHA (CLICK)
グッ
GU (TUG)
GYU (YANK)
ギュッ

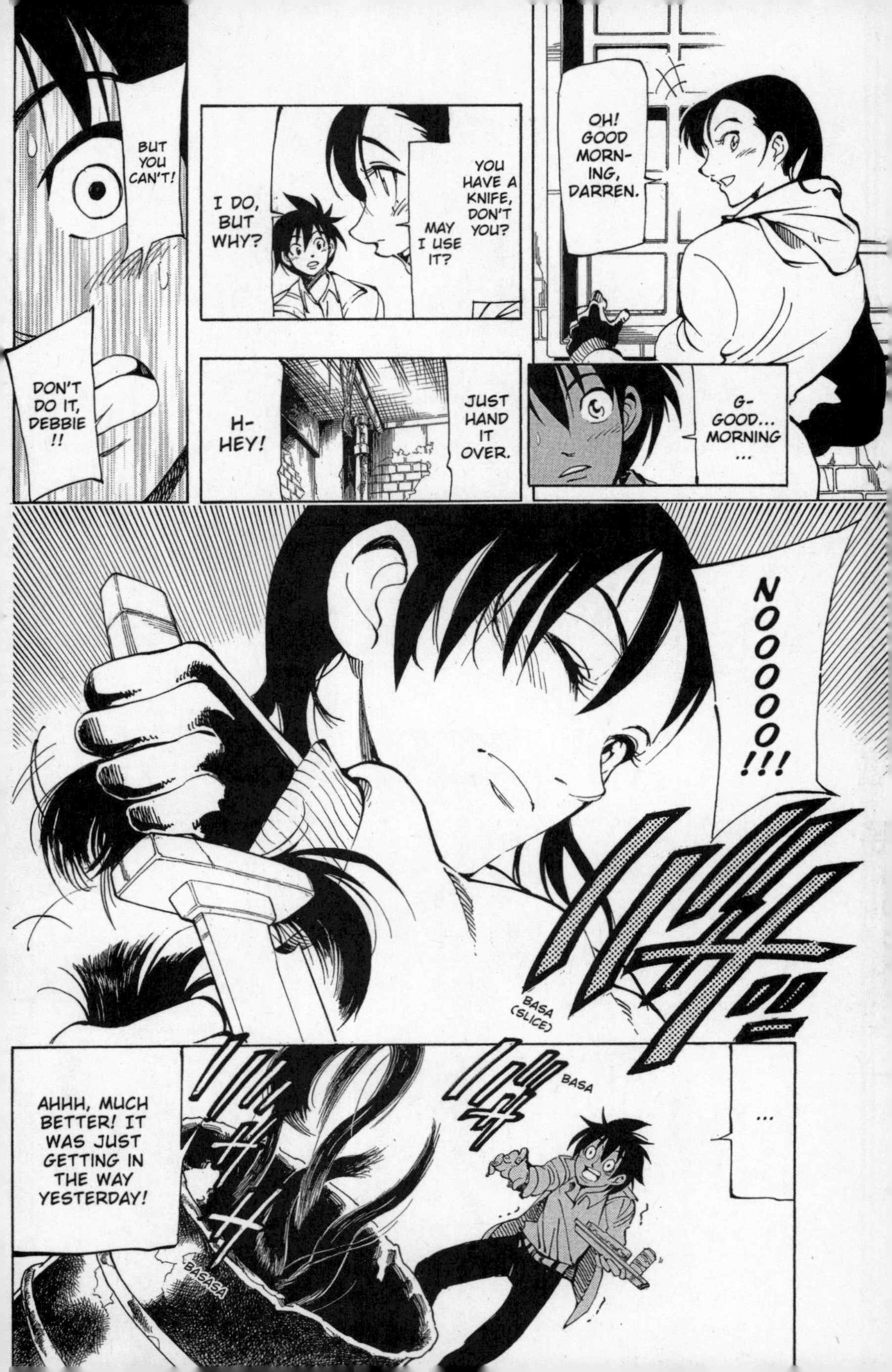
OH! GOOD MORNING, DARREN.
G-GOOD... MORNING...
YOU HAVE A KNIFE, DON'T YOU?
MAY I USE IT?
I DO, BUT WHY?
JUST HAND IT OVER.
H-HEY!
BUT YOU CAN'T!
DON'T DO IT, DEBBIE!!
NOOOOOO!!!
BASA (SLICE)
...
BASA
AHHH, MUCH BETTER! IT WAS JUST GETTING IN THE WAY YESTERDAY!
BASASA

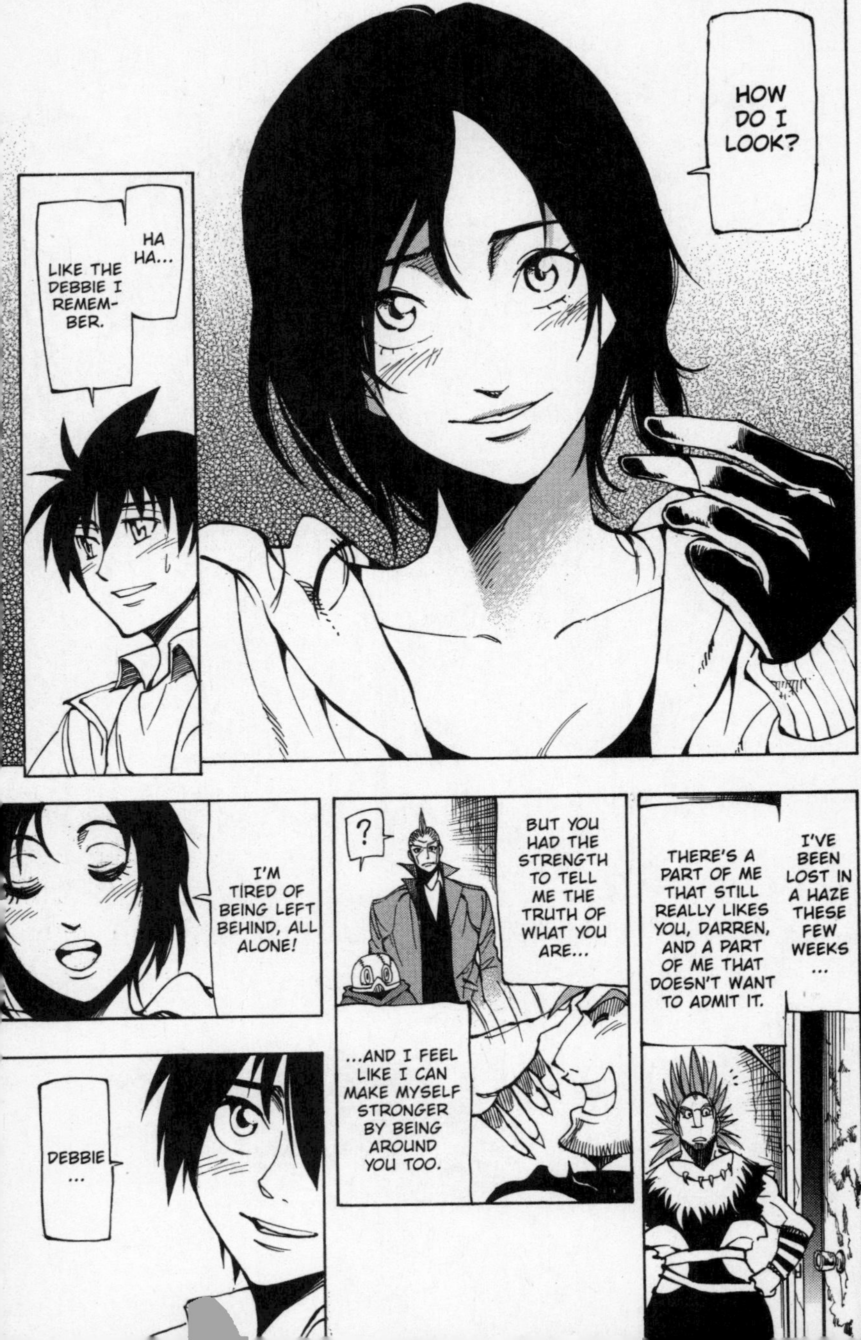
HOW DO I LOOK?
HA HA...
LIKE THE DEBBIE I REMEMBER.
I'VE BEEN LOST IN A HAZE THESE FEW WEEKS ...
THERE'S A PART OF ME THAT STILL REALLY LIKES YOU, DARREN, AND A PART OF ME THAT DOESN'T WANT TO ADMIT IT.
BUT YOU HAD THE STRENGTH TO TELL ME THE TRUTH OF WHAT YOU ARE...
?
...AND I FEEL LIKE I CAN MAKE MYSELF STRONGER BY BEING AROUND YOU TOO.
I'M TIRED OF BEING LEFT BEHIND, ALL ALONE!
DEBBIE ...

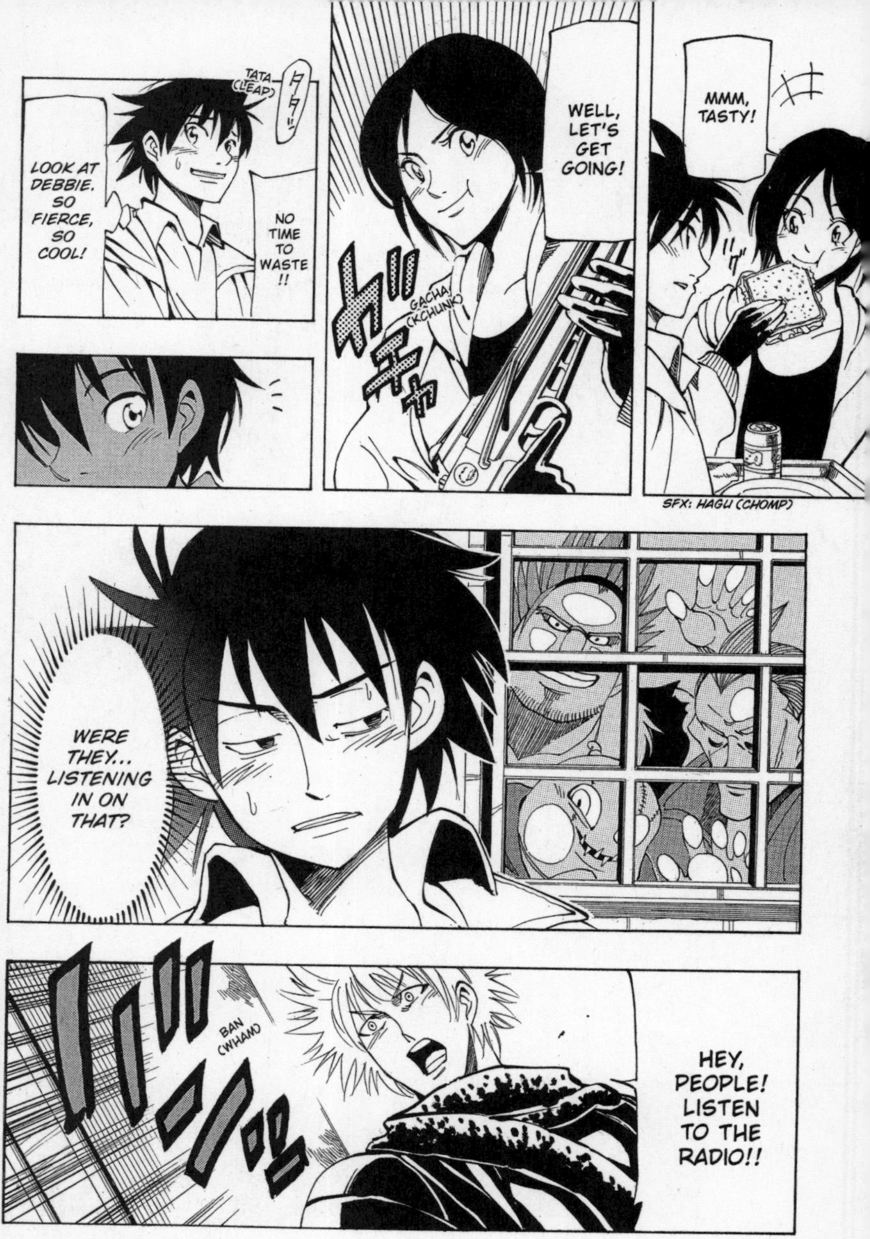
MMM, TASTY!
SFX: HAGU (CHOMP)
WELL, LET'S GET GOING!
GACHA (KCHUNK)
TATA (LEAP)
NO TIME TO WASTE!!
LOOK AT DEBBIE. SO FIERCE, SO COOL!
WERE THEY... LISTENING IN ON THAT?
HEY, PEOPLE! LISTEN TO THE RADIO!!
BAN (WHAM)

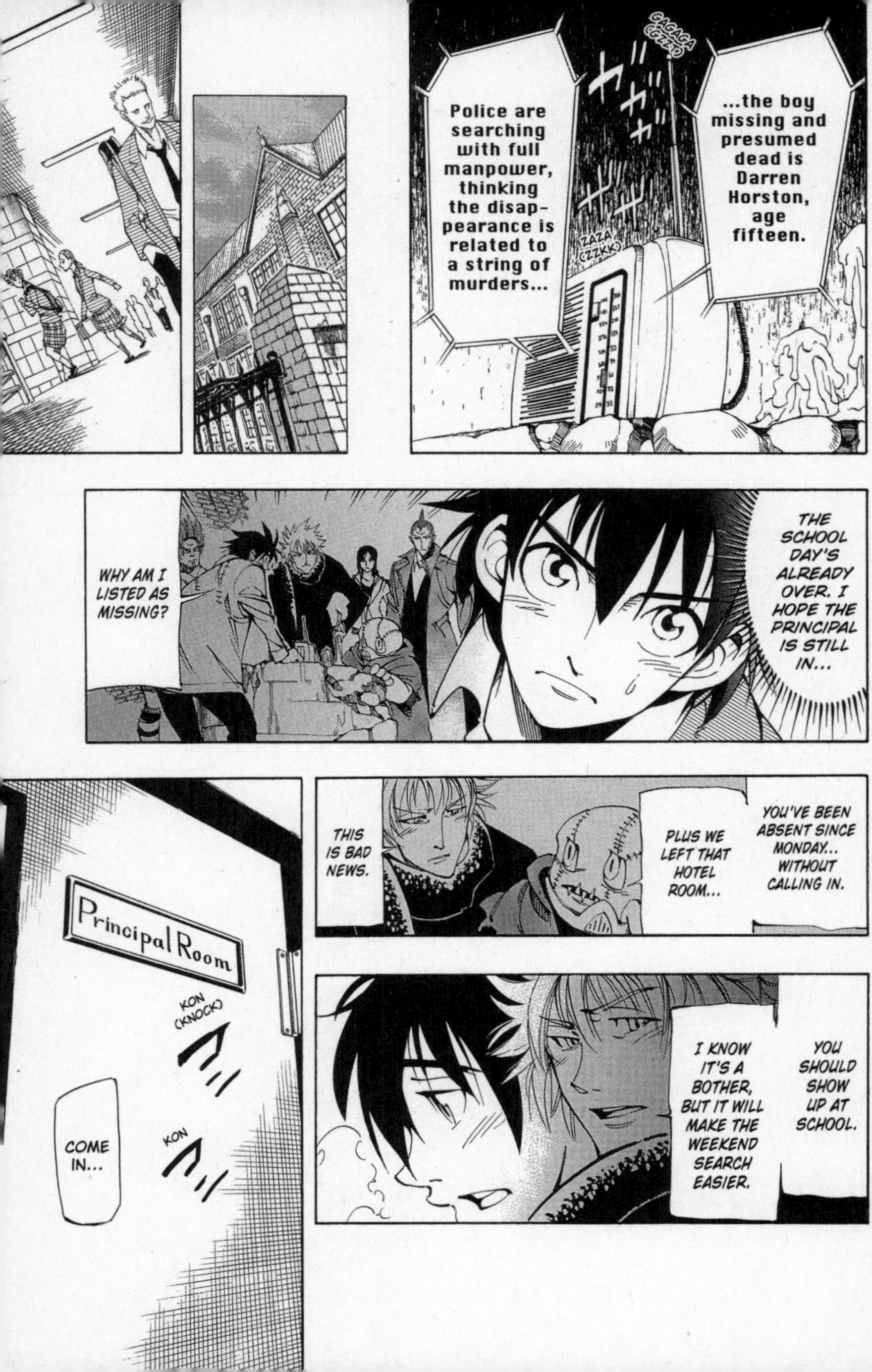
GAGAGA (GZZT)
...the boy missing and presumed dead is Darren Horston, age fifteen.
ZAZA (ZZKK)
Police are searching with full manpower, thinking the disap- pearance is related to a string of murders...
THE SCHOOL DAY'S ALREADY OVER. I HOPE THE PRINCIPAL IS STILL IN...
WHY AM I LISTED AS MISSING?
YOU'VE BEEN ABSENT SINCE MONDAY... WITHOUT CALLING IN.
PLUS WE LEFT THAT HOTEL ROOM...
THIS IS BAD NEWS.
YOU SHOULD SHOW UP AT SCHOOL.
I KNOW IT'S A BOTHER, BUT IT WILL MAKE THE WEEKEND SEARCH EASIER.
Principal Room
KON (KNOCK)
KON
COME IN...

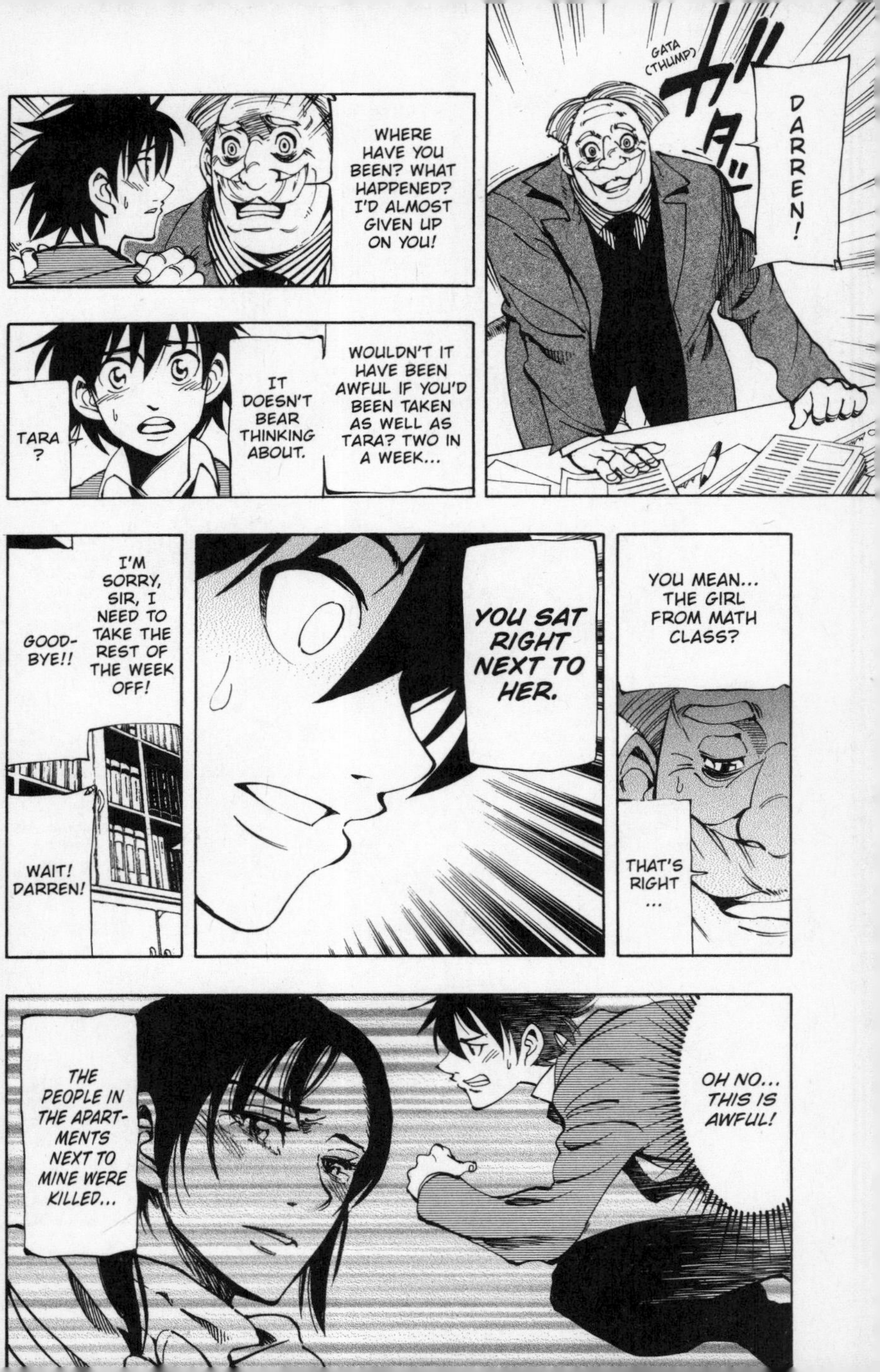
GATA (THUMP)
DARREN!
WHERE HAVE YOU BEEN? WHAT HAPPENED? I'D ALMOST GIVEN UP ON YOU!
WOULDN'T IT HAVE BEEN AWFUL IF YOU'D BEEN TAKEN AS WELL AS TARA? TWO IN A WEEK...
IT DOESN'T BEAR THINKING ABOUT.
TARA?
YOU MEAN... THE GIRL FROM MATH CLASS?
THAT'S RIGHT...
YOU SAT RIGHT NEXT TO HER.
I'M SORRY, SIR, I NEED TO TAKE THE REST OF THE WEEK OFF!
GOOD-BYE!!
WAIT! DARREN!
OH NO... THIS IS AWFUL!
THE PEOPLE IN THE APART-MENTS NEXT TO MINE WERE KILLED...

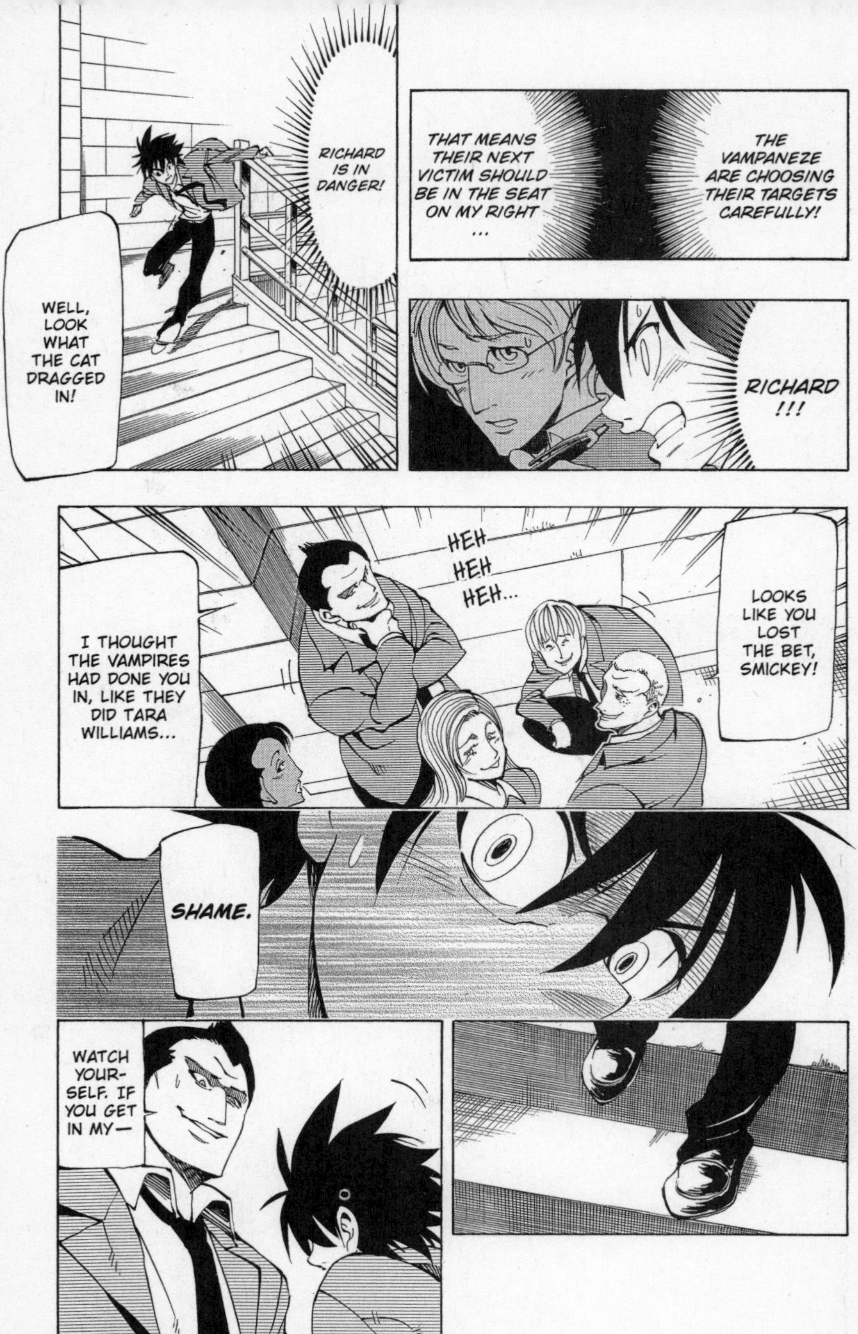
THE VAMPANEZE ARE CHOOSING THEIR TARGETS CAREFULLY!
THAT MEANS THEIR NEXT VICTIM SHOULD BE IN THE SEAT ON MY RIGHT ...
RICHARD !!!
RICHARD IS IN DANGER!
WELL, LOOK WHAT THE CAT DRAGGED IN!
LOOKS LIKE YOU LOST THE BET, SMICKEY!
HEH HEH HEH...
I THOUGHT THE VAMPIRES HAD DONE YOU IN, LIKE THEY DID TARA WILLIAMS...
SHAME.
WATCH YOUR-SELF. IF YOU GET IN MY—

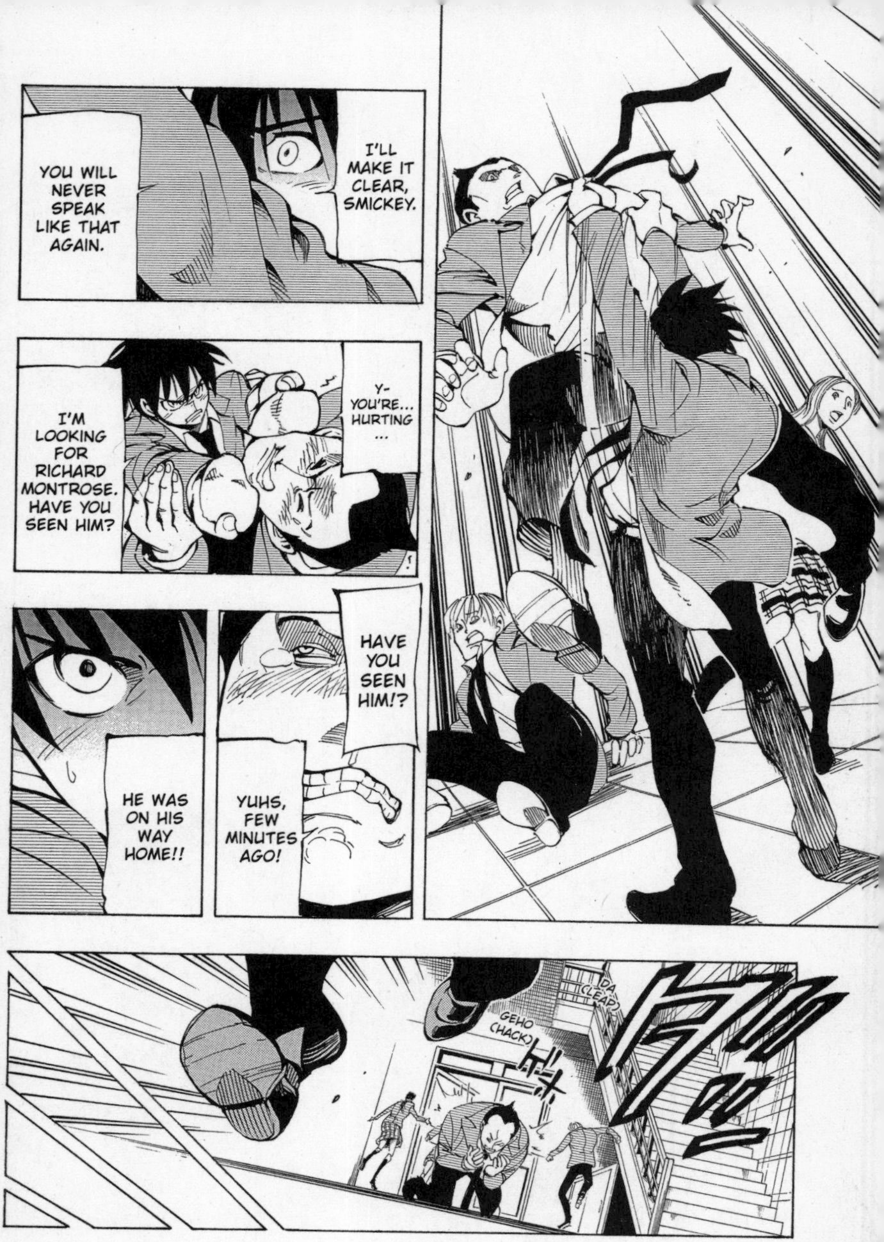
I'LL MAKE IT CLEAR, SMICKEY.
YOU WILL NEVER SPEAK LIKE THAT AGAIN.
Y- YOU'RE... HURTING ...
I'M LOOKING FOR RICHARD MONTROSE. HAVE YOU SEEN HIM?
HAVE YOU SEEN HIM!?
YUHS, FEW MINUTES AGO!
HE WAS ON HIS WAY HOME!!
DA (LEAP)
GEHO (HACK)

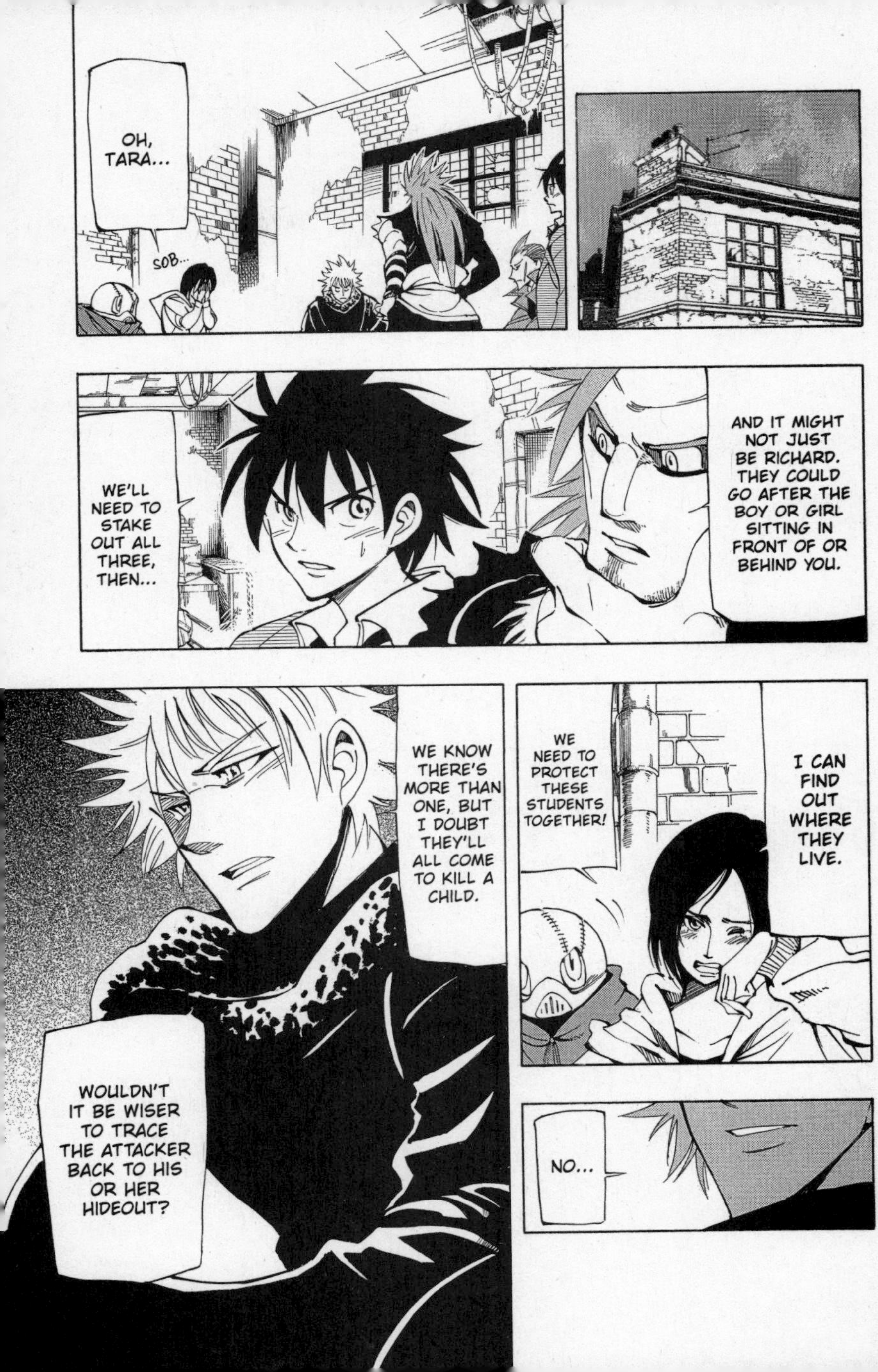
OH, TARA...
SOB...
AND IT MIGHT NOT JUST BE RICHARD. THEY COULD GO AFTER THE BOY OR GIRL SITTING IN FRONT OF OR BEHIND YOU.
WE'LL NEED TO STAKE OUT ALL THREE, THEN...
I CAN FIND OUT WHERE THEY LIVE.
WE NEED TO PROTECT THESE STUDENTS TOGETHER!
NO...
WE KNOW THERE'S MORE THAN ONE, BUT I DOUBT THEY'LL ALL COME TO KILL A CHILD.
WOULDN'T IT BE WISER TO TRACE THE ATTACKER BACK TO HIS OR HER HIDEOUT?

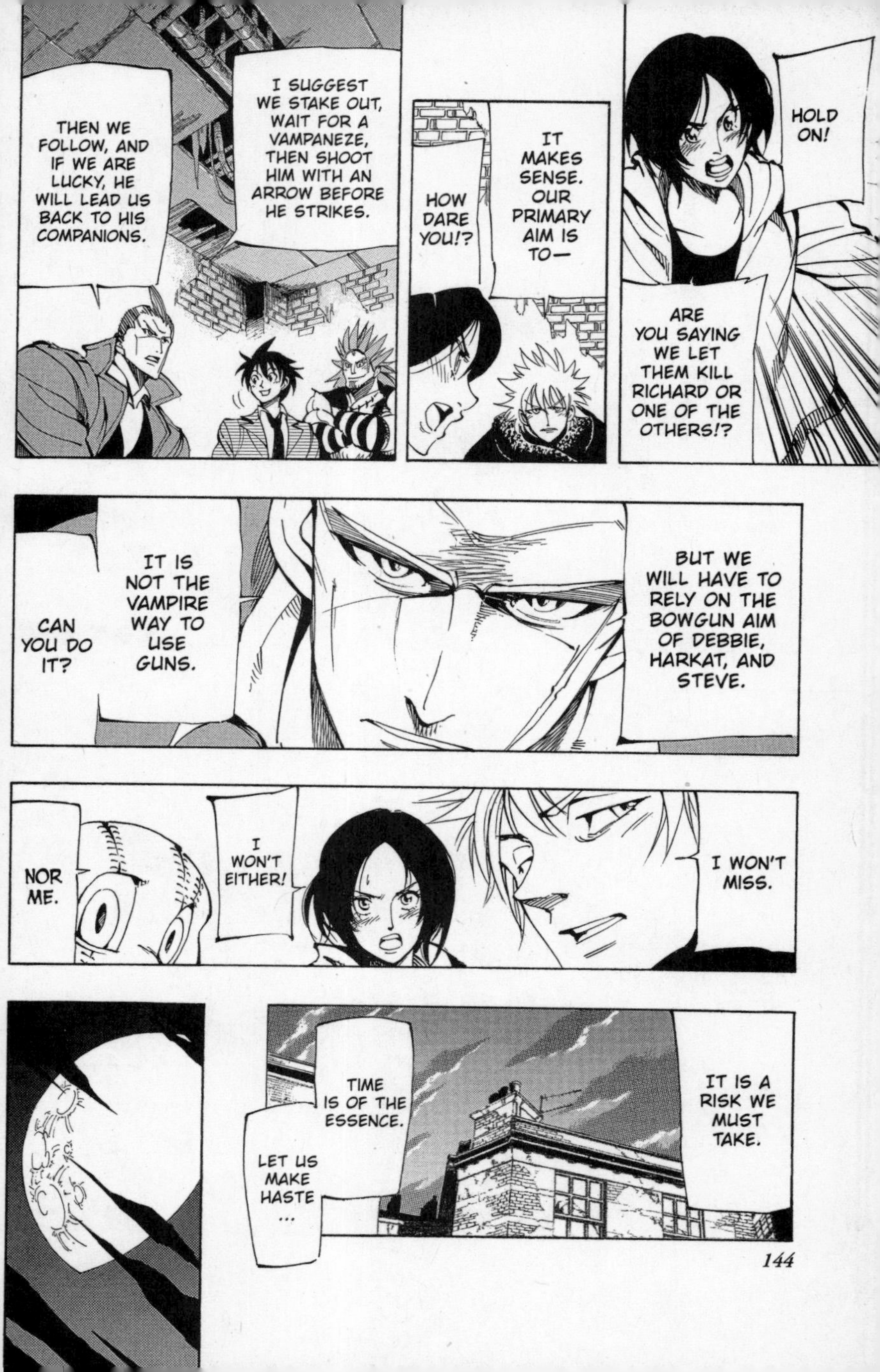
HOLD ON!
ARE YOU SAYING WE LET THEM KILL RICHARD OR ONE OF THE OTHERS!?
IT MAKES SENSE. OUR PRIMARY AIM IS TO—
HOW DARE YOU!?
I SUGGEST WE STAKE OUT, WAIT FOR A VAMPANEZE, THEN SHOOT HIM WITH AN ARROW BEFORE HE STRIKES.
THEN WE FOLLOW, AND IF WE ARE LUCKY, HE WILL LEAD US BACK TO HIS COMPANIONS.
BUT WE WILL HAVE TO RELY ON THE BOWGUN AIM OF DEBBIE, HARKAT, AND STEVE.
IT IS NOT THE VAMPIRE WAY TO USE GUNS.
CAN YOU DO IT?
I WON'T MISS.
I WON'T EITHER!
NOR ME.
IT IS A RISK WE MUST TAKE.
TIME IS OF THE ESSENCE.
LET US MAKE HASTE ...

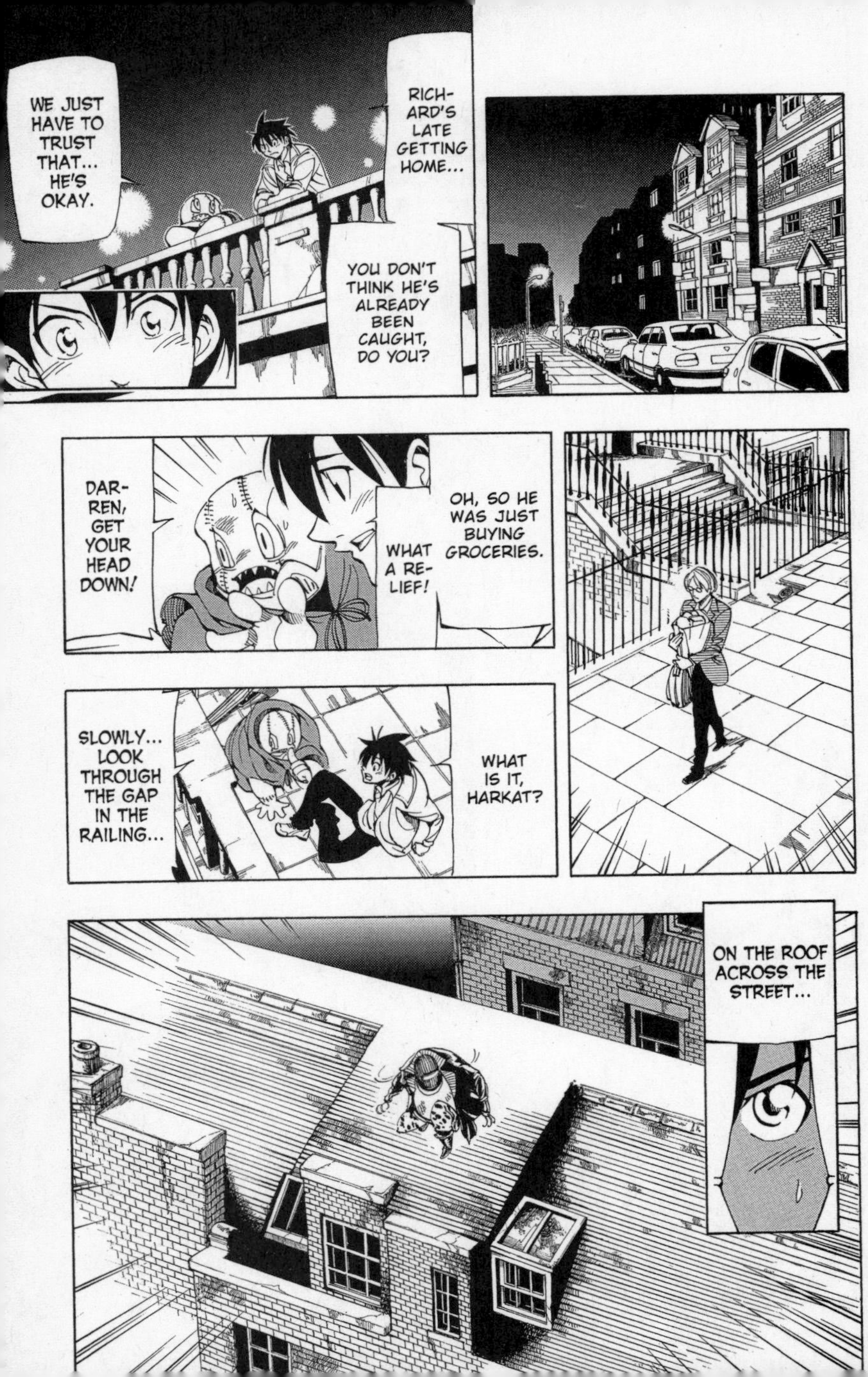
RICH-ARD'S LATE GETTING HOME...
YOU DON'T THINK HE'S ALREADY BEEN CAUGHT, DO YOU?
WE JUST HAVE TO TRUST THAT... HE'S OKAY.
OH, SO HE WAS JUST BUYING GROCERIES.
WHAT A RE-LIEF!
DAR-REN, GET YOUR HEAD DOWN!
WHAT IS IT, HARKAT?
SLOWLY... LOOK THROUGH THE GAP IN THE RAILING...
ON THE ROOF ACROSS THE STREET...

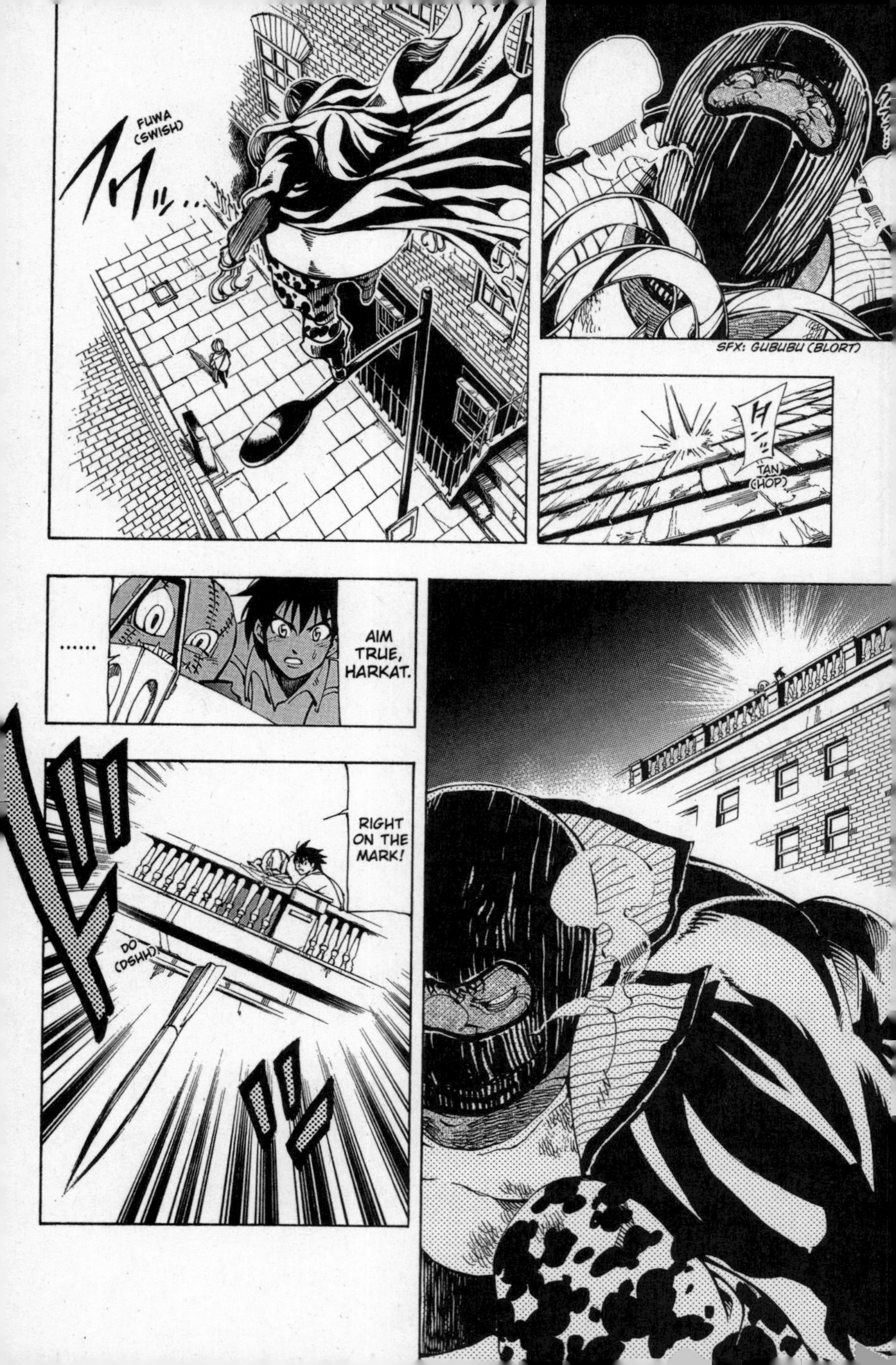
SFX: GUBUBU (BLORT)
TAN (HOP)
FUWA (SWISH)
AIM TRUE, HARKAT.
......
RIGHT ON THE MARK!
DO (DSHH)

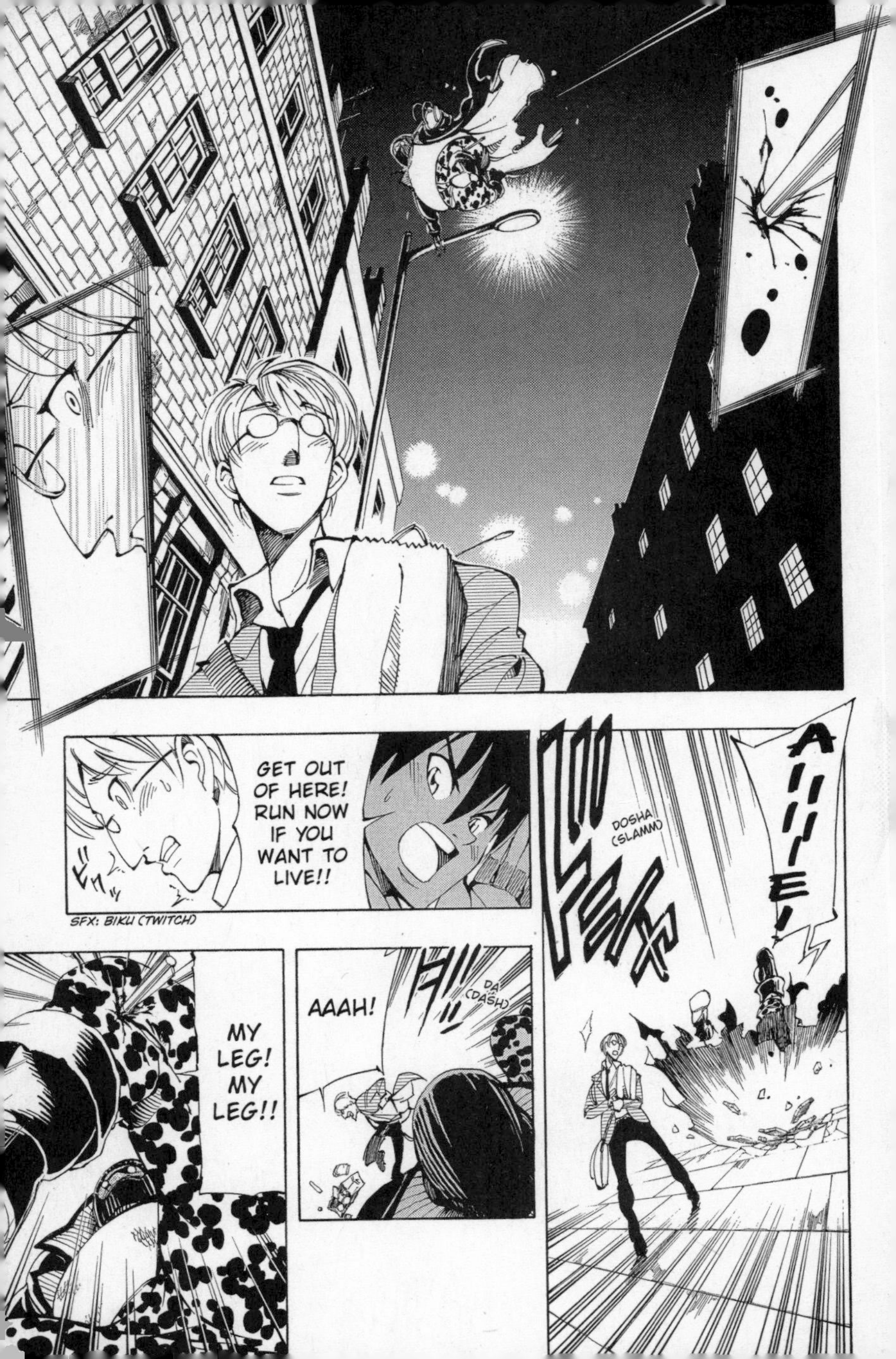
AIIIEE!
DOSHA (SLAMM)
GET OUT OF HERE! RUN NOW IF YOU WANT TO LIVE!!
SFX: BIKU (TWITCH)
AAAH!
DA (DASH)
MY LEG! MY LEG!!

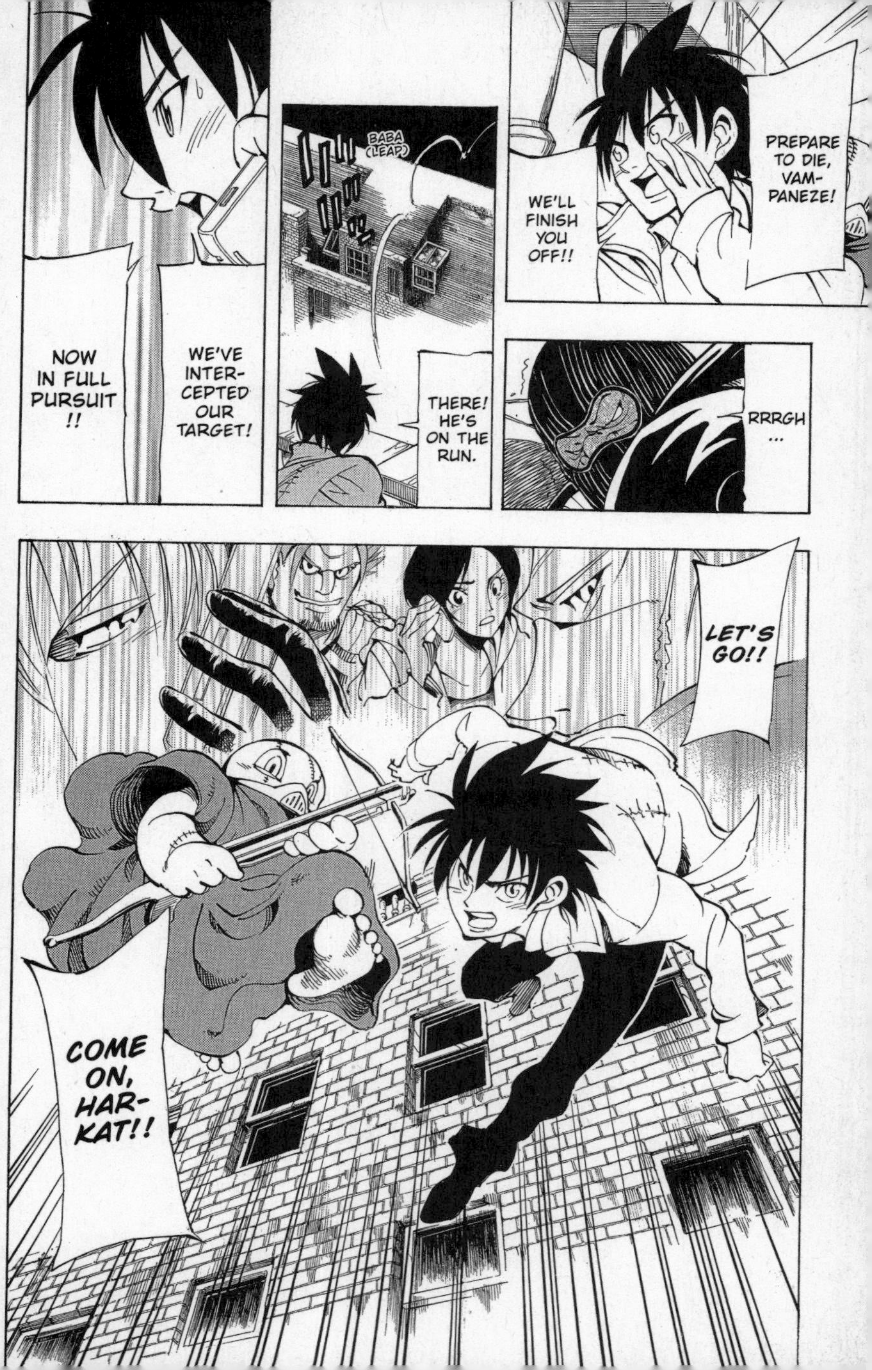
PREPARE TO DIE, VAMPANEZE!
WE'LL FINISH YOU OFF!!
RRRGH ...
BABA (LEAP)
THERE! HE'S ON THE RUN.
WE'VE INTERCEPTED OUR TARGET!
NOW IN FULL PURSUIT!!
LET'S GO!!
COME ON, HARKAT!!

CHAPTER 73:
ANGER AND
HATRED

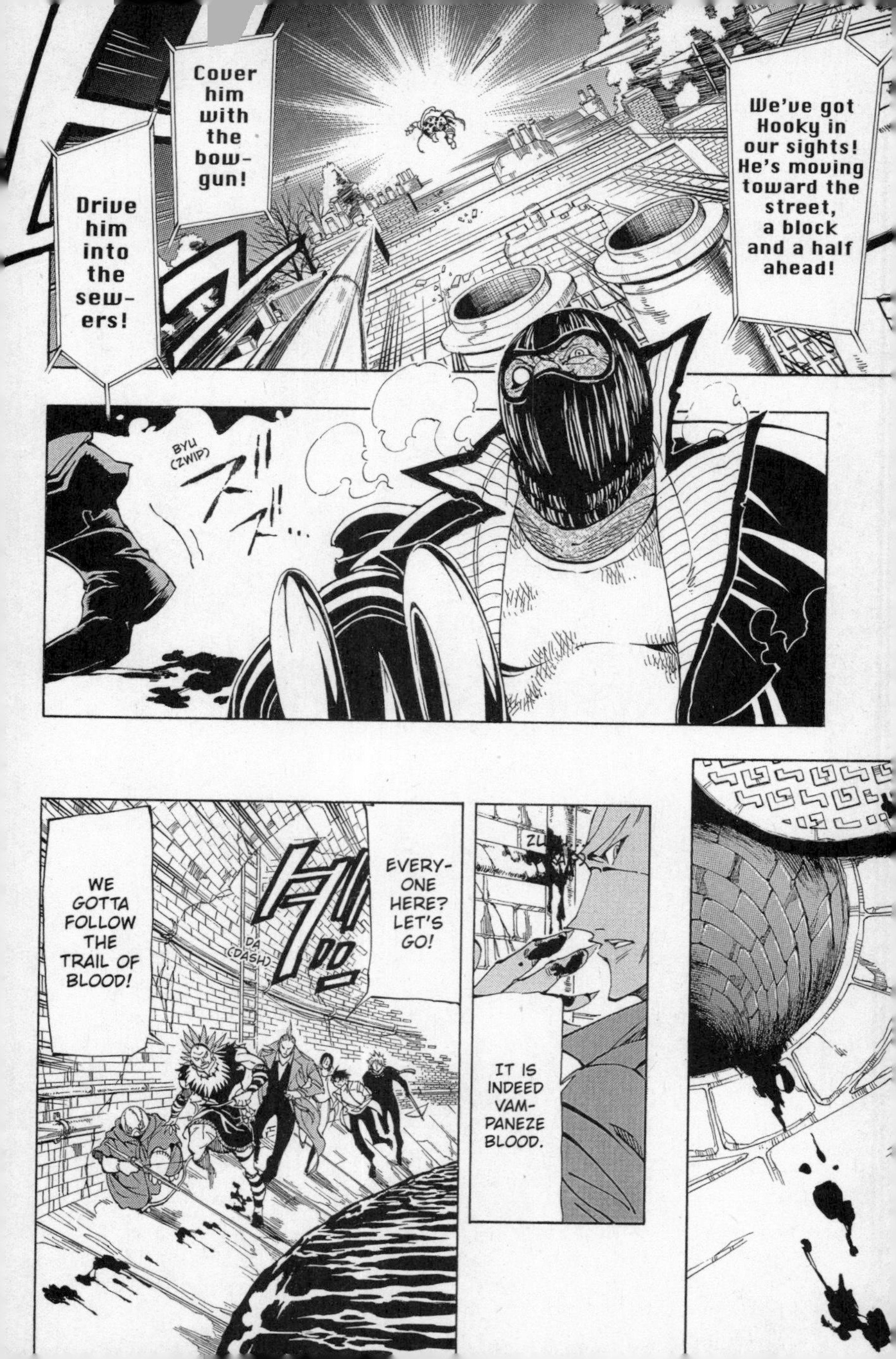
We've got Hooky in our sights! He's moving toward the street, a block and a half ahead!
Cover him with the bow-gun!
Drive him into the sewers!
BYU (ZWIP)
IT IS INDEED VAMPANEZE BLOOD.
EVERYONE HERE? LET'S GO!
DA (DASH)
WE GOTTA FOLLOW THE TRAIL OF BLOOD!

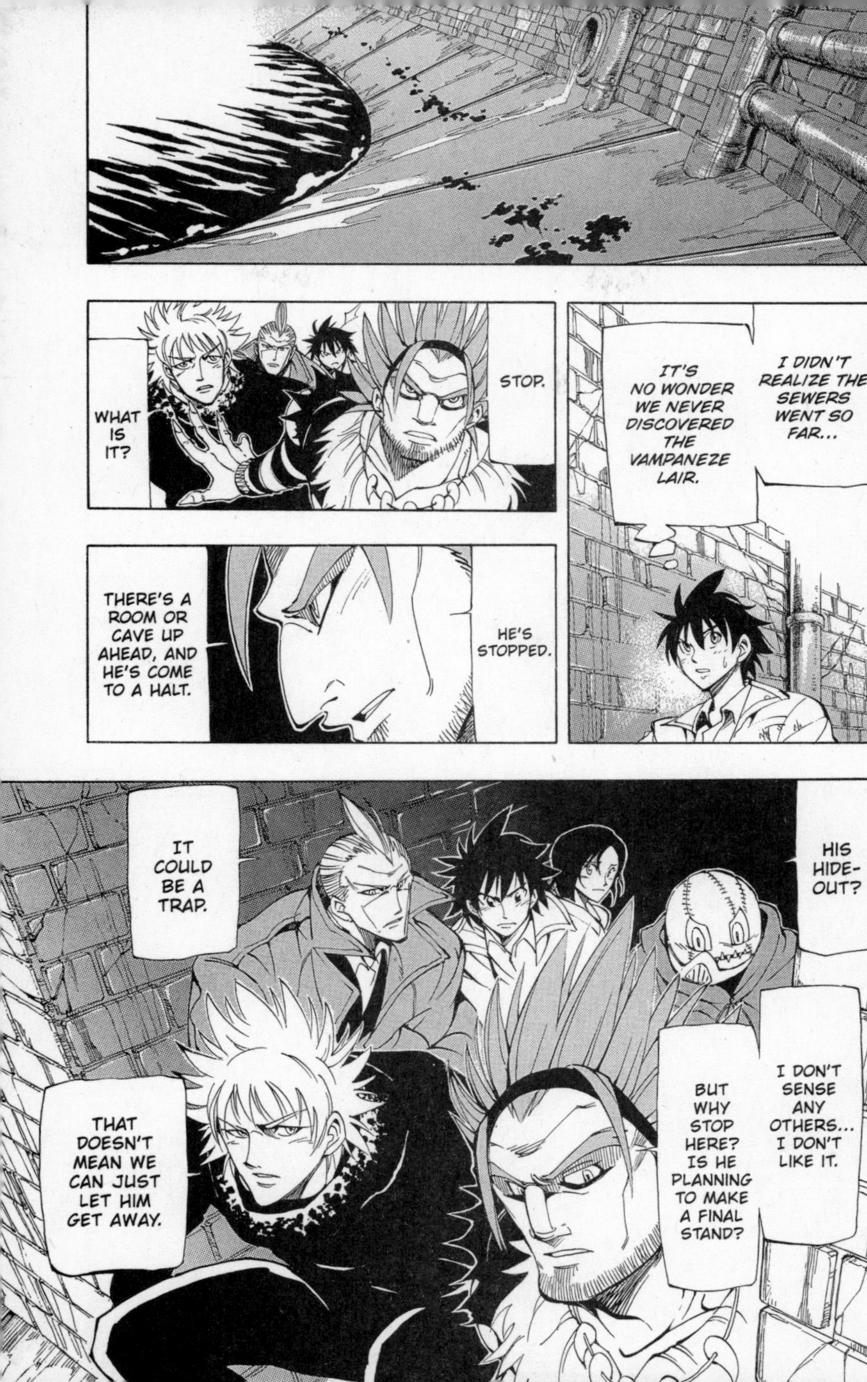
I DIDN'T REALIZE THE SEWERS WENT SO FAR...
IT'S NO WONDER WE NEVER DISCOVERED THE VAMPANEZE LAIR.
STOP.
WHAT IS IT?
HE'S STOPPED.
THERE'S A ROOM OR CAVE UP AHEAD, AND HE'S COME TO A HALT.
HIS HIDE-OUT?
IT COULD BE A TRAP.
I DON'T SENSE ANY OTHERS... I DON'T LIKE IT.
BUT WHY STOP HERE? IS HE PLANNING TO MAKE A FINAL STAND?
THAT DOESN'T MEAN WE CAN JUST LET HIM GET AWAY.

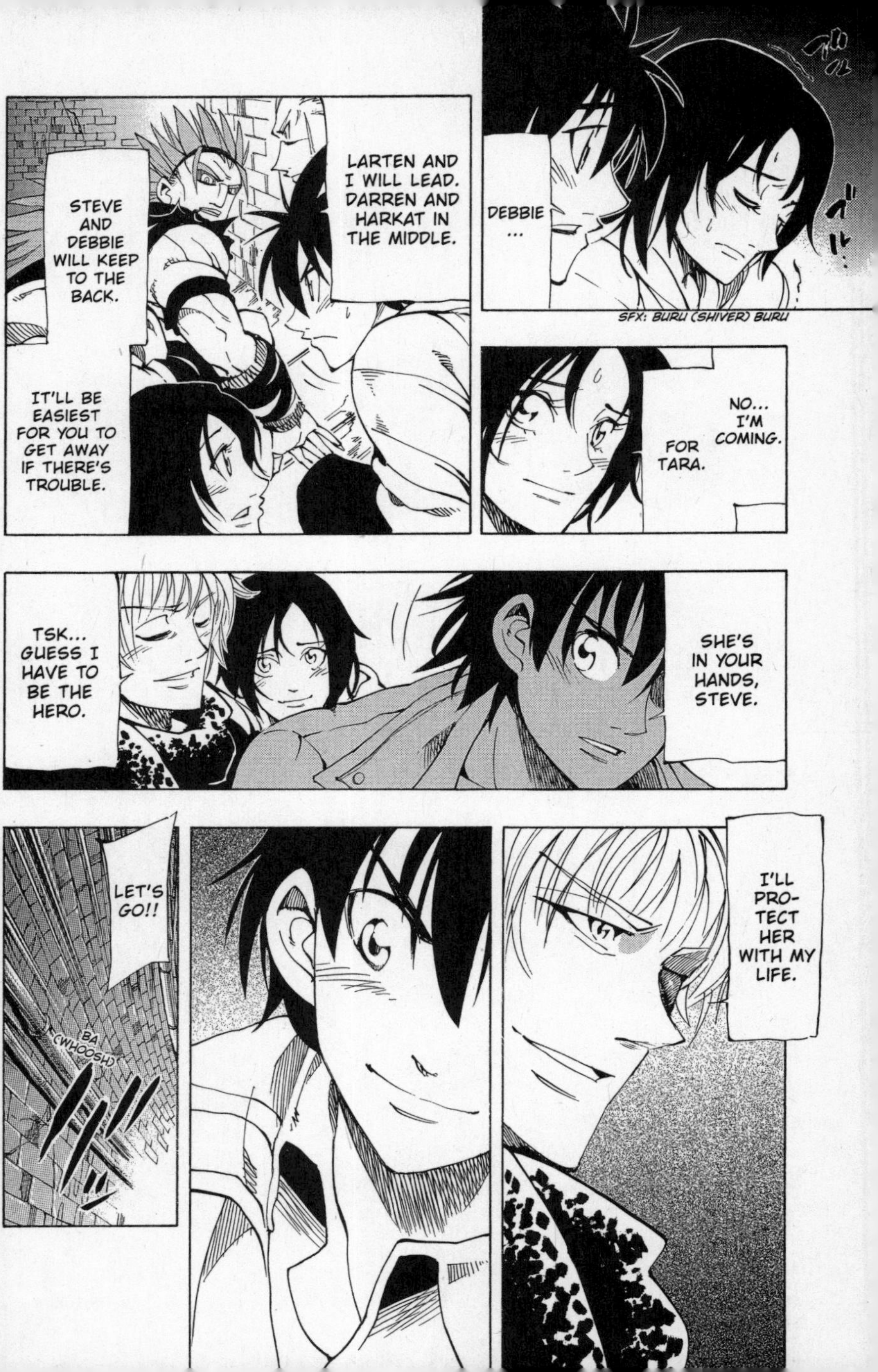
DEBBIE ...
SFX: BURU (SHIVER) BURU
NO... I'M COMING.
FOR TARA.
LARTEN AND I WILL LEAD. DARREN AND HARKAT IN THE MIDDLE.
STEVE AND DEBBIE WILL KEEP TO THE BACK.
IT'LL BE EASIEST FOR YOU TO GET AWAY IF THERE'S TROUBLE.
SHE'S IN YOUR HANDS, STEVE.
TSK... GUESS I HAVE TO BE THE HERO.
I'LL PRO-TECT HER WITH MY LIFE.
LET'S GO!!
BA (WHOOSH)

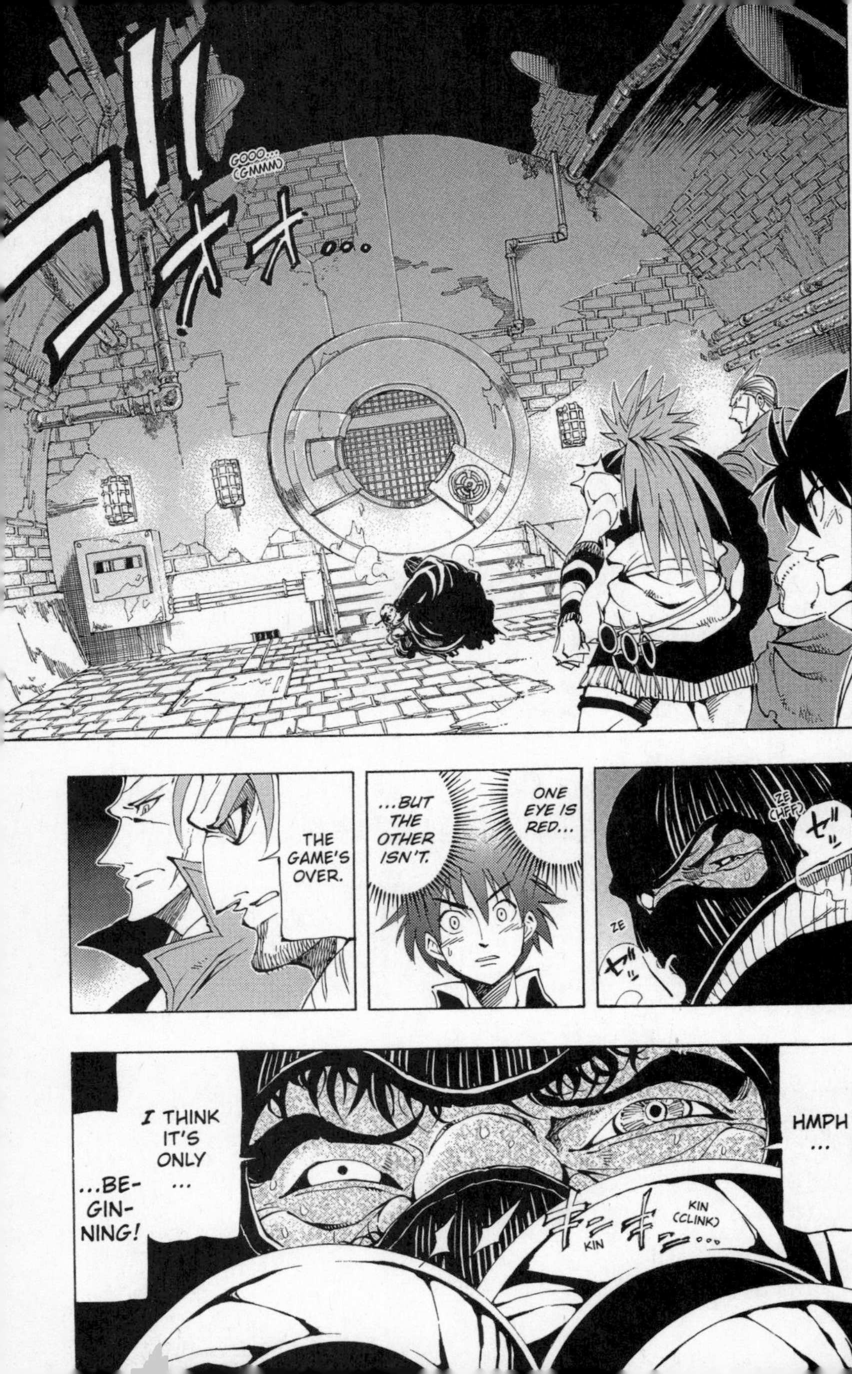
GOOO... (GMMM)
ZE (HFF)
ZE
ONE EYE IS RED...
...BUT THE OTHER ISN'T.
THE GAME'S OVER.
HMPH...
I THINK IT'S ONLY...
...BE-GIN-NING!
KIN (CLINK)
KIN

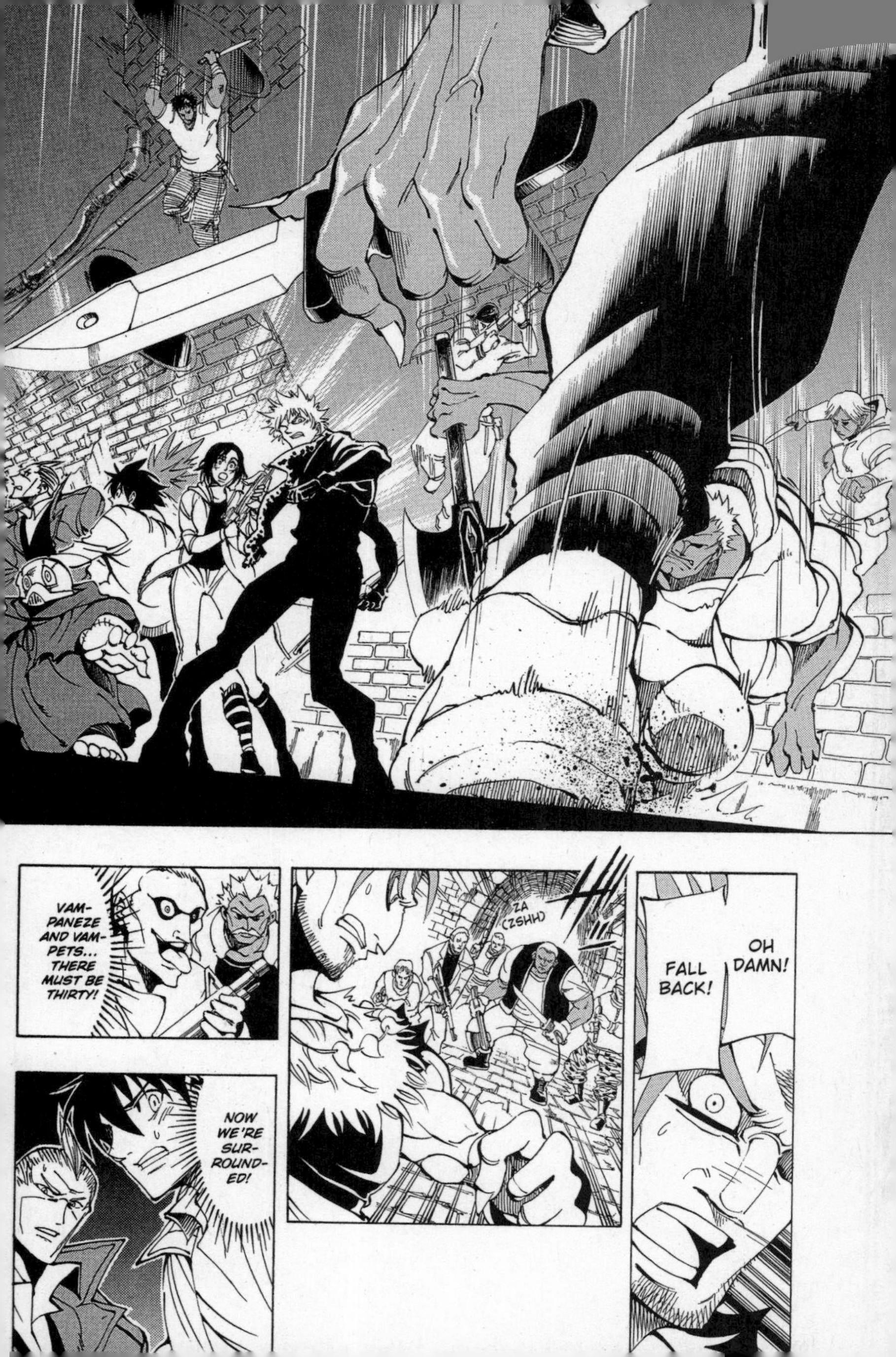

OH DAMN!
FALL BACK!
ZA ZSHH
VAMPANEZE AND VAMPETS... THERE MUST BE THIRTY!
NOW WE'RE SURROUNDED!

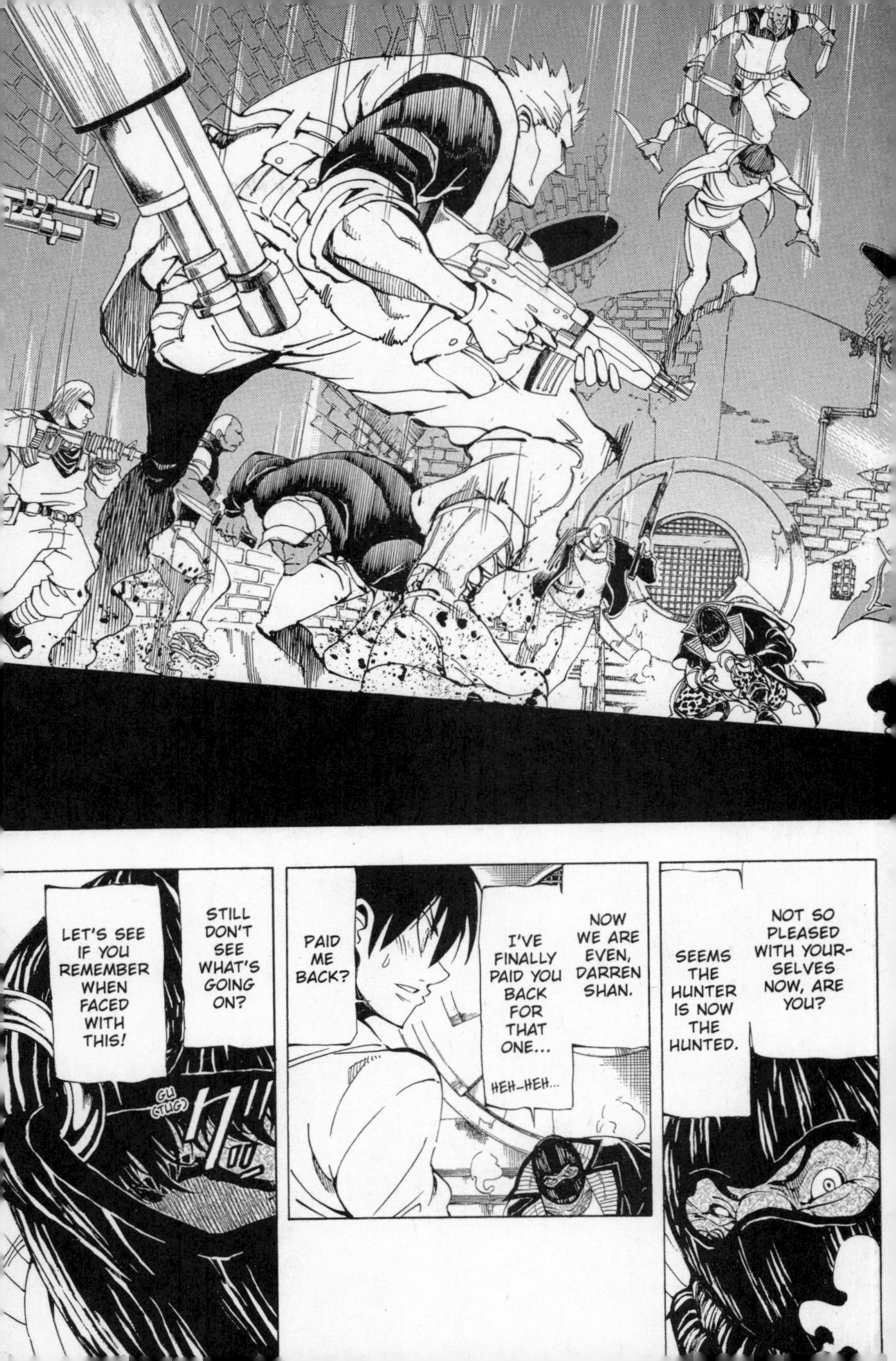
NOT SO PLEASED WITH YOUR-SELVES NOW, ARE YOU?
SEEMS THE HUNTER IS NOW THE HUNTED.
NOW WE ARE EVEN, DARREN SHAN.
I'VE FINALLY PAID YOU BACK FOR THAT ONE...
HEH-HEH...
PAID ME BACK?
STILL DON'T SEE WHAT'S GOING ON?
LET'S SEE IF YOU REMEMBER WHEN FACED WITH THIS!
GU (TUG)

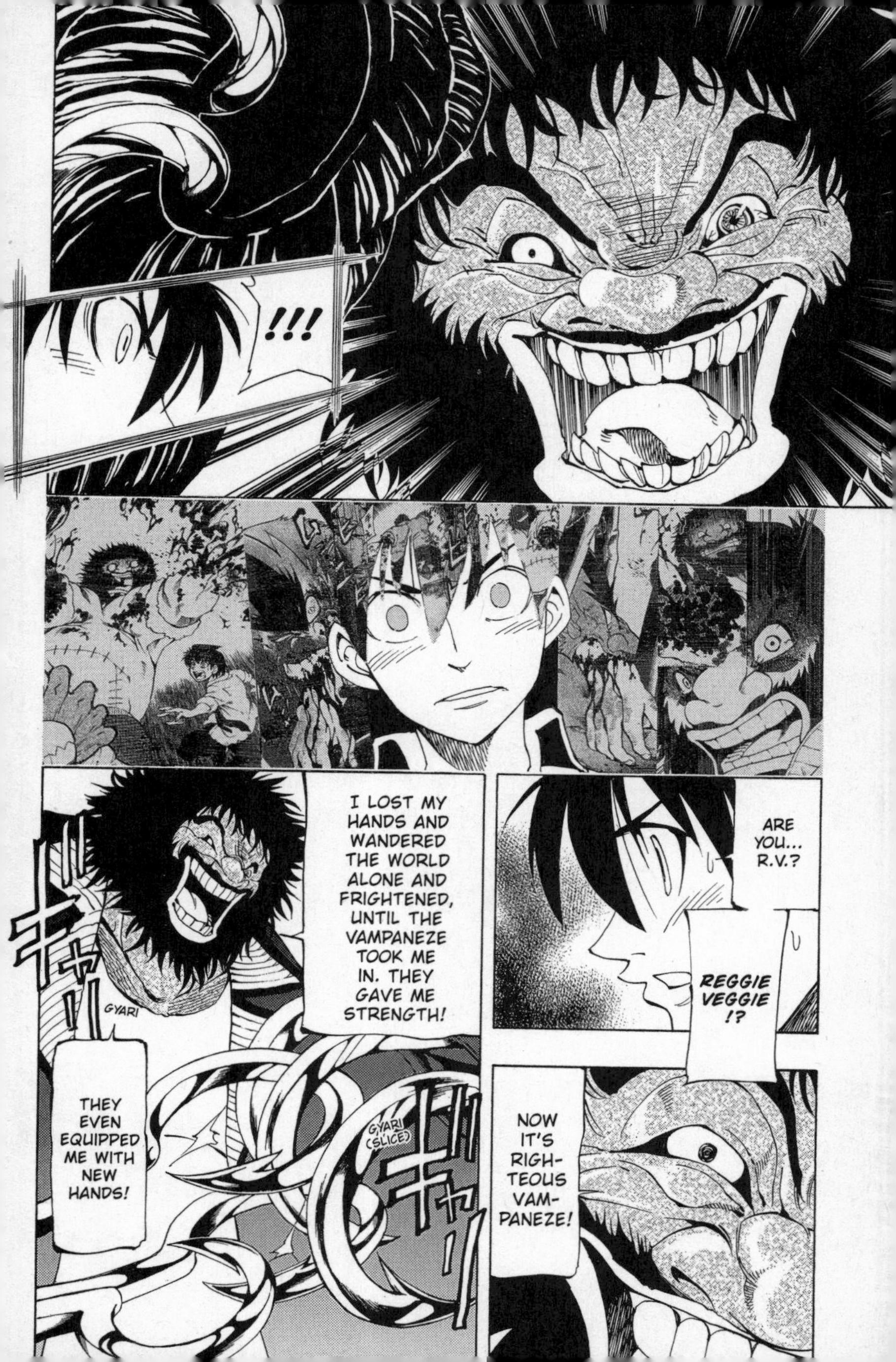
!!!
ARE YOU... R.V.?
REGGIE VEGGIE !?
NOW IT'S RIGHTEOUS VAMPANEZE!
I LOST MY HANDS AND WANDERED THE WORLD ALONE AND FRIGHTENED, UNTIL THE VAMPANEZE TOOK ME IN. THEY GAVE ME STRENGTH!
GYARI
THEY EVEN EQUIPPED ME WITH NEW HANDS!
GYARI (SLICE)

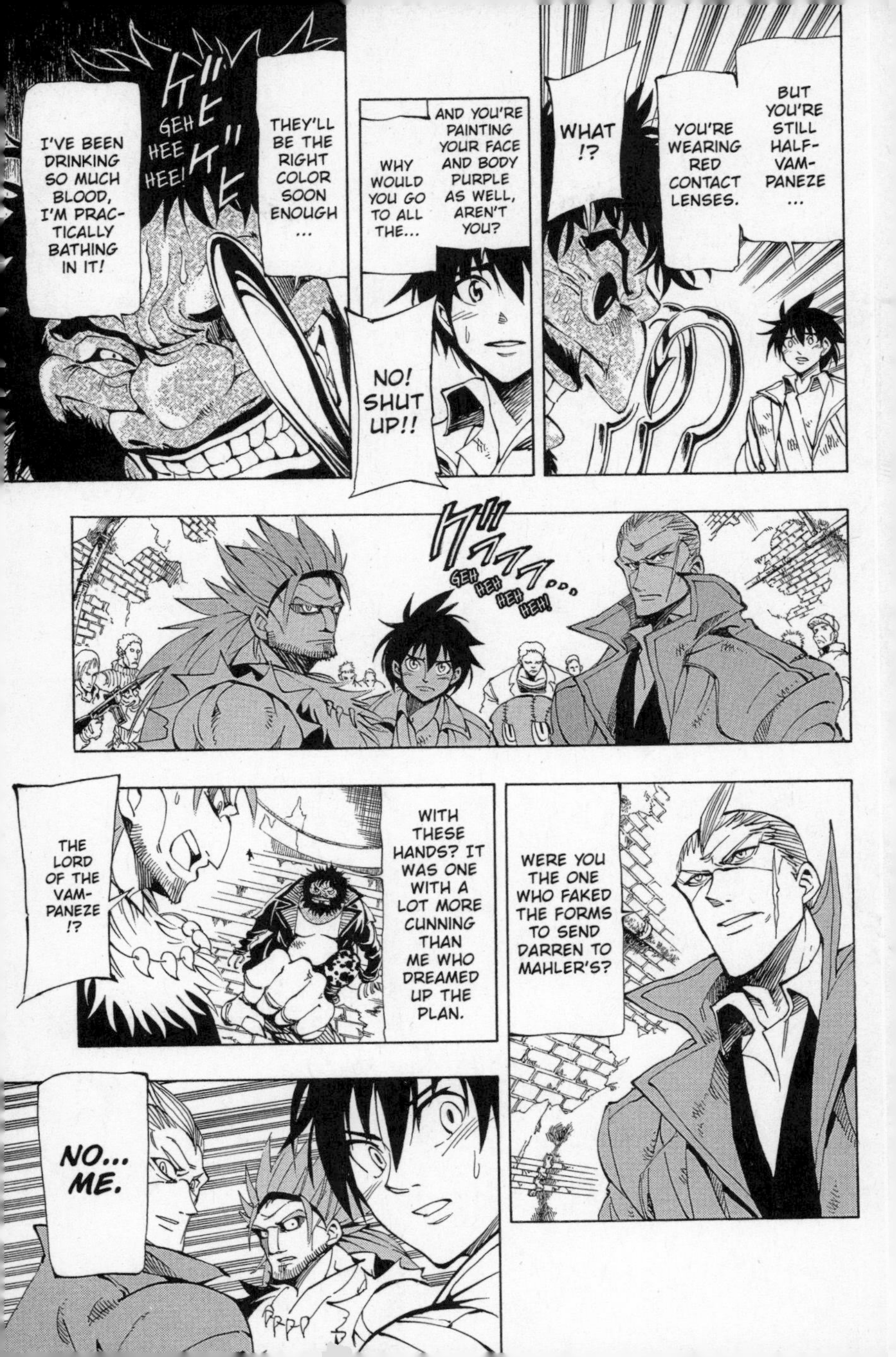
BUT YOU'RE STILL HALF-VAMPANEZE...
YOU'RE WEARING RED CONTACT LENSES.
WHAT!?
AND YOU'RE PAINTING YOUR FACE AND BODY PURPLE AS WELL, AREN'T YOU?
WHY WOULD YOU GO TO ALL THE...
NO! SHUT UP!!
THEY'LL BE THE RIGHT COLOR SOON ENOUGH...
GEH HEE HEE!
I'VE BEEN DRINKING SO MUCH BLOOD, I'M PRACTICALLY BATHING IN IT!
GEH HEH HEH HEH!
WERE YOU THE ONE WHO FAKED THE FORMS TO SEND DARREN TO MAHLER'S?
WITH THESE HANDS? IT WAS ONE WITH A LOT MORE CUNNING THAN ME WHO DREAMED UP THE PLAN.
THE LORD OF THE VAMPANEZE!?
NO... ME.

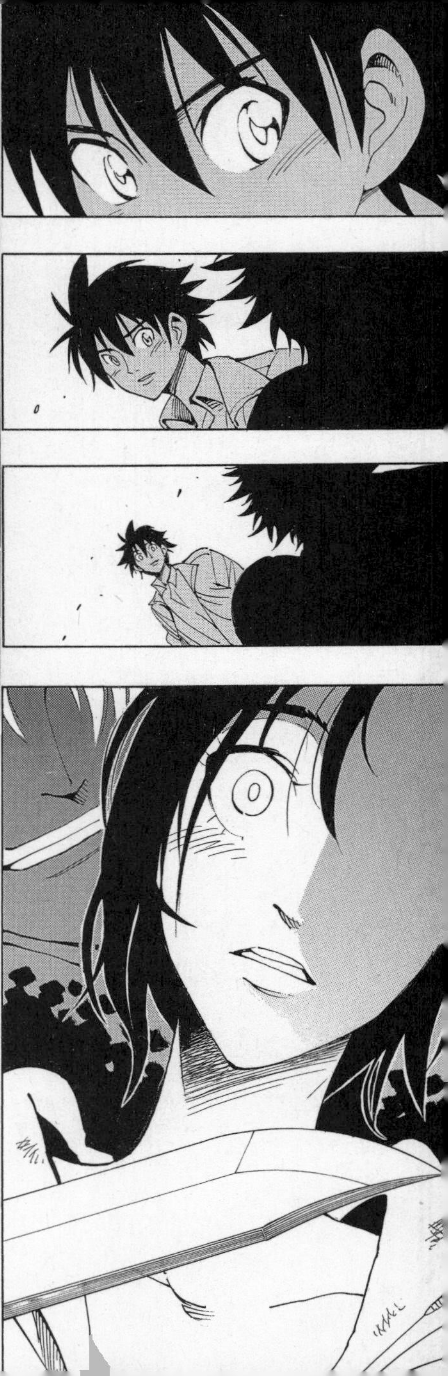
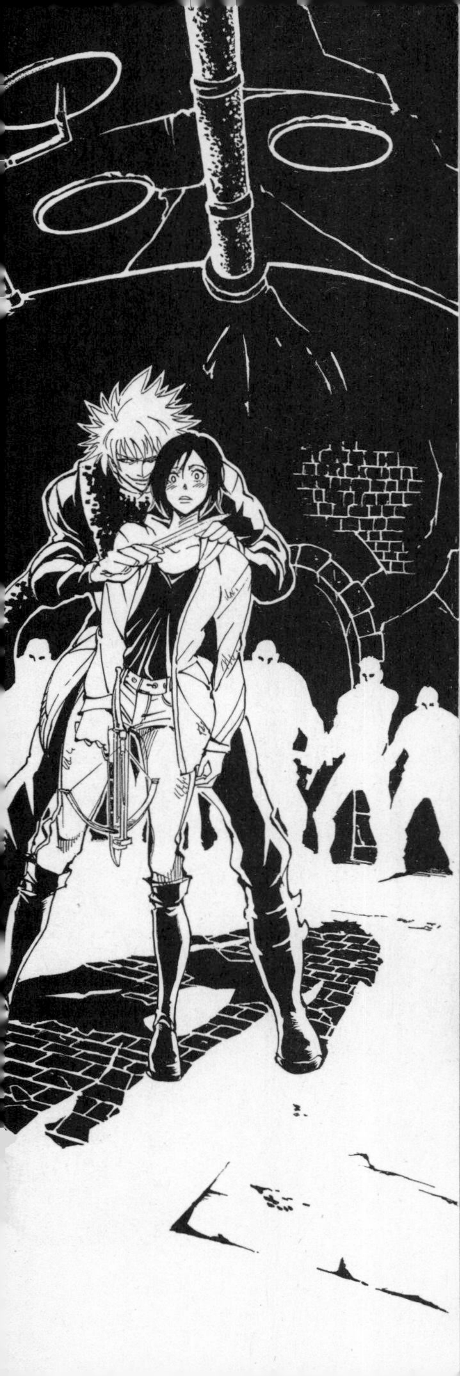

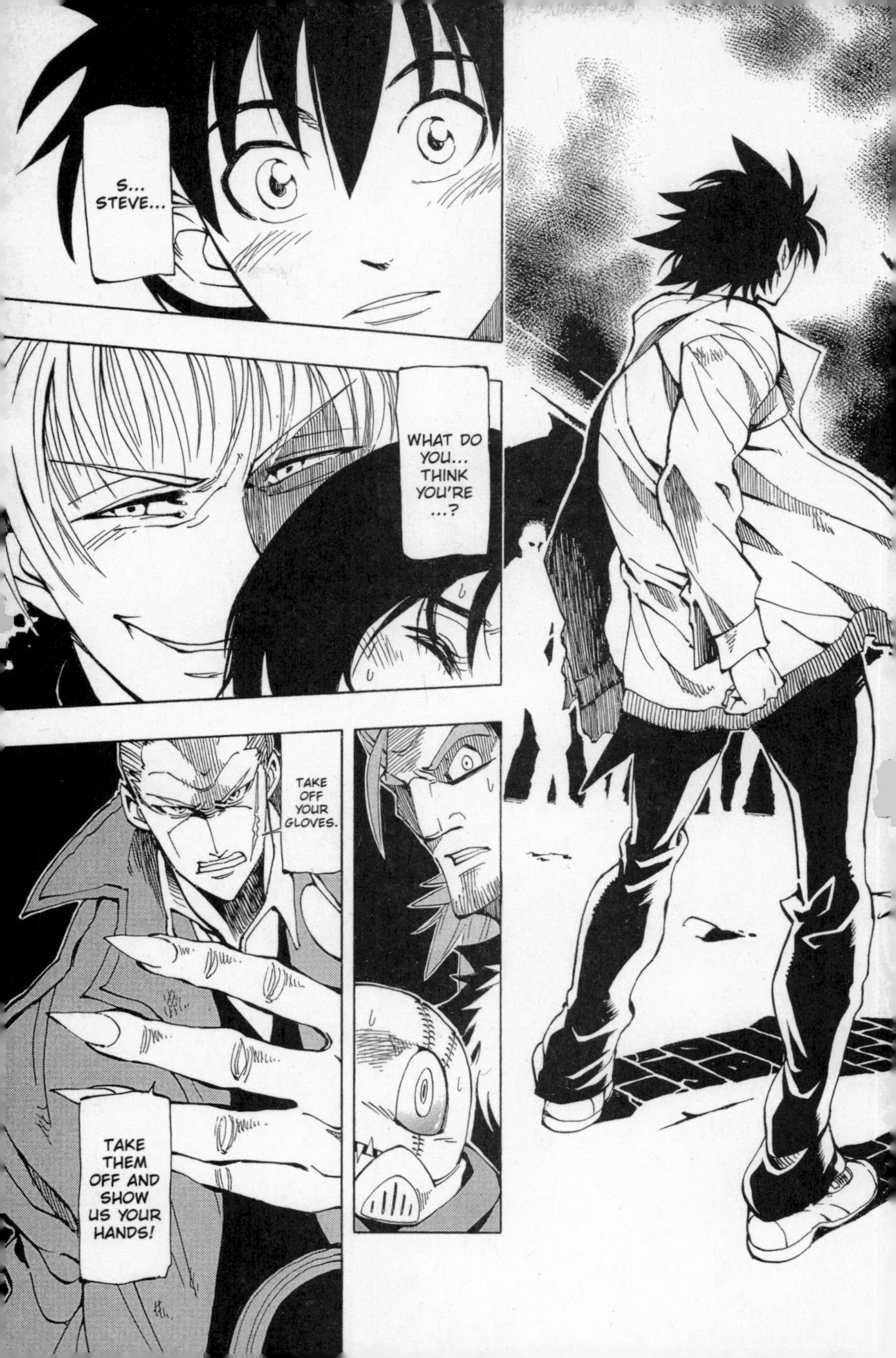
S... STEVE...
WHAT DO YOU... THINK YOU'RE ...?
TAKE OFF YOUR GLOVES.
TAKE THEM OFF AND SHOW US YOUR HANDS!

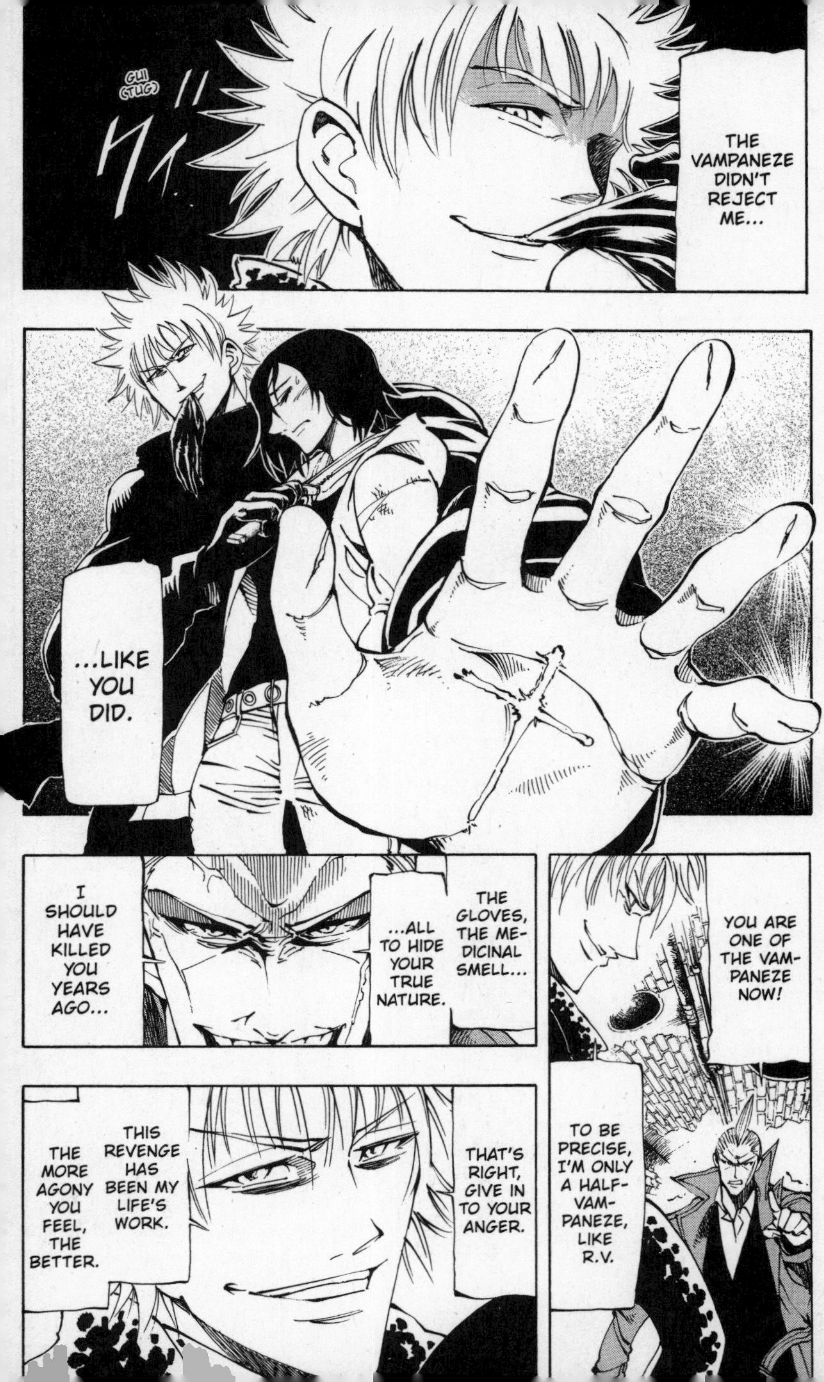
THE VAMPANEZE DIDN'T REJECT ME...
GUI (TUG)
...LIKE YOU DID.
YOU ARE ONE OF THE VAMPANEZE NOW!
THE GLOVES, THE MEDICINAL SMELL...
...ALL TO HIDE YOUR TRUE NATURE.
I SHOULD HAVE KILLED YOU YEARS AGO...
TO BE PRECISE, I'M ONLY A HALF-VAMPANEZE, LIKE R.V.
THAT'S RIGHT, GIVE IN TO YOUR ANGER.
THIS REVENGE HAS BEEN MY LIFE'S WORK.
THE MORE AGONY YOU FEEL, THE BETTER.

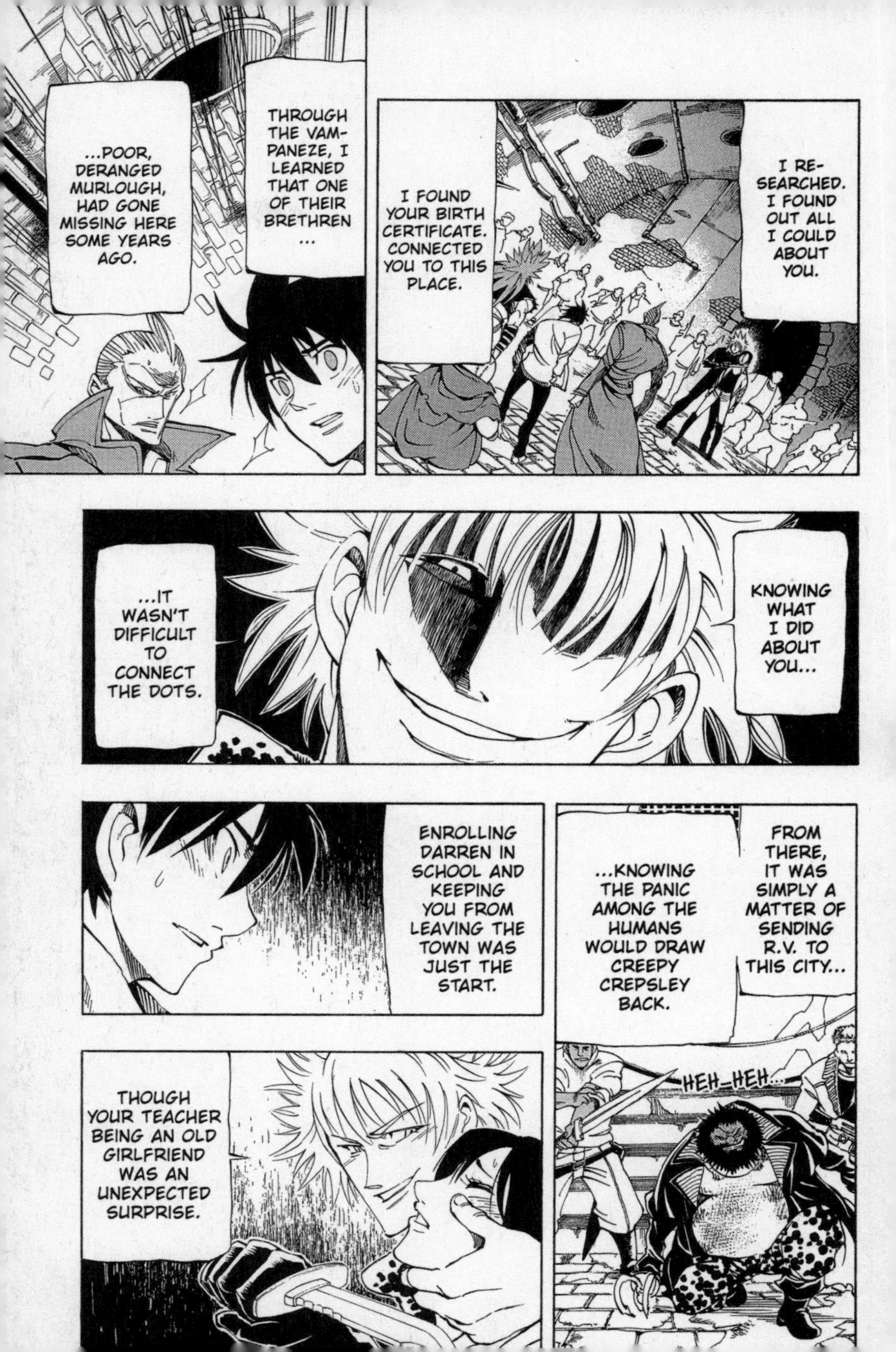
I RE-SEARCHED. I FOUND OUT ALL I COULD ABOUT YOU.
I FOUND YOUR BIRTH CERTIFICATE. CONNECTED YOU TO THIS PLACE.
THROUGH THE VAMPANEZE, I LEARNED THAT ONE OF THEIR BRETHREN ...
...POOR, DERANGED MURLOUGH, HAD GONE MISSING HERE SOME YEARS AGO.
KNOWING WHAT I DID ABOUT YOU...
...IT WASN'T DIFFICULT TO CONNECT THE DOTS.
FROM THERE, IT WAS SIMPLY A MATTER OF SENDING R.V. TO THIS CITY...
...KNOWING THE PANIC AMONG THE HUMANS WOULD DRAW CREEPY CREPSLEY BACK.
HEH-HEH...
ENROLLING DARREN IN SCHOOL AND KEEPING YOU FROM LEAVING THE TOWN WAS JUST THE START.
THOUGH YOUR TEACHER BEING AN OLD GIRLFRIEND WAS AN UNEXPECTED SURPRISE.

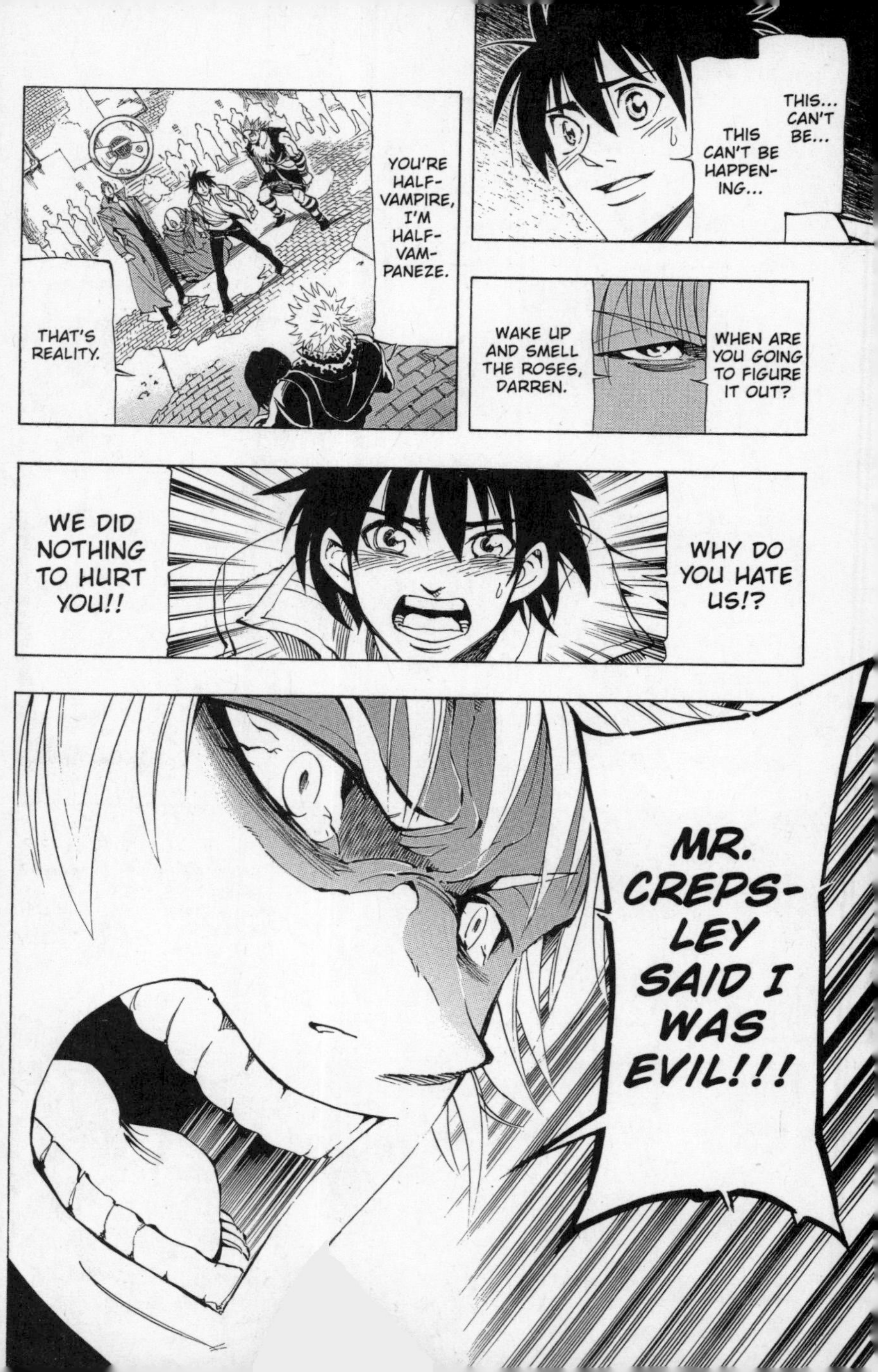
THIS... CAN'T BE...
THIS CAN'T BE HAPPEN-ING...
WHEN ARE YOU GOING TO FIGURE IT OUT?
WAKE UP AND SMELL THE ROSES, DARREN.
YOU'RE HALF-VAMPIRE, I'M HALF-VAM-PANEZE.
THAT'S REALITY.
WHY DO YOU HATE US!?
WE DID NOTHING TO HURT YOU!!
MR. CREPS-LEY SAID I WAS EVIL!!!

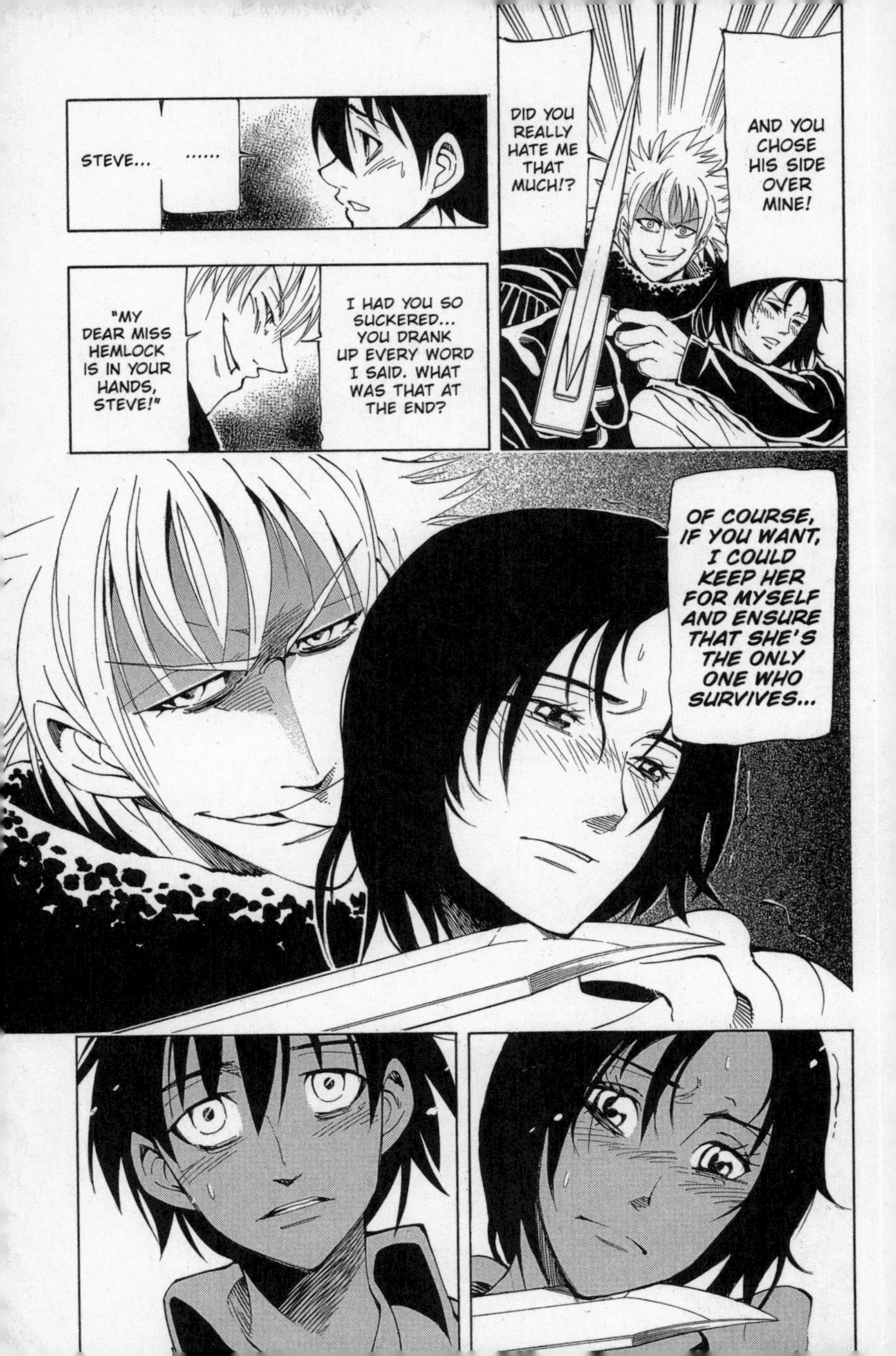
AND YOU CHOSE HIS SIDE OVER MINE!
DID YOU REALLY HATE ME THAT MUCH!?
......
STEVE...
I HAD YOU SO SUCKERED... YOU DRANK UP EVERY WORD I SAID. WHAT WAS THAT AT THE END?
"MY DEAR MISS HEMLOCK IS IN YOUR HANDS, STEVE!"
OF COURSE, IF YOU WANT, I COULD KEEP HER FOR MYSELF AND ENSURE THAT SHE'S THE ONLY ONE WHO SURVIVES...

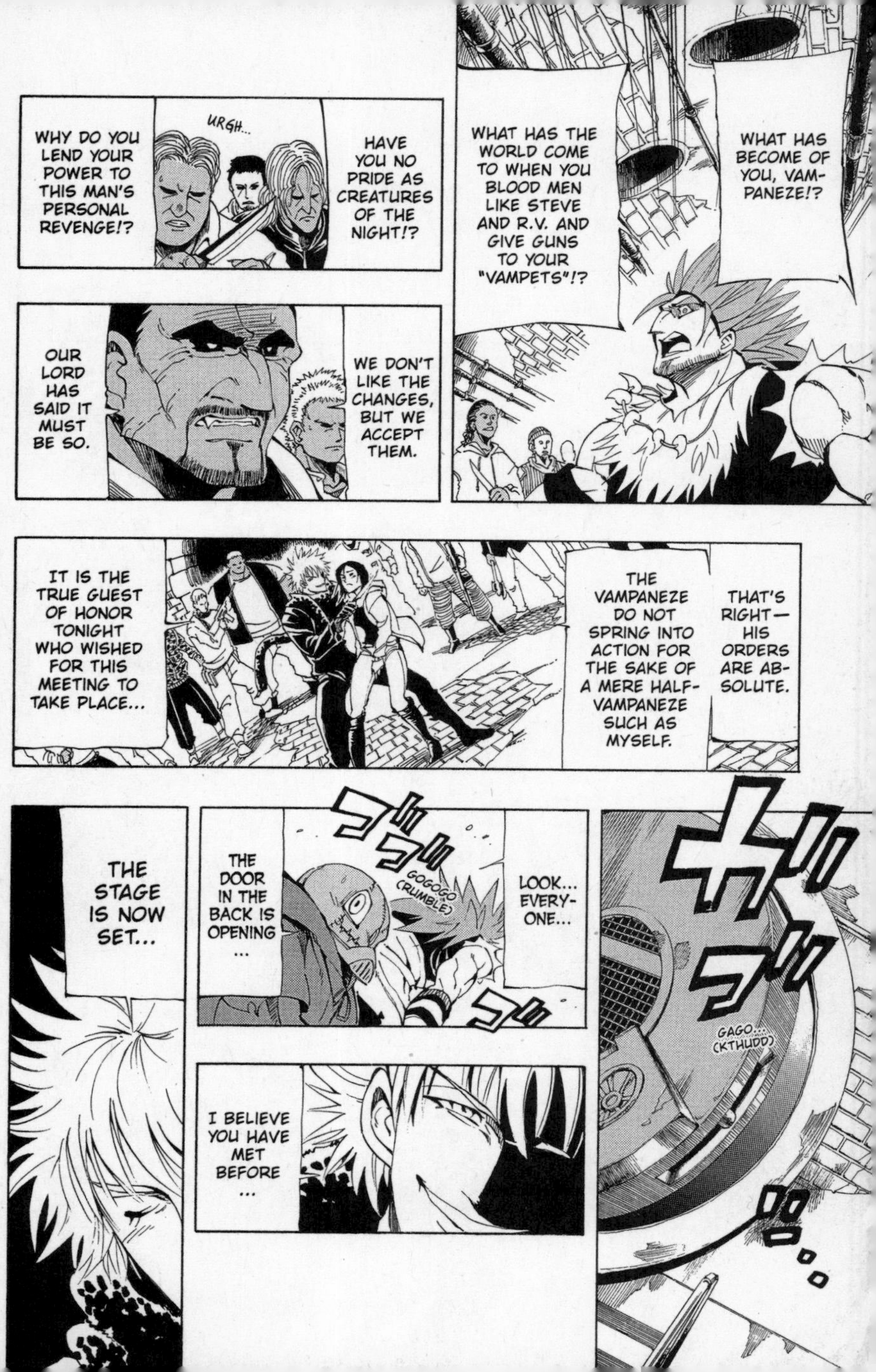
WHAT HAS BECOME OF YOU, VAMPANEZE!?
WHAT HAS THE WORLD COME TO WHEN YOU BLOOD MEN LIKE STEVE AND R.V. AND GIVE GUNS TO YOUR "VAMPETS"!?
HAVE YOU NO PRIDE AS CREATURES OF THE NIGHT!?
URGH...
WHY DO YOU LEND YOUR POWER TO THIS MAN'S PERSONAL REVENGE!?
WE DON'T LIKE THE CHANGES, BUT WE ACCEPT THEM.
OUR LORD HAS SAID IT MUST BE SO.
THAT'S RIGHT— HIS ORDERS ARE ABSOLUTE.
THE VAMPANEZE DO NOT SPRING INTO ACTION FOR THE SAKE OF A MERE HALF-VAMPANEZE SUCH AS MYSELF.
IT IS THE TRUE GUEST OF HONOR TONIGHT WHO WISHED FOR THIS MEETING TO TAKE PLACE...
GAGO... (KTHUDD)
LOOK... EVERYONE...
GOGOGO (RUMBLE)
THE DOOR IN THE BACK IS OPENING ...
I BELIEVE YOU HAVE MET BEFORE ...
THE STAGE IS NOW SET...

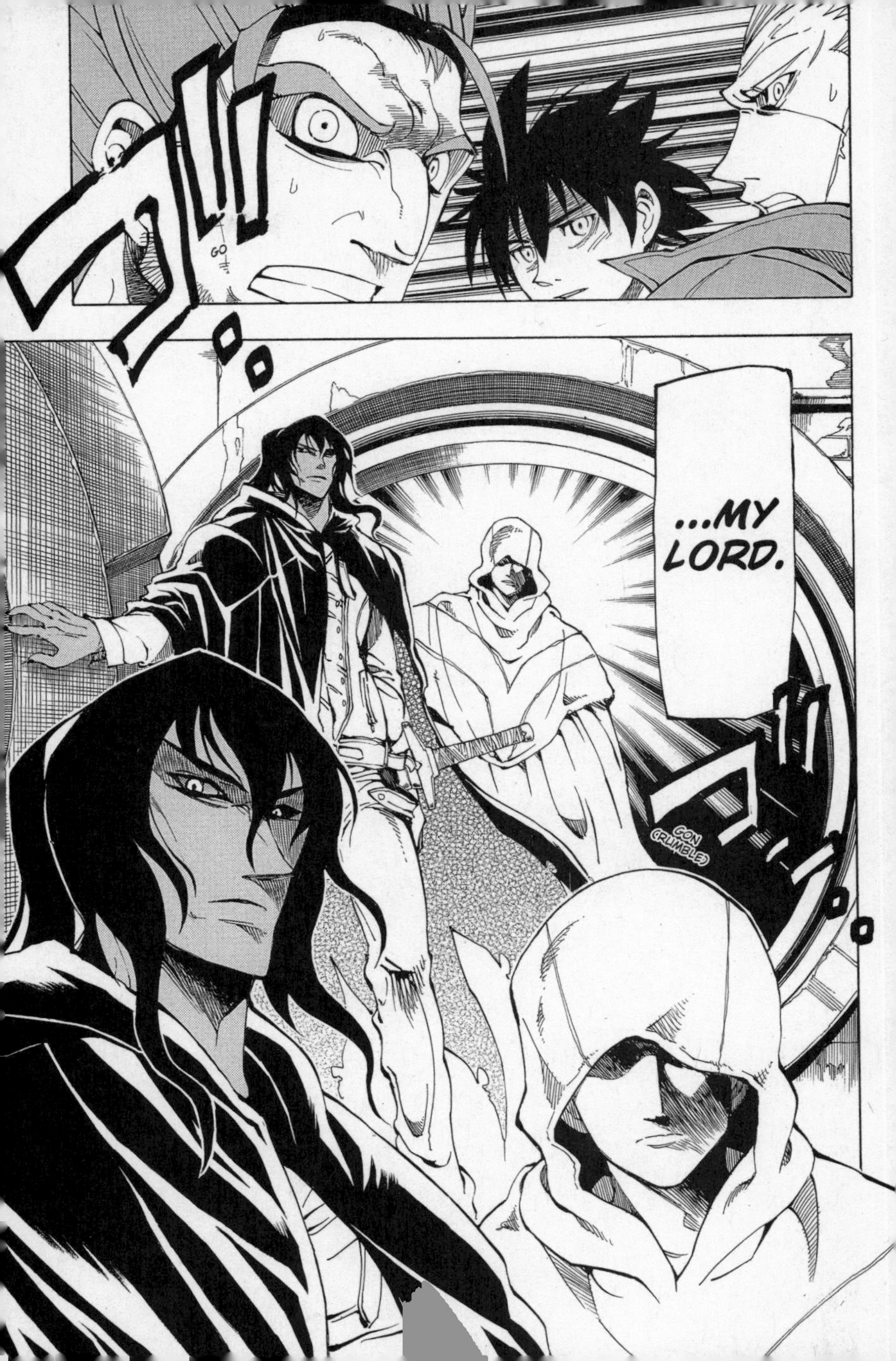
GO
...MY LORD.
GON (RUMBLE)

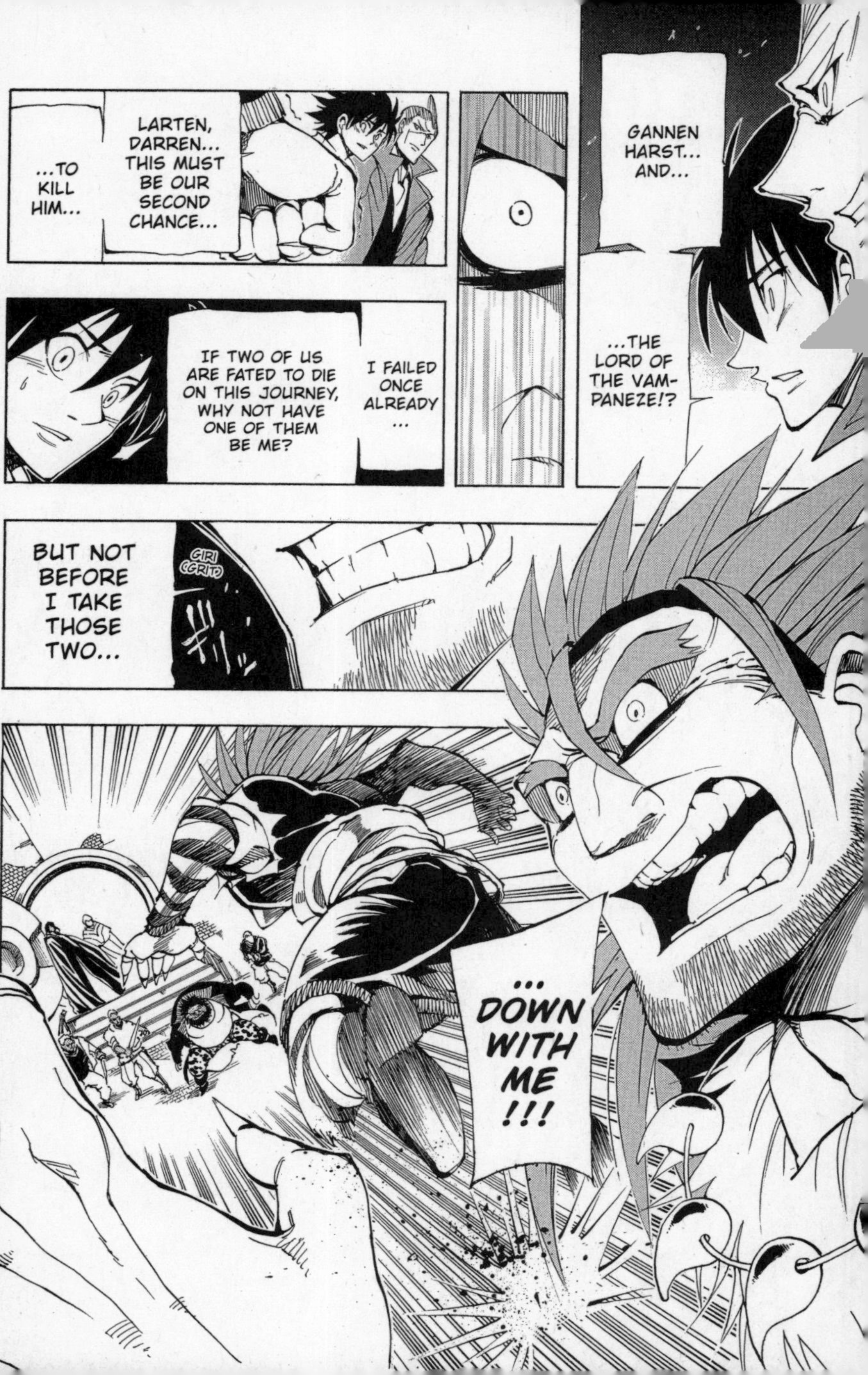
GANNEN HARST... AND...
...THE LORD OF THE VAMPANEZE!?
LARTEN, DARREN... THIS MUST BE OUR SECOND CHANCE...
...TO KILL HIM...
I FAILED ONCE ALREADY ...
IF TWO OF US ARE FATED TO DIE ON THIS JOURNEY, WHY NOT HAVE ONE OF THEM BE ME?
GIRI (GRIT)
BUT NOT BEFORE I TAKE THOSE TWO...
... DOWN WITH ME !!!

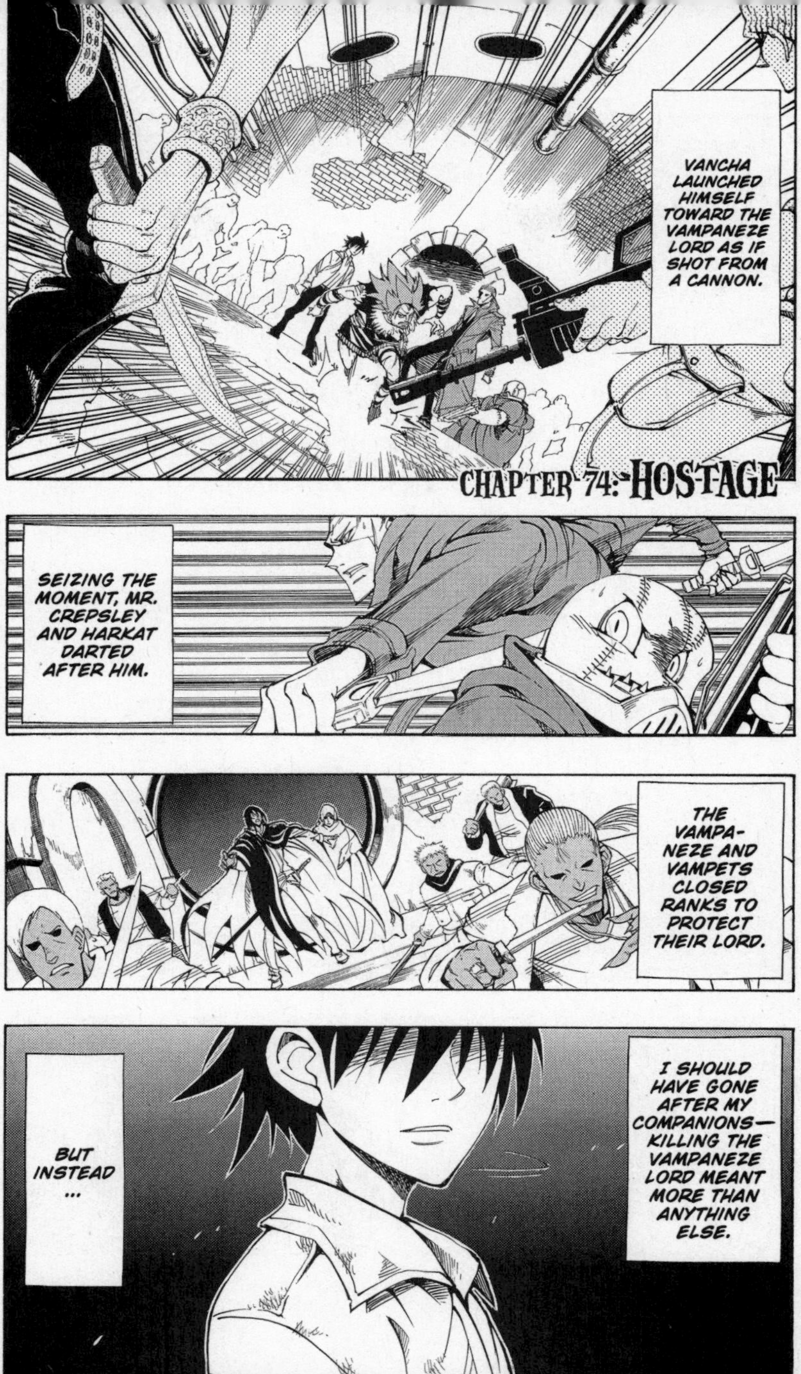
VANCHA LAUNCHED HIMSELF TOWARD THE VAMPANEZE LORD AS IF SHOT FROM A CANNON.
CHAPTER 74: HOSTAGE
SEIZING THE MOMENT, MR. CREPSLEY AND HARKAT DARTED AFTER HIM.
THE VAMPANEZE AND VAMPETS CLOSED RANKS TO PROTECT THEIR LORD.
I SHOULD HAVE GONE AFTER MY COMPANIONS— KILLING THE VAMPANEZE LORD MEANT MORE THAN ANYTHING ELSE.
BUT INSTEAD ...

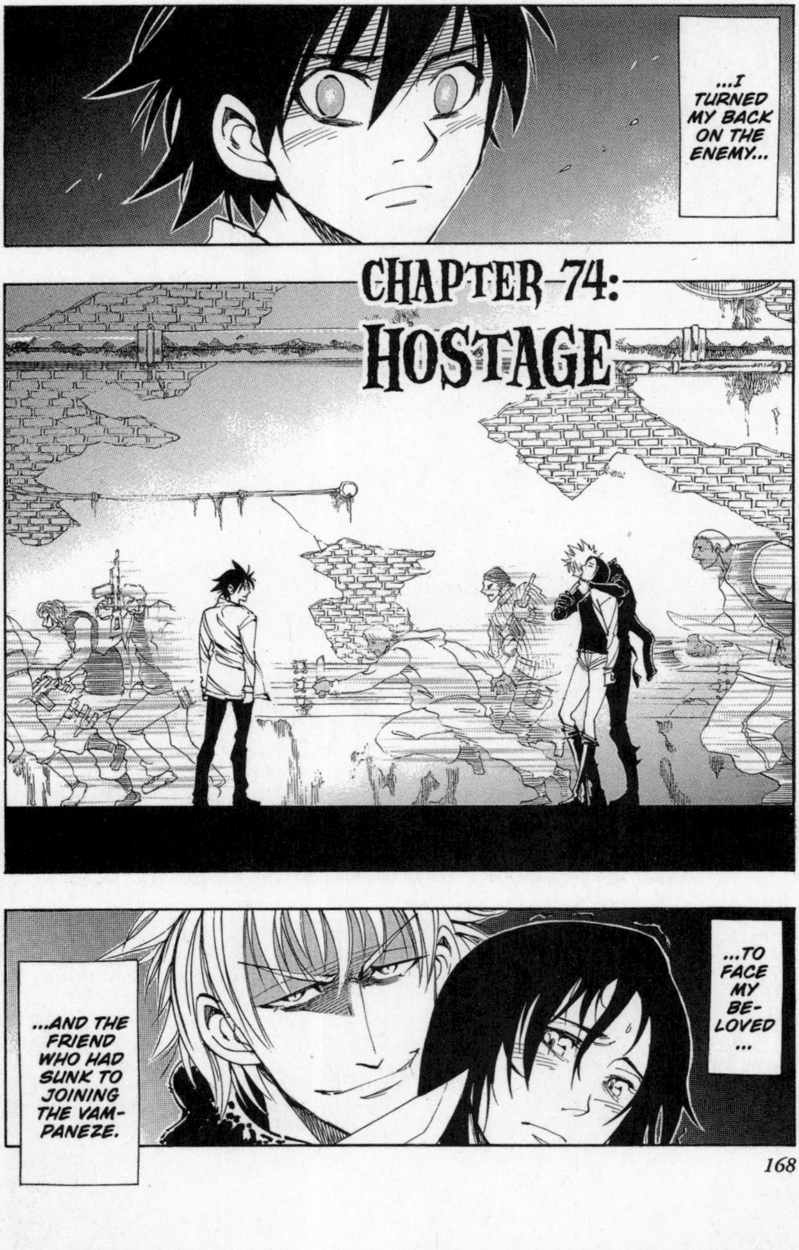
...I TURNED MY BACK ON THE ENEMY...
CHAPTER 74: HOSTAGE
...TO FACE MY BE-LOVED...
...AND THE FRIEND WHO HAD SUNK TO JOINING THE VAM-PANEZE.

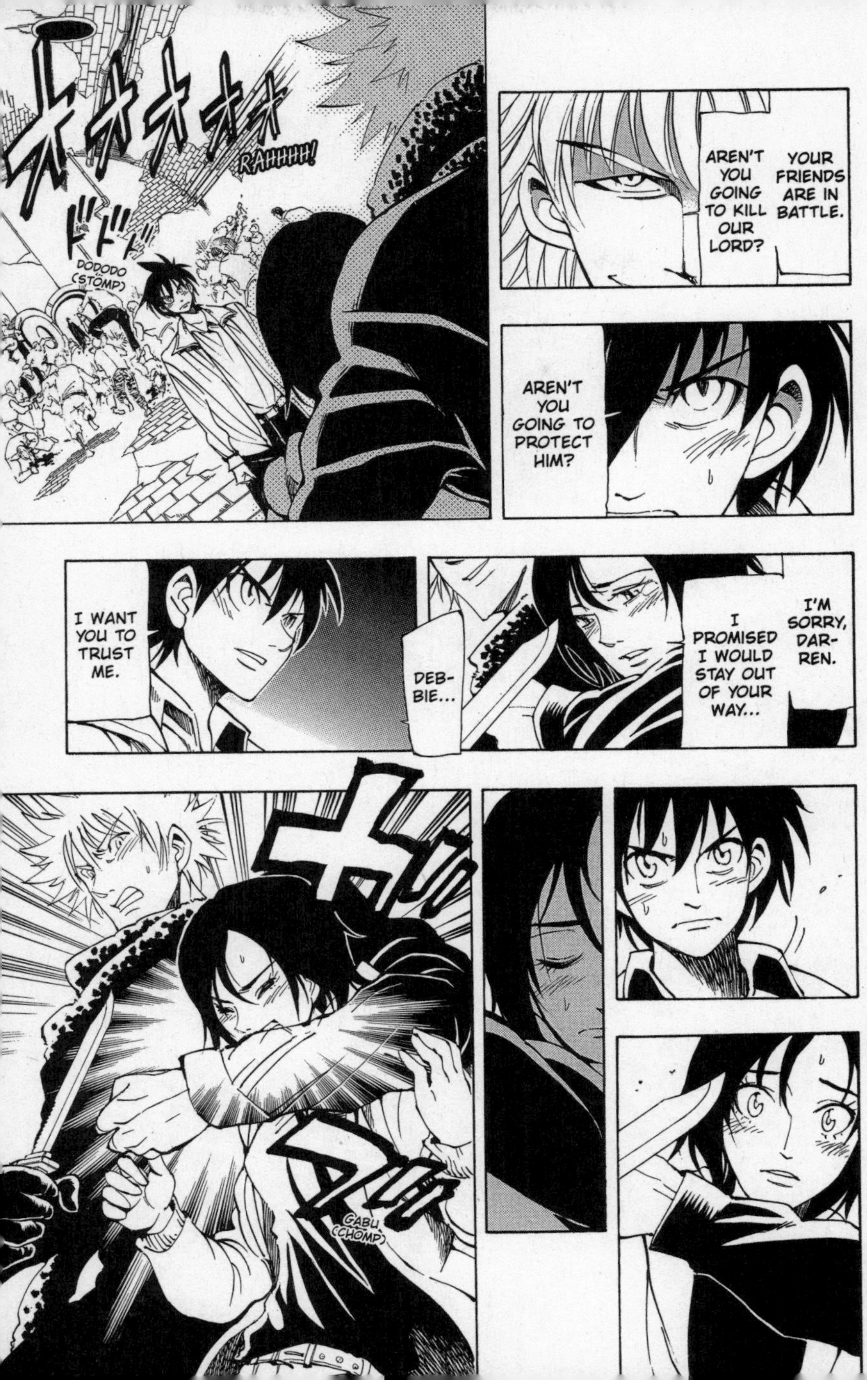
YOUR FRIENDS ARE IN BATTLE.
AREN'T YOU GOING TO KILL OUR LORD?
AREN'T YOU GOING TO PROTECT HIM?
オオオオオ
RAHHHH!
ドドド
DODODO (STOMP)
I'M SORRY, DARREN.
I PROMISED I WOULD STAY OUT OF YOUR WAY...
DEBBIE...
I WANT YOU TO TRUST ME.
GABU (CHOMP)

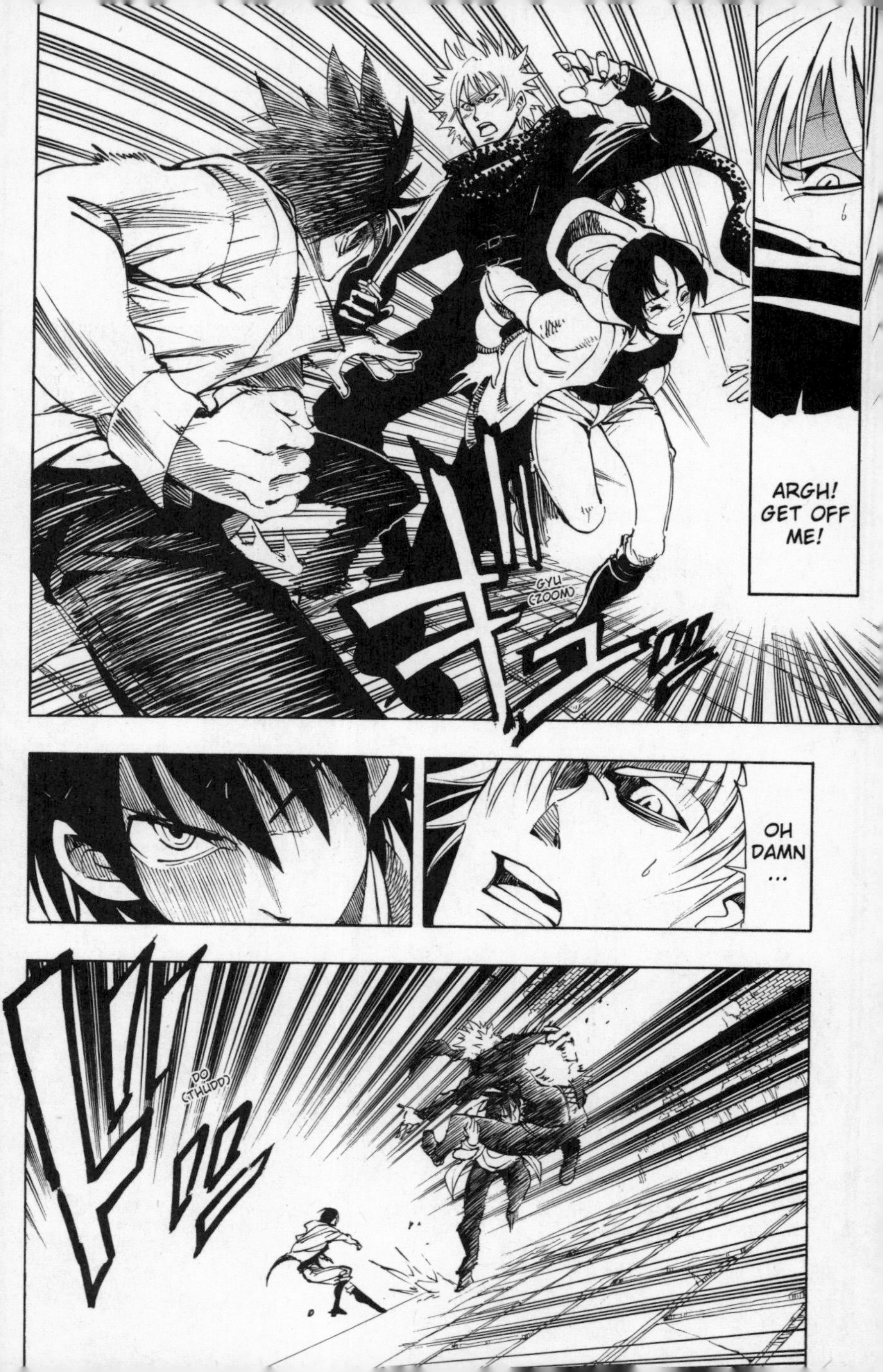

ARGH! GET OFF ME!
GYU (ZOOM)
OH DAMN ...
DO (THUDD)

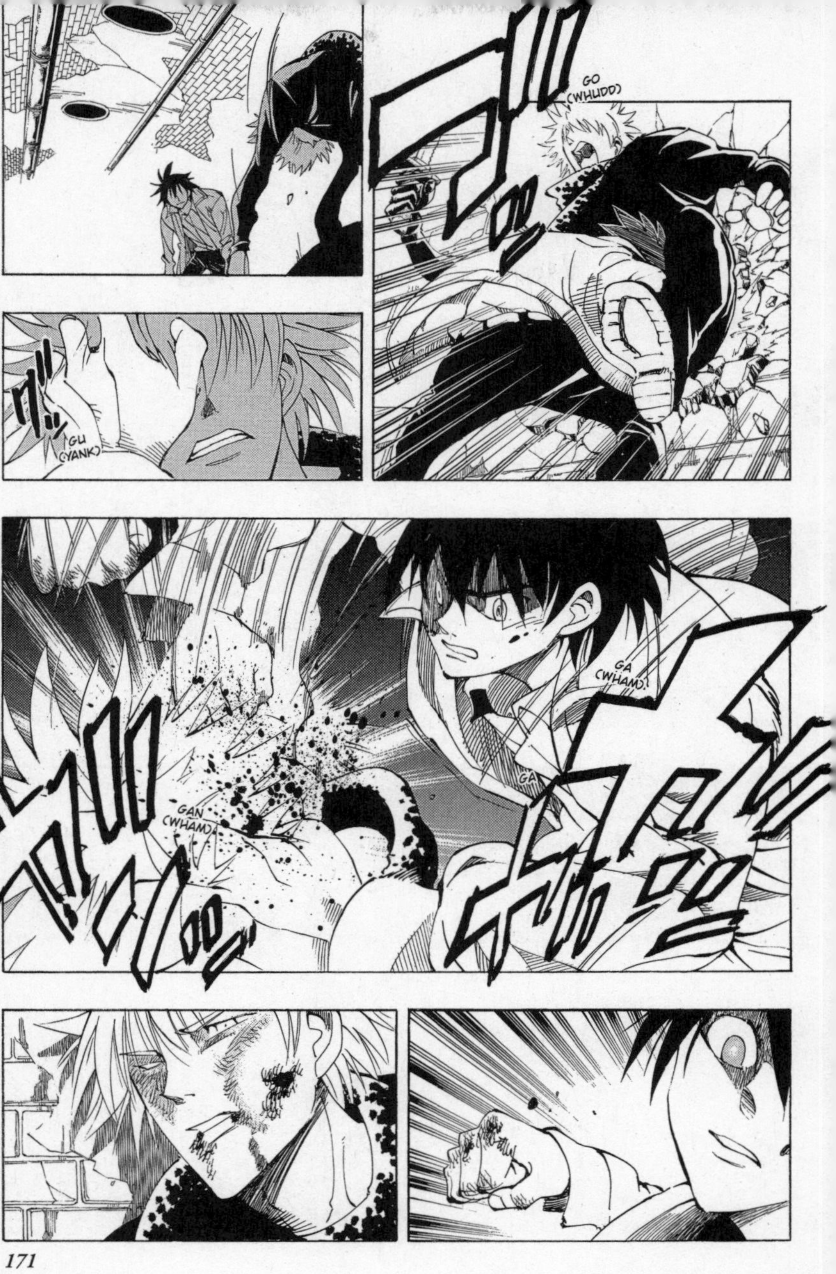
GO
(WHUDD)
GU
(YANK)
GA
(WHAM)
GA
GAN
(WHAM)

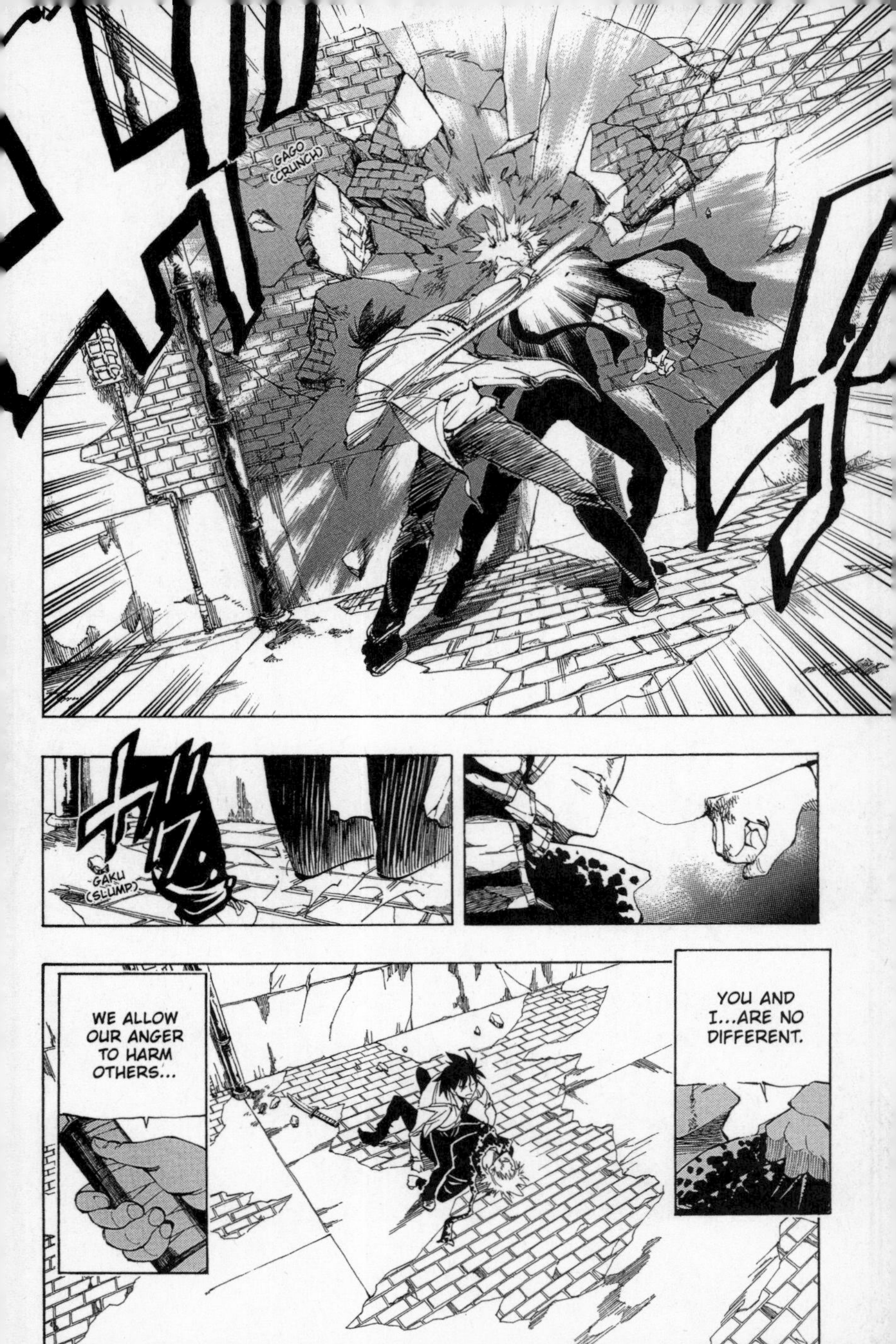
GAGO (CRUNCH)
GAKU (SLUMP)
YOU AND I...ARE NO DIFFERENT.
WE ALLOW OUR ANGER TO HARM OTHERS...

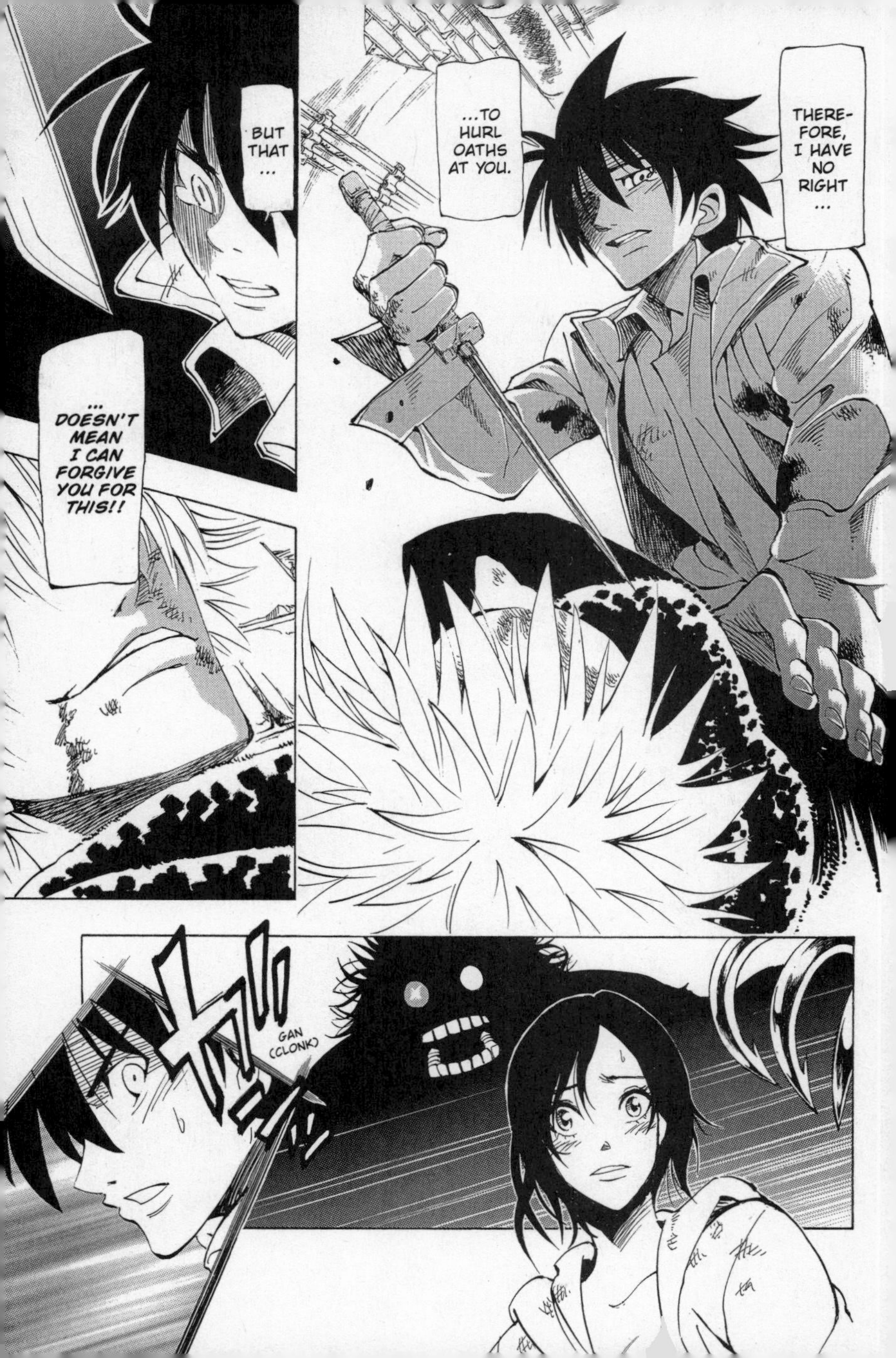
THERE-FORE, I HAVE NO RIGHT ...
...TO HURL OATHS AT YOU.
BUT THAT ...
... DOESN'T MEAN I CAN FORGIVE YOU FOR THIS!!
GAN (CLONK)

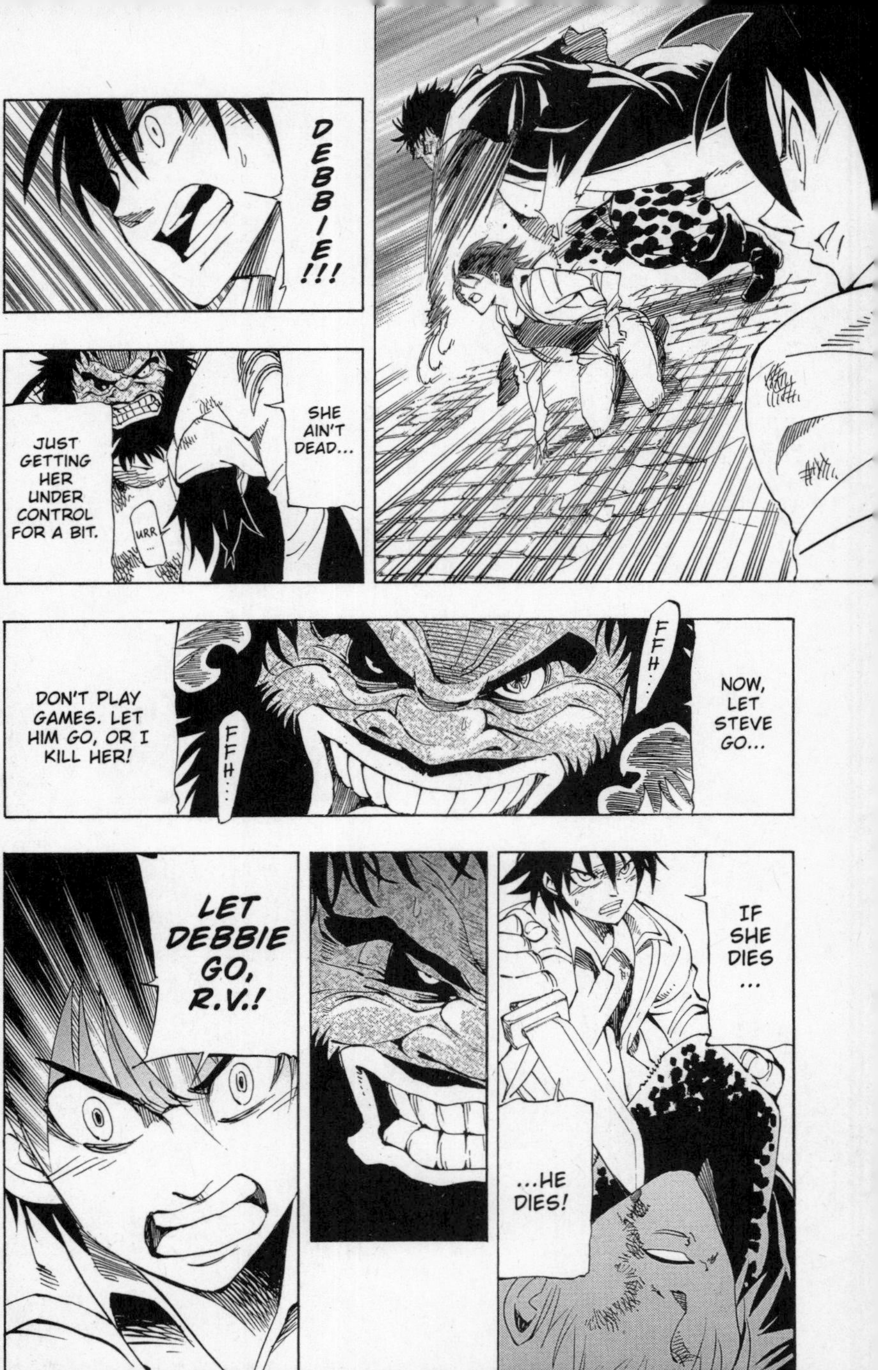
DEBBIE!!!
SHE AIN'T DEAD...
JUST GETTING HER UNDER CONTROL FOR A BIT.
URR...
FFH...
NOW, LET STEVE GO...
FFH...
DON'T PLAY GAMES. LET HIM GO, OR I KILL HER!
IF SHE DIES...
...HE DIES!
LET DEBBIE GO, R.V.!

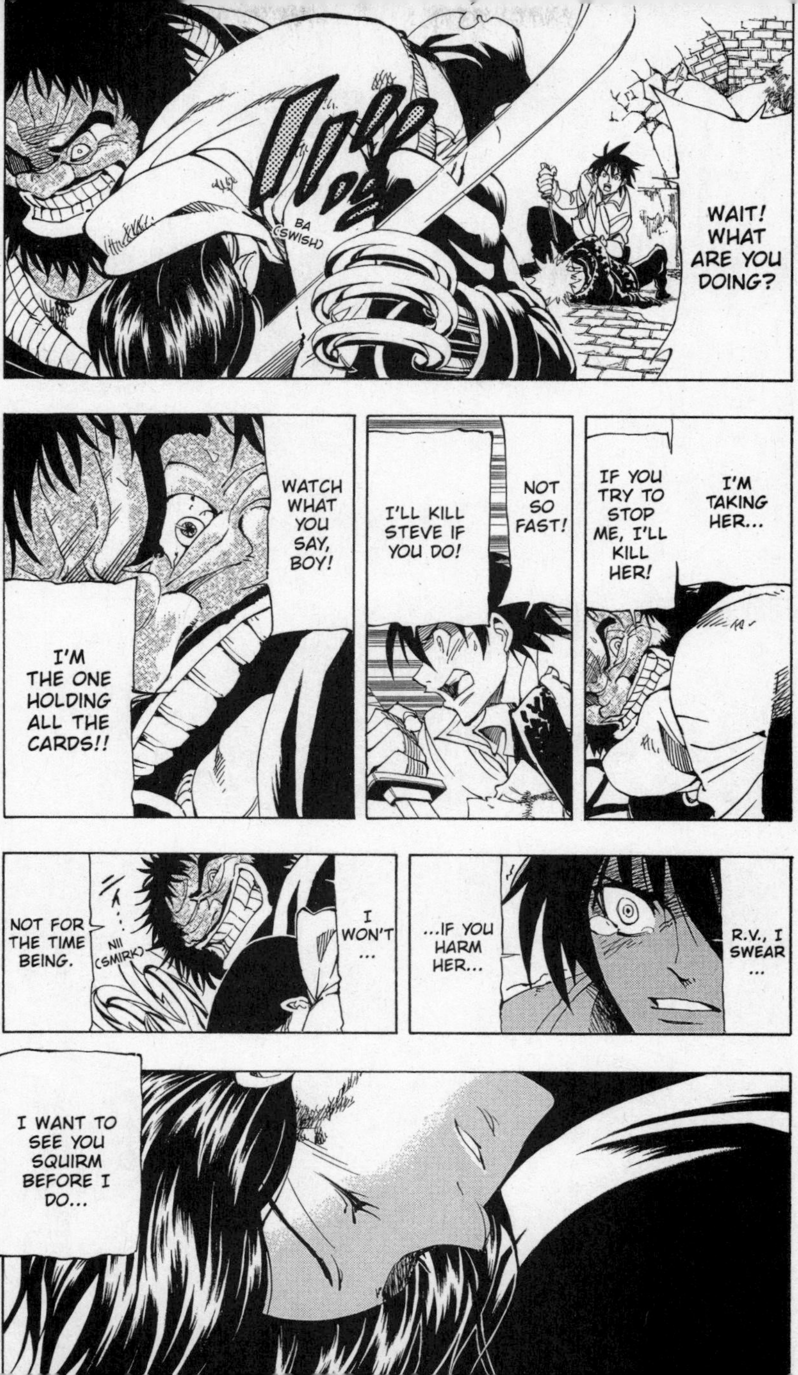
WAIT! WHAT ARE YOU DOING?
BA (SWISH)
I'M TAKING HER...
IF YOU TRY TO STOP ME, I'LL KILL HER!
NOT SO FAST!
I'LL KILL STEVE IF YOU DO!
WATCH WHAT YOU SAY, BOY!
I'M THE ONE HOLDING ALL THE CARDS!!
R.V., I SWEAR ...
...IF YOU HARM HER...
I WON'T ...
NII (SMIRK)
NOT FOR THE TIME BEING.
I WANT TO SEE YOU SQUIRM BEFORE I DO...

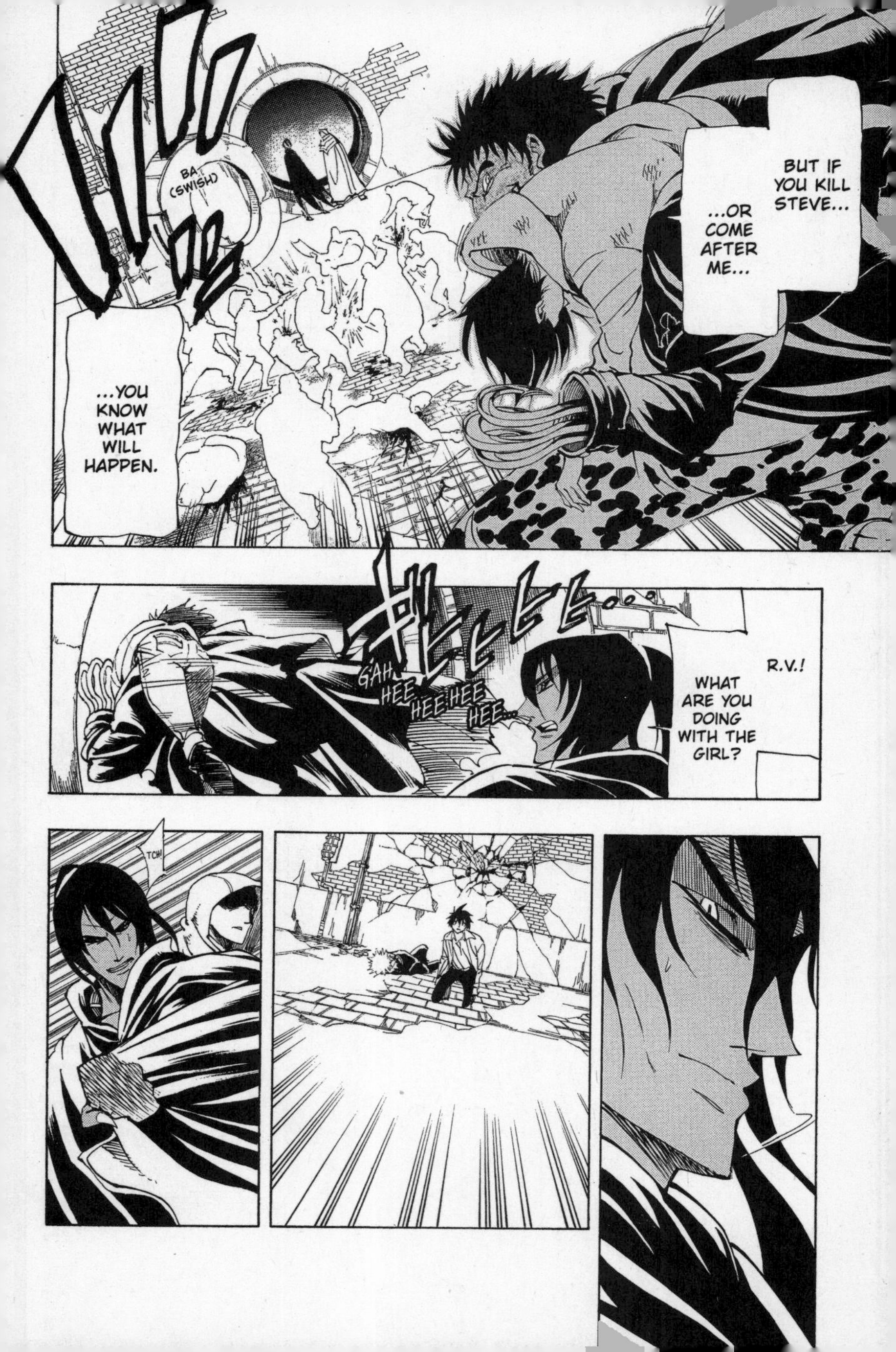
BUT IF YOU KILL STEVE...
...OR COME AFTER ME...
BA (SWISH)
...YOU KNOW WHAT WILL HAPPEN.
R.V.!
WHAT ARE YOU DOING WITH THE GIRL?
GAH HEE HEE HEE HEE...
TCH!

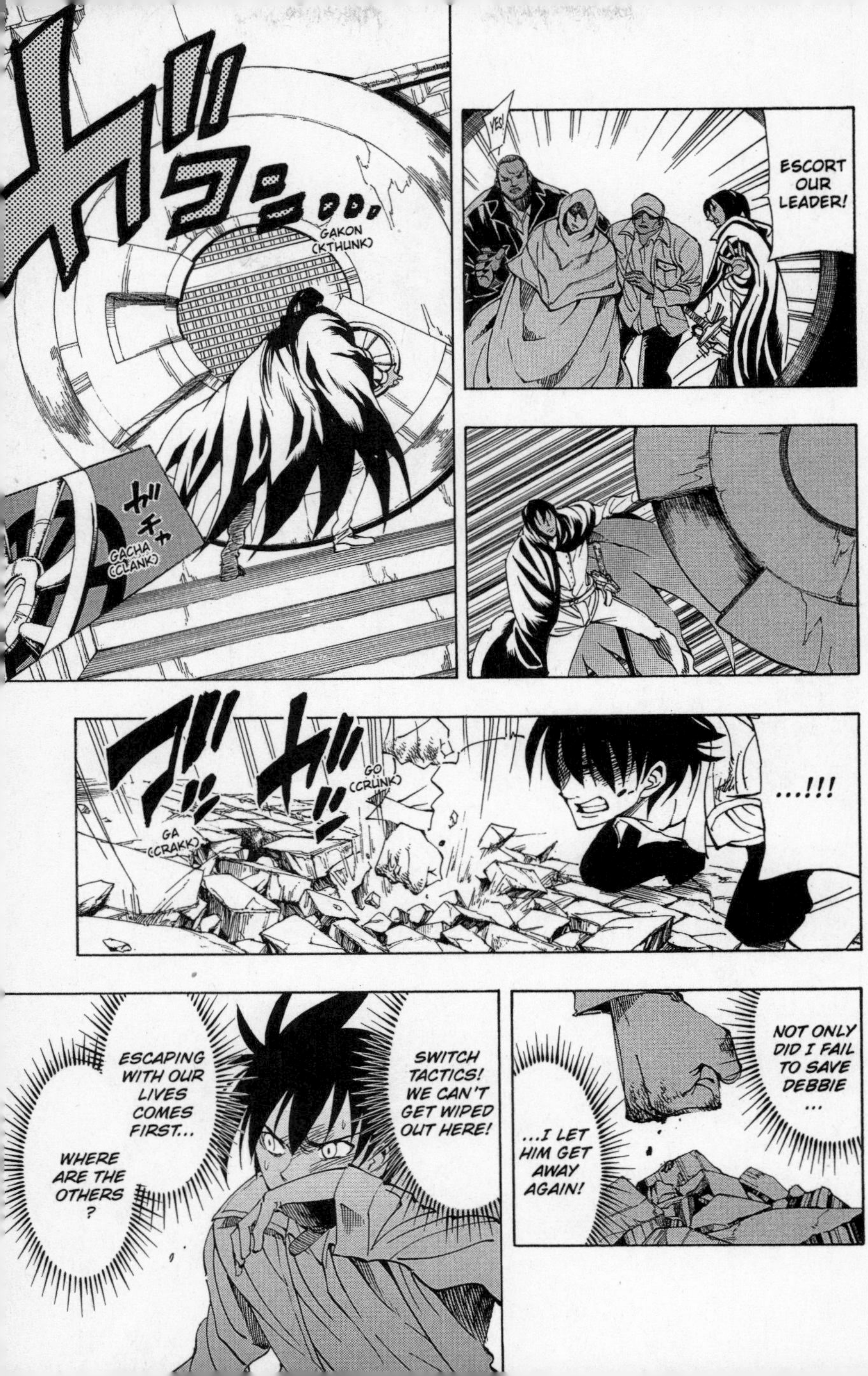

ESCORT OUR LEADER!
YES!
GAKON (KTHUNK)
GACHA (CLANK)
...!!!
GO (CRUNK)
GA (CRAKK)
NOT ONLY DID I FAIL TO SAVE DEBBIE...
...I LET HIM GET AWAY AGAIN!
SWITCH TACTICS! WE CAN'T GET WIPED OUT HERE!
ESCAPING WITH OUR LIVES COMES FIRST...
WHERE ARE THE OTHERS?

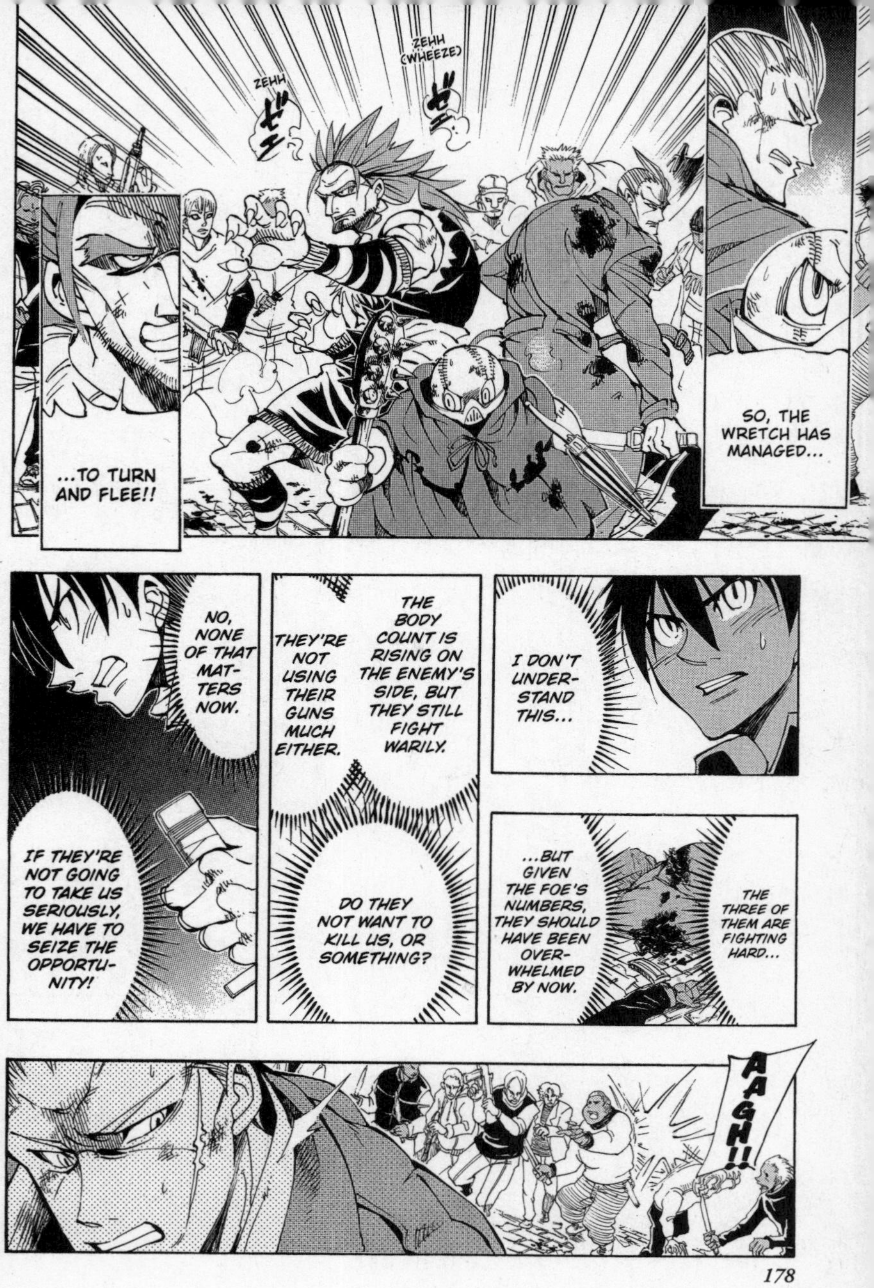
SO, THE WRETCH HAS MANAGED...
ZEHH (WHEEZE)
ZEHH
...TO TURN AND FLEE!!
I DON'T UNDER-STAND THIS...
THE THREE OF THEM ARE FIGHTING HARD...
...BUT GIVEN THE FOE'S NUMBERS, THEY SHOULD HAVE BEEN OVER-WHELMED BY NOW.
THE BODY COUNT IS RISING ON THE ENEMY'S SIDE, BUT THEY STILL FIGHT WARILY.
THEY'RE NOT USING THEIR GUNS MUCH EITHER.
DO THEY NOT WANT TO KILL US, OR SOMETHING?
NO, NONE OF THAT MAT-TERS NOW.
IF THEY'RE NOT GOING TO TAKE US SERIOUSLY, WE HAVE TO SEIZE THE OPPORTU-NITY!
AAGH!!

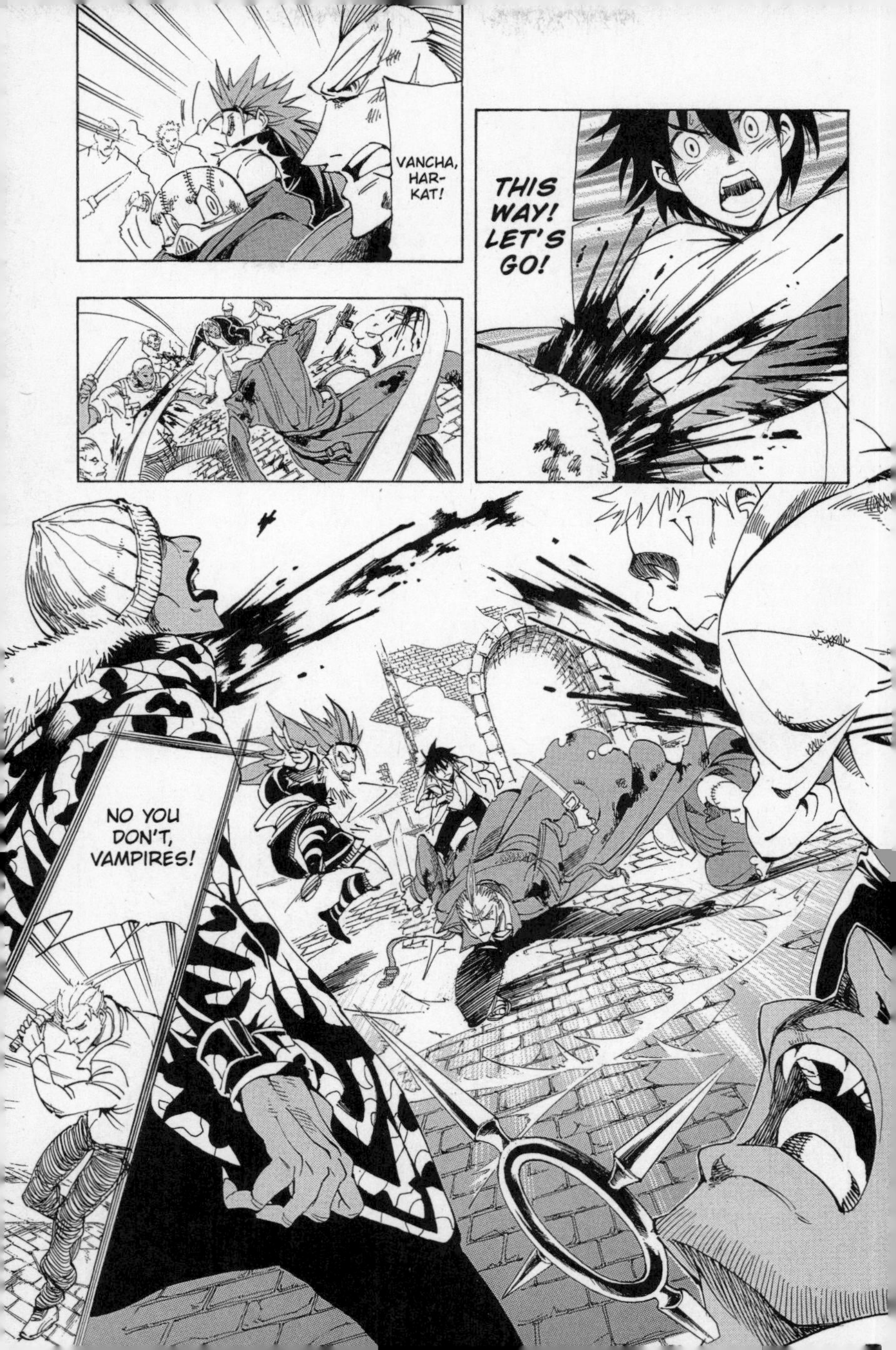
THIS WAY! LET'S GO!
VANCHA, HAR-KAT!
NO YOU DON'T, VAMPIRES!

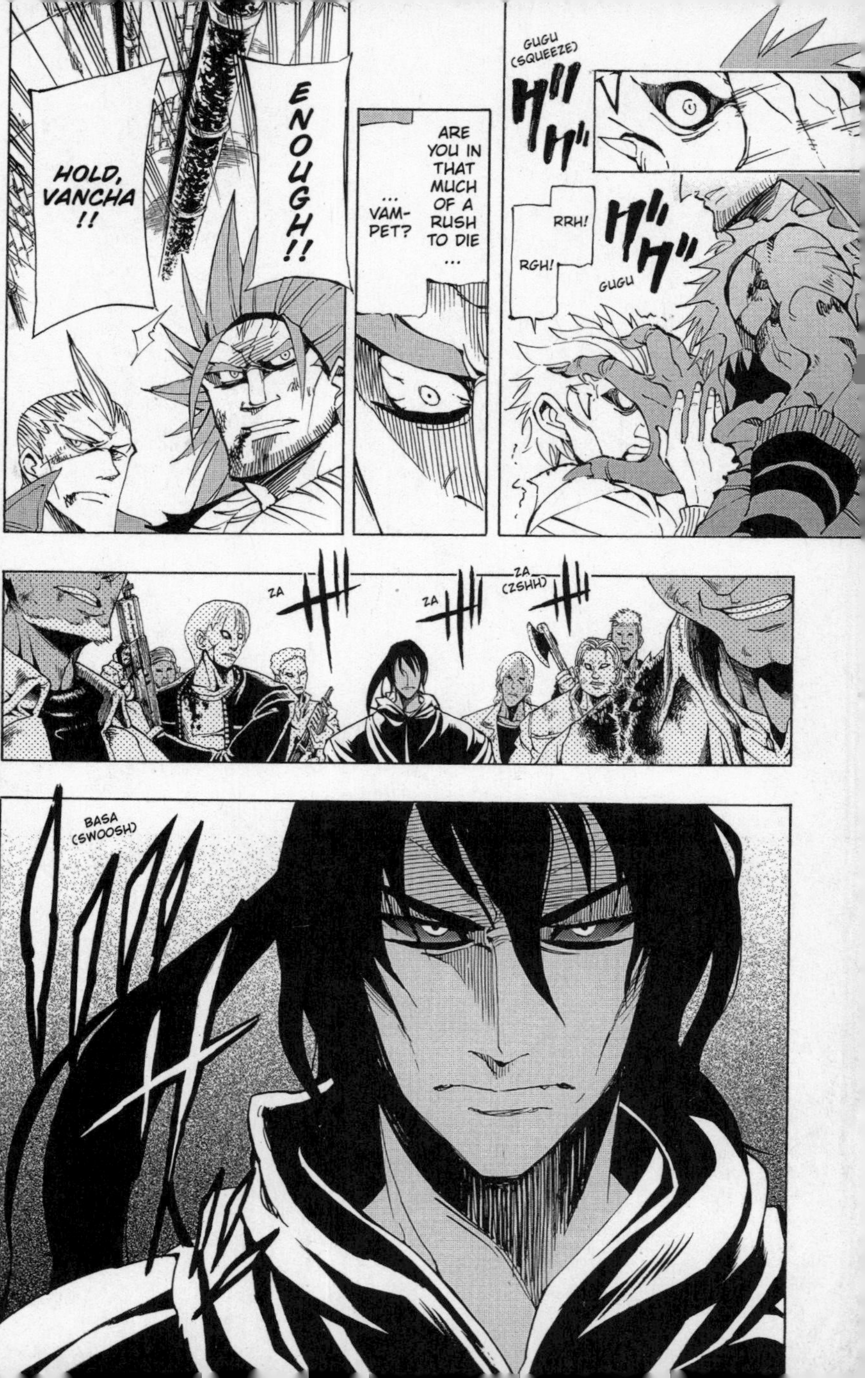

GUGU (SQUEEZE)
RRH!
RGH!
GUGU
ARE YOU IN THAT MUCH OF A RUSH TO DIE ...
... VAMPET?
ENOUGH!!
HOLD, VANCHA!!
ZA (ZSHH)
ZA
ZA
BASA (SWOOSH)

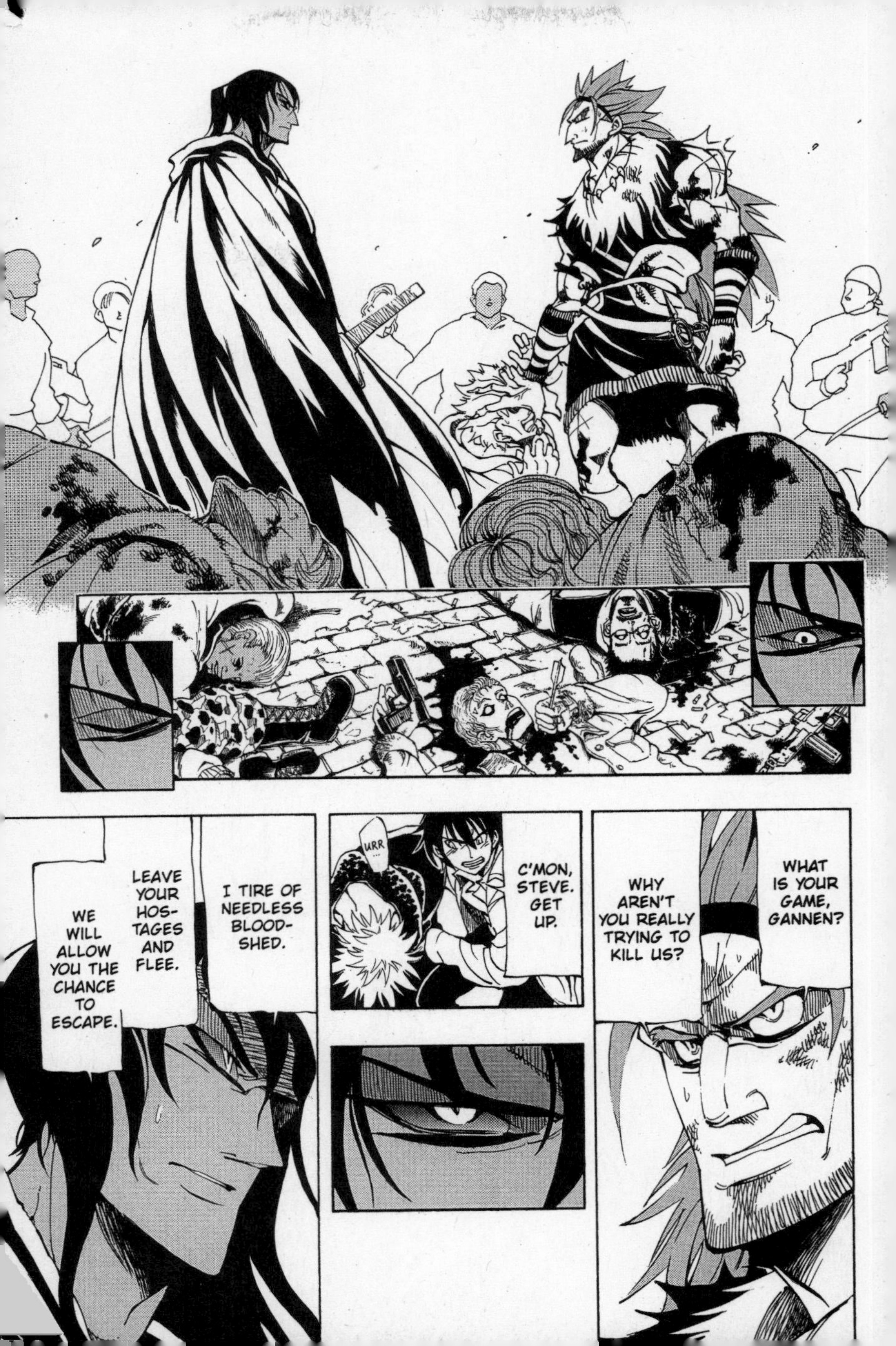
WHAT IS YOUR GAME, GANNEN?
WHY AREN'T YOU REALLY TRYING TO KILL US?
C'MON, STEVE. GET UP.
URR...
I TIRE OF NEEDLESS BLOOD-SHED.
LEAVE YOUR HOS-TAGES AND FLEE.
WE WILL ALLOW YOU THE CHANCE TO ESCAPE.

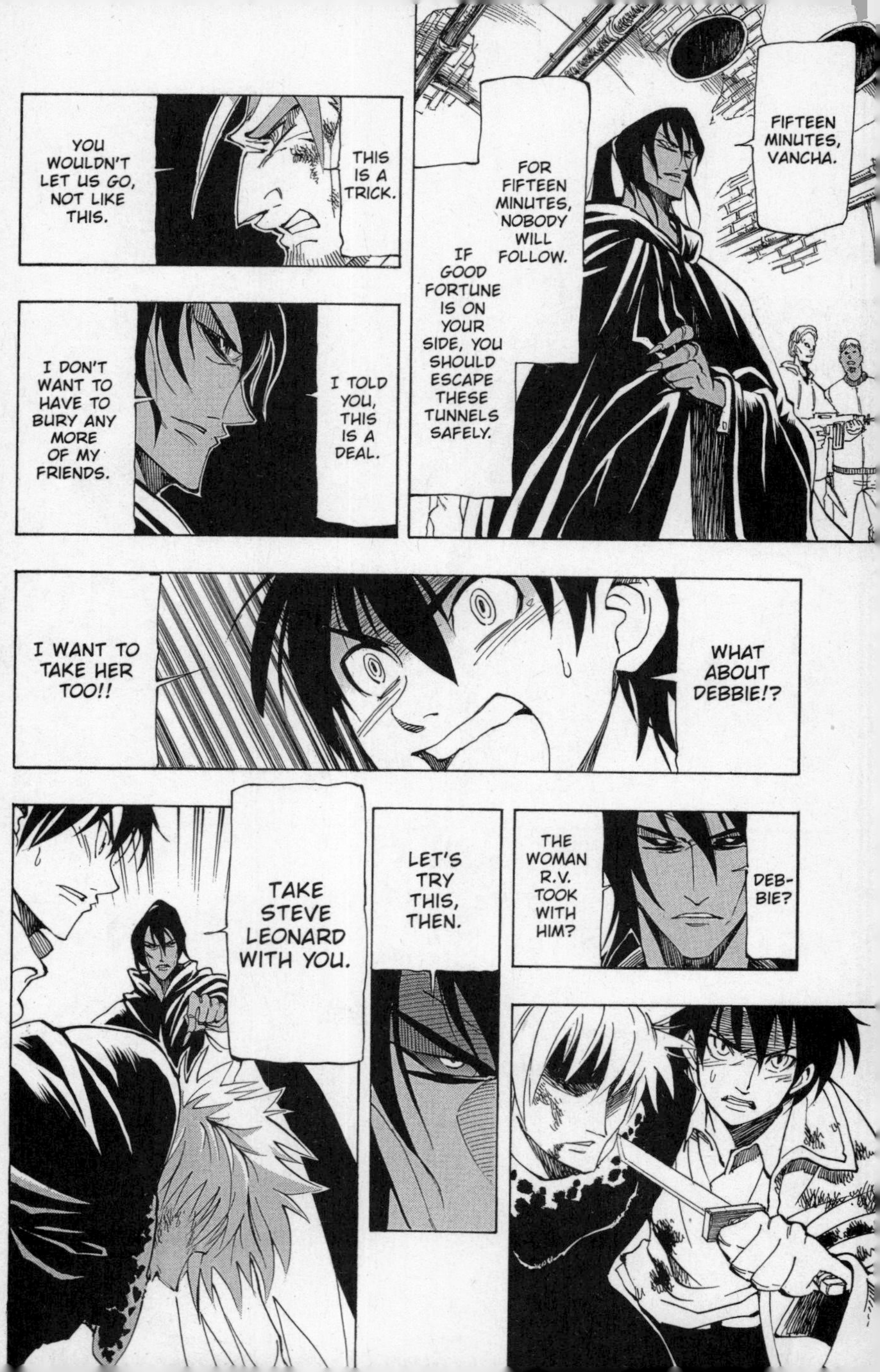
FIFTEEN MINUTES, VANCHA.
FOR FIFTEEN MINUTES, NOBODY WILL FOLLOW.
IF GOOD FORTUNE IS ON YOUR SIDE, YOU SHOULD ESCAPE THESE TUNNELS SAFELY.
THIS IS A TRICK.
YOU WOULDN'T LET US GO, NOT LIKE THIS.
I TOLD YOU, THIS IS A DEAL.
I DON'T WANT TO HAVE TO BURY ANY MORE OF MY FRIENDS.
WHAT ABOUT DEBBIE!?
I WANT TO TAKE HER TOO!!
DEB-BIE?
THE WOMAN R.V. TOOK WITH HIM?
LET'S TRY THIS, THEN.
TAKE STEVE LEONARD WITH YOU.

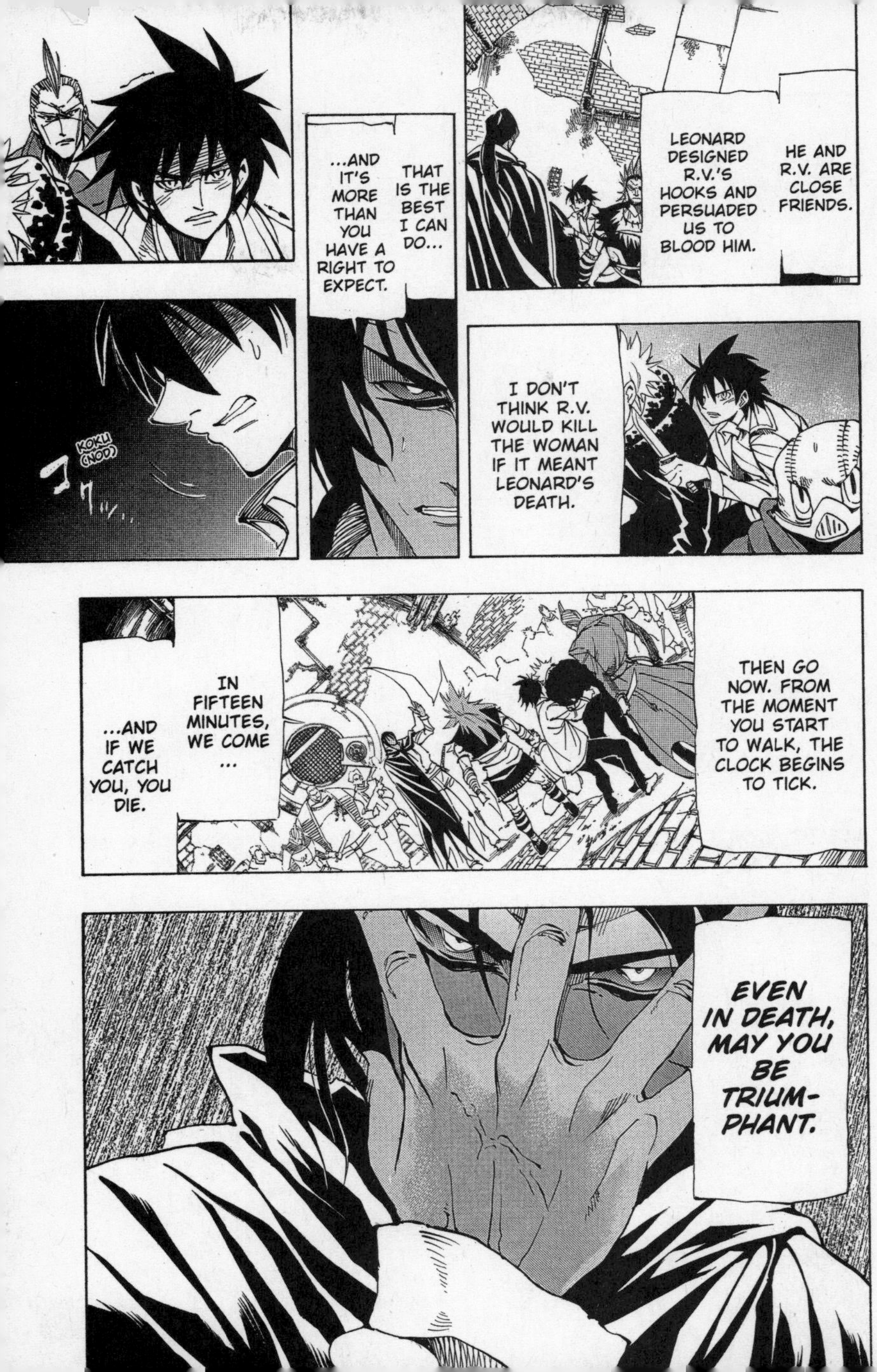
HE AND R.V. ARE CLOSE FRIENDS.
LEONARD DESIGNED R.V.'S HOOKS AND PERSUADED US TO BLOOD HIM.
I DON'T THINK R.V. WOULD KILL THE WOMAN IF IT MEANT LEONARD'S DEATH.
THAT IS THE BEST I CAN DO...
...AND IT'S MORE THAN YOU HAVE A RIGHT TO EXPECT.
KOKU (NOD)
THEN GO NOW. FROM THE MOMENT YOU START TO WALK, THE CLOCK BEGINS TO TICK.
IN FIFTEEN MINUTES, WE COME ...
...AND IF WE CATCH YOU, YOU DIE.
EVEN IN DEATH, MAY YOU BE TRIUM-PHANT.

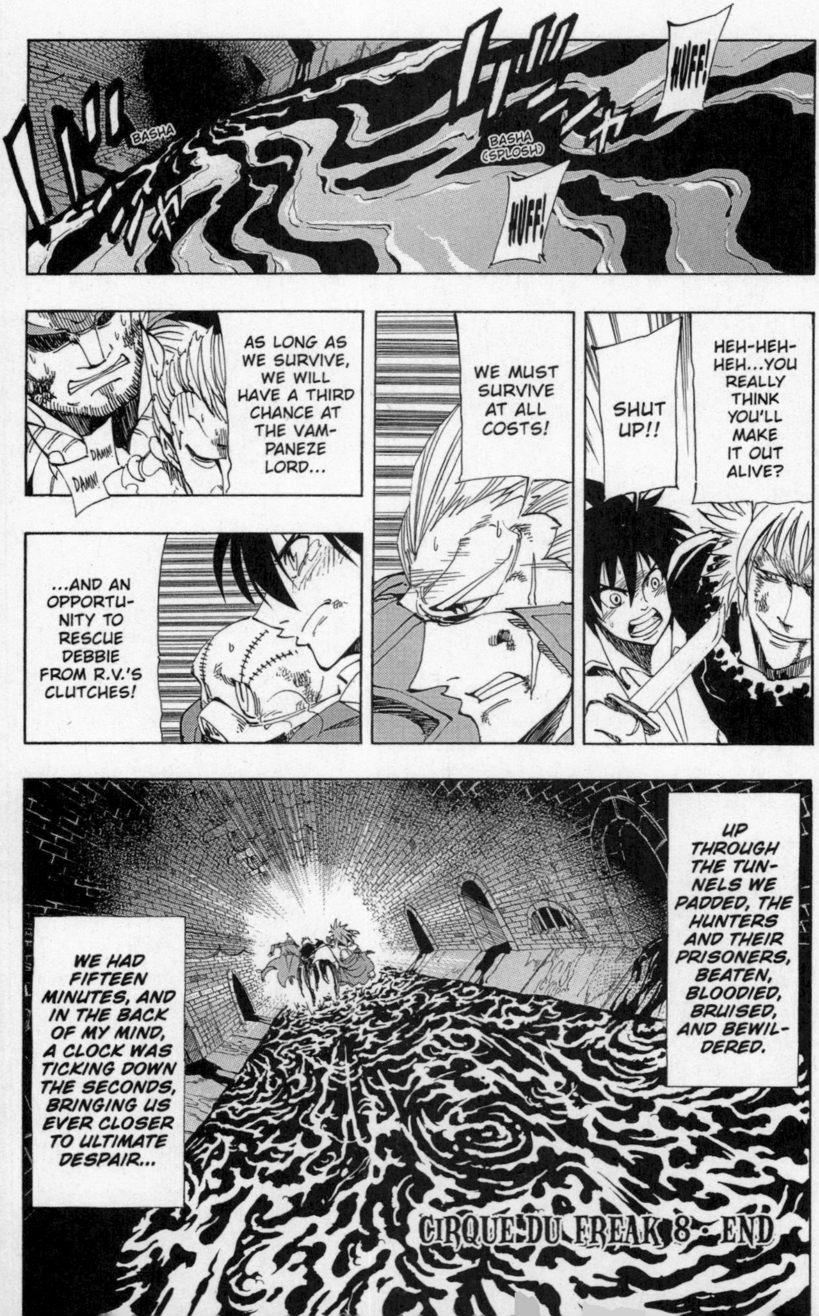
HUFF!
BASHA (SPLOSH)
HUFF!
BASHA
HEH-HEH-HEH...YOU REALLY THINK YOU'LL MAKE IT OUT ALIVE?
SHUT UP!!
WE MUST SURVIVE AT ALL COSTS!
AS LONG AS WE SURVIVE, WE WILL HAVE A THIRD CHANCE AT THE VAMPANEZE LORD...
DAMN!
DAMN!
...AND AN OPPORTUNITY TO RESCUE DEBBIE FROM R.V.'S CLUTCHES!
UP THROUGH THE TUNNELS WE PADDED, THE HUNTERS AND THEIR PRISONERS, BEATEN, BLOODIED, BRUISED, AND BEWILDERED.
WE HAD FIFTEEN MINUTES, AND IN THE BACK OF MY MIND, A CLOCK WAS TICKING DOWN THE SECONDS, BRINGING US EVER CLOSER TO ULTIMATE DESPAIR...
CIRQUE DU FREAK 8 · END

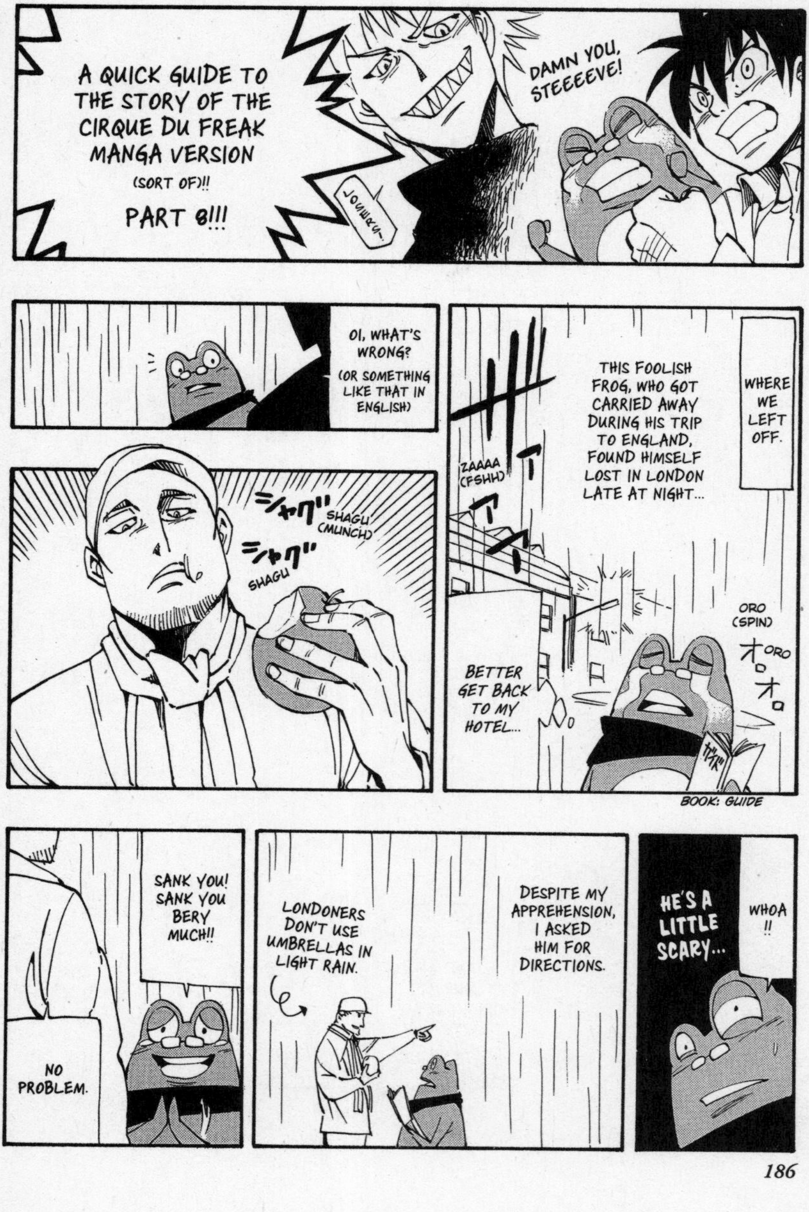
DAMN YOU, STEEEEVE!
A QUICK GUIDE TO THE STORY OF THE CIRQUE DU FREAK MANGA VERSION (SORT OF)!!
PART 8!!!
WHERE WE LEFT OFF.
THIS FOOLISH FROG, WHO GOT CARRIED AWAY DURING HIS TRIP TO ENGLAND, FOUND HIMSELF LOST IN LONDON LATE AT NIGHT...
ZAAAA (FSHH)
ORO (SPIN)
ORO
BETTER GET BACK TO MY HOTEL...
OI, WHAT'S WRONG? (OR SOMETHING LIKE THAT IN ENGLISH)
シャグ SHAGU (MUNCH)
シャグ SHAGU
WHOA!!
HE'S A LITTLE SCARY...
DESPITE MY APPREHENSION, I ASKED HIM FOR DIRECTIONS.
LONDONERS DON'T USE UMBRELLAS IN LIGHT RAIN.
SANK YOU! SANK YOU BERY MUCH!!
NO PROBLEM.
BOOK: GUIDE

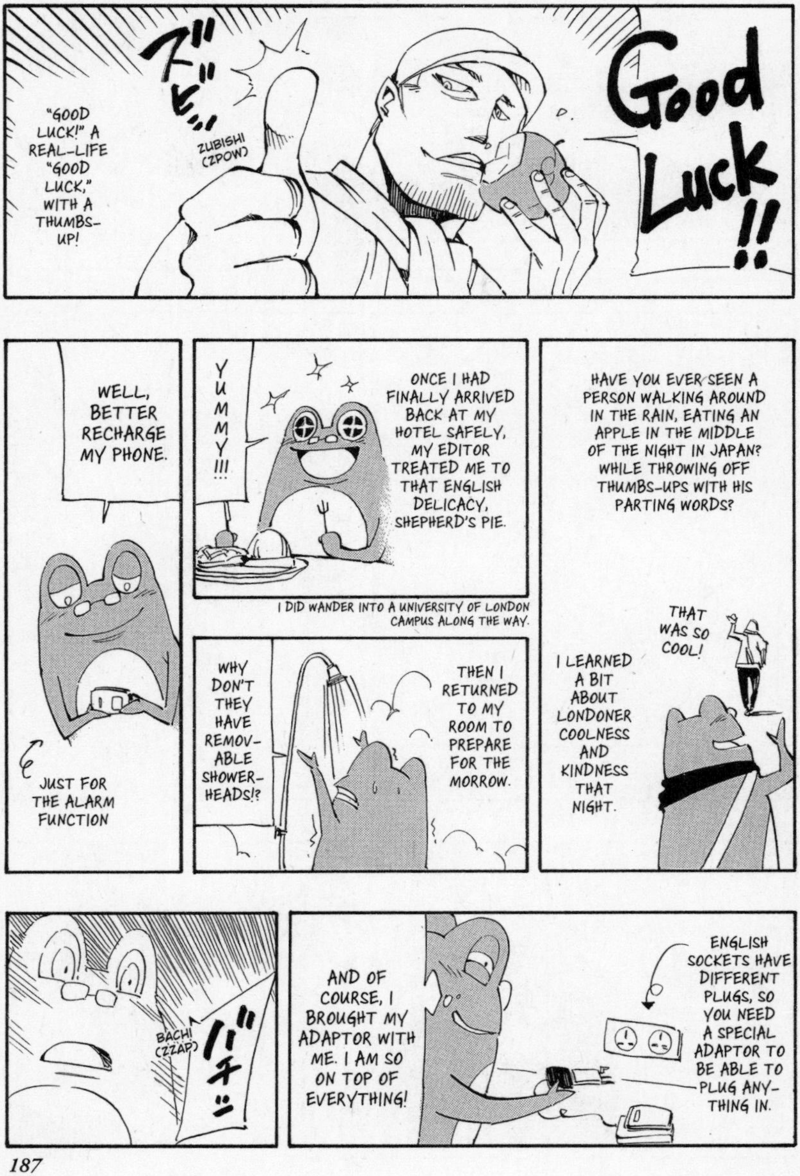
Good Luck!!
ズビッ
ZUBISHI (ZPOW)
"GOOD LUCK!" A REAL-LIFE "GOOD LUCK," WITH A THUMBS-UP!
HAVE YOU EVER SEEN A PERSON WALKING AROUND IN THE RAIN, EATING AN APPLE IN THE MIDDLE OF THE NIGHT IN JAPAN? WHILE THROWING OFF THUMBS-UPS WITH HIS PARTING WORDS?
THAT WAS SO COOL!
I LEARNED A BIT ABOUT LONDONER COOLNESS AND KINDNESS THAT NIGHT.
ONCE I HAD FINALLY ARRIVED BACK AT MY HOTEL SAFELY, MY EDITOR TREATED ME TO THAT ENGLISH DELICACY, SHEPHERD'S PIE.
YUMMY!!!
I DID WANDER INTO A UNIVERSITY OF LONDON CAMPUS ALONG THE WAY.
THEN I RETURNED TO MY ROOM TO PREPARE FOR THE MORROW.
WHY DON'T THEY HAVE REMOVABLE SHOWER-HEADS!?
WELL, BETTER RECHARGE MY PHONE.
JUST FOR THE ALARM FUNCTION
ENGLISH SOCKETS HAVE DIFFERENT PLUGS, SO YOU NEED A SPECIAL ADAPTOR TO BE ABLE TO PLUG ANYTHING IN.
AND OF COURSE, I BROUGHT MY ADAPTOR WITH ME. I AM SO ON TOP OF EVERYTHING!
バチッ
BACHI (ZZAP)

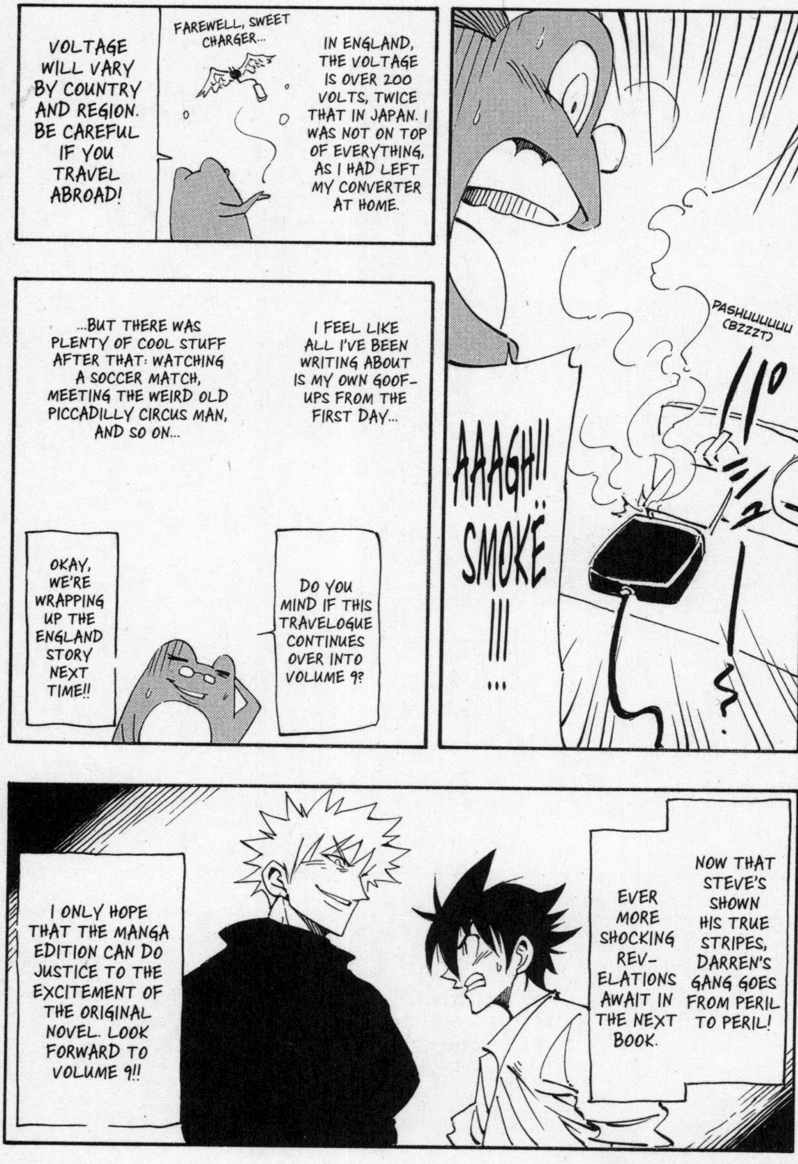
PASHUUUUUU (BZZZT)
AAAGH!! SMOKE!!!...
IN ENGLAND, THE VOLTAGE IS OVER 200 VOLTS, TWICE THAT IN JAPAN. I WAS NOT ON TOP OF EVERYTHING, AS I HAD LEFT MY CONVERTER AT HOME.
FAREWELL, SWEET CHARGER...
VOLTAGE WILL VARY BY COUNTRY AND REGION. BE CAREFUL IF YOU TRAVEL ABROAD!
I FEEL LIKE ALL I'VE BEEN WRITING ABOUT IS MY OWN GOOF-UPS FROM THE FIRST DAY...
...BUT THERE WAS PLENTY OF COOL STUFF AFTER THAT: WATCHING A SOCCER MATCH, MEETING THE WEIRD OLD PICCADILLY CIRCUS MAN, AND SO ON...
DO YOU MIND IF THIS TRAVELOGUE CONTINUES OVER INTO VOLUME 9?
OKAY, WE'RE WRAPPING UP THE ENGLAND STORY NEXT TIME!!
NOW THAT STEVE'S SHOWN HIS TRUE STRIPES, DARREN'S GANG GOES FROM PERIL TO PERIL!
EVER MORE SHOCKING REV-ELATIONS AWAIT IN THE NEXT BOOK.
I ONLY HOPE THAT THE MANGA EDITION CAN DO JUSTICE TO THE EXCITEMENT OF THE ORIGINAL NOVEL. LOOK FORWARD TO VOLUME 9!!

The End

MESSAGE FROM TAKAHIRO ARAI

IT'S BEEN ANNOUNCED: DARREN SHAN IS GETTING A HOLLYWOOD MOVIE MAKEOVER! AS I'M ONLY DRAWING A MANGA BASED ON THE ORIGINAL NOVELS, I'VE REALLY GOT NOTHING TO DO WITH ANY OF THIS, BUT I STILL CAN'T HELP BUT FEEL AS PROUD AS IF MY OWN STORY WAS MADE INTO A MOVIE!! THE CASTING IS ALREADY MOSTLY COMPLETE, AND I CAN'T WAIT TO FIND OUT MORE. I HOPE IT COMES OUT SOOOOOON!!!

THE VAMPIRE'S ASSISTANT IS NOW AVAILABLE IN STORES!

CIRQUE DU FREAK ⑧

DARREN SHAN
TAKAHIRO ARAI

Translation: Stephen Paul • Lettering: AndWorld Design
Art Direction: Hitoshi SHIRAYAMA
Original Cover Design: Shigeru ANZAI + Bay Bridge Studio

DARREN SHAN Vol. 8 © 2008 by Darren Shan, Takahiro ARAI. All rights reserved. Original Japanese edition published in Japan in 2008 by Shogakukan Inc., Tokyo. Artworks reproduction rights in U.S.A. and Canada arranged with Shogakukan Inc. through Tuttle-Mori Agency, Inc., Tokyo.

English translation © 2011 Darren Shan

Yen Press
1290 Avenue of the Americas
New York, NY 10104

Visit us at yenpress.com
facebook.com/yenpress
twitter.com/yenpress
yenpress.tumblr.com
instagram.com/yenpress

First Yen Press Edition: March 2011

Yen Press is an imprint of Yen Press, LLC.
The Yen Press name and logo are trademarks of Yen Press, LLC.

ISBN: 978-0-316-17608-8

10 9 8 7 6

BVG

Printed in the United States of America

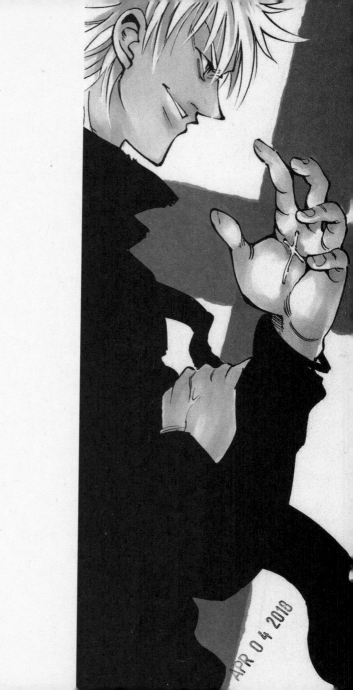

APR 0 4 2018